BLOOD FEUD

THE LEGENDS OF ANSU

J.W. WEBB

Acknowledgement for:

John Jarrold, for editing

Roger Garland, the late Tolkien artist, for the illustrations

Ravven, for the cover design

Chris Kocher, for proofreading

Crystal Sarakas, for book design

Map Illustration by Hanna Sandvig: www.bookcoverbakey.com

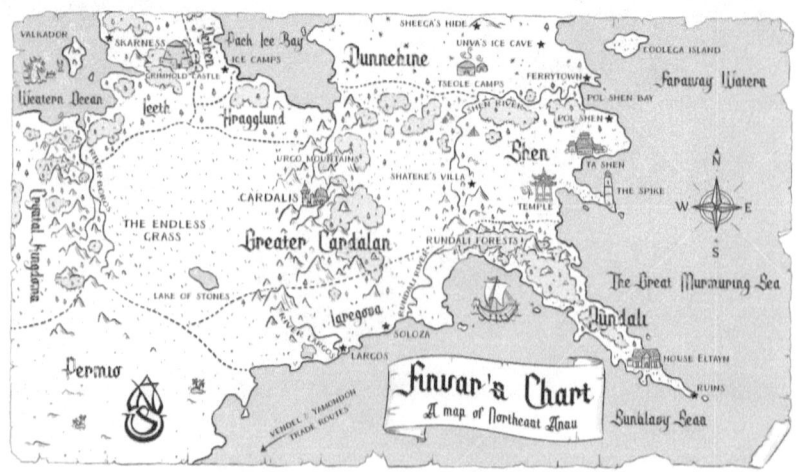

For Sally Oldfield, Singer-Songwriter –

Your enchanting voice and wondrous songs shone the light that guided this lost traveler through the dark lands, until he found this world—Ansu—waiting.
Thanks, Sally...

The sketches in this book, and throughout the entire Legends of Ansu series, are by Roger Garland, the late Tolkien artist.

A wonderful man I was proud to know.

Would you trade your soul to save your life?

The Crimson Lady knows that's the only way to find the man she wants to kill, the mercenary known as Corin an Fol.

Sign up to the J.W. Webb VIP Lounge newsletter and receive this exciting tale! More details are at the back of this book.

A NOTE FROM THE AUTHOR

Blood Feud is the ninth novel in the ongoing Legends of Ansu fantasy series. That said, this new book works well as a stand-alone and introduction to the world. The characters in Blood Feud, and the two novels that will follow, take place one thousand years after the conclusion of THE EMERALD QUEEN. So why not dive in right here and see what you think? If you enjoy this book, I hope you'll check out the others in the series. You'll like them too.

BLOOD FEUD

PROLOGUE

PROLOGUE|THE Curse

Bera gazed out from the cabin as the flakes swirled and settled, hiding the track through the woods, obscuring the tree line and sky above. She gazed up into that blanket of white, hearing the cry of geese winging south somewhere far above. *Lucky birds—escaping from this place.*

No escape for her.

The wind cried chill. Far off, deeper in the forest, she heard wolf voices calling out to each other. Bera wiped the damp from her hair and stamped her feet. She should go inside, see to young Jaran. He'd be hungry again soon. Her son was always hungry. Like his father, Jaran came from fighting stock—the Jarle's eldest son was the best warrior on the island. But where was Hrelgi now? What had come over him, tramping off to the hall in such a manner, with the promise of winter storm to come? That temper would ruin them all.

Her husband had left three hours ago, and night beckoned.

Night was no longer safe. Not even for him. It was scarce ten miles to the hall where Hrelgi's father held power.

Or tried to . . .

A short trip—even in this weather—and Hrelgi was strong and clad in the finest wool and furs. He should be here with them. Hrelgi's business with the Jarle could have waited until morning. Jaran needed his father.

Bera chewed her lip and shivered as the wild creatures called out from the forest. Not that she was worried about those—for her or her beloved. They were just beasts. Hrelgi was more than a match for any creature or man. Stalwart and steadfast—unlike his brother and father, both lesser men in Bera's opinion. But she who now resided inside that hall was another matter.

Sheega.

Bera repressed a shiver when she thought of that woman. It was all so strange, *uncanny even*. Sheega. The beautiful enigmatic foreigner had appeared like a spectre out of the mist, a mere two weeks before the untimely death of Casla, Jarle Hrund's beloved spouse.

Poor Casla had been found floating face down, drowned in the river. No witnesses, just a body floating out to sea, seen by fishers leaving at dawn. She'd been a good swimmer, Casla. *Strange.*

Jarle Hrund should be in mourning. Instead, the old fool was caught like a wasp in amber. Hooked and trapped by those canny blue eyes and that clever, beautiful face. Sheega ruled the hall these days. Word was, she came from cursed Dunnehine far to the east. Bera could believe it. The woman was as frightening as the rumors of that strange land.

She'd warned Hrelgi to stay put. "Don't provoke that woman.

Your father's folly is not your affair," she'd yelled at him as Hrelgi had strode off through the snow, his axe hanging at waist belt and a short bow slung across his shoulders.

He'd turned once and blown her a kiss, his fair hair lifting in the wind. "I'll return before dusk, sweetheart," he'd told her. *The liar.*

Bera glanced up again. Quiet, calm. The wind had eased back, and an icy chill settled in the crack of willow branches surrounding her. She knew something was amiss. Call it female intuition, but every fiber in her body urged her to wrap Jaran in swaddling furs and leave this place. *But where to go, and what about her man?*

She heard a scream from inside and felt an icy chill cramp her stomach.

Jaran was crying. That boy never wept. She ran into the room, blinking as warmth and hearth-light dazzled her. Jaran lay face down on the floor. He'd fallen from the cot. He wasn't crying now. He was gazing up at her with those knowing blue eyes. His gaze shifted to the door, left ajar from her passage. Bera turned as the wind returned sharply and blasted the coals across the little room. A man stood there. Tall, stooped. His face shadowed by a hood, and gloved hands reaching out for the boy.

"I've come to take your son." The man's voice was crow-raw as he stooped over mother and child.

Bera shrieked and reached for her hidden knife. Grabbing its bone handle, she stabbed upward at his shadowy face.

He didn't blink, but a gloved fist snatched the knife from her grasp with eerie speed. "You don't need that," the stranger said with that rope-rough voice. "I am not your enemy, woman—but rather one who would help you."

"Unlikely words for a spectre in the eve of night," Bera hissed, and gazing down at Jaran marked how quiet and calm he was. Unafraid. Curious. *A warrior.* The child seemed at ease in the presence of this stranger. Reluctantly, she tore her gaze from Jaran and glared up at the man holding her knife. So hard to see his face inside that hood.

He flipped the blade deftly through gloved fingers, then tossed it into the oak mantle, where it quivered twice and settled. Jaran giggled as though approving.

"We're short on time, Bera Ormesdottir," the raw voice barked, making her jump. "They are coming for the boy—Jaran will be charcoal embers by dawn if you tarry here."

"What madness is this?" Bera lashed out with a fist.

Again, he was quicker, catching her wrist and lowering her arm, none too gently. He slapped her face with his free hand. "Give me the boy."

"My husband will be here soon," she said. "He'll cut out your knave's heart for striking a Jarle's daughter."

The stranger laughed, his cold gray eyes blazing like winter stars. "Hrelgi cannot help you, girl. *She* will cast the runes. Soon the hunt will range out, by order of your father the Jarle, and led by your husband's brother."

"How do you know this? What is it that they hunt?" Bera felt the icy stab of dread again. *Hrelgi.*

"Hasn't long to live." The uncanny stranger nodded briskly, his sharp eyes pinning her gaze. "I can save you, Bera. But first I must take this boy."

THE LAKE WAS A MILE WIDE BUT EASILY CROSSED IN THIS chill, the ice set hard and thick beneath his crunching boots. Hrelgi strode across without a downwards glance. Confident, eager to face what he knew would prove a trial.

But if he didn't act—then who? The strong keep going in all weather, he told himself that evening. It was the northern way. Pride and strength.

Bera had raged at him. He'd wanted to comfort her, ease her worries—but some things needed to be addressed without delay. Things that had got out of hand. Hrelgi had picked up his pace as he'd reached the lake's end, the icy wind stinging cheeks and brow. A bleak evening—even for Valkador, the wintry wind casting sleet in his eyes, watering the rims. And dusk pulling the last wan light from the sky. A few stars studded the vastness over-head, as the last snow clouds left the island to assault the coast of Leeth, a score of miles to the east.

The hall loomed ahead. A gray shape resembling a sleeping beast atop the round rise of the hill. The ancient home of the Jarles since the legendary days of Barin Farranger and Taic the Strong.

The firs were cut back from the garth, open fields glittered with rime, and the thin track wound up above the iced water of the lake to the settlement, comprising hall, harbor, and village. Jarle Hrund's people were nowhere to be seen. That wasn't surprising on a day like this. Nor would the hall be full—not with *her* inside.

Hrelgi reached the path and trotted up, leaving the crusty surface of the lake behind. No guard blocked his way, and he growled at his father's negligence.

He arrived at the hall and forced open the heavy doors

leading in. Firelight greeted him with a bright, blazing glare. It was hot inside, stuffy. Hrelgi glanced around, blinking as smoke stung his eyes.

At first, the hall seemed empty. Rushes and pine straw were strewn across its spacious floor, tapestries adorning the walls, and runes carved deep into the beams supporting roof and gable.

Then he saw her lying there, half-clad in russet and pine, a slow and clever smile on her lovely face. Those sharp pale blue eyes narrowed like a cat's as Hrelgi approached.

"You took your time getting here," Sheega said. Her smile broadened and she shifted slightly, allowing her gown to slip up above her knees, awarding a brief view of shapely legs and a darkness hinting what lay between. "Do I not excite you, Hrundsson?"

"Where is Father?" Hrelgi demanded gruffly, as Sheega rose to her knees and brushed back her long smoky-black hair with a pale beringed hand.

"Sleeping," she yawned. "I'm left here all alone—such is your father's consideration for his new wife. A woeful shame when a woman needs so much more. *Look at me.*"

He didn't want to, but turned and stared at those crafty eyes. Uncanny pale blue, large, compelling and mercurial. There was power in that gaze. Dark knowledge. Her smile broadened. "Come sit with me, Hrelgi Hrundsson. We are kin now—share a cup of mulled wine. We should be friends . . . or mayhap lovers." Her lip quivered at the corner and a hand brushed her thigh.

"I should stab you and save us all," Hrelgi muttered, standing fists clenched by his side, his rising anger muted by her savage beauty and calm hypnotic gaze.

Those eyes flashed darker for a moment. "Ill is it for a son to speak so cruelly of his new mother—a woman who would be his friend."

"You are no kin of mine, witch." Hrelgi tore his eyes from that gaze. At last he understood the power this woman had over his father. "I've come to warn you. Go while you can. Return to your bleak wasteland—I know you hail from Dunnehine. Let my father be. Leave this island, else—"

"—else what?" Sheega stood in one swift movement and gazed at him, her eyes blazing pale-blue fire. "What will you do, ungrateful fool? I would offer you more than you could imagine —yet you spurn my advances like a dotard."

"You are betrothed to my father the Jarle, and yet you blatantly lust over his son. Not only that—I've good reason to believe you killed my mother too. I should kill you." But he knew the words were pointless. She was spinning her web around him—fast. First father, now son.

"Then fucking kill me," she said with sudden viciousness, unclasping her brooch and letting the russet gown drop to the floor. She stood there naked and proud, her body flawless and white.

The long hair trailing around her shoulders and partly covering her breasts.

Hrelgi reached for his sword, and she laughed. "You really mean it—don't you, Hrelgi? You blame *me* for your mother's sad demise, for your father's weakness?"

"You're responsible for both," he said, struggling to gets the words out. "Everything turned sour when you arrived on this island."

Her lip quirked again. She walked toward him, placing cold hands on his shoulders, pressing her hips against his rising manhood. "You should be Jarle, Hrelgi. You are strong. Your

father is a broken stick, his glory days spent, seed dry and fruitless. You cannot blame me for my needs—am I not a beautiful
woman? Are you not aroused, *my love?*" She reached down and
slid a hand inside his belt, fumbling.

Hrelgi gasped at that chill touch. He pushed Sheega away
and then slapped her cheek hard, sending the woman sprawling
across the floor. Her head struck stone, and a small bead of blood
showed at her temple. She turned on him then, rising to her
knees, hissing and snarling— her pale eyes darkening to cobalt
slits of fury.

"You'll regret that, churl." Her eyes blazed blue fire. She
reached down, scooped up an object, then rose to her feet. Hrelgi
saw she held a rune carved in the shape of a bear. *Barin's Curse.*
Terror gripped his stomach. He'd heard the tales of his ancestor
and the witch who cursed his family.

Sheega bit into the rune with her teeth and spat bloody
phlegm. Then she swore vehemently and cast the rune at his
feet.

"You too are cursed, Hrelgi Hrundsson." She spoke the
words as though they were choking her. "Come full dark, your
form will change horribly. You have the manners of a bear, so a
bear you shall become." Then she laughed—a witch's cackle.

"What have you done?" Hrelgi felt his knees tremble and
buckle as all strength left him. He reached for his sword but
lacked the will to draw it from the scabbard. "What have you
done to me?"

"Your father won't last the week." She smiled savagely. "The
winter chill's inside him. Poor, noble Hrelgi, trying to do the
right thing. What a waste! But not to worry, your brother's as
comely as you are, perhaps weaker—but not nearly so stupid-
proud. Erlund Hrundsson can warm my bed, while your bear-

corpse rots on yonder barrow. Go hence, fool—else I call the guards at my ravishment!"

The words tore like barbs inside him, and try as he might Hrelgi could do nothing except flee the hall on shaking legs, the ghost of her laughter riding across his back. He reached the frozen lake, slipped on it, found his feet again. Staggering like a blind drunken fool, as the sky turned green and purple, the Giants' Dance flickering high above.

Must warn Bera before it's too late. But he'd not covered a mile before the horns sounded and the wild frenzied baying of hounds announced the hunt had begun.

SHEEGA WATCHED WITH SHINING EYES AS THE WARRIORS surrounded the great white bear, their spears jabbing and poking, looking for weak points. Beside her, the Jarle looked worn out from lack of sleep and something else. A deep-rooted horror.

Your turn next, Hrund.

The dogs snarled and circled, and the spears stabbed deep. The monster collapsed at last, stumbling on the crimson-stained ice. Sheega laughed as they hewed its head off beneath the stars of that bitter night. Then the hunters' leader, Erlund, raised the monstrous head high in both hands as a bloody trophy.

"See, Father—I've slain a beast of legend." Erlund grinned, but Jarle Hrund said nothing. Sheega whooped approval, clapped her gloved hands and rode out across the ice to meet the hunters. High above, the sky flickered and shimmered, heavenly curtains shifting from red through purple to green—the phenomena they called the "Giants' Dance."

"Such brave men." She smiled at Erlund, whose ruddy face

was flushed with excitement. "Such valor. This calls for a feast! Come, warriors, let your Jarle's new bride entertain you while you drink and eat and share bold battle stories. It's not every day we put paid to a terrible menace. I swear this is the same mad creature that has decimated the cattle these last wintry weeks."

THROUGHOUT THAT LONG NIGHT, THE FEAST RAGED furious in the hall. Maidens drank alongside their carles, as the well-fed hounds lolled idle by the blazing firepits. Jarle Hrund's eyes blinked back sleep.

"I wish Hrelgi were here," he said to the stunning woman seated at his side.

Sheega's face revealed nothing. "That boy never respected you." She clapped loudly as they brought in haunches of dark steaming meat. Sheega had said that the beast would give the warriors strength. Each man should eat from the creature's cooked flesh before retiring.

Erlund ate first, tearing into a haunch with his teeth, the rare bloody meat dripping from his mouth. His carles followed, laughing.

"What about you, beloved husband? Are you not in need of strength?" Sheega passed a platter across with the beast's half-cooked heart still seeping blood. "Come partake as a leader should—the monster's heart is yours, my Jarle."

"I am not hungry," Hrund said, but she held the plate out with both hands until he relented with a nod. "Since it pleases you, lady." He grabbed the steaming flesh and bit down, chewing into the squelching meat until it dribbled from his mouth.

Sheega watched intently, her face sharp and urgent.

It grew deathly quiet in the hall.

She stood, pulling her heavy red cloak around her shoulders to banish the sudden chill.

"It is done," she said. "You all belong to me now." Ashen faces gaped from the firelight as she walked across to the table, like a queen gliding past admiring minions. Sheega grabbed a haunch of meat in both fists and tugged at it until it broke apart.

"Know you what this is?" Sheega laughed at them. No one answered, so she scooped up a gobbet of flesh from the floor and held it crackling above the fire.

"Hrelgi Hrundsson—or rather all that's left of him." She laughed louder, seeing Erlund's face blanch white. "Yes, brave Erlund the hunter—it was your brother's own flesh on which you feasted!"

Jarle Hrund roared and rose to his feet. He seized an eating knife and leaped towards Sheega, his mouth contorted in rage. The knife cut through air.

Sheega danced sideways and caught is hand, twisting the blade free from his grasp. She caught the knife before it reached the floor and stabbed up, hard and fast, jabbing Jarle Hrund's neck and tearing deeper, red and raw.

Hrund stumbled, clutching his throat. He reached for her, then sprawled on his face. Sheega spat and kicked him as the Jarle's body quivered once, then stilled.

"Father!" Erlund had his sword levelled at Sheega but stood frozen, braced feet rooted to the spot. "*Father . . .*"

Sheega tossed the knife into the fire. She reached inside her cloak and produced an object she brandished in her fist. A rune of power. She held it up to the firelight.

"You are mine, and this island, Valkador, is mine," Sheega told the silent watchers in the hall. "Come, brave Erlund—I have need of you. And you others." She motioned the score of fighting men still seated stunned on the benches, their wives and women having fled when the Jarle was killed. "Go hence, warriors—seek out Hrelgi's wife and child. Kill them both and bring me the child's heart."

They left her, grim shadows fading from the hall. Sheega gazed down at Hrund's dead face. She smiled as she watched the blood seeping through the rushes. It had been a most satisfying feast. And now the island called Valkador was hers.

NEXT MORNING, SHEEGA WATCHED THE THIN STRAGGLE OF men approaching over the ice. Pathetic, worn-out things. Beside her, Erlund looked exhausted—she'd allowed him little sleep last night.

"What news?" said Erlund, the new Jarle of Valkador, as his lady studied the arrivals. The men looked tired, defeated, their haunted eyes avoiding her gaze.

The nearest, Gornt, loomed close. "The cabin was empty," he said. "Bera Ormesdottir and the child—no sign."

"I want them found and killed," said Sheega, her pale face flushed with anger. She spurred her horse and rode out to confront the returning warriors. "You fools will not rest until they are dead. Know that I own your frail, broken souls forever."

Later, she stood in her chamber aside the great hall. By the door hung the copper mirror, recently summoned by her last enchantment. No longer any need for denial. Sheega the Enchantress had done well. Her age-old enemies had sought her ruin, but instead she had escaped from those warlocks in distant

Dunnehine, roaming the wild lands for years as a vengeful spirit until she heard tell of this island—Valkador.

A haven, perfect for her dark purpose. The goblin face inside the mirror gazed back at her. She brushed the surface. Gantallian's face faded, replaced by her own smiling reflection.

Three hundred years old, and you don't look a day over thirty.

"I need that child dead," she told the polished glass that shimmered like rippling water, then glazed over before the twisted copper face returned.

He is protected, but a time will come when you can reach him. Gantallian's voice was a scrape of metal on bone. The goblin was vindictive as ever. She'd promised to free him one day.

"How long must I wait?" Sheega rapped the glass again.

The imp shifted and spat at her, his red eyes angry. *In twenty-seven years, the stars will align again and Jaran's destiny will become apparent. Only then can you destroy him, or in turn be destroyed . . .*

"Then wait I shall, Gantallian," Sheega said, and left mirror and goblin behind.

THE STRANGER LED THEM UP THE STEEP TRACK TOWARD THE black hole yawning ahead. A deep, dank cave cut into the cliff-side, a hundred foot above the water. Bera glanced back and down, seeing the iron-gray breakers crashing on rocks below. She could just make out the tiny boat he'd used to ferry them across from the island. They were in Leeth, a land once ruled by her ancestors' enemies. Desolate and remote—a home to eagle, boar, and bear.

The man, who called himself the Traveler, turned at the cave entrance. "This is your new home," he told Bera. "You will be safe here. I will return for the boy when enough moons have passed."

"Who are you?" Bera demanded. "What do you want with my son?" He ignored her, turning and walking away, back down the steep track toward the distant waiting boat. "You're not taking Jaran," she called after him, but the Traveler had vanished from sight.

PART ONE

***

Shen and Cardalan

1

HOLMGANG

TWENTY-SEVEN YEARS Later

Gromaki stood on the island, his dark eyes scanning the spot where sea met sky— peering at a smudge of gloom in the far distance.

Still waiting for that skiff to arrive. *Bastard's taking his time.* An hour Gromaki had stood there, flexing muscles to keep off the chill. Late winter in eastern Dunnehine awarded scant comfort. The damp, raw chill seeped into gaps in Gromaki's clothing, and the dismal breeze watered his eyes and stung his battle-hardened features.

"Any sign yet?" The voice was a grunt of discomfort and annoyance away to his left.

"Shut up, Easec," Gromaki said without turning around. His men were to remain hidden. They weren't part of the arrangement. Honorable men didn't do this—but Gromaki needed insurance. The man he would fight and kill today had a certain reputation. Holmgang was good and well, but he needed gold more than honor. The King of Leeth would pay him ample once this devious deed was done.

He shifted, wiped salty wet from his eyes. The sea had gathered chop, and fresh drizzle smudged the shoreline off to his right. *What a shithole.* Even Leeth had a better climate than this. He stood framed by dark pines, their coned heads sighing as the wind stiffened to an icy gale.

At last, Gromaki saw something. A dancing speck on the water. It had to be a boat braving wave and weather, moving swiftly, making for the remote skerry where Gromaki and his three hidden men waited.

"He's coming," Gromaki growled. "Hide yourselves well— they say he's a cunning bastard. You lads stand to get rich if you keep your wits. Let me down, and I'll cut you open and drag your guts out along this beach for the gulls." No response— they'd seen Gromaki do this.

A seasoned fighter from eastern Leeth, Gromaki had won three bouts in the Carda Games in Cardalis a dozen years back. *His glory days.* Since then he'd given too much time to drink and false women—lost all his coin. Still, no regrets. Gromaki was tough and fit. Only forty, hard as the wilderness he hailed from.

King Erlund of Leeth had heard of his prowess and sent a man to Shen, where Gromaki served as one of the hated Sapphire Guard, the foreign auxiliary corps charged with guarding the Shen River outposts against Cardalan attack. A dreary monotonous task of watching and reporting back in foul weather, only the odd skirmish to brighten the long winter months.

Gromaki had soon tired of that posting. When the letter came fresh from a courier in the dead of night, he'd been happy to comply. The new king of Leeth wanted a man dead and was willing to pay a king's ransom in gold. The only problem was, the man was Jaran Saerk. A hero of the frontier wars, and a fellow countryman from Leeth. Gromaki had no idea how and what Jaran had done to command such a price. That didn't matter. Gold spoke volumes. He'd do the deed, collect payment, and disappear.

The skiff approach through the murk and drizzle. Gromaki made out the huddled shapes of two men, one large and hunched forward, the other diminutive. The smaller man would be the ferryman. That one wouldn't hang around and was of no account. Holmgangs were banned in Shen—it was the reason why they'd settled for this remote skerry just north of the border. If word got out to the Magister and his police . . .

Gromaki smiled grimly. They wouldn't hear it from him. He'd be long gone, riding west, the wanted man's head tied neatly in a sack. Erlund of Grimhold would need proof, else Gromaki's own head would serve instead. He'd heard the rumors about that king.

As the small craft beached on the pebbles, Gromaki studied his challenger. The brute they called Saerk in the barracks. A nickname he'd earned by tearing off his steel shirt in the rage of battle and slaying a dozen Cards single-handed, the legendary bear scar showing vivid on his chest. Like him, Jaran was a guardsman in the Sapphire Empresses' Auxiliaries. But unlike Gromaki, Saerk had been recently honored and promoted for efficient work against Ran Calla's forces across the river.

Gromaki had done his homework. He knew enough about this man. It was why he'd brought his people—something he'd never usually do. Three Shen lads and local thugs. Gang members from Pol Shen dockyards. Do anything for coin, and good fighters to boot.

This Jaran had been in Shen for years and gained a fearsome reputation, his violent rages during battle hinted at a berserker, like those ancient savages who fought naked and chewed their shields in the distant days of great King Hal.

Jaran Saerk was an enigma in the army. Subtle, soft-speaking and patient, for a Northman. Gromaki had dug deep to little avail. The man was a loner who spoke seldom and kept his own council—but not one to be crossed. He had a temper, they'd said, even among comrades. Marked by a bear as a child, apparently. A great white bear from the frozen north, the rumors said. He wore that scar like a badge of pride. Gromaki had seen Jaran wrestle twice. The man was iron strong, and quick to boot. But he had flesh, and flesh could be pierced.

It had only taken an insult. A staged quarrel that Gromaki instigated. Then a proposal to meet on this small outcrop. Man to man using sword, axe and spear. *The old way.* No shields allowed. Holmgangs had specific rules. Proud Jaran had readily complied.

Gromaki stamped his feet and forced warmth into his limbs as he watched the big man leap from the boat after a curt word to his companion. Moments later, the other fellow was rowing past rocks, doubtless seeking shelter alongside Gromaki's own vessel while the fight lasted. Gromaki smiled grimly. It wouldn't last long.

His challenger approached, loping up the rise to where Gromaki waited with axe resting in callused palms. He studied his adversary as Jaran loomed close. A huge man, taller than him by a head, and Gromaki was nearly six feet in height. Jaran had broad shoulders and a finely honed frame from constant fighting.

He looked energetic, showing catlike grace as he loped, half-trotting up the rise. He wore steel-studded leather trousers, doeskin boots, and a long blue cloak clasped with silver shaped in the image of a bear. His long, fair hair blew around his face. He wore no helmet, but Gromaki noticed the axe and sword hanging from his waist belt, half hidden by the heavy cloak.

Gromaki smiled, stowed his axe in the belt loop, and reached over for the spear, thrust base-down into the sandy soil. He tugged it free and readied.

Jaran Saerk stopped ten paces short and watched him with calm, pale-blue eyes. His face was broad and strong. Handsome —women might think. Those eyes were sharp, the stubble on his chin slightly darker than his hair. Jaran unclasped the silver bear broach, allowing the blue cloak to drop silent to the ground. He wore no shirt beneath, and his huge chest and shoulders were tanned from years of sun, wind and rain.

When Gromaki saw the horrific scar so close up, he almost had second thoughts. It was true what they'd told him. This man had been torn open by a bear in his youth. The rumor was that he'd killed the mad creature with his bare hands. Gromaki hadn't believed that, but now . . .

The scar was impressive. Ugly. A mass of torn flesh, resembling claw prints cutting deep through his left shoulder, breast and upper belly. Vainly enhanced by the tattooing, a bright blue and red mix of runes and Shen spirals that must have taken the artist over a week. A fearsome sight, and a warrior clearly in his prime.

Gromaki levelled his spear and spat in the dirt. *I'm ready.*

Jaran Saerk folded his massive arms and smiled. "You've still time to apologize—yes?" he said, his feet braced wide and brawny arms still folded. He looked at ease, bored even.

Gromaki tensed, then lightning-swift hurled the spear. A good, clean throw. Jaran knocked the weapon aside with his forearm, the only movement he'd made. A dismissive, arrogant flick as though he was brushing a fly from his arm. "I'll take that for a 'no,' then." He reached casually for his axe.

"Now!" Gromaki yelled, and his three companions leaped out from their hides. Crossbows twanged and bolts thudded into sand. Jaran Saerk had disappeared.

Gromaki circled. *Where the fuck is he?* A man screamed to his left. *Hotei?* Then, over to his right, he heard a thud, and he turned to see Het's shaggy head resting by a tussock.

A roar followed, then another scream as Easec stumbled into sight, his body split open through chain mail, the large rent spilling blood and entrails. Jaran stepped forth behind him, axe in left hand, sword in right. He kicked the crossbow at Gromaki in disdain. Three men dead in as many seconds. The stories were true—this man was a legend. But Gromaki was no craven, and he wanted that gold. He strode forward, his own axe swinging.

Jaran caught that weapon mid-swing with his free hand and tugged Gromaki close, pulling him off balance. He lifted the Gromaki from his feet and butted him hard in the face, mashing his nose.

Jaran let go and Gromaki fell back, spitting blood, his vision blurred. He steadied himself, blinked and made to swing again. *You'll pay for that, bastard.*

The swing went wide. Then Gromaki gasped as Jaran's axe thudded into his stomach. Jaran twisted the blade and pulled the weapon free. Gromaki screamed and stumbled to his knees. A kick in his face sent him sprawling.

Jaran Saerk gazed down at the man called Gromaki. He hadn't known him well. A recent addition to the Empress's Auxiliaries. From Leeth, like most the auxiliaries were. A trouble-maker and lout, and a treacherous one to boot.

"Finish it," Gromaki said, clearly finding it hard to speak with the broken jaw and oozing gash in his belly. Jaran smiled instead and placed his boot in that gaping hole, making it squelch and ooze. Gromaki screamed again.

"Who sent you, *assassin*?" Jaran's deep voice was laden with irony.

"Fuck you." Time for the boot once more, and again Gromaki screamed.

"I'm in no rush," Jaran said, turning his head, hearing a shout from down by the shore.

"You done up there, big lad?"

"Not yet," Jaran called out dismissively.

"Well hurry up, I'm fucking frozen."

"The ferryman's cold." Jaran smiled down at Gromaki. "Poor little fellow. He's a tad grumpy. Best you tell me who paid you, *assassin*, lest I have Finvar run up here to cut off your manhood. He's from Dunnehine, or thereabout—you know what they're like. *Spiteful*." The boot squelched in again.

"The . . . *king*," Gromaki coughed blood as the agony ripped into him.

"I don't know any kings," Jaran said. "I think he's lying," he yelled, turning as a shadow loomed close.

The ferryman emerged silently beside him.

"You shouldn't sneak up on people like that," Jaran said. "Could prove hazardous for your health."

"Looks like a liar," Finvar the ferryman said, ignoring Jaran's last comment. "Kill him, Jaran Saerk, and let's be off before it

gets dark. And what took you so long—a man of your reputation? Too damn cold for exchanging pleasantries." He then saw
the other corpses shredded across the ground. "Oh . . . I see. An
ambush. That's not good. Hard to trust people these days, and
him a bloody Northman too. I know how integrity and honor
are so important to you large lads."

Jaran pointedly ignored the ferryman and continued to focus
on Gromaki. "Tell me of this king. Do so swiftly, and I'll ease
your pain."

"The King of Leeth." Gromaki's face was paling. He'd be
dead before long.

"Leeth? Hah, that wilderness has no king. Hasn't for decades.
Try harder."

"It does . . . now . . . Erlund held a thing. United the
Northmen and settled old scores. Rethin and Hragglund
complied to pay him scot." Gromaki's words were whispers
forced through chokes. "Aided . . . by sorcery, they say." He spat
that word out. "He rules supreme from Grimhold Castle . . . has
for over . . . five years. I . . . was . . ." Jaran reached down and
sliced open the dying man's throat. Gromaki shuddered and
stilled.

"Well, that was helpful," the wiry Finvar said. "He was just
getting chatty."

"Shut up, ferryman," Jaran said. "I need to think."

"I'd sooner you do that on the boat. I'm ready to depart
whenever you are." Finvar turned away and trotted back to the
boat.

Jaran ignored him and stared down at Gromaki's corpse.
There was only one Erlund he'd heard of. Not a common name
since that curse. *That* Erlund had killed Jaran's father almost
three score years ago. Uncle Erlund, who'd become the puppet of

a witch—or so his mother had hinted before the Traveler urged her to be quiet. He'd assumed that Erlund was long dead—vanished like all rumor of his ancient island home. Valkador. Another name he hadn't heard in years, and only twice in childhood.

Could this new king be that same individual? Had to be. *Only thing that makes sense.* "Looks like I'm going back there," he said quietly, kicking Gromaki one last time.

He shrugged. Life was strange. He had no memory of Valkador. He'd only been a babe when the Traveler fled the island with his mother. Bera had hinted about what had happened that night, but had said very little about the detail, especially after the Traveler returned. That had been years ago, and Jaran's memory was hazy. Those two had their secrets. Bera had said they were protecting him against someone, and that to mention names would draw their attention.

He loved her, but over time Jaran came to doubt Bera's exile story as another fable spun by the trickster who had come for him when he was a boy. The Traveler, he'd called himself. A strange individual, wise in lore. Had some kind of hold over his mother.

Valkador was a myth, the Traveler had told him. At fifteen, Jaran had stolen a skiff and sailed across those waters seeking the truth. He'd returned confused and bitter. There was no island, only fog and endless seas. Bera had raged at him upon his return, branding him a reckless fool. They'd quarreled bitterly. The Traveler arrived that same week and smoothed things over with his glib-easy tongue.

There was no Valkador, the Traveler had said as he led Jaran out to the wilderness for that first training. It was a fable. The real truth of Jaran's past was lost to time, he'd said. Even Bera couldn't remember, as she too had been bewitched. Resentful of his mother, Jaran had believed the Traveler. There was no island. Bera had lied to him. *But why?*

He turned, hearing the flap of wings and saw a gull swoop past. It settled on a dead tree and preened its feathers.

Jaran felt a shiver. He gazed at the bird for a moment and shrugged again. The gull watched him, then shrieked noisily and took wing, angling off at speed into the gray. Jaran cursed, cleaned his weapons, and then scooped up his cloak and threw it over his shoulders, before ambling back down to the water's edge where Finvar waited impatiently.

"You look glum," the jaunty, freckled-faced man said.

"You'll be glum with my sword up your arse," Jaran told him.

"I'm just saying."

"Don't talk, ferryman. *Row.*"

Finvar manned the oars with dexterity. He was grinning for some reason Jaran couldn't guess, and commenced singing a bawdy song. Jaran watched him mournfully.

"Please stop that," Jaran said. "You've a voice like a dying toad."

"I like singing," Finvar said. "You don't want me to talk and I have to do something to pass the time."

"I would have thought rowing was sufficient."

"I've a curious mind," Finvar said. "It's a bit of a curse. You see, I get in a lot of trouble because folk don't understand me."

"I can imagine."

"You know what I think it is?" Finvar stowed an oar and rubbed his arms.

"I don't care."

"I'm a warm soul with a giving heart. And this is a cold, hard world."

"I heard you were a thief and a killer, and that you would do anything for coin—even clean floors in taverns."

Finvar looked pained. "I've been through a rough patch, is all."

"Midnight Cutting Crew."

"No longer a member." Finvar blew on his hands and grabbed both oars again. "Fuck, but it's cold." The coast was looming close. Jaran saw the harbor lights—they'd be back in town inside an hour.

He studied his companion. Finvar was tough and wiry, his dark, smoky hair both curly and frizzled. His constant banter and gap-tooth smiles masked a canny ruthlessness. Jaran knew he was a wanted man in several states. And his old chums were after him too, the infamous highwaymen and robbers known as the Midnight Cutting Crew, or Cutters for short. Finvar Droll —or "Drolly Fin," as he was sometimes called—was fast running out of options. He'd leapt at the chance of earning some sly coin by rowing the famous Jaran Saerk across to Dunnehine on some illegal Northman business. Jaran had explained about Holmgangs, but such definitions were lost on Finvar.

"Why don't you just knife the fat bastard when he's asleep?" Finvar had asked when Jaran asked him for help.

"We don't do that," he'd replied. "Northmen are not sly cowards like you weasel easterners."

Finvar had grinned at him, hearing that. "Of course, I'd be happy to help."

Jaran snapped back to the present when Finvar resumed his song. This was proving a long evening. He thought about the fight and what the dying Gromaki had told him. He needed time to process. That was impossible with Finvar's racket in his ear.

Instead, Jaran gazed out across the water, dismal weather and storm clouds mustering in the east.

"I'm tired of winter," Finvar said, after finishing a particularly dreary song. "Ready for some sunshine."

"It's always winter here," Jaran said.

"And you a Northman? I thought you'd like this gloomy climate."

"I didn't say I liked it not. But it's brighter back west. This coast is always so gloomy."

"I've heard tell that Valkador's a beautiful island." Finvar's smile had faded, replaced by a sharp glance. "Where you hail from, isn't it?"

Jaran fingered his axe and glared at the ferryman. "And what would you know about that?" This was the second surprise today. *Valkador and Erlund.* Names from his shadowy past. Forgotten, or lost to time—especially here in the east where they never looked beyond their own borders. Clearly there was more to this rogue rowing him ashore than he had assumed. But what did Finvar want? "Are you a spy, or eavesdropper? The place you mentioned doesn't exist—I'm from Leeth, as I told you."

"I know what you told me, Northman," Finvar leaned over and spat in the water. "But I'm from a place where people know how to read signs. I've heard of Valkador and believe it very real. It's not just that. I know your story, or rather I can guess. Your famous scar, the way you carry yourself. There are tales among my folk of such a one."

"Dunnehine," Jaran snorted. "What, are you a fucking wizard as well as a cutpurse and thief? I hear little good about your country, ferryman."

Finvar's face was bleak. "I'm not from Dunnehine, but I'll

forgive the insult. You weren't to know." Jaran raised a brow at this angry change of tone. "I'm from Coolega Island."

"And where is that?" Jaran watched the harbor lights winking. Time to get off this tub and seek out an ale house. He had some hard thinking to do.

"Off the coast of Dunnehine," Finvar muttered. "North. Three days hard sail. Not my original home—like you, I'm an exile from a different place."

"What nonsense have you heard about me? About this . . . Valkador?"

Finvar's face relaxed, and his freckly grin returned. "I'd rather talk by a warm fire with a large ale, and maybe a lass or two for company. My lips grow numb out here."

"I think you're full of shit, ferryman," Jaran said, resuming his watch of the land swelling ahead.

"I could help you," Finvar said. "Find your home, or prove its existence. I know you've doubts."

Jaran stared at the ferryman long and hard. This was proving a vexing day. And he didn't like puzzles that he couldn't solve. How could this knave know about him? Jaran scarcely recalled the words his mother had spoken all those years ago. Three names lost to time: Hrelgi, Erlund, and Valkador. The father he'd lost, the uncle who'd killed him. And the fabled island where it had happened. He rubbed his face as weariness clouded his vision. "Why make such an extravagant offer?" he asked eventually.

"Because at the moment I can really use a big, violent friend," Finvar said.

ALMOST AN HOUR LATER, THE FERRYMAN EASED THE SKIFF
into Pol Shen Harbor. Jaran wasn't overly surprised to see the
Harbor Master standing at the end of the dock surrounded by a
squad of Imperial Police. Hard to be secretive in Shen. Someone
always knew what you were doing.

"Good evening!" Finvar called up cheerfully as the police
grabbed the boat's sides and pulled it over.

"Drolly Fin" —the Harbor Master's face was disapproving
—"save yourself a flogging or worse, and report where you've
taken this man. The word *Holmgang* comes to mind."

Finvar glanced at Jaran. "Sorry, mate. Word will out." And
then he told the harbor master all about their sojourn to the
skerry and the brutal fight that followed.

2

SAVARNA AND VIAN

THE WAGON CREAKED AND RATTLED, hitting every pothole on the Imperial Highway. The two guards glared at Savarna as though the noise and jolts were her fault. She ignored them. They were minions, persons of no account.

She was to meet the Empress this evening. Had been summoned. Impressive for a recently captured slave. But Savarna had certain talents and the Empress had got word.

Another pothole. That one was deep, and the entire carriage shook. One guard cursed, while the other kept glaring at her. She risked a smile: "Time of the month, soldier?"

His glare deepened. They would be flogging her or worse, were it not for the orders that had just arrived that morning. The man beside her sniggered slightly. The Magister's aide had a sense of humor that his soldiers clearly lacked.

Savarna had been a slave only a week and hadn't adjusted well. They'd tried chaining her, but when she tore out the overseer's tongue with her teeth, the others held back, notifying the masters. It wasn't until she performed the skin-shift that they

decided this slave needed to be reported to the top officials up in
Pol Shen, the Imperial City. Thirty miles distant according to the
last milestone, where they'd stopped for mundane necessities.
Aside from those, her escort and guards hadn't tarried on the
way, eager to shed the responsibility of their burden. It was no
common thing, slaves changing skin color.

"Your death will prove an entertainment, I feel." The aide's
voice was nasal. Savarna wondered if he had a head cold. His face
was thin, as though it had been squeezed on either side by a
Yamondon wrestler's hands. An unhappy-looking man, despite
his pretense of humor. But then the Shen were always miserable.
One of the soldiers grinned at her—the biggest of the two, who
she'd just insulted. "I'd heard your kind were long extinct," the
aide continued, smiling across at his soldier.

"My . . . *kind?*" Savarna stifled a yawn. "What are you saying
—I'm not human?"

He didn't respond but shuffled awkwardly beside her, and the
guards looked grim again. "Not fully human and possessed by
evil spirits, like all Rundali?" Savarna said. "Have to have them
burnt from my soul."

"After slow questioning," the big soldier said. She'd scared
them back at the camp. It was why they hated her and were
trying to goad her. She wasn't taking the bait.

"*Torture* and burning? I'd have thought Imperial Shen would
have learned more sophisticated pastimes during its twenty-thou-
sand-year lineage. But you Shen are not who you were back then,
are you? You're decadent, depraved, and weak—a sad reflection
of your former selves. Like your fucking roads—cracking open
from within." The wagon struck another pothole to emphasize
her point.

The thin-faced man at her side fidgeted again, and his

soldiers' scowls deepened. They didn't know how to deal with her. Nobody did. The Empress's *people* had summoned this wild young woman. They couldn't intervene—not so much as lay a finger on her. That would mean slow death in one of the Magister's rooms of correction. And their feeble attempts at scaring her were risible.

The Magister's aide shuffled again. He was about to speak when the wagon came to a crashing halt. The soldiers lurched forward, bumping into Savarna and her escort.

"Must have thrown a wheel," she said, laughing as the soldiers shuffled back on their seats. "You people should spend more money on your roads." She looked at the screen masking the tree-lined highway outside. There were voices out there—shouts, getting louder. *Fighting?* Men fighting. Hard not to recognize the clash of steel on wood and leather.

They were under attack. An ambush. Savarna smiled, suddenly enjoying the morning.

"Go see," the aide ordered the biggest soldier out. He nodded briefly and pushed open the carriage door. He didn't get far. The arrow pierced his throat, and he tumbled from the carriage. The other soldier grabbed his Jian blades, while the aide shouted and fumbled for his ritual knife.

Savarna got there first. She wrested the thin blade from his weak grasp and plunged it into his side. The aide screamed, so she stabbed again, and a third time until he wept and slid from the seat.

The second soldier was torn between his comrade's death and the confusion in the carriage. He tried to stand but there wasn't room, and his swords were useless in here. He glared at Savarna briefly and then leapt outside. She heard him running off before a short yell announced he hadn't got far.

The sound of heavy boots approached. She waited, and then the carriage door creaked wide. A face appeared—heavy set, scarred and brutal, shaggy black hair and thick moustache. This was no educated Shen. Either a bandit, escaped slave, Cardalan deserter from the frontier, or—more likely this close to the city —one of the several robber gangs working the roads.

The rough face smiled, so Savarna smiled back. "Come see this," he said. He turned, yelled to someone out there. More boots approaching, and then two more faces much like his. Moustaches, long shaggy black hair, scars and earrings. Evil grins showing bad teeth.

"It's kind of you to drop by," Savarna said, flicking the bloody knife through her fingers. The men leered at her.

"Rundali," the first one said. "Tell by the color of her hair."

"She's a rare beauty," said the second man. "Fetch a fine price. That bright red mane and gold-flecked brown eyes. Exotic."

"Pass me that knife, please," the first man she'd seen said in a calm, reasonable manner. He looked like the leader, older, and the other two stepped back to allow him into the carriage. The big brigand took seat opposite her and stared down at the dying aide, wriggling and weeping on the floor.

Savarna tossed the knife between her fingers and the brigand raised a brow. "You are a circus girl." He barked a laugh, then stamped hard on the aide's neck, snapping the bone. "His mewing was annoying me," he said, flashing her a grin. "I'm Gurtei. These lads are Roile and Mulci. The other boys are mopping up the rest of your people."

"My people?" Savarna deftly switched hands with the knife again.

"A large train of seven carriages usually means someone

important in tow. I don't think it was him. Doesn't look important. Please give me that knife. I won't ask a third time."

She flicked the blade again defiantly. "What happens now?" she asked.

Gurtei made an impatient gesture with both hands. "Depends on you. Toss that aside and come outside quietly. Then you can meet the full team, and share some hot food and warmth. We'll most likes sell you, as Roile said—but we can at least be civil until then. One has to make an income in these difficult times."

"What if I stab you like I just stabbed that?" Her eyes flicked to the dead aide, his blood seeping from the carriage to the damp ground outside.

Gurtei smiled. He was missing two front teeth. "Circus trickster or not, you're not in my league, girl. If you don't comply, we'll have to get rough."

Savarna flashed him a grin, then she stabbed hard and fast at Gurtei's neck. He was quicker than she expected. He shifted sideways, catching her wrist and wrenching the knife free. Then he leaned forward and punched her hard in the face.

"Help me drag her outside, lads," Gurtei shouted to his men. "This one needs some training." Before he took a proper hold, Savarna spun around and elbowed his right ear, knocking him back. She kicked Roile in the face as he re-emerged, and then leapt out from the carriage.

She struck loose stone and rolled on impact, found her feet again, and lithely twisted out of range of Mulci's questing Jian blades. She dived into the brush hemming the highway and ran full pelt into the deeper woods beyond, switching side to side, avoiding any arrows they might shoot.

"Catch that bitch!" she heard Gurtei's weary voice yelling after his men.

It was two hours later and almost dusk when they dragged her back to camp. Roile had three broken fingers, and Mulci's left eye was black and puffy. Two of the other robbers were in worse states, and one of them wouldn't be siring children any time soon.

They dragged her close to the fire. The camp was a mile back from the road, hidden from prying eyes, and a further ten miles from where they'd ambushed the train. Two of the robbers forced Savarna to her knees, then shoved her face down in the dirt.

She rolled, but Gurtei's boot kept her pinned in place. He leaned forward with interest, noticing the small brand on her ankle. Still red and the flesh around it swollen, though the pain had faded to a dull nagging. "You were a slave?"

Savarna didn't respond but glared up at him in silence. "I'm from a high-born family," she said eventually. "A Shen slaver party raided our estate, killed the men, and made all the women slaves. My family is no more. Butchered or captured, chained to the plow, or whoring their new masters."

"But you put up a fight and got extra attention," Gurtei grunted. "Rundali—I've heard of those woods surrounding your country. Dangerous place, they say."

"It is for you foreigners," she said.

"Well, here's the thing." Gurtei smiled pragmatically. "I'm liking you more than I did, girl. You've spirit and some fighting skills—and we're always looking for new talent. Especially now you've buggered up three of the lads. Rosin's eye's a mess, and Sumil can't walk properly."

"You want me to join your gang?" Savarna laughed like a crow, and the faces surrounding her looked confused and angry.

"What's funny?" Gurtei asked her. "You should be honored. The Midnight Cutting Crew don't usually employ women— except for nighttime pleasures, of course. And you'll have plenty of opportunity to share those, should you wish to."

"Thanks for the offer, but I've other plans," she said, and Gurtei laughed this time.

"A runaway slave with *other* plans. What have we got here, lads?"

"We should strip the bitch and stake her out in front of the fire," Roile said. "Take turns, and then cut her throat. Look what she did to my hand. Three broken nubbins and one half bitten through."

"You were careless, Roile—so shut up and sit down," Gurtei said. He turned to Savarna again. "He does have a point. Maybe we should cut our losses and do away with you. Or perhaps sell you promptly in Ferrytown."

"Where's that?" she asked.

"A small trading town across the bay from Pol Shen. It's in Dunnehine, so free from Shen interference. We conduct a lot of business there."

"Happy for you," Savarna said. "Thing is—I'm to meet the Empress. She demanded it herself. Those fools were delivering me hence."

Gurtei stared at her long and hard. "Why would Exalted, Sun-Shines-Out-Her-Arse, Imperial Rasnei summon a recently captured slave girl to her court? How would she even know about you?"

"I have certain . . . *talents*."

"Why not show us?"

"You might not appreciate them."

"We're all big lads here. Go on—be a sport."

"Tomorrow, and only if you don't sell me in Ferrytown," Savarna said.

"Agreed." Gurtei turned to those others gathered around the fire. "Think that's fair, lads?" Several nodded and a few looked askance. "We'll let you pick your time."

"Good. Don't say I didn't warn you."

Gurtei raised a brow. "What do they call you, strange one?"

"Savarna." It was as though her name held a power they couldn't comprehend. A secret. After she told them, those members of the Midnight Cutting Crew seated around the fire grew very quiet. Most made excuses and headed for their blankets, while others took their turn to watch the camp. Soon only Gurtei sat over the fire, his hands deftly whittling a stick and poking its end in the embers.

"I need to meet the Empress," Savarna said in a quiet whisper meant only for his ears. "So that I can kill her."

Gurtei nodded then yawned. "We'll talk about it in the morning. Suffice to say you have my curiosity. I won't sell you, but have a care. The other lads might."

"They will die first," Savarna told him. "And if by chance a fellow did get lucky, there is always my brother."

"Your brother?"

"Vian will come."

"I thought your kin all dead?"

"Vian lives—I would know if it were otherwise."

She stood and smiled down at him briefly before retiring to the blanket they'd given her for warmth. She rolled up and closed her eyes, content in the knowledge she would be left in peace. She'd spooked them enough for one day. Tomorrow was another matter. *Where are you, beloved?* She whispered his name and let sleep carry her down to those golden swaying pastures.

I'M HERE . . .

Vian stiffened and responded in a whisper, as her words floated through his quick mind. *Savarna*—she needed him. They must have captured her along with the rest of the womenfolk, taken her north. His sister and twin. They would pay for that —those Shen.

Vian had buried the other members of his family this morning. He hadn't wept. His kind seldom did. But his silent rage had left the servants terrified and shaking as they assisted him. Two survivors who'd been out fishing on the lake when the raiders came. He'd found them wandering aimless, like mad fools, and slapped some sense back into them.

Hulo, the oldest, told Vian his nephew Coru had arrived back at the villa a few days after the atrocity, discovering the carnage. Coru had ridden north and reported back to his uncle. Hulo said the boy had seen a crew of slavers leading women up the road toward the mountains. A Shen slaving party. They were ranging wider these days, now that Cardalan had conquered most of the surrounding lands.

Once he'd performed the rites and seen to his kin in proper fashion, Vian turned to Hulo and his nephew. "Shen slavers— you're certain? Not Cards? Or distant Vendeli, and Yamondon up from the coast?"

"They were Shen, Lord," Hulo said. "I am certain of it. Coru here glimpsed them riding the north way. They'd be heading up through the passes to avoid entanglement in our forests."

"The overseers wore Imperial blue, Lord," the younger servant said. "They were striking our womenfolk as they led them away. I could only watch on." His young face was a mask of self-loathing and anger. "It was nearly two weeks ago. We've done nothing."

"You did well, both of you. Staying alive." Vian rested his palms on their shoulders. "And I'm sure you've lost loved ones too. Go mourn for them, and with my blessing. Don't worry about the captives. They'll be back safe and free within a week —this I swear."

"What of you, Lord?" Old Hulo's eyes were rimmed with tears. "You can't fight them all."

"I've a journey to undertake," Vian said, dusting down his tunic. "Someone to find, others to kill. But first I'll catch up with those slavers, send a clear message north."

He left them without further word. Returning to the villa, Vian sought out his weapons, still resting on the half-burnt pergola where he'd first seen the ruins and remains of his ancestral home. House Eltayn was no more. *Time to go.* Vian grabbed a spear, his twin Jian swords, and a curved knife, plus the package he always carried containing his silver flute.

Vian ran. His strong legs carried him through the rice fields, past the lakeshore and up into the foothills. He ran all day and into the night, his anger cooling as he focused on a plan. Vian slowed to a walk as he reached the mountain passes. Once there, he studied the signs. Easy for one such as he. And they were careless, these Shen. Unheeding of any pursuit. Who would dare?

But they were as ignorant as they were cruel. And very soon they'd pay full dividends.

It took almost a week. Vian caught up with them one crisp dawn, high in the mountain passes, the snow painting their tracks for him to follow in haste. A week-long chase with scarce sleep and little rest, but he wasn't weary. It took a lot to tire Vian Eltayn, and his controlled rage kept burning like a twisting knife inside, driving him forward.

A bright, clear morning. The mountain's shoulders flanking the path, green pines rising up to meet the snow-clad peaks, their faces glinting in the sun. Vian slowed to a walk, hearing shouts. He darted from the road, seeing the Shen horses tethered to trees. There were men up and about, stretching, yawning, and swearing coarsely at each other. He counted seven, clad in blue cloaks and leather.

Then Vian noted the tall one pointing and giving orders, the blue silk over-shirt marking him clearly as a Shen master and the leader of this sorry crew. Finally, he saw what he sought—the bundles of female misery lashed in a group at the far side of the camp, except three who were weeping near the fire, their clothes torn and ragged. Obviously, these three had been the entertainment last night.

Vian counted twenty women. Savarna wasn't there. But then he knew she wouldn't be. He walked through the trees making no sound. Like a shadow, Vian freed the horses first and whispered in their ears. They would wait for his command before fleeing.

He approached the camp, flexed his arms and stabbed his spear's base hard into the earth. Swords out, Vian walked into the camp. Men turned and swore, seeing him strolling toward them. They yelled and reached for weapons, but Vian was upon them, cutting, whirling, stabbing and slicing—a dancer dealing death with either hand.

He cut, danced away. Ran back, danced in again, and leaping forward struck once more. The twin swords dripped crimson. Vian's rage cooled as he sliced the head from the last slaver clad in blue painted leather. That left the leader, currently running for the cover of the pines.

Vian ran after him. He leapt, twisted his lithe body, and crashed into the overseer's back with both heels slamming down. The man sprawled face-first and skidded through snow. Vian landed bird-light beside him, balanced with feet braced even and swords held parallel.

One of the three girls who weren't lashed had caught up with him, her eyes wide in disbelief. "Lord . . .?"

"Free the rest." Vian motioned she leave him be. The girl nodded and sped back to the camp, her soft mushy tread announcing her departure.

"Your turn." Vian kicked the overseer until the man was forced onto his back, staring up with terrified eyes.

"You came from nowhere," he said.

"I'm a ghost," Vian said. "Your people used to call us ghosts, back when you hunted us in packs."

"Aikashi?" The man's face paled visibly.

"In my blood." Vian smiled down at him. "We can do this two ways. You can talk and die quickly, or else I can sate my appetite and take my leisure. I'm happy either way—you'll tell me everything eventually."

The slaver chose the first option, and moments later Vian returned to the camp where the freed women shivered and huddled close. Vian recognized one or two of the older ones.

They'd been around before he'd left for his long sojourn in distant lands. Chiarra and Mjorde.

Chiarra rose to her knees and bowed her head to the floor. "Gods bless us that you live, Lord. They have the lady Savarna. She killed some of his men, so the slaver's soldiers took her north."

"I know." He smiled. "That's not your concern. Are you strong enough to go home? I cannot look after you."

"We will be fine," Chiarra said. "They didn't hurt us, Lord. Not much anyway."

"The horses await you," Vian said. "Save for one I'll need. Go, find the warmth. Old Hulo and his nephew are back at the villa. There's work to be done there. I expect to see improvements on my return."

It took a while, but they mastered the horses easily enough. Vian waved to Chiarra as she led the party of women and girls back down the mountain pass. Hopefully most of them would survive the journey home and eventually recover from their ordeal.

Vian turned away, reclaimed his spear and sack, and approached the last horse. "I need to push you hard, my friend," he told the beast. "That slaver worked for a man called Shateke, perhaps your owner. You can lead me to him, boy."

Vian vaulted on the gelding's back and urged the big horse on up the track as fresh snowfall dusted the way ahead and the sky darkened to vengeful violet.

3

FERRYTOWN

Jaran Saerk allowed the harbor police to escort him back to the city barracks. No point making a fuss—they liked their rules in Shen. He knew Holmgangs were forbidden. He'd been careful, but it seemed not careful enough when trusting that ferryman. Honor had required he acted when that troll Gromaki insulted him. To do nothing was beneath contempt, and to kill him in a drunken brawl, or sly knife in the gut—far worse. A warrior's honor and strength were everything. And Holmgangs were the northern way. A tradition left from his ancestors—the kings of Leeth.

No one spoke as Jaran was ushered into the Correction Administrators' chamber. Tin Lous, the duty officer, stood fidgeting with his wispy moustache. He looked edgy and nervous. The Shen didn't like Northmen, considered them oafish and unsubtle. Vulgar, and lacking the nuances and intricacies of an ancient culture such as Shen's. But Northmen were needed to help hold back the rising incursions from the cursed Cardalan Republic, or "Cards" as they were contemptuously called.

Tin Lous fumbled and fiddled with papers and details on his highly polished desk. Eventually he turned and awarded Jaran a frown through thin round spectacles. "This has to go further," he said. "I'll need to file a report to your superiors."

"If you say so." Jaran shrugged, and the little man turned his face away. Jaran smiled wryly—they were all intimated by him, these Shen. "Rules are to be obeyed—yes, Secretary."

"I'm not the Secretary. I'm an administrator in his service. And, yes, it's protocol." Tin Lous rubbed his skinny fingers and wiped them on his silk gown. It left a stain on the expensive yellow cloth.

"Well then," Jaran said. "Here I am—all yours, administrator, and ready for chastisement."

"We will have to secure you in the Correction Rooms until the Imperial Magister decides on your punishment. An unfortunate business, I'm sorry to say."

"It's fine—I'm in need of a rest," Jaran said.

"Hmm." Tin Lous rubbed those greasy palms again. He turned to his police, the two who remained. "Escort this . . . *Northman*. Lock him in the retaining cell where he can await word of his punishment." He turned away briskly.

"I hope your day improves," Jaran said to Tin Lous's back, as the gray-clad police led him through a maze of offices and rooms, down a long corridor, and finally into a dark, square room walled with bars framing a lone cot, a rush lamp that wasn't lit, and a murky bucket in the corner.

"You can leave." Jaran walked inside and flicked his fingers at the police, who shifted uncomfortably.

"We have to stay," the biggest one said.

"Fine, you can watch me have a shit." Jaran reached for the bucket.

Hours later, he heard shouting and heavy boots approaching from the corridor beyond. Jaran smiled. Northmen were easily recognizable by their tread. Shen feet brushed the ground like leafy whispers. Northmen stomped, none more than the one approaching.

Hranic Finehair's florid face was furious as he pushed passed the two police guards who'd leapt to their feet in alarm. "What is this nonsense?" He chewed his red beard and struck the bars, making them rattle.

Tin Lous appeared, his thin face more miserable than before. "Holmgang."

"What?" Hranic turned and glared at the officer. Jaran smiled at both of them from the shelter of his cage.

"Please calm down, Captain Hranic, and let me explain," Tin Lous said, rubbing ink-stained hands.

"Do so quickly." Hranic rounded on him. The renowned captain of the auxiliaries was not a man to cross. He was nearly a tall as Jaran, a mass of battle scars crisscrossing his arms and face. A bull of a man, cloaked and booted, sword and axe belted at either side of his waist. His thick, matted beard and long, waxen hair were both braided and combed to perfection.

Tin Lous stepped forward, rubbing the stubble on his chin. "A skerry off Dunnehine," he said. "A local rogue took coin to row this one across. The man sent prompt word to us, insisting his service had been requested and he wasn't about to refuse a Northman. We agreed to spare the wretch, allowing him keep his coin, as it was your man who broke the rules and doubtlessly intimidated the other."

Jaran raised a brow, looking at the two of them. He'd pay the talkative ferryman a visit at some point when this nonsense was forgotten.

"Leave me alone with Jaran Saerk," Hranic said. Tin Lous looked uncomfortable, and his guards shuffled awkwardly. "Just piss off." Hranic glared at all three, until Tin Lous clicked his tongue and snapped his fingers, bidding the two police follow.

"My superior, Soma Ghee, will hear about this," Tin Lous muttered before leaving the room. "I am an important man, and your tone should show some respect, Captain Finehair." Hranic ignored him and turned to face Jaran.

Jaran grinned at him. "Poor little fellow."

"You have nothing to smile about," Hranic replied, glaring at him.

Life is funny," Jaran said. "There's always something to smile about, especially with these little Shen."

"Who will have you flogged, or worse, in a few days' time."

"I don't think that will happen, Captain." Jaran seated himself on the bed, lay back and folded his arms behind his neck. He closed his eyes, feigned weariness.

"You broke their stupid rules," Hranic said. "Holmgangs and private vendettas are forbidden in Shen, but then you know that, Jaran Saerk. How long have you been stationed here in Pol Shen?"

"Too long." Jaran opened an eye. "Months. I'm ready to return to the river postings."

"I could certainly use you there," Hranic said. "The bastard Cards are getting bolder week by week. But your Empress Herself requested the best fighters remain here in Pol Shen. There's something going on in this city that stinks. Like you, lad, I'd much rather be away at the river. The Cards are cunts. But they're good honest fighters and worthy of killing. I'd consider offering service to Ran Calla himself, were he to part with coin as easily as these Shen. But I've heard that warlord's the frugal type."

"Well then, bust me out of here, and we're on our way."

"That would mean execution for both of us in the Imperial Sapphire Square. Not your sharpest idea, Jaran Saerk."

"How do they expect to win this war if they execute their best fighters?"

"The Shen are complex." Hranic rubbed his face. "We'll never understand them. Suffice to say their protocols are not to be broken. If Magister Chulan hears about this business, things will get far worse. Take your punishment, Jaran. Put up and shut up. You've endured far worse. Your bloody scar's proof enough. Then, when things calm down, I'll get you away from Pol Shen as fast as I can."

Jaran shrugged as though considering the idea. "What do you know about this man Gromaki?"

"Very little." Hranic rubbed his chin. "From Leeth like yourself."

"Big fucking country."

Hranic nodded. The captain came from Hraggland, a desolate lake-strewn land bordering Leeth and Rethen. Like that land, Hraggland was a new Jarledom that had once been ruled by the kings of Leeth.

"Gromaki was a former mercenary who kept to himself," Hranic said. "I asked around, but no one knew much about him. Only been here in northeastern Shen three months."

"Sent to kill me."

"What's that?"

"A message from my long-lost uncle—so Gromaki said."

Hranic looked puzzled. "Why would your uncle want you killed?"

"I mean to find that out," Jaran said.

"And why stage a Holmgang? An efficient assassin would strike in the dark with knives."

"Gromaki had some honor left." Jaran shrugged. "He was a good fighter, his men not so much."

"His *men?*"

"Gromaki had three fellows hidden behind bushes as insurance."

"And you call him honorable?"

"To a point . . ." The door creaked open and a tall, serious-looking Shen in a long blue gown gave them both a measured look. Jaran recognized Soma Ghee, the Magister's private secretary. A man much feared and best avoided.

Ghee folded his arms inside flared embroidered sleeves. He smiled at Hranic, ignoring Jaran. "Captain, good day to you." Ghee's voce was reedy but menacing. Tin Lous appeared behind him, looking increasingly worried.

"Soma Ghee." Hranic nodded. "Why is my best fighter incarcerated in this place?"

Ghee smiled patiently. "An unfortunate business, but Imperial Rules must be obeyed. Your man is to be stripped and flogged in front of the Empress Herself as an example to her Sapphire Guard. Discipline is what keeps us civilized, unlike that rabble in the west—sometimes you auxiliaries forget that. He also will be ritually branded."

"What?" Hranic said, while Jaran barked back a laugh.

Jaran turned and locked gaze with the Secretary. "No one's branding me."

Ghee smiled thinly. "It is unfortunate. Alas, yes, but our Magister got word and wanted to make an example out of you. Loyalty and absolute obedience to the Empress are paramount.

You Northman are wayward and reckless. You need reining in, and that requires chastisement." He turned to Hranic. "Magister Chulan's examiners will come for this one in the morning. You are not to intervene, Captain, else you join your foolish charge on the Plinth of Correction. Good day!"

The Secretary and Tin Lous left, and the two police followed, leaving Hranic and Jaran staring at each other.

"Nothing I can do," Hranic said. "I'm sorry, lad. Bastard Shen."

Jaran said nothing for a moment. Then he smiled. "Since you won't help me, you might as well go, Captain. Once this is done, I'm enlisting in Calla's army. The winning side. Perhaps we'll meet at the river—I'll seek you out personally."

Hranic Finehair glared at him for a moment and then nodded. "So be it." He left without further word.

The hours passed slowly as Jaran's mind worked on a plan. It was hopeless. He wouldn't slip their nets; the Shen were too thorough. So that meant he had to die. And before he'd got to kill his uncle, or even find out what was going on in Leeth. What a waste. But no one was going to flog him, or touch his skin with searing iron. They would die first, and then he would die, probably slowly. It was the manner of things here in the east.

He sighed. It must've been night outside—the cell darkened and no one bothered lighting the lamp. He heard the guards talking quietly for a time, then silence. For several hours, he stared into space, before he jerked forward.

A soft noise. *Mice?*

No—it was footsteps. Someone approached very quietly.

Someone who shouldn't be here. The door creaked open, and Finvar the Ferryman grinned at him.

"Let me out so I can kill you," Jaran said.

"I was afraid you'd take it that way." Finvar crouched to the floor and folded his arms.

"You reported me to the harbor police."

"Of course, I did—I'm not fucking daft. They'd have found out what we were up to, and I'd have been sitting with you sharing that bucket. Didn't seem like the best plan."

Jaran glanced at the bucket. "What?"

"I told you I needed a friend."

"Well, maybe you should have got a puppy or a cat—they like cats in Shen."

Finvar grinned at him and shook his head. "You've a strange sense of humor, Northman."

"All right, then, free me and I won't kill you."

"Promise?"

"Yes—I'm a Northman. My word is—"

"—save the bollocks for when we're in the boat."

"Boat? We're getting back in your bloody boat?"

"Yes—and we had better do it quickly else those police wake up, and our dear friend recovers from the braining I gave him." Finvar flicked a knife in his hands. He approached the barred door of Jaran's cell.

"How?"

Finvar thrust the blade into the crack above the lock. He twisted and wriggled the knife for a few seconds, and the lock clicked and the door sprang open. "Like that."

"Impressive." Jaran stepped outside the cell.

"You'll find me a useful companion," Finvar said. Jaran stared at him, for once lost for words.

THE SKIFF WAITED FOR THEM AT THE OTHER END OF THE harbor. They'd vacated Tin Lous's offices without any bother. Jaran noted the three guards face-first on the floor, and he saw Lous lashed to his chair, mouth stuffed with straw, his eyes bug-huge and terrified. And so he should be, *poor sod*. Wouldn't go well for Tin Lous when Magister Chulan got word.

A short sprint through dark streets saw them to the harbor. "This way," Finvar whispered, grinning like a madcap child performing his latest prank.

"Where are we heading?" Jaran asked. He glanced inside the boat, then laughed seeing his war axe and sword lying there. "You are an efficient fellow."

"Ferrytown." Finvar grabbed an oar and poled them out from the wharf.

"Where is that?"

"Dunnehine. I heard you like the climate there." Finvar eased the craft through the waterways and reedy creeks leading out to the wide bay beyond. Lamps glinted as they passed. Jaran worried that guards would see them, but all was still in Pol Shen harbor.

"Near the Holmgang skerry?"

"Nope. Other way. It's a trading town across the bay, west not north," Finvar said. "A rough place." He grinned. "Rogue Shen, army deserters, Northmen, and Cardalan spies, even the odd crazy Tseole, all trading, eavesdropping, and killing each other in No Man's Land."

"Sounds like my kind of town."

"Shithole," Finvar said. "Take us till morning to get there. Once we're free of this harbor, I'll set the sail."

"What happens at Ferrytown?"

"We purchase nags and supplies."

"I'm not good on a horse."

Finvar grinned again. "You just sit and point its front end forward. Way I see it, Northman, you need to leave Shen as much as I do. We're both wanted men. You for desertion, me for . . . other things."

"I did not desert."

"The Empress won't see it that way, old son." He rolled his eyes. "You Northmen are so prickly. Don't look so glum—I only insult my friends. And take hold of these oars, I'm bloody knackered."

An hour later, the shrinking twinkling harbor lights were lost to gloom. Ahead, Pol Shen Bay opened wide; its flat surface glittered as the stars' reflection danced across the water. Serenely beautiful, cold and still.

Jaran stared at his wiry companion. "So why are you leaving the city? You seem like the sort that does well in crowded streets."

"I fell out with my former mates." He shrugged. "A misunderstanding. But, hey—nothing good lasts forever."

"Yes, I remember—you said you were a Cutter."

"I scouted for the Crew." Finvar flicked an earring. "Good fellows, the Cutters—though liable to hold grudges. We had an altercation. Doubt I'll see them again. Keep rowing or I'll start singing."

"Stinks here." Savarna crinkled her nose as the drab huts of some forlorn settlement blurred into view. The night was black and sooty. Cold rain soaked the puddle track, and heavy clouds hung overhead. Depressing and drear. Despite that bitter damp, the stench grew stronger and almost gagged her.

"Worse in summer." Gurtei turned his head and grinned her way. The Cutters and their "captive" rode horses in single file toward the cluster of buildings hemmed by a fence of stakes and a large wooden gate blocking the way ahead, the doors barred with iron.

"Just as well you're not selling me here," Savarna yelled from behind Gurtei, as she rode up close. "Doubt you'd get much coin."

"You'd be surprised," Gurtei said. "All manner of people frequent Ferrytown. Pol Shen is just across the bay, a short paddle, and only three score miles by road. And beyond Ferrytown in all other directions lies the vastness of Dunnehine, a hive of horny warlocks and lonely Tseole, who'd so love to tousle those lustrous red locks."

"Just remember, I sleep with a dagger in both hands," she said. "And I can perform some witchy shit, too."

"Yep," he said. "Noticed that. They'd most likes make you a queen in Dunnehine."

The gatekeeper blinked at them and opened both gates. "Late for visitors," he grumbled. "Taverns are full, fighting's started already." He had a long face, made longer by his dismal expression staring at them beneath the lamp. "You won't profit none, staying till morning. Unless you want to doss in the shite like the donkeys."

"We're just passing through." Gurtei tossed a small bag of coins to the gatekeeper, who snatched it from the air with a deft paw.

"Stupidest thing I've heard all week," the gatekeeper replied. "Nothing but snow beyond here. You'll freeze before the next tavern. Tell me your names and I'll see if I can book some lodging till dawn—cost you no more than it should this late in hour." He held up his palm again, expecting coin. Instead, his eyes widened as Gurtei's curved blade tickled his throat.

"You've been more than considerate, but our business is our own. And no need to mention our passing." Gurtei withdrew the blade as they rode through the gates. He slammed it in the scabbard, and Savarna saw the gatekeeper glaring at them beneath his lantern as they filed past.

"Was that sensible, pissing him off?"

"No," Gurtei said. "But I enjoyed doing it. And he was talking crap. There's always lodging in this town—any hour, if you're willing to pay. That tosser was after more coin. They're all like that here—you have to draw the line right. It's a fine balance between a fat purse and a slit throat. That fool knew he'd pushed it."

Savarna shrugged and glanced either side at low-roofed, dirty-looking houses lining their way. She saw a few skinny dogs lurking under sheds, a smithy lit by lamplight and flames, with a large occupant still at work inside despite it being well past midnight. They rode on, passing what she suspected was a brothel and three dreary taverns. The Cutters stopped outside the third one and dismounted from their horses.

"Home for a few days," Gurtei said.

"Then what?"

"We'll sell you," Gurtei laughed, and she laughed back.

THE LODGING WAS CRAMPED AND UNCOMFORTABLE, BUT AT least it was dry, and warm to a point. The insects biting her skin weren't welcome, but Savarna had put up with far worse over the last few weeks. The men left her after a harsh word from Gurtei, who seemed to be her friend—for the moment, at least. Roile and two of the others glared at her. Savarna paid them no heed, but she'd sleep with her stolen knife close by.

She stretched out as best she could in the creaking cot and stared out the drab widow. A gibbous moon fell free from clouds, spilling silver on the filthy street below. She saw three men down there, walking with swords in hands. She leaned close, looked the other way down the street. Five stood waiting, one holding a crossbow.

Not my concern. Minutes later, there were shouts and the brief clash of steel. Then silence, broken occasionally by her companions snoring and coughing in the dark. Savarna couldn't sleep, so she watched the moon rise over the nearest roof. An owl settled and stared at her from that gable. She shivered. She knew a sign when she saw it.

Something would happen here. Something . . . profound. She was in Ferrytown for a reason. Her instinct told her the events taking place tomorrow would change the course of her life. Savarna sat up on the cot, crossed her legs, and pushed her long hair back behind her face. She felt a heightened sense, a tingle of excitement. Anticipation, too.

She smiled as the strange feeling sent tingles up her spine. She sat by that window until dawn's pale glimmer promised a dry day at least.

THE SKY PINKENED OVER WATER AS JARAN GAZED EAST. FAR off, he could still see the tiny glimmer of Pol Shen. He turned his attention to the land ahead. Here storm clouds were breaking up and marching off north. A jetty and ropes were a half-mile away.

"Yep, nearly there." Finvar opened an eye. He'd been motionless the entire trip as Jaran worked the oars. Jaran enjoyed the exercise, and it had given him time to think.

"You're awake now the work is done," he said.

"Saving my strength for Ferrytown." Finvar winked at him. "There may be a feisty lass or two to sooth my aching bones . . ."

"Purchase nags and goods and move on, you said."

"I know what I said"—Finvar gesticulated—"but a man is entitled to some recreation along the way. You have to seize the moment when it comes, Biggun. We're out of Shen, so we should celebrate that achievement, at least. We're free as the wind, you and I, and me with still enough coin."

"For nags . . ." Jaran grinned at his wiry companion.

"You're no fucking fun, Northman."

"That's been said before." Jaran coughed back the damp air. "Then what you going to do?" He gazed over his shoulder and saw they were fast approaching the shoreline. The jetty was off to their left. He adjusted, cursed Finvar for not mentioning it, and then pushed hard on the oars.

Jaran was ready to get back on his feet. His thinking hadn't helped much. Didn't have a plan aside from what he'd told Hranic Finehair in anger.

"What do you mean—*what am I going to do?*" Finvar snorted. "We're a team, Northman. We'll stock up, ride west and see what happens. Life is for living, old chum. Why bother with plans? Things usually work out whether or not you prepare." He looked past Jaran's right shoulder. "You're straying again."

Jaran sighed. "It would be helpful if you told me where the

fucking jetty is without me turning and craning my head every minute."

"Don't get prickly, I thought you knew what you were doing."

Jaran ignored him, and after a few more minutes they tied off and clambered onto the battered wharf. Jaran retrieved his weapons and stretched. He looked up, seeing the moon slide free from clouds. Away east over water, the sky had deepened to rose-pink with scarlet flecks.

"Storm warning," Finvar said, looking back that way. "Methinks we should stay clear of Shen for a while."

Once free of the rustic wharf and jetty, a lane led off into woods. They walked briskly, Jaran garbed in blue cloak and heavy trousers, with sword and axe swinging from his broad, studded belt. Finvar carried a horse bow across his shoulder, his curved sword and various throwing daggers all hidden by a shabby green cloak.

The moon lit their way until the light grew behind them and morning arrived. Jaran studied the terrain. Ahead ranged dark hills, their slopes and crowns coated with white, and hosts of tiny pines gathered beneath like a mustering army of green.

Nearer, in the middle distance, he saw thin trails of smoke curling up into the gray. Ferrytown, he assumed. They were close. Since it was obvious Finvar wasn't going to enlighten him on any plan, Jaran tried again once they were in town. "What do I need to know?"

"Bad town, unpleasant people—especially the women."

Jaran looked up at the sky and cursed. "Just tell me when I need to hit someone," he said.

The gatekeeper yawned and blinked as they approached. He

saw the size of Jaran and pulled back the gates. "Morning," he said, as Jaran passed through without a word his way.

"How's the town, Gatey?" Finvar tossed the man a copper penny.

"Tight bastard," the gatekeeper said, biting down hard on the coin. "'Tis busy as usual. You boys staying?" Jaran turned and looked at him, and the gatekeeper held up both hands. "Just making chat this fine northern morning, don't take offence," he muttered as they left him be.

"You were right. This is a shithole," Jaran said as they strode side by side along the one grubby street, an array of wooden huts and buildings flanking either side.

"Ferrytown has its moments," Finvar said. "Ale's cheap here, and the wenches willing."

"Well I'm not lingering." Jaran glared at a man who stood leaning against a worn picket fence, a curved sword at his side and beringed fingers on the hilt. "I'll relieve you of some of that coin, purchase my own nag and be about my business."

Finvar stopped and looked at him. "We can't rush this, Jaran." His lean tough face was serious for once, the look showed a keen intelligence Jaran hadn't noticed before. "Don't want to draw attention to ourselves. And I was joking about the women. We'll amble through town, get mounts, and ride north of the River Shen."

"I'm going to Leeth," Jaran said, walking on. "I've an uncle to visit."

"And you'll need my help with that."

Jaran stopped again. "No, ferryman—I will not. We part beyond the river. My vengeance is my affair. You should go back to the city, maybe a different city. You're a clever fellow—I'm sure you'll fare well enough."

Finvar grinned up at him. "We'll see."

They strolled past a grubby shack where a wild-haired woman was seated amid clutter and bundles. Smoke curled up around her shrouding the face. A large gray cat stared at Jaran from the table where its mistress rested her elbows. She was drinking a brew, her long, dark hair trailing across shoulders whilst draped in a shabby coat.

The woman glanced up suddenly as they passed her. She smiled savagely, her features harsh and weathered, the skin red raw from a life of toil. She tossed the remains of her brew in the filth. "The three who must become one," she said, her voice rougher than the ragged coat and boots she wore. "Bear, Hawk, and the Tigress is coming."

"There are two of us," Jaran said, as he stopped to survey her. Those sharp brown eyes stared at him unblinking, like the cat's beside her.

"You shouldn't indulge her." Finvar made to move on, but the woman spoke again, causing them both to turn her way.

"Strength, cunning, and spell craft—you'll need all three skills to defeat her." She slipped a dirty finger under a blanket and produced three playing cards. Beside him, Finvar fidgeted, but Jaran held the woman's gaze in his own.

"Come on," Finvar said, but Jaran remained put.

"This one knows . . . something." Jaran approached her table. The cat hissed and jumped off, but the woman smiled up at him. She had perfect teeth, and the smile made her look younger. Jaran gazed down at the cards as she placed them face up on the table. They were torn and faded, but etched on their surface were the sketches of three animals: an orange striped cat hunting, a hawk in flight, and a white bear standing on its hind legs. When

Jaran saw the bear card he shivered, felt the scar on his chest tingle.

"Yes," she said. "I see the pattern emerging here. These three cards tell the story."

Finvar swore, but Jaran placed both palms on the table and glared down at the woman. "You mock us. What do you know, woman? Tell me, else my rage proves your end."

But the woman showed no fear despite his rising anger, the scar burning on his chest, and a memory from his childhood. A terrible happening that still returned in nightmares. A great white bear falling upon him, his young body already torn by wolves. The bear had saved him, but had left its mark.

"The shadow of the white bear watches over you," the woman said. "Your spirit animal is strong, Jaran. He is a legend. But he cannot save you against her entrapments. Much less, the hawk spirit saves this one. Or the tiger she who comes. Only together can you defeat her."

Finvar paled visibly beside him. His companion looked scared for the first time since they'd met. "This one's from the wastes, Jaran. Don't let her trap you with her snares. Let's move on."

Jaran ignored him. "I'm looking for my uncle, not a woman. You're wide off the mark, witch. A charlatan who belongs in a circus. We're not that far from Pol Shen—you most likes heard of me and guessed my name." Jaran made to strike her face, but she rammed a sharp finger into his chest, causing him to stop.

"Your uncle is part of the pattern, yes. But you cannot reach him before they get to you—those three will soon be heading east along the trade roads."

"Three? More hired killers." Jaran snorted. "Let them come."

"Come they will." The woman held his gaze like a spider

traps fly. "Your cousins, Jaran Saerk—each one a match for you. They seek the White Bear's shadow."

"Erlund's sons?"

"The same." She grabbed his arm with her other hand, her black eyes glinting like damp coal in firelight. "You must kill those brothers first, your uncle too. Then her. Only by killing her can you reclaim what was lost."

"What is that?"

"Your home, Jaran Saerk. This one knows, for his own destiny runs alongside, as does the woman's."

"Where can I find my uncle—tell me that much," Jaran urged her. "Which castle?

"Grimhold, the ancient seat of the kings of Leeth. King Erlund rules there at this time."

"King." Jaran spat on her table and shook himself free of her grasp. "Soon to be a dead king."

"You better leave," she said, her eyes misting over. "There'll be all kinds of trouble here shortly." She flipped the cards over on their backs, revealing dirty brown paper, no more. "Perhaps I was mistaken," she said, her face sad, appearing older and careworn again. "You'd better go. They are coming."

Finvar took the hint and started walking briskly toward the nearest tavern. Jaran turned to follow, but the woman grabbed his arm again. Her face was concerned, and showed a sincerity he hadn't marked before. "Be careful, warrior. She is cunning and will kill you. She'll never give up until she has you in her nets, Jaran. Remember this—only together can you defeat her."

"Who is this woman you speak of?" Jaran asked, but she shrugged and shambled off to linger beneath the battered roof of her lean-to. She fussed with kettle and fire, the gray cat on a chair beside her. Jaran saw Finvar waiting for him outside the nearest tavern.

"I'll come back and kill you if you've lied to me," Jaran told the woman, and left her watching him in silence as he strode across to join his friend.

"Come on—let's get some horses and get out of here, else that witch put a hex on us," Finvar said, his tough face still shaken. "You don't mess with the Dunnehine, Northman. You can't kill witches with swords."

"I'd find a way," Jaran said, and the pair commenced walking briskly toward the far end of town where Finvar said the trading corrals, livestock markets, and stables could be found.

They stopped abruptly when three men walked out from the last tavern and blocked their way. The nearest and biggest was grinning.

"Drolly Fin, well bugger me senseless—look who it is, lads." The man to his left wasn't smiling. He was watching Jaran, his hard, brown eyes quick and dangerous.

Finvar grinned up at Jaran. He had cheered up again after the encounter with the Dunnehine woman. "My old crew. Had no idea they'd be here. This might take some explaining."

Jaran remained glum. He wanted to be gone from here, riding west, hard and fast. His uncle had sent three sons to find him. His cousins. He'd find them first and rip out their hearts. Then he'd make for Grimhold Castle, wherever that was. A long journey he was more than ready to commence. But Ferrytown wasn't ready for him to leave yet.

Finvar folded his tattooed arms. "I can explain, Gurtei," he said to the apparent leader, a broad, hard fighter with a thick wad of moustache hiding his lips and drooping below the chin.

Jaran saw four more tough-looking characters had wandered

out into the street. He studied them dourly. "We've scant time for this," Jaran muttered, fingering his axe head. They were rangy, clad in fur and mail. Most sported moustaches like their leader, and pony tails. Others wore their hair free, trailing down their backs, long and shaggy. Jaran noted that two carried bows. Those two stayed back. Jaran would kill most of them, but those arrows would stop him eventually.

Finvar was yakking beside him, but Jaran could tell these men wanted a fight. Not his fight, but one he would finish. And one that would most likely prove his last.

The leader fingered his moustache and stared his way. "We've no quarrel with you, Northman," he said, his voice a rough croak as though he smoked too much tobacco.

Jaran dropped his hands to his side, left held axe while right gripped sword. He smiled at the leader, and Finvar grinned beside him. "You travel with a thief and a card cheat," the leader said, folding arms and spitting in the dirt. Close by, Jaran heard dogs yapping and whining. He registered the sound of more men on their way.

"You're a bad loser, Gurt," Finvar said. "Besides, it was Dorley there's fault." The man beside the leader paled visibly.

"Fuck you, Droll," that one said, reaching for the saber hanging at his side. Jaran watched him as the man's fingers drummed the leather hilt while the dark eyes flickered his way.

"This here Northman is Jaran Saerk," Finvar said cheerfully, as though playing for time. "You might have heard of him, Gurt."

"Don't much matter if we have. Our quarrel is with you, Fin. You alone." The leader smiled at Jaran. "So come over here and let me slit your gizzard open."

"A misunderstanding, Gurt." Finvar's smile fled his face. "You should have let me explain—"

Jaran, tiring of the impasse, leaped forward at speed and punched the man Dorley, knocking him backward through the air and crashing into a building where he crumpled and lay still. Silence followed that clatter. Everyone was staring at Jaran in disbelief, including three women and a gimp who had just appeared to watch the show.

"Fuck, but you're quick, as well as big and strong," Finvar said.

"I didn't like his expression," Jaran said, ignoring the two crossbowmen, their weapons both aimed at his chest.

"Finvar's right—that was quick," the leader said, scratching an ear. "Doubt you can dodge an arrow though, size of you."

"Let's give it a try." Jaran smiled at Finvar, who gazed up at him askance.

"Shoot him, lads," the leader said, as Jaran dived for cover.

SAVARNA ROLLED FREE OF THE BLANKET AND GLIDED TO HER feet when she heard the yells and clash of steel. She recognized one of the hoarse shouts as Gurtei's. Curious, she grabbed her stolen knife and ventured outside, where Ferrytown's shabby street looked almost welcoming, its drabness lifted by a weak, pale sun.

She approached warily, saw the fighters close by and smiled. Doubtless a quarrel with another gang. As convenient a time for her to slip away as any she'd likely get. She stole back inside the tavern. No one around, so she gathered her garments and purloined some of the Cutters' gear. Some knives, a crossbow and a bag of dried jerky—plus a gourd full of brandy.

She left without sound, distancing herself from the noise of steel clashing on steel. It sounded like a dozen or so men were fighting. Strange, this early in the day.

Savarna loped cat-like down the street toward the far stable where the Cutters had left the horses. She'd free them all and steal the best. Then she'd make for Pol Shen. After that came the tricky part—meeting the Empress and plunging a dagger in her gut. Hopefully, Vian would catch up with her in that city and help. Savarna knew he was coming, her twin.

She reached the stables. A man stood there smoking and leaning against a door. She emerged, he blinked. Savarna kicked him in the bollocks and he sprawled. She made for where the horses stood snorting steam, reached for the nearest then stopped when someone laughed.

Savarna turned. A woman watched her from the shadows. Small and dark with hard, canny features. She was swaddled in a shabby coat, and her eyes were black as coals. She laughed again, and then spat bloody phlegm in the dirt.

"What do you want?" Savarna hissed at the woman. "What is funny?"

"You are." The woman's voice was crow raw. "Trying to escape your destiny."

"Not that it's any of your damn business," Savarna said, "but I'm confronting my destiny, not fleeing."

"Vian will confront the Shen." The smile faded from the woman's face, replaced by a cruel expression. "Your path winds in the other direction."

Vian. His name spoken on a stranger's lips. Savarna froze. She knew the stories about Dunnehine, the land they'd just entered. Clearly this was a seer—or worse, a witch. She needed to be careful. The woman might have answers that could help her.

"What do you know of my brother?"

"Vian is far away, but getting nearer."

"Where is he?"

The woman ignored her question and craned her head to where the sound of fighting rose. "You should go help," the woman told her.

"Why? They are not my friends." But the woman laughed again and faded into the gloom behind the stables.

Voices behind her. Armed men approaching. Savarna turned and saw four big individuals coming her way from the street. These weren't Cutters or any local gang. They were soldiers, tough and durable. Confident in stride and purpose. They wore chainmail and carried spears, with large, curved swords hanging by their sides.

They caught up with her before she could flee. Three others blocked the road at the end of the corral. The nearest approached, lifted the helmet from his face, revealing tough features and flat, brown eyes.

"You're Cardalan regulars," Savarna said, then ducked as the man's hand swiped at her face. She kicked out, catching his knee, but hardly impacting the steel.

"Lively bitch," one of them said, his voice sounding foreign and guttural. "Keep the whole troop busy taming her."

Savarna leaped for cover, but a fist knocked her sideways. She stumbled to her feet, then a boot struck her face and she sprawled backwards. Someone laughed. She retched up blood and rolled over. The leader stood over her, a leather whip curled in his hands. He was grinning. The grin vanished when a loud crash announced a newcomer in the stables.

Savarna blinked. Was that a bear roaring? She heard crashing, groans, a man's death scream, steel striking steel. Then a newcomer's freckled smiling face loomed over her, grabbing her arm.

"I'm Drolly Fin," the gap-tooth stranger said. "That noisy destructive bugger is Jaran Saerk. He killed those bastards single handed—doesn't mess around. You'd best run away with us, lassie, the horses have already bolted. And there are plenty more of these Cardalan bastards coming our way."

4

RANNING

SHE WALKED THE BEACH, as was her habit, the sea crashing to her left and seabirds swooping overhead. Far out across the ocean, lightning seared the water's surface and broiling clouds trawled the horizon. Sheega stopped for a time, stood and gazed, the strengthening wind lifting and tossing her smoky black hair across her face.

She drew a deep breath. How she loved winter in the north. Short cruel days and long starry nights when the Giants' Dance braided the heavens with distant thunder and vivid color, reminding her of her lost home in distant Dunnehine.

The storm was swelling in size. She felt beads of icy rain as the wind picked up speed, blowing drifts of spume and turning the ebbing waves into spindles of white dancing froth.

Sheega walked on, her mercurial mind on many matters. For twenty-seven years, she'd ruled this island. She wasn't loved by the few families who remained, but they suffered neither sickness nor war and should be content. The fact that they weren't wasn't her concern. They stayed out of her way. Sheega honored the annual rites as she must, but mostly she kept to the great hall, and the people of Valkador to their fisher huts and homesteads. The arrangement suited her well enough.

She stopped on a whim, again turned and surveyed the waves marching off, darkening like spilt ink until they were swallowed by the storm.

Something is out there.

Sheega felt a strange sense of expectation, a quickening of the pulse. A rare feeling of excitement. Then she saw a shimmer, a dark mass forming in the center of that storm. The shape shifted and blurred until it became a man. A colossal figure striding across the water. Sensuata the Sea God about His affairs.

If the giant saw her on that beach, He made no sign, but strode across the horizon fading into the deeper gloom, a mile-wide net dragging behind His shoulders.

There is meaning in this. A warning. Sheega had lived long enough to read the signs when they came. *Signals.* Then she saw the bird winging fast toward her.

The gull settled on her shoulder, a spark of white under the darkening sky. It spoke the words she'd taught it in that harsh language. Once its message was delivered, the bird lifted to wind and took wing far away, a bright dart searing into the storm and vanishing as swiftly as it had appeared.

Sheega watched the bird disappear, her face bleaker than the storm.

He lives yet.

She walked on, her mood turned grim. Erlund had failed her again. Three sons they had between them, but the father no longer served her needs. She'd grown bored and sent him to Leeth where he ruled as king in her name. He'd seemed relieved to go. She laughed harshly—no one could bear her moods for long.

Sheega should have ripped out his heart, but Erlund still had uses, the primary one being to find and kill the baby he should have smothered nearly three decades prior. But she needed a new Jarle. A bright lover to warm her bed. There was little choice among the terrified fishers and townsfolk of the island. Gornt and the older thanes had left with Erlund. A few remained, but these dreaded her as much as the other islanders. They'd witnessed the swift fall of Hrund's family, the self-loathing and bitterness of the only survivor—Erlund. They served her well enough as guards, but were terse and edgy, and often drunk.

But then Erlund wasn't the only survivor of that family. *Jaran Hrelgisson lives* . . .

The goblin in the mirror had told her to wait, curse it, and Sheega had complied, though grudgingly. But this was the eve of the aforementioned year, and her time was running out. Late last summer, one of her birds—a raven this time—returned with news of a Northman from Leeth called Jaran Saerk making renown as a fighter in the eastern wars. Sheega hadn't hesitated but tasked Erlund to find and finish him immediately.

A man was sent. That same man was now a corpse—the gull had told her. And Jaran would know he was hunted. Sheega clenched her small fists and screamed at the skies in sheer frustration. People always let you down, especially *mortals*.

The distant shape of the god had blurred into a dark mass again. She paid Him no heed. Sheega was from Dunnehine, a land of eternal winter ruled by ice-warlocks and shamans who dwelt in tents at the northern rim of the world. She'd lived there for long years and gained great power with her many sacrifices, runic trances, and demon-couplings.

At last, powerful enough, she'd raised a horde summoned from Faerie and ruled over half of that land, until the remaining warlocks allied against her—summoning their own spooks and casting her out, branding Sheega the "Ice-Witch Eternal." True to their nature, the allies from Faerie deserted her. She'd been stripped, whipped bloody, and driven from the land. Cast naked and broken into the frozen river that bordered Leeth. Left to drown in its thawing spring waters.

But Sheega had lived. She was hard to kill. Her cunning, hatred, and rapacious hunger melded into a savagery that demanded compensation. She walked the lands for years, plying her crafts, and even helping the lonely folk who dwelt in the wilds with ailments and illness.

The evil seed inside Sheega grew. She would have her vengeance against those who had cast her out, and take back her home. But that would take many years. First, she needed a base, a refuge and haven where she could rule again, preen her feathers and mend her inner wounds, repair the torn fabric that was her soul.

Valkador. Of course, she'd always known about the island far to the west, beyond the wild countries of the Northmen that bordered her own land. It was rumored an island of proud warriors, ocean farers and occasional marauders, who'd had plied the many seas for over a thousand years, since the days of their first Jarle, Barin—himself a victim of her own ancestor, Helga Kregat.

Valkador was perfect for her purpose. Their current Jarle was weak, unlike his ancestors. Jarle Hrund had a roving eye, so when she'd appeared, a lost wandering maiden alone in his forests, the Jarle had fallen quickly for her poisonous charms.

That left Casla, the Jarle's wife. Sheega had dealt with her easily enough too.

Once Hrund was dead and the island was hers, Sheega had summoned Gantallian from Yffarn after entrapping him with spell runes. A renegade from his people, the rogue imp had been thrown out of Faerie for grave felonies at the goblin court. Sheega, scrying the underworld, had seen him sobbing down there. A talented trickster—even by goblin standards—Gantallian was wise in lore. She'd promised to release him, and with no other choice, Gantallian had sworn to assist her. With the goblin's aid, Sheega set up her mirror and scrying station, resuming her age-old studies and concentrating her powers on the long game of bringing down the warlocks who had cast her out.

As insurance, in case they should become aware, Sheega wove a mist around Valkador and bid none save Erlund and their three sons leave to sail through.

Valkador was self-sufficient, its climate fertile, with ample herds of deer and cattle for meat, and many rivers and lakes containing countless fish. After Erlund left for Leeth with her sons, Sheega tightened her nets around the island so no straying ship from another dimension would find them by chance. Her enemy, the ancient being called Rune, had manipulated the world fabric, causing a rupture. Sometimes things got through. She could leave nothing to chance. She'd struck fast and trapped Rune in her nets.

Those first tasks completed, Sheega grew stronger. The mist around the island deepened, interlocked like steely nets. Valkador faded from memory, the very word confusing most mortal minds —thanks to Gantallian's cunning and her spell craft. The island became a fable, a myth. An imaginary realm, much like Laras

Lassladen from the distant time of the Crystal Kings, long millennia ago.

Her mind shifted back to the present. *Breaking through . . .* The creepy feeling returned. *I'm not alone.* Sheega turned sharply, saw a figure striding free of the waves. Man-sized. Not the Sea God this time, but surely one of His people. A tall man he appeared, fair of face yet not fully human.

He glided toward her with uncommon grace, his milky-white eyes flecked with silver and shining with promise. Sheega knew of his kind and wondered how he'd navigated the nets and found her alone on the beach.

The spirit-man approached and she drank in his muscular frame. The lithe limbs, those rippling, shifting muscles, the skin shifting from green to honey-gold. As he got closer, she recognized the quicksilver glimmer in his milky eyes that marked him as Faen, one of the ancient folk. *Elves,* they called them in Dunnehine. Dangerous beings, artful and conniving, beautiful and deadly. A creature of Faerie the Twilight Realm. The Faen's skin shimmered gold-green, his hair was long and fine, golden as barley on southern fields in summertime.

"I am Ranning," the tall stranger said, his voice rich and deep. She smiled, feeling the need rising from below. He stood before her, his wet hair smelling of brine and his honey-hued skin tingling and shifting, as though glowing from inside, a candle or flame breaking to get out. "I've come to share your bed and make you my queen." He smiled, his eyes shimmering like tiny stars inside their milky corona.

"The Sea God sent you?" she asked breathlessly, after he kissed her long and hard, his filed teeth biting her mouth until the blood trickled from her chin. Laughing, she rolled on top of him, straddling his body, her hard, questing fingers probing his damp, clammy flesh. They'd made love savagely on that icy wet beach as the sleet pummeled their bodies. He sated her needs time and again. At last, thought Sheega, a creature worthy of her loving.

"Not Him," Ranning said eventually, his milky gaze shifting far away. "Like you, I'm a stray—an outcast from the far corners of the world. Ansu is changing, my kind fading like mist in morning sun. My realm was below the waters, and my mother is Rann, one of Sensuata's daughters. That God is not pleased with me. He drove me from His domain. Doubtless Sensuata was warning you of my arrival. I am *perilous*, you see. A creature of the dark."

"I'll take my chances with that," Sheega said, smiling darkly. "It's said that I too, harbor a blackness in my soul."

Later, in the hall while they drank alone by roaring fires, Sheega informed Ranning of the news the gull had brought. Together the Ice-Witch and her Faerie lover put a plan in place, should the weak fool Erlund Hrundsson fail her yet again.

KING ERLUND OF LEETH WATCHED THE DOGS SNARL AND bite each other as his huge, brutal sons placed bets. The boys weren't like him. Those three had more of their mother in them. They didn't feel the cold of this unusually bitter winter, as did he. They lived for fighting, wenching, and drinking. Little else appeased their violent nature. Blunt tools, unruly and untrustworthy. Erlund knew he'd sired three monsters—but with a mother like Sheega, how else would the boys turn out?

He'd been so relieved when she openly tired of his attempt to satisfy her incessant—and increasingly challenging, and complex

—needs. Grateful even, when she announced he'd rule over here as her eyes in the east. A puppet king in a violent, troubled land. No matter—he was free of her. *Almost.* And now the bleak mass of rugged mountain, moor, and woods they called Leeth was his to rule and tax. The home of his ancestors before they'd found Valkador.

You can't return—Sheega had told him. *Valkador is hidden from such as you.* He hadn't cared. To be free of her was more than enough. But Erlund needed to work on his sons. Gorn had killed a man last week, one of Erlund's housecarls, while boasting at his cups. Valgarn and Holtarn had raped girls in the town and villages. All three boys were hated and feared by his guards, the carles, and local folk. They couldn't stay here indefinitely.

At last, the brothers tired of their game, and the exhausted hounds took to sleeping. Bored, the three huge warriors scooped up their weapons, leaving the hall without a glance his way, doubtless in search of more ale and women down in the town.

Erlund stared into his cups. Grimhold Castle held many dark memories. A cold draft filtered down from the ceiling, a chill no blaze could hold off. The hour was late, and he was weary. But then Erlund was always tired these days. A shadow of the man he had once been. A clown king. At least in Valkador he'd been Jarle. He had held some real power, in her name—but still power. To govern, hold council at the Thing.

Here in Leeth, the new king ruled over strangers who despised him as much as they detested his boys. They all knew rumors about Sheega, though none dare mention her name, or Valkador. To utter that name was to risk her wrath, or bring such bad luck that would ruin families and drown ships. Easier to believe the island no longer existed. Forget, lest she become aware. The Ice-Witch's shadowy reputation ensured no one challenged Erlund's seat of power, however hollow. Potential rivals had crumbled like rotten wood at the mention of her name. Erlund was wealthy and powerful, his rule unchallenged. He should have been content with that, but the worm inside would never stop biting. He was what he was. *Kinslayer.* The past had teeth that wouldn't let go.

Erlund sipped the warm ale, a broken shell who despised this world and everything in it—especially himself.

I killed my brother, betrayed my land.

A sudden shimmer and flicker re-ignited the fire, shooting sparks in his eyes. Erlund blinked. He felt that icy dread, *so familiar.* She might be on that island, but his wife could still reach him anytime she wanted too. Her claws were longer, far longer, than the creeping shadows of Grimhold Castle in the depth of winter.

The flames took shape and her face appeared. Cold, pale-blue eyes stabbing out at him in accusation. *You failed again.* Sheega's brittle voice sucked the heat from that struggling fire.

Erlund shivered, reached for his cup of ale again. The dogs woke, yelped and circled, and then ran out into the hallway with tails between legs. The shadows above flickered and distorted as the sconces blinked and then were gone, as though invisible fingers had snuffed them out all at once around the feasting hall.

Your nephew lives, she said. *The fool you sent is dead.*

"I will send another." Erlund choked on his ale. So dark in the hall, gloomy and quiet.

No—you will send our sons forth and deal with this like a man. They are ready for the world, though it may not be ready for them. Through your failure, Jaran will learn of his past. There are only two outcomes—kill him or succumb to his revenge. I'm leaving this to you, husband. Finish the task you started and don't fail me a third time.

The eyes flickered and vanished, and the fire returned to honest flame.

THE NEXT MORNING, KING ERLUND SUMMONED HIS THREE sons. He felt better, had a plan. And besides, Sheega had done him a favor. He could send the boys away at last. They'd be someone else's problem.

The three ambled in, blue eyes sulky and red-rimmed from too much ale and not enough sleep. "The hour is early, Father," Gorn said, grumbling, his mouth half full of meat. He loomed in front of Erlund, the other two beside him. None of them looked pleased to see their father. Mighty, strong men in their prime. Experts with every weapon, trained by his best carles. But more importantly, they possessed Sheega's cunning and ruthlessness.

And then there was the deep dark rage she placed in them as children. The battle fury they called berserkergang. *Someone else's problem . . .*

"I heard from your mother," Erlund said, keeping his eyes neutral.

"Is she here?" Holtarn, the youngest, sounded excited.

"If she were here, I would know," said Gorn, the firstborn and biggest. He cuffed his brother's ear and Holtarn glared at him.

"We've a task for you," Erlund said as they continued to quarrel and jab each other, Valgarn having joined the nonsense. They stopped and glared down at him.

"As long as it involves lots of ale and horny women." Valgarn grinned. "Then we're your men, Father."

"A journey east," Erlund said. "Adventure, and a chance to earn reputation at last. You boys could be the greatest warriors of our age. There's a war far away in Shen. A thousand miles, they say—I've never been."

They looked interested, but Gorn shrugged. "Plenty of fighting here, among the fringes. And Hragglund and Rethen both need subduing. Leeth still has its share of remote home-steaders that secretly hold out against your rule. Then there is Dunnehine, and the lands to the south no one ever mentions."

"Aye—why journey to the edge of the world when we can reap glory closer to home? Besides, I like it here," Valgarn said.

"Because there's a man I want you to find and kill," Erlund said quietly.

"One man?" Gorn sniggered, and the brothers grinned at each other.

"You're having a laugh with us," Holtarn said.

"His name's Jaran Hrelgisson, and he's your cousin." Erlund rubbed his tired eyes.

"Didn't know we had a cousin," Gorn said.

"He should be dead, but Jaran killed the man I sent after him, himself a reputable slayer from the border regions. Hrel-gisson needs to stop breathing—your mother fears him."

"Fuck off, Mother's not afraid of anything." Gorn spat on the floor.

"She fears this Jaran," Erlund persisted despite their looming snarls. "If he isn't dealt with this year, he will come for her, the gods on his side. Your mother has seen her death in his eyes. She will die, as will all of us, unless he is killed first. I killed his father

—your Uncle Hrelgi. He most likely knows that now and will be wanting revenge."

The three knew the tale, though they had been born a few years after the events. Valgarn looked bored. "We know you helped mother kill the old Jarle and warm your arse on his seat. What of it?"

Erlund sighed. Gorn was the strongest, but Valgarn the middle brother was sharper than the other two. This boy was a thinker, as well as a murderous thug like his siblings. Neither Sheega or Erlund had seen cause to mention the woman Bera and her tiny child to their sons, or the stranger called the Traveler rumored to have saved them that day.

"Hrelgi's wife escaped that day. We searched far and wide for the woman and her baby son, to scant avail. Bera vanished, and no word of her plight has ever reached me. But her son lives and thrives in Shen, carving out a name as a mighty warrior."

"Our long-lost cousin." Valgarn grinned, seeming interested at last. "A blood feud in the family." He licked his lips.

"He must perish, or we will. Come on, what say you? A simple task it may prove—but somehow I doubt it. Jaran's already a legend in Shen. They call him Saerk. Like you three, he has the rage. There are stories about a bear, a scar. Your mother's heard rumors. Bera's brat has been fighting out there for ten years, but it wasn't until recently that we knew where he was—hence your task." Erlund waved a hand. "Go east and kill your cousin. Once that's done, join in that war. Doesn't matter which side, though I've heard Cardalan is winning. Earn fame and riches, but report back to me first with Jaran Hrelgisson's head. Yes . . .?"

"I'm interested," Holtarn said, after a moment.

"Gorn? Valgarn?"

"Yeah," Gorn said. "We'll kill him. Tell Mother we'll do your dirty work for you." He spat again and kicked one of the hounds that had settled by his feet. The animal yelped and crawled under a table.

Valgarn nodded beside his brothers. "I'm in."

"Good," Erlund said. "Take what weapons you require, and any servants for portage and assistance. A score of my younger carles can accompany you too—that should prevent ambushes by rogue Hraggs or the Rethe during the journey east. Head for Pol Shen—that's where you'll find news of your cousin. He serves in their empress's army."

Two hours later, Erlund gazed down from the battlements as the three riders led a troop of men along the road toward the line of dark hills in the middle distance. He grinned for the first time that week. His wife was across the sea, his sons faring east. It was time for an early ale and some quiet celebration.

Erlund's smile broadened. This was proving the best morning he'd had in years. With a bit of luck, he'd soon be rid of them for good. Those trolls had tempers that would get them killed sooner or later. As long as one of them killed Jaran Hrelgisson first, then she would leave Erlund be. And life as King of Leeth might finally be worth a damn.

5

THE SHEN RIVER

GURTEI BLINKED and spat blood on the street. He rolled over and found his feet, started crawling across to the stinking clutter of a midden at the far end of Ferrytown. Once safely hidden in the mess of corpses, carcasses, offal and general trash, he closed his eyes again and blacked out.

Sometime later, a boot woke him. Gurtei blinked, looked up, and saw gawky Roile standing over him.

"What the fuck happened?" Gurtei scratched his ear, still bleeding from the gash he'd received.

"We've ten men still standing," Roile spat. "The others are dead as leaves in winter. Big Rosen's got a gut wound—so he's most likes buggered too."

"What . . . happened?" Gurtei leaned forward and spewed in the shit. He had no memory of the last hour, on account of the blow he'd received on the side of his head.

"Cardalan War Party," Roile spat again.

Fucking Cards . . .Gurtei checked his body for wounds. He

counted three, but none would prove fatal. *I'll live.* "Why were they here?"

"How should I know?" Roile hawked and spat a third time, his hard face taut with spent rage and confusion. "We've lost most of our men, Gurt. It's a fucking disaster."

"Where are the Cards now?"

"Gone," Roile said. "They pretty much cleared everything out from Ferrytown and took off, leaving me and some of the lads for dead, though they gutted anyone moving. Efficient bastards, but not wanting to stick around. That's why I'm alive. Their officers seemed anxious, ready to be gone."

"What about Fin and that big northern twat?"

"No idea," Roile said. "Things got confusing when the gang-fuck started." He showed bloody teeth in a wry smile. "How fare you, Gurt?"

"Been better. Where are the other lads, those still breathing?"

"Sheltering inside the tavern, nursing their wounds, and finishing the bitter dregs left by those Card bastards."

"Best we join them, then." Gurtei rolled to his knees and then stumbled onto his feet. The street was spinning, so he braced his legs until it settled.

"Then what?" Roile stood staring at him with rage-torn, bloodshot eyes.

"We find Finvar the Droll and cut him open."

"Wasn't his fault."

"Don't care. I need someone to blame," Gurtei said, as Roile shoved an arm under his shoulder and helped his leader stagger toward the nearest tavern.

Unva smiled at the corpses as she scurried past, her coat blowing in the chilly breeze. It had started, the pieces introduced to the board. She shuffled to the edge of the town, saw the remnant of Gurtei's men loitering and tending to their wounds in the last tavern. They didn't see her. Unva held out her left hand, the three playing cards spread wide. She spoke the rune tongue and the cards crumpled, caught alight and fell as blazing cinders to the ground. She stamped on the ashes.

Once clear of Ferrytown, Unva turned north on the road. She uttered the changing charm, her voice hoarse with the chill. Unva's gaunt body blurred and shimmered. She became a she-wolf, her jaws slavering. She loped off into the growing dark. Beyond those far hills, the other warlocks would be waiting. Her allies against the Ice-Witch. There was much at stake, as this was the appointed year. Their age-old enemy, Sheega the Sorceress, would return soon. The Warlock Guild of Dunnehine needed to be ready when she did.

Savarna watched the flames crackle as night fell deep in the wild. The men seated nearby were silent. The small one had finally stopped chattering and was smoking a pipe a few feet away. The other man, the large violent-looking one, crouched cross-legged, broodily staring into the flames as though hypnotized by their flickering dance.

"That was an interesting day," Drolly Fin said, after removing his pipe and spitting in the fire. "Poor old Gurt—doubt he survived."

"You knew Gurtei?" Savarna glanced his way.

"I worked with him and his boys."

"Stole from them, he means." Big Jaran stared at the other man with a wry expression. The two made for strange comrades in Savarna's opinion. No doubt a story there, but not one that concerned her. A night's shared shelter with these two, and she'd be off about her business. Returning to Shen, killing the Empress.

But these oddballs intrigued her. The smoky-haired one was garrulous and shifty-looking. The huge blond was clearly some renowned warrior, with his axe, sword, and proud, haughty expression. How they'd come to be a team in the wild, she couldn't begin to grasp.

"It was a misunderstanding," Drolly Fin was saying. "That tosspot Dorley—the lanky one you hit, Jaran—he's a shit-stirrer, like Roile. Those two set me against old Gurt. I liked Gurt. Shame, we had some good times on the road." Savarna and the big man ignored him, so Fin shoved the pipe back in his mouth and stretched out his legs. "Think I'm for sleeping soon," he said. "That's if there's rest to be found for my poor bones in this bloody chill."

Savarna gazed up at the stars above. Earlier, the sky had blazed with shimmering lights, filling her with wonder. *The Giants' Dance*, Jaran had called it. A common occurrence in the north, apparently. Beautiful, yet disturbing to behold.

"Striped cat." Jaran looked her way suddenly, a half-grin on his tough face, the long hair lifting in the night breeze.

"What's that?" Savarna said, blinking alert. She noted how blue his eyes were, clear and sharp, paler than most men's. Intelligent for one of his type. A thinker as well as a fighter, she deemed.

"That witch in Ferrytown, you met her, too," Jaran said. "She told us the . . . *Tigress* . . . was on her way. Finvar says that's a large stripy orange cat, but then he's full of shit."

"There are tigers in my country," Savarna said, feeling a cold tremor flush through her veins. *Vian and I—the tiger cubs.* That's what her father had always called them, his darling fierce twins. His *Aikashi* . . . So unlike the other children. "Big cats," she added, evasively. "They eat people. I've not seen many near our home. They live mostly in the jungle forests skirting the mountains of my land."

"She said that you had a tiger's spirit guiding you, as Fin here has a hawk, and myself, a bear."

Savarna shrugged indifference, not in the mood for making conversation. She needed to sleep, or at least think through her next move. But he kept staring at her with those pale blue eyes, an irritating half-smile on his lips.

"I don't know what you want me to say," Savarna said. "The woman was clearly touched, or insane—or else cursed, and cursing us too, for good measure. I don't know much about you and your skinny friend, warrior. And I don't really give a shit. We'll part ways in the morning—so why not get some rest, and let me sleep too."

"I'm not skinny." Fin opened an eye. "All muscle here. Sinew." They both ignored him.

"You're safer with us, woman," Jaran said. "We're heading west, skirting the river. The Shen don't like us anymore."

"Good for you." Savarna rolled to her knees and yawned. "I'm going in the other direction."

"The sea?"

"Pol Shen—I have business in that city."

His infuriating smile broadened. "That's a silly idea, I'm thinking."

"I don't give a shit what you're thinking. No doubt you're an impressive fellow with that axe and sword you carry, but I have certain talents, too."

"Yep, the witch in Ferrytown hinted as much."

Savarna rolled her eyes. "What is it you want from me?" The blond giant confused her. Neither he nor his scrawny companion had made a pass at her. A relief, as she hadn't wanted to kill them, but a surprise, too. And this Jaran's constant probing was grinding on her nerves. She was tired, confused. Missed her twin. Drolly Fin was right—it had been an *interesting* day. A day of change, followed by a night and morning of violence and more strange encounters.

Jaran dropped his gaze from her and sighed. "Nothing," he said eventually. "Go to sleep, woman, clearly you're in need of some."

Savarna stared hard at him for a moment, and then nodded. She rolled closer to the fire and huddled for warmth. Close by, Drolly Fin's snores were gathering pace. She stared at Jaran for a time as he sat brooding by the flames, his hard face expressionless, those pale eyes far away, lost in distant thought.

"Good night, Northman," she whispered before closing her eyes.

JARAN LET HIS MIND WANDER AS THE FLAMES DIED DOWN and their smoke trail faded to a whisper. To his left, Finvar snored enthusiastically, but the woman lay silent as the night surrounding them. Jaran knew she wasn't sleeping. *Strange girl.* Exotic to behold, with her dark olive skin, deep red hair, and gold-flecked brown eyes. A beauty, some might say. Too bony and angular for Jaran's taste. He liked well-built women with curves aplenty. This lass was all muscle. Lanky and jaunty. And somewhat ungrateful, if truth be told.

A captive, or runaway slave. Not broken yet, judging by her haughty manner and tone. Perhaps recently bought. Aristocratic, and very foreign. *Rundali*, Fin had told him. A distant land far south of here, bordering Shen. Jaran knew nothing about the place. Hot and steamy, apparently.

Jaran gazed at her prone shape for long moments, feeling a return of the loneliness that haunted him at times. Since that far-off day when he'd left his mother, her tear-stained face calling out his name. Her shouts, small fists beating his chest. He had left Bera alone in that cave more than ten years past. His sad, crazy mother—alone with her foiled vengeance, bitterness and rage. And her dark secrets, too.

A shuffle, the shadows hiding her shape moved. Jaran shifted uncomfortably, returned his gaze to the fire. His uncle wanted him dead. The King of Leeth was his uncle. Erlund. The seer said he'd sent his three sons to kill Jaran after Gromaki failed. *Why?* What threat was Jaran to this king? Three days ago, Jaran didn't even know he had an uncle. He knew nothing of his heritage. He'd asked his mother so many times, but she'd never told him anything after mentioning Valkador once or twice in those early years before the Traveler came. It was part of the anger he'd felt toward her, and also the reason he'd left.

Nor had the canny Traveler mentioned his past, when he'd found Jaran broken and bloodied by that bear in the wood. The man knew Bera—those two had shared knowledge, but not friendship. Jaran had questioned the Traveler when he'd fared east with the man before joining Shen's army. Like his mother, the Traveler had told him nothing, only hinting that he came from noble stock. "You are not yet ready for that knowledge, boy," he'd said before their parting at the Shen River.

Valkador. That was part of it. Mother had mentioned that name in her sleep a few times, he remembered. And strangely, Finvar knew of it too—an island near Leeth. *Where I'm from.* Too many mysteries. Jaran heard the shuffle beside him again.

Savarna rolled to her knees, the thick crimson curls spilling across her dusky features, those gold-flecked brown eyes sleepy but calm. She flashed him a smile.

"I can't sleep," she said.

"Cold?"

"Yes, very, but my mind is racing." She rose to her feet, waved her arms back and forth to warm herself. "Care if I join you?"

"Be my guest," Jaran said.

"You've nice manners for a Northman," she said, sitting beside him, her lean, tanned body brushing against his arm.

"Have you known many?"

"You're the first—and I don't know you." She showed that sleepy grin again.

"No one knows me," Jaran said. "Not even myself."

"I'm called Savarna," she said after a moment's quiet. "I was captured by raiders. Shen slavers who took my people north. I fought them, killed some—so they separated me from the others."

"I'll bet." Jaran smiled.

"Their leader said he saw potential in me," she said. "He sold me to another man with high connections in Pol Shen. Word was sent north, and during our journey I learnt that their Empress had summoned me, after hearing what happened in the Rundali Passes. So I was told."

"And you want to kill Rasnei for what they did to you, and your people." He smiled, but gently this time, not mocking.

"She rules Shen—those people were her slavers. So, yes, I want . . . I mean, I *am* going to kill her."

"That will prove difficult, also hard on you."

"I don't expect to survive," Savarna said. "That doesn't matter. It's duty. My family was butchered, all save the younger women and some of the servants. I only have my brother."

"And, where is he?"

"Vian is coming." She flashed him that smile again.

Jaran said nothing for a time. Savarna had a strangeness he couldn't fathom. Almost, he felt like another being dwelt deep inside her. A savage violent creature, feral, yet latent. Buried within. *The Tigress?* She seemed to him a volcano on the edge of eruption.

He shrugged away the thoughts, poked the dying fire with a stick. Finvar's snores flared up again and then eased back. "Be dawn soon," Jaran said eventually.

"And you are the bear?"

Jaran raised an eyebrow. "So that witch in Ferrytown said. Or rather—a bear's spirit watches over me."

"I still think she was mad," Savarna said. "And even if she was sane, she would know I was from Rundali. We have a certain look and reputation."

Jaran shrugged. "That woman knew things about my past. Important things I need to learn. Fin has some knowledge, too. There's more to that skinny tosser than meets the eye, and I've yet to question him thoroughly." Jaran turned and stared hard at her face. Those fierce gold-brown eyes didn't flinch. "I was marked by a bear once."

"Marked?"

Jaran nodded and unclasped his woolen cloak. He tugged the thick tunic and mail shirt over his head. He sat there bare-chested, the woman's eyes wide, and her lips parting slightly as she studied his body.

"A bear did that?"

"When I was sixteen winters," Jaran said. "A white bear from the ice realm. He saved me."

"*Saved you?*" she laughed. "I'm sorry, I'm a bit confused. Judging by that scar, the brute nearly tore you in half."

"He marked me, yes. A branding. A badge of honor—the way I see it. I'd been attacked by wolves in the forest. The white bear killed them all, and then turned on me."

"And somehow you survived."

"I know it sounds absurd, but that bear gifted me strength. The scar is part of who I am. They call me Jaran Saerk, some-times the White Bear. Saerk is short for *Baresaerk,* after the ancient warriors who fought naked and were feared by all because of their terrible battle rage."

"That's why you tattooed the surrounding skin? To empha-size the . . . *branding.* A touch vain, no?"

"Not me. The Traveler did that with a reindeer horn, sharp-ened into needle points—said it was necessary for rune protection."

"And who is he?"

Jaran didn't answer. Away east, a dim light heralded morning. Finvar's eyes blinked open and he rolled and sat up yawning. Then he reached across for flint and stone, lit his pipe and shoved it in his mouth. "Morning," he said, after several puffs.

Savarna leaned against Jaran's body. She rolled up her jerkin sleeve, showing him the recent brand. "I'm marked too." She smiled. "Arm and ankle. We have that much in common, North-man. But unlike you, I'm not proud of it."

"You cannot kill the Empress of Shen." Jaran glanced at the small, red brand, and then shifted his gaze to her fierce eyes.

"I am obliged to try," Savarna said. "And my brother, too."

"Even so, and summoned or not—you won't get a weapon close to her person. Rasnei has guards everywhere. Some are Northmen like me, but mostly they're special Shen warriors, highly skilled in weaponry and unarmed combat. The Empress also has her councilors and spies. Then there is Chulan."

"I've heard that name," Savarna said. "One of the slavers mentioned it."

"The Imperial Magister," Jaran said. "Chulan is the real power in Shen. Rasnei is just a symbol, last in an ancient fading line of rulers. She has absolute power, and yet controls nothing. Chulan, on the other hand . . ."

"Well, then I shall kill him too," Savarna said, and Jaran laughed. "I don't need a weapon," she added. "I told you—I've certain skills."

"Again, I do not doubt that," Jaran said. "But you cannot go to Pol Shen, summoned or not. Finvar's old gang murdered your escort. You will be hunted, as will they. Once caught, your elegant head will be removed from your shoulders slowly with a toothed saw. It's what Chulan's special police do to outlaws in Shen."

"I have to try," she said. "Family is everything."

"We're your family now. Stay with us a day or so. Strays should stick together in a place like this," Jaran said. "At least, until we find some sort of settlement. I know nothing about this country, but Fin does."

"Why is he your friend?"

"He isn't. But he did rescue me from Pol Shen's rooms of correction, where I'd been placed for misdemeanors."

"You'll have to tell me more," she said.

"Only if you stay with us," Jaran smiled. "As for that one"—he motioned to Finvar, who had wandered off into the bushes—"he's playing his own game, and I've not yet worked out what that is."

They said nothing as Finvar returned fumbling with his breeches. "Another fine day in the wilderness," he said, grinning. "You two seem to be getting along nicely."

"This one was chilly," Jaran said, as Savarna glared at Finvar.

His grin broadened. "Well, here we are," Finvar said. "Three lost souls in the wild. No horses, no blankets, and scant grub."

"Speak for yourself," Savarna said. "I'm not lost."

"What's the plan?" Finvar asked, ignoring her hostile response as he fumbled inside his jerkin, producing some strands of dried beef. He tossed them over, and Jaran caught them with a deft hand. He shoved one in his mouth and gave the other two pieces to the woman. She crunched down on them hungrily.

Finvar produced another strip and tore at it with his teeth. "Last one," he said between mouthfuls.

Jaran stood up and stretched. "She wants to go Pol Shen," he told Finvar.

"Not keen on that idea," Finvar said. "Just left the place."

"You aren't invited," Savarna said. "You boys can go your own way."

"You're not much with gratitude, are you?" Finvar said. "Can you imagine what those Cards would have done to you? The Shen are perverse, but Calla's lads are damn vicious too, belief me."

Savarna didn't respond, but Jaran was curious. "What do you know of Ran Calla?"

"The 'Wolf,' they call him," Finvar spat. "Takes after his great-grandfather Carda who led the rebellion that toppled the Ptarnian Empire. He's ambitious and ruthless. Unlike his other forebearers, content to wallow in the newfound wealth of greater Cardalan, Ran Calla wants Shen and won't stop until it's in his grasp."

"There has always been war between the two lands," Jaran said. "The Shen have always held the river. Can't see that changing anytime soon."

"You, Northman, lack vision," Finvar said. "Calla will not stop until Shen is destroyed. He's like a rabid wolf."

"How is it you know all this, small one?" Savarna was staring hard at Finvar.

Finvar's flint eyes shot her way. "Because I worked in Cardalis City a few years back. The legendary City in the Clouds. Once the home of the mad God Emperors. *Caranaxis*, they called it back then."

"What were you doing there?" Jaran asked, gazing about. It was past time they got moving. Those Cardalan soldiers might be heading their way.

"Keeping my eyes open and mouth shut."

"Find that hard to believe," Savarna said.

"I don't think your girlfriend likes me." Finvar grinned, then the smile faded from his lips. Before they could respond, he produced a knife and tossed it past Jaran's head. "I saw some-thing," he said. They didn't respond. Embarrassed, Finvar walked over and retrieved his knife. "We're in Dunnehine," he said. "You can't trust the shadows here. We need to leave while we still can."

"I'm heading east," Jaran told Savarna. "You're welcome to

come, should you change your mind about Pol Shen. Finvar's coming along too—though I'm not entirely sure why."

"I'm not changing my mind or direction," she replied. "I'm returning to Ferrytown, then on to Pol Shen. Been nice knowing you pair."

"Alas, but that's no longer an option," Finvar said. He'd been staring back at the way they'd come, as morning light revealed gray skies, a skein of geese cutting chevrons high above while calling out to each over in mournful trumpet voices.

Not the only sound. Jaran cursed as the noise of hoofs drumming earth grew louder. The Cards were on their way. "Nowhere to hide in this terrain," Jaran said. "Perhaps we should make for the river. Try swimming."

"It's a mile's run south, and then a half-mile's swim across freezing water," Finvar said. "Not your best idea, Northman."

"What do you suggest—fly?"

"We can stay put and fight," Savarna said quietly, and the two men looked at her.

"Girl's got a death wish," Finvar said, but Jaran was grinning, his axe and sword in either hand.

"I don't feel like running," he said. "Or swimming."

Finvar reached for his bow. "Then let us go say hello," he said, walking off toward the cloud of dust announcing the riders' swift approach.

Storga Kull reined in his horse abruptly, and his men followed suit. They knew the stories about this land. Any strange sighting might not be as it seemed. Normally, spotting three strangers on the road in enemy land would have spurred him on to skewer them. But in Dunnehine—were the stories true—you had to be cautious. These three could be shamans, or worse, spirits or fetches. Warlocks even.

His second, Baltarg, rode alongside. "Tseole?" he asked.

"The small one, perhaps," Storga Kull said. "The other is a Northman, the woman I'm not sure."

"Spirits of the slain." Baltarg looked edgy.

"Let's go see," Storga said, urging his pony forward, the thirty riders following behind. Storga didn't want to be here. Not his idea to enter this land, but Ran Calla had insisted, and the warlord was not one to refuse.

"Take your men to the ocean," Calla had told him in his tent two weeks ago. The warlord had been visiting his warriors stationed in the frontier, the wide Shen River a few miles east. "I need to assess the possibilities of invasion from the Dunnehine coast. If Pol Shen City falls, then their entire land will crumple."

They'd ridden north the next day for mile upon mile, eventually reaching a series of great bends in the river, the region where its course veered slowly east toward the distant ocean, marking the northern boundary of Shen.

From there, they'd ridden along the Dunnehine banks until spying the distant lights of Ferrytown. They'd attacked that morning, making sure no one survived. Once that task was done, Storga Kull had led a few men to the nearby jetties and docks to examine the possibility of launching an attack from there. After that, they'd ridden east until reaching the coastline proper. A broken line of cliffs splintering off into small islands, nowhere in sight looked suitable for an army to camp.

Their reconnaissance done, Storga decided Ferrytown would serve well enough for the purpose. He'd report that back to Calla on his return. The Ran would then decide whether risking his whole army in Dunnehine was worth breaking the stalemate of the ceaseless Shen River skirmishes. Storga was glad that wasn't his decision to make, but he still prayed to Mighty Kullaan of the Skies that he not get sent back here anytime soon.

Job done, and with Ferrytown's streets scoured of life, the riders had left at first light. Storga Kull's plan was to maintain a steady trot until they reached Greater Cardalan. But plans change.

He watched the three strangers carefully. They showed no fear, and the large one looked very dangerous. Had they escaped from Ferrytown? If so, he had men to question and discipline. But these three were an unlikely crew. Curious—and if he was honest to himself, a little shaken—he guided his mount across, stopping short of bowshot as he noticed the weapon in the smaller man's grasp.

Storga Kull raised a palm facing outwards. The small bowman looked to his bigger friend who shrugged, then nodded. The bowman lowered his weapon, the arrow still on nock. "Let me go speak to them," Baltarg said, riding up alongside again.

"No." Storga Kull would not have his second look braver than himself, even if there was trickery here. "I will go, but watch that archer. Shoot him if he levels that weapon again."

"Why not shoot him now?" Baltarg asked, but they both knew the answer to that. These three might not be human, and there could be sorcery here.

Storga Kull took a deep breath and slipped from his saddle. He walked, arms wide on either side, making toward the waiting three, his twin sabers rattling on his studded belt. He felt awkward walking, but then like most Cardalan war chiefs, Storga Kull spent more hours in a saddle than he did on his feet. He stopped when he could see their faces clearly.

"I am Storga Kull, Third Captain of the Dawn Riders, beloved warriors of Greater Cardalan. Tell me who you are and why you are here, then I shall decide whether to kill you."

The archer grinned. "Methinks I'll put an arrow in you first."

"You could do that," Storga said. "But my archers would cripple you, and then my other men would continue the process at leisure, same for your comrades."

Jaran walked past Finvar who stood, bow half-drawn, to his right. Savarna remained put, no fear in her eyes, only defiance. The stocky hard-faced officer watched him with small, distrusting eyes. Jaran stopped several paces short. "Are you a coward?" he asked, swinging axe and sword in circles, and then sheathed them, sword back in scabbard, axe clanging into loop.

Storga's eyes narrowed. "Not wise insulting me."

"It was a simple question," Jaran said. "I meant no offense. It's just, I weary of your arrogance. You and your men must be held accountable for your actions."

"What actions?" Storga Kull barked a laugh. "You are a proud, foolish fellow, even for a Northman. I could fight you —but why should I bother? I thought perhaps you three might be wayward spirits on this empty road. Dunnehine is infested by such, they say. But I see you are just vagrants. I shall order my men to cut you apart."

He made to turn, but Jaran's voice stopped him. "Don't walk away from me, fat man. If you are a coward—run. If not, then draw those sabers and let us settle this as honorable men."

Jaran never received an answer. Instead, Storga Kull coughed as an arrow pierced his throat. Jaran's eyes darted to Fin, as fresh shafts struck the Cardalan archers Storga had ordered to protect him. Further shafts found other riders, until the rest wheeled their mounts about and cantered back toward Ferrytown.

A small man clad in dun trousers and floppy jacket appeared from the dead grasses where he'd lain hidden. Three others stood behind him, and more were emerging in the heathland beyond. They appeared as shadows made from the mist. Jaran wondered if these were Dunnehine fetches, but they looked solid enough when they approached.

The nearest shouldered his horn bow as he approached the spot where Jaran and his two companions stood in stunned silence. Close by, Storga Kull's body was still twitching, while further away were screams as the last of his men tumbled from their horses, their bodies full of arrows.

"There is meaning in this," the smallish man stopped to survey them briefly before glancing down at Storga's corpse. He kicked the body, then reached down smoothly and jerked the shaft free. "You three wanderers are welcome in our camp."

"Jaran." Finvar shot him a wary glance.

"Are you Dunnehine warlocks?" Jaran asked.

"We are Tseole," the man said. "Driven from our lands by men like these." He kicked the corpse again. "Forced to scratch out a living in this blighted country, while keeping two eyes out for the Others, those you call the Dunnehine."

Finvar's eyes were wide. "Tseole? I thought your people a myth. A nomad race who'd been wiped out by the God Emperors centuries past."

The man smiled bitterly. "Not far from the truth, Finvar the Droll. There are few of us left living these days. The Cardalan warlords seemed happy to continue where the God Emperors left off. No one likes the Tseole."

"How do you know his name?" It was Savarna who had spoken.

The archer turned her way. "I know all your names, Savarna Eltayn. You three were expected."

"By whom?" Jaran asked, feeling edgy again.

"Our shaman, Odel. He told us to wait until the Cards returned, and kill them before they hurt you."

"What does this Odel want with us?" Savarna asked.

"To reveal to you your destiny."

6

RASNEI

Rasnei Cai Ti-Shen, thirty-third ruler of the Ti Dynasty, surveyed her courtroom with cold, impassive eyes. There were over a hundred people gathered down there, small figures milling around. Some issuing commands, others cowering—all were a dozen feet below her and over fifty distant, as was proper.

Only her chosen bodyguard, and a few of the Secretary's officers, were allowed in her presence. And Magister Chulan, of course, when he paid his weekly visit. He was down there, surrounded by courtiers and servants, plus slaves and other minions—always a cloud of people around that one. She could see the Magister leaning over a table reading something, his black gown and flat, square cap rendering him crow-like. A small, neat man whom everyone feared. Even herself, should she care to admit it.

Rasnei was no fool. Twenty-seven years old, and born to power. Her family had ruled for nearly four hundred years, snatching the throne from the mighty Shaan dynasty by employing a toxic mixture of cunning and diplomacy over time, and using paid assassins with daggers, or artful placements of poison. The Ti dynasty was as ruthless as the one it had over-thrown. Rasnei was no exception.

But unlike her forebearers, Rasnei could only rely on herself. She had to be sharper than her ancestors. Shen was changing, and quickly. No one could be trusted in court these days.

Her revered father had aloofly left politics to his lowly advi-sors. Rasnei preferred to stay ahead of such intrigue. And she didn't trust Magister Chulan, a wily old fox who wielded far more influence in court than he had in her father's time.

Rasnei couldn't count the number of rulers who'd sat upon the Sapphire Throne since the first dynasty millennia past. But she did know that only three of them had been women, and two of those in ancient times when Shen was young. The last empress had been Samalca Shaan, famous for outwitting her many would-be assassins, herself an accomplished poisoner and artful intriguer. But those skills hadn't saved Samalca. Her Magister's trusted slaves had drowned the empress in her own milk bath. They'd killed her other servants and all the guards too, before they were slain themselves. Predictably, Chun Ga—the Magister at that time—emerged as the new emperor.

Rasnei determined she wouldn't share such a fate. She had her spies, careful servants and slaves, who listened and reported back frequently. But Magister Chulan had far more. And he owned the armies too. All five Imperial Cadres were in Chulan's pocket, him and his Secretary and Magistrate, the oily but capable Soma Ghee.

Rasnei had her Sapphire Guard made up of auxiliaries. Good fighters, but loathed and despised by the regular cadres as unwashed vulgar oafs. Most were foreigners, though some came from distant rural parts of her domain, peasants with no chance of joining the regulars.

Rasnei liked the Northmen best. These giants were proud, honest and loyal. Ferocious fighters. Some, like their captain, Hranic Finehair, had served since her father's time. Hranic reported to her directly—something that Chulan frowned upon, she knew. The Northmen were hated by her courtiers, but unlike those scheming cockroaches, the big warriors from the west were fiercely loyal to her alone.

Rasnei gazed down at the piazza. Naked slaves were constructing a platform for the ritual execution. She didn't know the man—Tin Lous. One of the Soma Ghee's Correction Masters. An administrator and minor civil servant of small account. The man had let some dangerous prisoners escape, Chulan had informed her. Such carelessness would cost him his head. Chulan had suggested the ritual saw, accompanied by soft flute music, and some intricate dance routines by his erotic performers. She hadn't declined the notion.

Rasnei didn't care what they did to the man. The escaped criminals interested her more. Especially as one of them had been a fighter in her auxiliaries. And not just any fighter. A legend, apparently, who had almost single-handedly held back the Cardalan scourge time and again during their constant raids along the Shen River.

Jaran Saerk. He'd been presented to her once, nine years ago —not long after she'd become ruler, still clad in her mourning black silk. A proud, handsome giant with piercing pale-blue eyes. Their eyes always fascinated Rasnei. She remembered he'd had sad eyes that day, though the emotion was well-hidden beneath his warrior pride. He'd looked about seventeen then, maybe younger. It was hard to tell with Northmen.

The other escapee was a known thief. Finvar the Droll had slipped Chulan's nets on several occasions. But he'd received a pardon after some useful espionage he'd carried out in distant Cardalis. He'd also reported that Jaran Saerk had killed another Northman in Holmgang, a thing forbidden in her realm. Northmen had served the Shen for years, and both races had profited by the relationship. But there were rules.

A hard and fast one was a ban on Holmgangs. If a soldier —any soldier—had a grievance, he was to report to his superior, and that one would pursue the correct channels. Holmgangs were for savages—they belonged to a distant time.

Rasnei heard the soft scurry of feet approaching.

"So sorry," said Mawla Tei, her preferred courtesan, who kneeled and lowered her pretty forehead to the dais. The servant was behind Rasnei and out of sight from any prying eyes below. Rasnei always had her people use the secret doors behind her chambers. She didn't doubt that Chulan knew where these were, but even he wouldn't pry in there. *Yet*...

Rasnei bid the girl rise. Mawla Tei bowed again and then sprang to her toes. She was a beauty—but more importantly, sharp and quick at learning and very discreet.

"Speak," Rasnei said, a slight wave of her hand.

"Exalted One, Captain Hranic is here. He says please forgive, but it's urgent." The bow again.

Rasnei was intrigued. Hranic Finehair usually stayed well away when Chulan was at court. Like all of his kind, the Auxiliaries leader had a temper, preferred fighting to intrigue, and was very wary of the Magister and his oily servants, especially Ghee. For him to seek her Imperial attentions at such a busy time was diverting.

"Where is Finehair?"

"Forgive me, he is being served tea in your outer chambers. Shall I summon him?"

"No—I'll go." She rose gracefully, noted Chulan caught her eye from afar. Never missed a thing, that one. Chulan bowed low, as did everyone else down there. Rasnei swept her cool gaze over the courtroom piazza and turned to her servant.

"Mawla Tei, keep an eye on the Magister. If he approaches, let me know." She left the girl and slipped away from sight, leaving the dais and gliding, like the flowing silk she wore, through the backdoors into her expansive chamber area. Servants and slaves prostrated themselves as she breezed past, her blue silk gown brushing the marble mosaics, and her arms neatly folded, hands hidden inside funneled sleeves.

Captain Hranic leaped to his feet when she emerged in the outer chamber. The tea cup looked ridiculously tiny in his Northman's paw. He spilled some, and she almost smiled.

He started to speak, but she raised a hand. Hranic bowed. These Northmen was clueless at protocol. Another source of amusement. Chulan insisted they should remain at the Shen River where most were posted. Rasnei ignored such advice, deeming it prudent to keep some of the best ones close by.

The Auxiliaries alone, with her inner-house servants, could be trusted.

She bid him relax and seated herself gracefully on a sedan. A servant brought her tea, but she ignored the piping-hot liquid and the girl faded from view, her movements soft as summer breezes.

"Your news couldn't wait, Captain?"

Hranic saluted her. "Highness." *They never get it right.* "There was an ambush on the highway, several murders."

Rasnei's brow flicked in annoyance. "Magister Chulan deals with these provincial matters. Report the incident to him."

Hranic looked uncomfortable. "Highness . . . I . . . a woman escaped, someone you had ordered brought before you. A Rundali slave, recently captured, currently roaming the country-side at large with the Midnight Cutting Crew."

"How intriguing." Rasnei faintly recalled hearing about a woman who had killed three slavers in the southlands. Word had reached her that this creature possessed unearthly combat skills that had enabled her first escape, until the slaver's people caught up with her again and caged the vixen. Soma Ghee had suggested they bring her to court for interrogation. Rasnei had liked the idea, and ordered her brought hence by Imperial Carriage, escorted by one of the Secretary's trusted aides and a squad of soldiers.

"A random raid, you think—or contrived?"

"Hard to say, Highness." Hranic fidgeted, stroked his forked beard, and then dropped his rough hands by his side, as though realizing he shouldn't be moving. "Those Cutters are devious killers. Try as we might, they always elude our traps."

"Well find them, especially the prisoner . . . Rundali?"

"Yes, Highness—it looked like she did some of the killing. The Secretary's aide was stabbed before the carriage door was opened."

Rasnei reached for her tea. "This is hardly urgent news, Captain." She stared at him until he dropped his gaze. "What else?"

"One of my men has . . . eloped."

"Eloped? Ah—yes, Jaran Saerk escaped from the Correction Rooms." She smiled thinly. "The Magister is vexed, and the fool responsible is about to lose his head, slowly." She smiled slightly. "How did this happen?"

"The same villain that reported his Holmgang broke in to the Correction Center and freed him. A concerted effort, obviously, and there are complications as this man—Finvar Droll—is a former member of the Cutters."

"You think the two incidents are connected, Captain?"

"I remain uncertain, Highness. It does seem an odd coincidence. But there is more."

"I thought there might be." Rasnei sipped the tea again. "Continue."

"Ferrytown."

"What of it?" Her eyes narrowed, the man looked nervous, unusual for a Northman.

"The trading town across Pol Shen Bay—"

"I know where it is," she snapped.

He nodded, chewed his moustache and continued. "Attacked, two nights ago."

"By whom—the Midnight Cutting Crew again?" Her sarcasm cut crisp waves through the air.

"They were involved, as was Jaran Saerk, but so were the Cards."

Rasnei spilt her tea as her arms stiffened in shock. The servant appeared and fussed, she glared at her, and the girl vanished behind the screen. "Cardalan. Ran Calla? The enemy was there?"

"Across the river, yes, Highness. A scouting party, I suspect. Ran Calla grows overbold." He lowered his voice to a whisper. "The Cards are winning this war, Highness."

"You think Calla is planning invasion, via Ferrytown or

thereabouts?" The servant girl reappeared and, at a nod from Rasnei, refilled the tea before vanishing again. Rasnei sipped carefully. "You didn't think to inform Magister Chulan about this?"

Hranic shifted his feet.

"Sit," she ordered, weary of his mournful expression. "Drink some tea, then tell me what really concerns you."

Hranic complied clumsily. After several slurps that had her wincing inwardly, the Auxiliary Captain placed the tiny cup and saucer on a side table with infinite care. She suppressed a smirk. Most comical watching that.

"I . . . do not trust Magister Chulan, Highness." She said nothing, so he stood up again and fidgeted. "I think he might be a traitor."

Rasnei's face blanched white. To distrust Chulan was prudent. To accuse him of treachery was both reckless and impertinent beyond words. She saw fear in Hranic's eyes. A word or signal from her would see the Northman taken to the saw, replacing the fool they were preparing down there.

"That, Captain, is a most grievous accusation," Rasnei said. "What proof have you?"

"None," he said. "Just suspicions. A hunch."

"You would risk slow torture and your neck for a hunch, Captain?"

"I would, Highness."

"Very well, then, you were wise to come here." Rasnei straightened and arched her delicate fingers, the long emerald-blue painted nails were filed to pointed precision. "Speak your mind, and it will not go beyond these walls."

He nodded, his gaze sweeping the screens and doors nervously. "Soma Ghee travelled to the Shen River last month, and the previous one."

"He is allowed to do that."

"Ghee was seen handing a scroll over to men at the crossing. The same men took the raft across to Cardalan on that night, so my captains at the front informed me."

Rasnei sipped her tea. "Even if Ghee is a traitor, that doesn't implicate Chulan."

"Ghee works for Chulan, Highness—reports to him directly. Those two men are tight and close."

"This we know, Captain. But why would either man —however ambitious—sell secrets to our enemy? I'm not overly familiar with Soma Ghee, but Chulan is loyal to Shen beyond all else."

"Shen, yes—but, I suspect, not its empress," Hranic said quietly.

Her gaze pinned him for a moment. She nodded. "This too is known to us. Continue."

"Pol Shen is rotting from within, Highness. Your court, this entire city, functions on bribery and deception."

"Again, that's nothing new in Shen," Rasnei said.

"But it is far worse than the time I served your father. Chulan simpers and placates you, Highness. But I suspect he wants your throne and will pay any price—even selling us out to that wolf Calla."

"Calla would destroy Shen if he could," Rasnei said. "That would not benefit Magister Chulan overmuch."

"He is a master of compromise, Highness. I think—"

He stopped abruptly when the courtesan Mawla Tei appeared, bowed three times and whispered in Rasnei's ear. Rasnei nodded. She rose and handed her tea to the other servant, freshly back from the screen.

"We thank you for your report, Captain Hranic. I will send

instruction via courier in a few hours. You may leave us." Hranic nodded and briskly departed behind the screens. Rasnei watched him leave and then made her imperial way back to the throne and dais.

Magister Chulan greeted her at the entrance. She stopped, surveying him with chilly eyes. He bowed. "Please forgive the intrusion, Exalted One." He smiled. "The executioner and his people are awaiting your command."

She nodded, disliking how he hovered close, his sharp, black eyes scanning the back of the dais. Rasnei took to her throne, Chulan standing behind her. She waved a dismissive hand, cheers followed, then soft music. After that, the screams took over.

VIAN REINED IN, SEEING THE TEMPLE'S ROOF SHIMMERING in heat haze. After a long ride, the horse was trembling with exhaustion beneath him.

"We'll rest here for a time." Vian didn't want to push the animal beyond recovery, even though every muscle in his body urged him to drive the beast harder.

It was scarce a dozen miles to the coast and the estates owned by the wealthy noble called Shateke, the same man who ran six teams of slaver gangs throughout southern Shen. But Vian needed rest, too. He was hungry and tired. He guided the horse down the twisted track, the copper temple hovering ahead, deserted and remote.

The roofs curved up at the corners, a stone dragon seated on each. Beneath them were four copper walls linked by ivory-colored pillars, more dragons and gryphons carved on each, and a single arched alcove leading inside. Vian dismounted and tied his horse to a rail at the roadside. He vaulted the rail and strode inside the temple. Far beyond, the murmuring sea crashed and surged into dreamy distance.

Inside the temple was a wooden statue of the Goddess, her eyes painted jade green. A beaded rug stretched the tiled floor in front. Aside that, there was a three-legged stool and a spittoon bowl, together with drying towel. Vian wondered who tended this remote place.

He kneeled, folded his legs beneath him, and tucked his hands beneath his armpits. He closed his eyes and focused.

For long minutes, Vian sat there, rocking his body slightly, as his fargaze searched the northern lands. He saw a town cloaked in gray clouds—fires burning, too. A witchy-woman's harsh face glared back at him, and Vian recognized a challenge. The woman was blocking his search, and he couldn't reach Savarna.

Frustrated, Vian rose to his feet smoothly and left the temple behind. He found some wild berries and filled his belly while the horse cropped the grass nearby. Then he rested for a time, letting the warm breeze and soft surge of the distant ocean lull his frayed nerves and senses.

Vian pictured her face. Those gold flecked eyes, the long red hair—so like his own. Savarna was hidden from him for the moment, but he would find her. Before that, he would glean everything he could from the man he held responsible.

7

RANNING'S GIFT

VALGARN STOOD at the prow as the small craft clipped across the river, the bright winter sun blazing above, gulls mewling and swooping, the sharp wind in his face. He smiled, enjoying the short crossing from Hragglund's eastern hills over to the bleakness and shadow of Dunnehine ahead. A host of firs waited to greet him and his two brothers, as the pilot guided his boat into a shamble of jetties, docks, and fisher huts. Beyond these, a thin road wound up into the dark mass of trees, vanishing from sight.

The brothers had done well. The three great northern kingdoms lay behind them, and the brooding mystery of Dunnehine and Shen ahead. Valgarn grinned at Gorn. They had reached their mother's country, a place feared more than any other land. A grim vastness of shimmering lights through midnight skies. A cold, cruel country riddled with troll caves and stalked by wandering shamans. Dunnehine stretched beyond the Hragg River for countless miles until greeting the distant sea north of Shen. The brothers had studied the old maps before departure and decided this their best route.

Weak, common men might shun Dunnehine, but Erlund's sons were not feeble like his carles or warriors. Their mother's birthplace held no dread for them. "Avoid Cardalan," King Erlund had said. "Cross the wide realms until you reach the Shen River, then follow that to the sea."

A long, hard ride, but they had six good horses—three for riding, the others for weaponry, equipment, and fare. Their men had refused to cross the river. Gorn had killed two. Despite that and threats, their dread of Dunnehine ensured the other faint-hearts stayed put.

That meant hard work for the brothers. Such an arduous undertaking involved hauling barrels of beer and copious haunches of dried meat. Valgarn wasn't worried— they could buy servants in Shen, or anywhere men lived. Let those cravens run back to King Erlund. Valgarn and his brothers would carve the blood eagle on their backs when they returned.

The silent pilot shored his craft, and they leapt onto the dock. Valgarn tossed the waterman a coin. He bit it and nodded, looking relieved to be heading back. The crossing was rarely used, but hunters and fishers sometimes scoured the far river bank for fare and game when times were hard. The huts over here were for drying skins, and a necessary shelter should the weather turn foul, as it so often did this far north.

Valgarn turned to his brothers as they mounted their horses. "Best we ride until nightfall. Those look like troll woods to me."

Gorn laughed. "I'll protect you, brother, should one come a-visiting."

"Fuck off." Valgarn struck his eldest brother's saddle as he vaulted onto his own beast's back. "You and Holt will most like shaft any troll passing—judging by the wenches you lie with." All three brothers laughed, then cussed and urged their mounts forward, the packhorses lashed behind, off the dock platform and onto the murky road twisting up toward the wooden maze beyond.

They cleared the woods before dark and rode across low rolling hills, the odd dead lightning tree marking the way ahead. That night, as Valgarn lay wrapped in his blanket by the cracking glow of firelight, the wonder they called the Giants' Dance flashed green and purple, glowing shifting lights flickering out across the heavens. Valgarn knew it was a good omen. A sign from their mother. The shaman-gods of Dunnehine were welcoming them home.

SHEEGA GAZED UP AT THE DANCING LIGHTS, THE SKY flickering all around. For three days and nights, she had wandered the empty beaches of the island, seeing nothing save spindrift and ocean, the odd seal lounging.

Her lover had returned to his banished domain for a time. The Sea God was ranging far off through distant oceans, he'd told her. There were things Ranning needed to fetch from the depths. She missed his watery sinewy touch and urgent sex thrusting inside her. Aside that, she enjoyed the solitude of Valkador in winter.

She walked briskly, leaving the beach and ocean behind, turning for home where firelight and hearth would warm her ancient bones. The Giants' Dance flickered above, its reflection mirrored in the lake as she neared the hall. Nothing stirred, no creature or person would be out at this hour save perhaps a wolf or owl away in the forests and hills. She'd been back to Bera's cottage once or twice, trying to see what had happened there, so long ago. The signs he'd left—the Traveler.

She'd scryed for Bera, finding nothing. Doubtless her guide had warned her that to mention Sheega's name or mutter Valkador would announce her presence, and Sheega could finish the work at last. It irked her that Hrelgi's wife still lived, though it was hardly important. The Traveler played his own game. What remained crucial was that Bera's son died within the next twelve moons.

Her own sons were out there, his cousins, out to slay him. She'd seen their rough faces reflected in the mirror, the same eerie skies above their heads. They would kill Jaran for her, and then deal with their father the king. Erlund would have outlived his usefulness by then. Ranning would hold this island, allowing her to cross over finally, and then she'd wait up in Leeth and plan her revenge against her enemies: the Traveler, the Siren, the Dream-chaser, Unva and the others. Her arch-foes, the seven warlocks of Dunnehine.

The Traveler was crafty, and the Siren cruel. Neither would be a match for her once her full powers returned after Jaran's death, though. The others even less so. Unva in particular she hated. They had been lovers once. But Unva had sold her out to the Traveler, given her position away that bleak night when the warlocks turned Sheega's world inside out. The other warlocks would perish, but Unva she would keep for a time. Perhaps like Gantallian, trapped inside a mirror. Compressed, dried out and screaming. It was a pleasant thought.

Ahead, the hall loomed like a prowling beast crowning the hill, the woods cut away and the stockade and yards gleamed stark under that flickering sky. Sheega felt old this evening. She could tell the three Norns were spinning their threads, weaving busy against her. Those sisters would cause her undoing if they could. Sheega had many enemies—you didn't get to her age without being loathed. Especially when sorcery was the only coinage for survival.

Sheega saw the fires blazing in the hall as she walked up, untied her snow boots and kicked them off. She dropped her coat by the door, walked up to the fire and poured a large flagon from the heated wine, clasping the cup in her white, icy hands.

Her eyes narrowed at a flicker of gold by the fire.

Who comes?

The flicker shimmered and became a blur, manifested to a man. Ranning stood there. A wet mass of weed dripped from his hands. He cast it down at her feet. Kelp and bladder wrack clustered like dead spiders, glistening in the firelight.

"What's that?" Sheega asked her lover, as his handsome face emerged from the gloom.

"A gift," he said. "And one that should prove useful. Long have I thought about your words. If we are to overcome all our enemies, we need assistance from my realm. These are dark spirits who served me down there. They cannot manifest above water, but with the right runes can be . . . altered."

"Altered? I see only kelp lying there."

Ranning smiled. "Do you doubt me, my love?" He reached down with liquid grace and scooped up a small piece of bladder wrack. Ranning squeezed the weed, and a wet pop squirted juice into his hand. The juice changed color and solidified, becoming a tiny manikin. Sheega watched in fascination as the man-figure grew larger, rising up until he stood naked and glistening beside them. She reached out and touched his wet blue skin. The moment her fingers made impact, the manlike figure imploded, and a rush of brine soaked the floor at her feet.

"You just wasted that one." Ranning looked angry. "They have souls."

"What must I do?"

"Cast the stones and speak the welding runes. Couple with each one in turn, and then they are yours." Ranning smiled, his anger vanishing as quickly as stormy seas settling in summer.

"I shall do as you ask," Sheega said. She unclasped her broach, allowing the heavy fur cloak drop. She stood naked before him.

Ranning took her in his arms. "I have missed your touch." He slid his fingers lower, working them nimbly, and then kneeled before her, as she gasped and allowed him to pleasure her in front of the fire.

Once they were done, Ranning scooped up the weed again and offered it to her.

"Today?" she asked.

"No, it needs to dry, and we want to wake them by the ocean —that will allow you time to arrange the correct runes."

"Then I must lie with each in turn." She caressed his chest as they lay together entwined on the floor. "A busy night ahead."

It turned out to be a busy week. Sheega raised the horse-head pole, its skull warding off any scrying counter-spells. She cast the stones, spoke the rough incantations, allowed the rune spell to take shape. Ranning, standing beside her, popped open the wrack, allowing the juicy inner brine to manifest and grow. Then, as the watery men took form, Sheega led them away into the trees and performed the necessary sealing rites.

There were twelve that crossed over successfully. Each one towered over Sheega and Ranning, far bigger even than her sons. Like Ranning, their skin was honey gold mixed with green, and their eyes a cloudy milky white. The *Witch-Guard,* Sheega called them. Her soldiers in the fight to come.

THE VAGABOND WOMAN SHUFFLED TOWARD THE VILLAGE, the filthy rags and shawl hiding her once-handsome features, and her bare feet sore on the frozen winter ground.

The long trek south along the coast had taken her months, living off carrion and seeds, seaweed, land plants, birds' eggs —anything she could find. At last, she reached the area where the new king held sway. Grimhold Castle was only a score of miles distant.

But she wasn't ready to finish the journey yet. Worn out by toil and travel, she needed to lie low, gather herbs and heal her body. She would have to be strong to properly perform her task in the town. With that in mind, the shabby, battered wretch left the nearby village alone and made for the deep woods. In their tangled midst, she set up a rudimentary camp surrounded by dense mossy pines. The vagabond woman would be safe there. No wolf or bear would cause her harm. She had her charms of protection, and the shadow of the bloody past hung over her. Once settled in, she'd wait for the appointed time.

8

ODEL

THE TSEOLE HAD INTRODUCED himself as Cuile, a leader of his people. He led them northwest for several miles leading up into snow-brushed hills, their slopes bare and empty. A long, hard trek, the snow thickened as they wound up through the hills. Afternoon arrived and faded to evening, the days so short in this northern winter land.

Jaran gazed past the furthest slopes where a gap showed a flat valley ahead. He saw lights flickering down there, the welcoming orange of firelight. As they approached, he noticed a score of cone-shaped tents hemmed by a round fence, the stakes sharpened, and a strong-looking wooden gate the only visible entrance. A shallow ditch revealed more stakes peeping up from the snow.

Cuile led them down to the gate where a Tseole dressed in a heavy coat of silver and blue waited, a long, white stick clutched in his gloved hands.

"Odel has come to greet you," their guide said. "It is a high honor our shaman shows you three."

Jaran glanced at Savarna, who shrugged. To his right, Finvar was unusually quiet. By his expression, Jaran suspected he thought these Tseole might cook them later tonight.

Odel the shaman watched their approach with dark eyes. His face was half-buried in the high hat he wore, its elk horns spreading out and wide. His skin was dark, and the long moustaches and whisper of hair that showed whiter the snow surrounding them. He struck his staff into the powdery ground. "Follow me."

"You're not coming?" Jaran noted how Cuile hung back.

"My task is done," he said, turning and leaving Jaran gazing after him.

"I said *follow*." Odel flicked his sharp gaze back where Finvar and Jaran stood hesitating. Savarna walked close behind the old man.

"I don't like this," Finvar said.

"We're here, and not lying near that river pierced full of arrows," Jaran said. "I take that as a good sign."

"Well, keep your wits about you," Finvar muttered, fingering his long knife. "That conniver might put a spell on us."

They caught up with Savarna, who seemed lost in thought as she followed Odel inside the largest tent, a round dome comprising stretched dried reindeer skins with a hole at the top where smoke wisped through, trailing off into the deepening dark.

A Tseole appeared, his leather clad arms crossed. "Leave your weapons with me," the wiry hunter said. Savarna flicked her stolen knife into his hands. Finvar glanced darkly at Jaran, who shrugged. He unsheathed his sword and passed it over, then the axe. The guard gestured that he should place them by the tent.

Finvar, still scowling, followed suit with his bow and sack of arrows.

"I'll take that dagger too," the guard said, his dark eyes unfriendly.

"If you insist," Finvar said, tossing the blade into the snow between the guard's feet. "I can use my teeth if I have to." The Tseole raised a brow but said nothing.

"Enough of your nonsense, Fin," Jaran said. "Let's learn all we can and move on."

"I admire your optimism," Finvar said. "But this is Dunnehine, so I do not share it. You first, big lad."

Jaran and Finvar stepped inside. The tent was bigger than it had looked, perhaps twenty feet in diameter. Bearskin rugs were strewn across the floor, and a single wicker rocking chair rested adjacent to the fire ring at the center of the tent.

Odel took the chair, leaning back into it and rocking slightly, his flinty-dark eyes hooded. He motioned for them to sit before him on the floor. Savarna complied readily enough, folding her legs beneath her and sinking low. Jaran crouched uncomfortably, whereas Finvar remained standing.

"Drolly Fin, you might like to sit," the shaman said, a thin smile smudging his lips that barely showed beneath that snow-white moustache. "This will take some time."

"I'd rather stand," Finvar said, but the shaman ignored him, and his gaze swept to Jaran and Savarna.

"Three lost children in the wilderness." Odel's raspy voice showed a hint of wry humor that was lost on Jaran. "Brought together by the Norns' will."

"Not for long," Savarna said. The shaman didn't respond.

Jaran relaxed and slunk down on his haunches, motioning

Finvar do the same. The small man glared at him and complied with a shrug.

"We are in your debt, Tseole," Jaran said. "I would thank you for sending those men to help us."

"Save you, you mean." Odel croaked a laugh. "You can believe me when I say it was a pleasure. Cuile and the other hunters had been following that Cardalan war party since they entered our land. We saw what they did in Ferrytown, witnessed them scout the bay. It seems Calla the Pugnacious is planning invasion. But that doesn't concern us here," he said, rocking gently, his eyes dark slits.

"Shen deserves its fate, overripe fruit that it's become," he continued. "What does concern we Tseole are marauders crossing our country, the small region that we retain. Long have the Tseole been persecuted. First the Ptarnians, and then the Cards who replaced them. Even Shen slavers upon occasion."

"What of the Dunnehine?" Jaran asked. "Don't they rule this land?"

"They are few and rarely encountered. Mostly they dwell on the ice rim where the white bears roam." Jaran felt a shiver flush through his veins hearing that. "They are a strange people, pale blue eyes, like yours Northman, but slanted, not round. They are a closed people, the Dunn. Canny in lore."

"Are you not also wise in runecraft?" Savarna asked. Jaran noted how she seemed more relaxed in the old man's company. He didn't share Finvar's concerns about being eaten or sacrificed, or else maybe cursed, but these people were strangers and that meant staying alert.

He studied her face, watched on as Savarna and the old man locked gazes for long moments. Eventually Odel nodded. "That is Vian's task, not yours, Savarna," he said quietly. Finvar and

Jaran exchanged baffled glances, but Savarna said nothing, though her face blanched and she chewed her lip. "Your way lies west with these two men," Odel told her.

"I'm going to Pol Shen," she said, and glared hard at Jaran to challenge that. He didn't, but instead noted how the old man smiled at her response. Jaran frowned. *What am I missing here?*

"We will see," Odel said, the thin smile fading. "Listen well, let me tell you what I know, and then you can eat and partake in parley with our hunters. Cuile will have the Yunna ready."

"Yunna?" Jaran shook his head again, but the old man didn't respond.

Odel sighed and stretched his back, causing the chair to rock wildly. He leaned forward, steading himself, poking the staff into the fire. "You know about the Great Happening?" he asked. They didn't respond, and Finvar scratched his ear.

"The Great . . . what?" Jaran asked.

"*Happening*," Odel tutted, and poked his staff into the flames again, this time sparks danced on the rugs. "Do they teach young people nothing of history these days?"

Jaran wanted to explain that he didn't know his own history, let alone that of the east lands.

Odel stared at their vacant expressions and rolled his eyes. "Pay attention—this concerns you," he said, glancing at Jaran and poking the fire a third time. "Over a thousand years ago, a war ravaged this entire world, shaking the heavens above. An event so seismic, even the old gods partook, resulting in their near-obliteration, and changing form and shape forever. Most of their minions fled the galaxy, but a few remained in the far north. Descendants of the ancient Faen. Others crashed through the dimensions to Faerie, the Otherworld where they still reside.

"Years later, the small group remaining became the

Dunnehine and kept mostly to themselves. They were spell-masters and artful connivers, always seeking to outwit each other up there in the frozen lands. There was a witch among them who grew wise in lore. Clever, ambitious, and greedy for yet more knowledge. With that, she could ensnare her kin and take control. The others were wary of the witch and eventually ordered she reveal her schemes. She would not, and instead made a bargain with the Faerie King, Aldorian. He sent a host forth to destroy the other 'United Warlocks,' as they called themselves, and still do."

"I'm fascinated," Jaran said. He wasn't and looked at his companions. Finvar's eyes were intent and Savarna still looked cross. No support there. Jaran chewed his lip. "Where are we going with this, shaman?"

"But King Aldorian proved unreliable," Odel continued, ignoring Jaran, "as the Faerie folk so often are. He called his people back, no longer trusting the witch. Thus, she was exposed and defeated, cast out of her home by the frozen seas. For years, the witch wandered alone throughout deserted countries, until she found refuge in a distant land. A fair island just off the far coast of Leeth." His eyes glinted at Jaran, who felt another tingle along his spine.

"Valkador," Odel nodded. "It exists Jaran, your lost home." Jaran looked at Finvar, who was staring at him with wide eyes. Savarna seemed lost in thought.

"I'm from Leeth," Jaran said. "Was raised in a cave. My mother—"

"—fled Valkador after your father was killed. She and one other saved you, Jaran Saerk. The Traveler, another warlock with his own agenda. Bera tried to protect you, but the Traveler saw your potential and persuaded you to fare east to Shen when you grew big enough."

"How do you know all this? You're saying this warlock is the wanderer I knew from my youth?" Jaran vaguely remembered the outline of a man with mysterious eyes and a cunning smile. Another addled memory that had faded like morning mist from the dawn of his past. Could this be the same man?

"Yes," Odel said, catching his look. "The same individual who claimed to have saved you from the bear—or was it the other way, Jaran *Saerk*?" The old man smiled. "The Traveler is a stray warlock. Like the witch who stole your heritage, he fell out with his kinfolk. The Dunnehine are not big on trusting. I suspect he erased your memory, too."

Savarna and Finvar were staring intently at Jaran, the old man still smiling. Irritated, Jaran stood and glanced around the tent. "But how do you, shaman, know all this—what of my mother . . . father? This witch killed him?"

"Your uncle killed him," Odel said quietly. "But the 'witch' provided the opportunity. Erlund was duped."

"Does Valkador still exist?" Finvar had clearly overcome his dread and was consumed by curiosity. "Can it still be reached?" He seemed keener to learn about Jaran's past than the Northman did himself.

"In one sense, yes." Odel's eyes misted over as he reached behind, retrieving a long pipe. This he lit and commenced puffing with enthusiasm. The visitors waited with anxious faces. Jaran folded his big arms and chewed his lip He felt intrigued, yet angry—was this crafty shaman playing him for a fool?

"The island can still be reached." Odel caught his glance and smiled again. "Though the way through is tricky, and no sea chart will take you there. She shrouded its shores in mist. A fog crafted by spell runes, and with the aid of a creature she captured. A mysterious but spell-crafty being called Rune."

"And why would she do that, this witch? Does she have a name? If so, then why not speak it?" Savarna asked impatiently, her gold-flecked eyes glancing at Jaran, who was struggling to make sense of it all.

"She does, and I won't. For good reason. She is in hiding from her family, the other warlocks who would find her if they can. Also, she fears the returning shadow of the white bear. There is a prophecy, you see." Odel's eyes were misting over and his voice grew faint. "I will sleep soon."

"Weren't you marked by a white bear?" Finvar stared hard at Jaran, who said nothing, his mind racing and emotions churning.

"He was," Odel said huskily. "The claws of destiny. The bear scar that links you to your past." Odel stared at Jaran again. "*She who I must not name* knows you will return, Jaran Saerk. It's why she sent her sons to find you."

"Erlund's sons," Jaran said, nodding. "This witch is wedded to the King of Leeth."

"No more—she chose another, someone more like herself. And nearly as dangerous."

"Why can't you tell me her name?" Jaran felt his face flush as the latent rage rose up from below. "Then I can go find her and hew her cursed head off."

"I'll not say her Faerie name—her real name—for it will alert the witch of your presence. You are not ready for that yet. Mortals call her Sheega, though she has several names. She is old, even for an enchantress."

"So how can I kill this Sheega?"

Odel chuckled. "You cannot," he said, pulling at the pipe.

The smoke was making the tent stuffy, and Jaran felt his lids grow heavy. The other two looked sleepy, their eyes blinking. "At least until the next conjunction."

"The next . . ." Finvar blinked.

"The nine planets are due to align again—the very first time since the Fall of Gol. The world fabric shifts and becomes thinner than at any other time. Things slip through. Chaos, limbo—everything merges together. Anything is possible at such a time. Sheega knows she is most vulnerable then, therefore even more dangerous. She will be searching for you with increasing urgency, needs you gone before that vulnerable time."

"What must I do?" Jaran asked, his arms folded and mind cloudy.

"Stay alive long enough to kill Sheega before she—or those she will keep sending—destroy you and your stolen heritage," Odel said. "You have your friends, Jaran Saerk. They too are part of the pattern. *The first stage.* You need knowledge that will give you power. With that, you can locate and free the creature Rune. He alone can unlock the spell-mesh, or *mist* that hides the island called Valkador from mortal eyes. To do that, you must first seek the archives in the Halls of Antiquity in Cardalis. If Calla hasn't destroyed the buildings, you will find what you need inside."

"I'm not going to Cardalis," Jaran said. "I'm paying a visit to Grimhold Castle in distant Leeth—I've a relative to kill. King Erlund can help me find his wife before I cut out his liver."

"Several relatives," Odel said, nodding. "Else they kill you. But first, you need that knowledge—the three of you, lest Erlund's brutal sons, and the others she will send succeed in her demands."

"What knowledge?" Jaran felt anger rising again. "All I need is a boat—if Valkador exists I'll find it, hidden by a witch's sorcery or not. My axe will shatter any nets or spells, and then cut her in two. But first, I'm killing Erlund."

Odel closed his eyes. "Make for Cardalis, Jaran Saerk. Heed my advice—it is well meant. The Halls of Antiquity will contain what you need. And before you ask—yes, I do have a vested interest. Sheega must die at the appointed hour, and by your hand alone—else she destroys us all, by allowing Faerie back into the world. Ansu was their domain once."

"Faerie." Finvar flashed him a wild look. "He means elves, trolls and such."

"Then after that's done, fare northwest to Leeth," Odel said, his voice barely a whisper. "But remember, King Erlund and his sons are but the first spoke of this spinning wheel. The closer you get to her, the more cunning she'll become, and the more terrible the beings she sets against you. You must act swiftly, Northman. Decisively, and only at the appointed hour—else your island heritage is lost forever, and your chance for vengeance fades like smoke in winter skies."

"It would help to know when this hour will be upon us," Savarna said. Her eyes appeared tired, but she was staring at Jaran with a look he hadn't seen before. He smiled at her and something passed between them.

"Rune," Odel said. "He has the codes. You need Rune. Find and free that creature, and you have all the answers you need."

"You said he's her prisoner," Jaran said. "How can we find him?"

The old man closed his eyes. "I'm done talking," he said. "You should take your ease with the hunters, make the most of company and warmth for the rest of this night."

Finvar rolled his eyes and turned to leave. Then Savarna rose gracefully to her feet, her eyes glancing his way again. Jaran stood and shook off weariness, his gaze still pinned on the shaman who rested back, arms behind his head, snowy brows knitted together.

"Why do you help me, really?" Jaran asked the shaman.

"Because the Norns tell me to," Odel said, without opening his eyes.

"And what of me—my brother?" Savarna asked, hovering by the entrance. "You know his name, warlock. Vian and I have a need for vengeance also."

An eye blinked open. "You will see him in time, don't fret. I've seen how Vian's path and your own lie in different directions for many moons. Go in peace, Savarna of the Rundali. I know the spirit that rises inside you. Understand that wild restlessness, *Aikashi* spawn. You'll find no rest in Shen, but like Jaran here, you will find answers in Cardalis. Farewell. We won't meet again in this world." Odel closed the eye, and Jaran knew that the Tseole shaman was asleep. The Tseole guard greeted them with their weapons. Jaran stowed sword and axe, while Savarna shoved the dagger up her sleeve.

He turned to Savarna. "I'm going to Pol Shen," she told him, but her face looked unsure.

Jaran shrugged, having heard more than enough for one night. "Let's go and see what's cooking," he said, and together they left the shaman's tent, the snores of its lone occupant blending with the crackles of the fire.

9

TYHO'S GIFT

Outside, a crowd gathered around a large fire. Jaran's nostrils flared, detecting the rich aroma of cooked meat. Close by, he saw Finvar crouched with three Tseole, one of whom was Cuile. Finvar was grinning. "You should try this shit," he said, as Jaran approached with Savarna, and one of the women offered him a horn of some white frothy liquid.

"What is that?" Jaran asked.

"Fermented goat's milk." The woman smiled, her nose ring glinting in the firelight. "We call it Yunna."

Jaran crouched down next to Finvar, who was talking in a very loud voice with the Tseole gathered around, and he took a wary sip.

"That's revolting," he grumbled, and Savarna laughed at his expression.

"Give it time." Finvar winked at Savarna. "It'll hit him in a moment. You want some, girl?"

"I'll pass, I think," Savarna said, still looking at Jaran.

It took about twenty minutes, but when he'd drank enough

of the foul stuff, Jaran felt a nice warm numb feeling creep over him. He found himself smiling, tucking into the steaming meat offered, and talking readily in a loud voice beside his new best friends.

Savarna kneeled quietly beside him. Eventually she partook, and the three of them mixed with the hunters until the night passed in a blurry haze. At some point, one of the Tseole must have led them to a tent. Finvar pitched head first into a cot and commenced snoring. Jaran lurched about in the dark crashing, until someone—Savarna, he realized eventually—lit a torch and placed it in the iron ring provided.

"How do you feel?" Her feral gold-flecked eyes were huge in the firelight.

"Strange," Jaran said, trying to focus and stop his head from spinning.

"I like the Tseole," Savarna said, as she removed her clothes and stood naked before him.

"Like what you see, Northman?" Savarna's voice was slightly slurred.

"I do," Jaran said, then closed his eyes as sleep overtook him.

NEXT MORNING, HER GAZE WAS AS FROSTY AS THE GROUND under feet. "It was that evil brew," she said. "You're not my type."

"What is she talking about?" Finvar grinned at him. His friend seemed unaffected by the cursed drink, whereas Jaran's head thudded—and he could tell Savarna's did too, judging by her miserable expression.

"Err . . . I'm not sure," he muttered, responding to Finvar's lingering smile. A comment that made his friend laugh, but only deepened Savarna's scowl.

"Where is everyone?" Finvar asked as Cuile appeared from a nearby tent flap. They'd woken and stirred when the wind picked up, its howling flapping their tent, allowing light to peep through. It was colder than yesterday, and dark clouds promised more snow.

"The feast ensured everyone will rest late," Cuile said. "You timed your visit well—that was a rare harvest we caught last week. Fresh meat gets scarce this late in the year."

"Where is Odel?" Jaran asked.

"You won't see him again," Cuile said.

"Still asleep in his tent, I guess." Savarna yawned, but she still looked angry. Something Jaran didn't understand.

"No, he has gone," Cuile said. "Odel departed after the feast. He watched you three for a time, seemed satisfied, and then informed me he was leaving at first light."

"Going where?" Savarna asked.

Cuile shrugged as though her question made no sense. "He is a shaman," the Tseole hunter said.

An hour later, snow falling all around them, Cuile and two other hunters led the three away from the Tseole camp. Jaran glanced back once, but the tents and stockade had already vanished in a blurry haze of white. *Probably should have stayed another day.* The weather looked to worsen that afternoon.

As if reading his mind, Cuile untied a sack he'd strapped across his back. "I asked if you could stay until the snow passed. Odel said time was running out, and the weather would only worsen. I brought these to aid your passage through our country and the deep hills beyond." He slung the sack in the snow and knelt, untied the gut bundling it together.

The package contained six flat lengths of wood turned up at one end. There were also six poles with discs and points in one end. "These are skis," Cuile said. "We Tseole use them to cross the snow. Tie them to your boots with the gut. The poles will assist your balance. The skis will help you across the worst of it." There was also a skin containing pressed dried meat, two flasks of half frozen water, and another large one containing Yunna.

"I'm not touching that," Savarna said, shooting Jaran another acid stare.

"That's fine. I'll have yours, sweetheart," Finvar said, ducking as her small, hard fist sailed for his head.

"This is where we part company," Cuile said, stopping with the other two Tseole as they reached the crown of a low hill. Ahead was a wide flat region fading into shimmering light, while away to their left, Jaran glimpsed the frozen blue ribbon of what must be the Shen River winding and curving around a series of bends.

"Range west across that white until you see high mountains," Cuile said. "Those will be the Urgo Heights—you'll find a road at their feet which will lead on down to distant Cardalis."

"How far?" Jaran asked him.

"A week, two perhaps, depending on weather—so go careful with your fare."

"That long?" Finvar looked worried.

"Either that, or you follow the Shen's curve south and enter Cardalan, take your chances in enemy lands. Either way, I wish you well," he said, and turned to leave.

"Cuile, stop." Jaran thrust out his hand. Cuile stared at him for a moment, puzzled, and then clasped it with a rough smile. "Thank you, Tseole, I will not forget this—it's good to know we have friends in the wilderness."

"I was merely obeying the shaman's wishes," Cuile said. "If he'd wanted you dead full of arrows, I'd have complied readily enough."

"Why spoil a beautiful moment?" Finvar said, as the Tseole hunters departed the crown of the hill and vanished in the white.

THEIR HOSTS' DEPARTURE LEFT THE THREE COMPANIONS staring at each other. "East or south?" Finvar said, eventually.

"I'd sooner stay clear of Cardalan for a while," Jaran said. "At least until the river frontiers are far behind us. What about you . . . woman?" Jaran grinned at Savarna. "Coming with us or going your own way?"

She glared at him and mouthed a curse. Finvar laughed, then quickly straightened his face, lest she strike him again. "I'll be trying these ski things out if you need me," he said, and quickly faded from view in the fresh cloud of snow.

"You still have nothing to say about last night?" Savarna asked, as Jaran kneeled to lash the first ski to his leg.

"It's a bit hazy? Lots of talk." He looked up at her scowling face. "Have I upset you somehow?"

"You Northmen are not very bright, are you?" Savarna said, chewing her lip. Jaran didn't know how to respond to that. He stood puzzledly watching her looming, until she sighed and, kneeling, cussed as she attempted strapping on a ski.

He watched her with a mournful expression. "Can I help you with that?"

"Piss off."

Jaran raised a brow and reached for the last set of skis. He looked at them warily. "Better than a horse," he said.

Savarna had the skis tied expertly while he was still fumbling.

He looked up, saw her smiling as she pushed her body forward, the poles gripped in each hand. "We can get some speed up with these," she said.

"Does that mean you're coming with us?" Jaran asked, risking another smile.

"Of course, I'm coming with you," she snapped. "Not much fucking choice, is there? You pair are too stupid to be left on your own."

"You don't mean that," Jaran said, and her face softened. "But why the sudden change of heart?"

"What do you think?" She stared at him for a moment and then shook her head in disbelief. "Bloody Northmen." Savarna launched her body forward roughly, the skis taking her away from him.

THE SKIS WERE TRICKY TO MANEUVER, AT LEAST FOR JARAN. Both Finvar and Savarna seemed to grasp the technique without trouble. Jaran kept getting stuck in the snow. He blamed it on being heavier than they were.

After the first day, he had the things under control. He even overtook Finvar once, and laughed—until his gut ties unraveled and he spilled into a snow-covered tussock.

They left the hills far behind and crossed that plateau of ice. An empty world where a wan sun glittered on ice during daylight, and at night the weird lights flickered and blazed in curtains of green, red and purple. At least Savarna was talking to him, though she never got too close.

"Those lights in the sky are unnerving," she said one time as they camped in a hollow they'd found amid the empty wastes. A clump of thorns nearby provided fuel for a fire, and Finvar's flint lit the spark. The three gazed up at the vivid colors shimmering and shifting high above.

"The Giants' Dance," Jaran said. "I remember seeing it often, as a boy." They looked at him, but Jaran grew silent, thinking of what Odel had told him—though much of that was blurred to memory because of the filthy Yunna. Like Savarna, he hadn't touched the stuff since the night in the camp. Finvar got stuck in every night. Jaran suspected the wiry goat had a cast-iron stomach. He never seemed the worse next morning.

Days past without change. The skis allowed for good progress —they were all proficient with practice, and the great ice plain covered every horizon. They had decided to make for the road of which Odel had spoken. Why risk Cardalan until they had to? The dried meat and salt kept them nourished but still left them hungry.

Jaran had counted ten freezing nights under that dancing sky before he woke to see mountains that morning. The Urgo Heights ranged like a blurry, black wall at the edge of vision. A long trek yet, but at least the initial destination was in sight.

As they got nearer, the ice plain broke into knots of hills, making progress much slower. These were wooded, and clusters of pines shrouded their passage as they wound up toward the distant dark mass of the mountains.

"Those heights look a tad gloomy," Finvar said one evening, as he'd returned from gathering firewood. "Like they're carved in obsidian."

"They are not over-welcoming," Savarna agreed, adding wood to the fire. They soon had a rare blaze underway. "What's the matter with you?" She looked up at Jaran, who was fidgeting, standing gazing across at the half-moon, lifting ghostly pale above a cluster of pines.

Somewhere far away, a wolf howled, an eerie sound they'd not heard in weeks. "It's nothing, a mood," Jaran said as she stared at him. He turned to Finvar, who was making himself comfortable by the fire. "Can I borrow your bow?"

"Where are you going?" both Finvar and the woman asked him.

"I smell elk in those woods," Jaran said. "I miss fresh meat, and a restlessness lies on me this evening."

Finvar passed his bow across and the sack of shafts. "Don't lose any, and don't get lost out there." Jaran nodded, turned to leave, but a small hand gripped his arm.

"Be careful," Savarna said, her gold-flecked eyes intent.

Jaran covered her hand with his paw. "Does this mean you like me again?" He grinned at her until she freed her hand and muttered something inaudible about the apparent stupidity of Northmen. He left the pair warming their hands by the fire.

JARAN WALKED TOWARD THE DISTANT HILLS. HE'D LEFT HIS skis behind, as unfettered boots would serve better in the woods. He walked silently for an hour, the woods deepening, closing in around him. Jaran saw elk tracks leading off. He strung the bow, picked up pace. High above, the white moon followed him winking down through the trees, as though watching his progress.

Night deepened, the tracks led on. At last, he spotted shapes moving, down in a break between trees. He counted three large elk.

Jaran approached carefully downwind. One of the beasts raised its antlered head, the others didn't stir. Jaran stepped out from the trees and loosed the bow with one fluid motion. The arrow shot true, striking the nearest animal in its flank.

The other beasts took flight, fading off into the trees as Jaran approached the dead elk. A clean kill—he was pleased. They would eat well tonight. He turned, felt an icy shiver running along his back.

Someone is watching.

Jaran stood for several moments surveying the trees, their shadows painted silver by the moons restless passage. He shivered as a wolf howled. The sound was closer this time, and others joined it.

Jaran felt a stab of icy fear, which shocked him—he was no stranger to the wilderness. Then he saw it, the flicker of firelight through the trees. He ranged closer, curiosity conflicting with dread. He stopped yards away.

A huge figure knelt by a roaring blaze. A shaggy-haired man he appeared, with corded muscle and barrel-chest. He wore a kilt, but no cloak to cover his naked torso. Like Jaran, the stranger bore many scars on that flesh. And on closer inspection, he saw the man had only one arm. A distant memory flickered through him. And a name.

Tyho. The one-armed warrior. A god of the north.

Jaran knew the god was testing him. Despite his fear, he stepped out and approached the crouched figure, who looked up casually as he walked close.

"Your friends worry that you've left them, Jaran Saerk." The voice was a gravel-scrape and thunder boom, those eyes glints of blazing sliver fire, the moonlight trapped inside.

"I needed time alone." Jaran shoulder-tossed the elk in front of the god as a gift. He heard it boded ill, meeting Tyho the War God alone in the wild. "Time to think."

"A gift for a gift." Tyho rose to his feet, standing massive before Jaran. He reached behind his back and produced a huge long-hafted axe. "Your enemies are closing. You will need Griner to kill them."

Jaran felt uneasy. Why would Tyho want to help him? And what would he ask for in return? Despite his misgivings, he gripped the weapon and thanked the god. Tyho pinned him with that terrible gaze. "Use it well. Griner belonged to Borian once, before that deity perished in the timeless wars. It serves you now —in the new struggle."

"You mean against the witch, Sheega?" Jaran hefted the axe. It was heavy, the intricate rune markings glinted on its beard. He sensed power in the weapon. Felt strength flowing into his arms. Strength and something else. A slow burning rage. "I will avenge my father," he told the god.

"You had best go back," Tyho said, his silver eyes blazing. "Your little camp is under attack."

10

DREAMS AND REVELATIONS

THE DREAM CAME FAST and hard. Snarls surrounding her, and the sound of tearing flesh. She heard screams in the night, fading off. Then Dream-Savarna saw them. At least a dozen great dogs, yellow fangs dripping, eyes ravenous and pointed ears the color of freshly spilt blood. They circled, bunched, snarling congealing into one bulk, the dozen or so heads snapping slavering jaws, and splitting apart again, and leaping down upon the place where she and Finvar lay.

Still in dream state, she rolled her feet as the flickering skies thundered and boomed overhead, a vast green curtain where faces gazed down upon her, and voices shouted from afar. The giant dogs surrounded her, slavering and snarling. Dream-Savarna heard a terrified shout, turned and saw Finvar staring at her, his mouth moving but face blurred. Then his features fell away, crumpling like parchment in flame. He screamed as though torn apart, his face faded. He became a bird, lean and sharp. Finvar the hawk took urgent wing, vanishing in the dark.

The dogs were upon her, teeth tearing and jaws dripping. She felt no pain, but rather a changing within. Like Fin's, her form —her *self*—was shifting. *Altering* . . .

What is happening to me . . .? Her dream voice cried out. A deeper voice answered inside her. *Aikashi, Aikashi!*

As the ghostly white hounds tore at her flesh, Savarna watched on, as though looking from afar, and unaffected. She felt calm inside the dream. In control. She witnessed her hands change shape, saw long, curved claws sprouting, witnessed and felt her body shrink low and then lengthen, then grow huge, and charged with violent power. She saw herself under the trees, a tigress, orange and silver—a great slayer from the jungles. The giant white dogs bayed and backed away, circling and snarling, retreating from the fire.

Then Dream-Savarna was on them. She felt the alien fierce joy rising from inside. The need to kill, to rip and tear. An ancient pleasure, part of something she didn't understand. *But liked* . . .

She clawed, bit and tore, her jaws dripping gore. The dogs were whining, her teeth and claws ripping them apart. Dream-Savarna roared as she killed, ripping dog flesh, tearing limb from limb, tasting foul blood in her jowls. Their snarls became whimpers, then distant howls. The moon spilled ghostly silver and their fire gutted to darkness. Somewhere far away, a bell tolled twice. That sound became thunder, then faded off, accompanied by a sudden icy rush of wind.

Silence. The wind whipped up the slope then vanished. She felt herself fading, falling into nothingness. Down and away . . .

Aikashi . . .

The tiger stared back at her, the shape fading like morning mist in sunshine. *We are one* . . .

A violent jolt shook her body, and she woke with a start.

Savarna opened her eyes. Jaran stood there. A huge long-hafted battleax gripped in both fists. His blue eyes shone wild with savage rage.

HE'D HEARD THE HOWLING THE MOMENT TYHO SPOKE. Jaran had turned toward the distant sound, then wheeled around again. Both the War God and his fire had vanished. Instead the howls rose higher. Great dog voices tearing through the quiet.

Jaran ran as though the night-gangers were riding on his back. Loping, sprinting, pushing through that snow, the heavy axe held high in both hands, as he vaulted over branches and crashed back toward their distant camp, cursing himself that he'd wandered so far.

Arriving back at last, Jaran saw Savarna sitting by the ashes, face scraped bloody, her hands covered in dripping gore. Finvar stood a way off. He looked terrified, his dark eyes flicking here and there and mouth gaping wide.

"What happened . . .?" Jaran reached down, quelling the rage inside. He stroked her disheveled hair. "*Dogs?*"

"Fucking big ones," Finvar said, as Savarna gazed up into his eyes, her face taut with anxiety, and something else—a kind of savage joy. "She killed them, Jaran," Finvar said, his voice shaky. "I saw her do it. But it wasn't her."

"You were a bird," Savarna blinked, turned her head towards Finvar. "You flew away, and I was happy about that, for I knew I needed to kill."

Jaran bit his lip and sat beside her. The rage had left and he felt exhausted. "Dogs," he said.

"Big ones," Finvar said again. "White and ghostly, with blood-colored ears."

"That's not good," Jaran said, placing Tyho's gift on the ground.

"Where did you steal that fucking great thing?" Finvar asked, his mouth still twitching as Jaran placed his arms around Savarna, hugging her close. She didn't pull away. Her expression was strange . . . *lost*.

"I met someone in the woods," Jaran said, as though he'd been on a fishing trip. "You . . . all right?" he asked Savarna. She nodded slowly, as though she was asking herself the same question.

"I feel . . . *different*," she said.

"We need to get moving," Jaran said, tired of the mysteries. "Daylight's here, and this region gives me the creeps."

"I'm hearing you," Finvar said.

"Yes—I'm ready," Savarna said.

THEY'D SHOULDERED THEIR SKIS AS THE HILLS WOUND UP steep through the tangle of trees ahead. Jaran passed close to the break where he'd seen Tyho. There was no sign of any disturbance where a fire might have been. He said nothing and walked faster, his strong legs pushing up through the snow—deep in places, in the dells and shadows of this wood. No one spoke as the day wore on. Savarna looked at him sometimes, and once when they stopped to drink, she placed her hand in his, and he brushed her face with an icy finger.

Finvar looked grimmer by the hour, and he'd taken to the Yunna early, sipping as he hobbled through the deeper drifts. By dusk they reached a high place, the sky had cleared and wide views revealed a drastic change of scenery.

The dark mountains loomed close, hovering like craggy broken teeth. Huge and oppressive, their black slopes hinted at darker things lurking within.

The waxing moon was almost full, its sheen painting the snowscape with silver crust. Jaran spied the ribbon of a road far below, a thin worm of gray running down from the north and disappearing into shadowy distance. His eyes followed the road's passage south. It wrapped around the base of the mountains, its gleaming surface clear of snow.

"We're almost there," Savarna said. It was the first time she'd spoken all day.

"A long way from Pol Shen," Jaran smiled at her. "And your vengeance."

She nodded. "I have decided to be patient, as other factors have come to play."

He looked at her face, saw she was biting her lip. "How fare you?" He could tell she didn't want to discuss last night's weird happening. That suited him well enough. Jaran was still edgy about Tyho, though the heavy axe he carried across his shoulder was no small comfort. But why had Tyho given him the weapon? The question troubled him, so he placed it in the back of his mind. *Focus on things you understand and keep moving forward.*

They'd reached the bottom of that rise before Savarna finally responded. "I feel strange. Like someone else resides inside my body."

Jaran nodded, and Finvar hearing their words kept a wary distance. "You fought the demon dogs in your dream," Jaran said. "But they were real enough, and Fin was there. A . . . bird, you said?"

"A hawk." She nodded. "I saw him change, Jaran, and then fly away. Much as I saw myself, or *felt* . . . changing, becoming that tiger."

"It seems the hag in Ferrytown was right," Jaran said. He spied the glimmer of road ahead. Not far now. "Come on, let's leave the ice behind us for a while."

The three companions reached the road by nightfall, exhausted and battered. They found what shelter they could beneath some ash trees, the grim flanks of the Urgo Heights looming above. Savarna lay wrapped in his arms that night. Jaran watched her face as she slept silent and still. He glanced across and saw Finvar watching him.

Jaran risked a smile but Finvar didn't respond. They would start the next stage of their journey tomorrow. Jaran was more than ready.

THE VIOLENT JOLT THREW HER BACKWARD, AS THE MIRROR distorted and Gantallian's metallic mocking voice echoed around her head. Sheega sprawled across the polished floor. Her hounds were dead, torn apart by the shadowy creature. She sensed a new threat. A challenge . . . and something she'd known long ago. An *Aikashi?* Surely that could not be? She felt fear for the first time in years.

The goblin face in the mirror mocked her. *They have left Dunnehine*, his metallic voice whispered viciously inside her mind. *You can no longer track them.*

Sheega rose to her feet and glared at Gantallian. "It's but a small matter. My sons will find Jaran and his new friends. Only a matter of time."

And time is passing all the while, mocked the voice.

"I still have a year," Sheega said. Her white hand struck the mirror's surface. Like water, it rippled and distorted, the goblin's face blurred and faded. "Mock all you like, imp—you'll never be free from me."

Time will tell . . . Gantallian's hollow voice came from a great distance.

THE SKY SHIMMERED AND BLURRED, AND SOMETHING SMALL broke through. A white gull, its feathers dripping blood. Valgarn reined in sharply, recognizing a message from their mother. The other two cursed. "What now?" Gorn asked.

The bird blurred and shifted, changed shape, becoming the sorceress. Sheega's pale face was drawn with concentration.

"Damn you, Mother—you've spooked the fucking horses," Valgarn yelled at the apparition, as his beast bucked and nearly threw him from the saddle. His brothers cussed and struggled to steady their own beasts, and one of the pack horses broke loose from Gorn's grip and galloped off into the white.

"Bollocks," Gorn said, watching it ride off. "That nag's carrying our grog."

"Change of plan," Sheega said, her voice sounding husky and far away. "The one you seek is heading south, making for Cardalis. I have informed your father, who will contact their ruler, Ran Calla, and make sure Jaran is apprehended and kept for you."

"We're going to Cardalan?" Holtarn spat in the snow, having finally got his horse under control. "That's good, I was getting pissed off with all this snow."

"We must be near Shen," Holtarn grumbled. "This journey has taken an age. And now you expect us to trek all the way back?"

"Jaran has two others with him." His mother's white face ignored Holtarn. "One appears to have basic shapeshifting ability. *The woman.*"

Valgarn grinned. "She can change all she likes, while these two hold her down and I teach her a lesson." Sheega's face shimmered and flashed. Valgarn saw anger there and cuffed Holtarn's head.

"Sheega is speaking."

"Do not let me down like your father." Sheega's pale eyes narrowed dangerously. "You three are useful, but I have better servants. Do not presume you are worth more than any other tool. Fulfill your task—kill Jaran Saerk and these others. Ware the woman—she, too, is perilous. Then you are free to join in Calla's war, or fight for Shen, whichever you prefer." Her face faded, the eyes extinguished like snuffed candles, and the white shadow of a bird lifted and fled into the endless skies beyond.

Valgarn stared at his brothers. Despite their bravado, he knew they were shaken by her words, not used to being treated harshly.

"Cardalan it is, then," Gorn said. "At least there'll be women there, and strong ale." Their barrels had run dry over a week ago, and the last keg was vanishing into the white, the mule clomping out of sight. The pack horse was gone and with it their last dregs and the dried jerky.

"Any idea where the fuck we are?" Holtarn asked, gazing about, his expression grim. None of them had shown much interest up to now. They'd had supplies enough to get to Shen, wherever that was. *East.* But weeks that seemed like months in Dunnehine had left them disorientated.

"We make south," Valgarn said, pointing vaguely in the direction he thought that lay. "That way we'll either reach the Shen River or be in Cardalan. Win-win. Once there, we'll introduce ourselves."

"Father says those Cards don't like Northmen," Holtarn said. "We might have to kill some before we reach that city." Holtarn fingered his axe.

"I was planning on killing Saerk," Gorn said. "But I don't much mind wetting my axe on a few Cards first."

"We'll keep our heads screwed on and won't upset the fuckers," Valgarn said, glaring at his younger brother. "Could be a good career for us with this Calla. And we'll get mother off our backs by sending Saerk's head in a sack to father. You two tossers ready?"

"Thirsty for ale," Gorn said.

"Yeah, and anything beats yomping through this fucking snow for another week," Holtarn said, kicking the powder from his boots.

"Shut up, Holt," Valgarn said. "Let's get moving. Yah!" He kicked his horse forward as the white skies started spilling more snow.

THE MOON GUIDED THEIR WAY, THREE WANDERERS ALONE ON the road. Savarna gazed up, seeing its silver sheen hovering high above. She felt strange and alone. Sad, yet also hopeful. Something was changing inside her. She couldn't deny her emotions any longer.

The dark mass of mountain loomed to her right, while the left awarded dim views of copses, snowy fields, and pastures. Two days faring south, and they were approaching the fertilized region north or Cardalis. Savarna guessed they must already be in Cardalan. Hard to tell in this world of white.

But toward the end of that second day, the snow vanished beneath their feet, replaced by cold, gray stone. They rounded a corner, the mountains bulging out, and the road sloping up and dropping away on the left. Savarna and her friends stopped and gazed in wonder having rounded that bend.

Dusk had fallen, and floating some miles in the distance were the myriad lights of what must be a large city.

"Cardalis," Finvar said. "Now I can see why they call it the 'City of the Clouds.' Civilization at last."

"Not sure I'm ready," Jaran said. "It's still a good distance, so we should make camp soon, enter the city at first light."

"No doubt they'll welcome us with mulled wine and fanfares," Fin said, a wry grin smearing his lips. They hadn't discussed how to get into the city.

That night, Savarna dreamed of Vian's face, his gold-flecked eyes gazing at her from a remote temple on a hill, the sea crashing far below. She called out his name in her dream, but her brother faded from sight. Then she saw him again, a lone figure walking a high path, the blue-green ocean churning close by.

Vian!

Her own dream-shout woke her, and she looked up into the blue-eyed gaze of Jaran Saerk.

"You were crying out in your sleep," he said. She nodded and he pulled her close.

11

THE WARLORD

Ran Calla leaned back and grinned as the hot bubbling water rose up over his broad shoulders and soaked his aching bones. A long, hard ride from the frontier. The bathhouses were the best things those Ptarnians had left them. He cared not for their temples and shrines, the many tiered gardens, the fountains and statues, and all the other wonders of ancient Caranaxis. The City of the Clouds, renamed Cardalis by his esteemed ancestor, Carda the Conqueror.

The current ruler—or Ran—disliked the decadent remnants of the former occupants. The Ptarnian God Emperors had all been insane, their people weak and worn out by ceaseless wars with the Crystal Kings in the west. Their so-called civilization had rotted from within. Much like Shen was doing now—with a little help from his men inside, of course. Old countries, their great days over and soon to be forgotten. It was time for Cardalan to seize control.

Calla waved away a slave offering wine. Too early in the day for such pleasures, though his sons always partook at this hour, idle sods. He heard voices and glanced along the length of the steaming pool. Seeing one of them—his current favorite —emerge from his massage, face red, a naked wench in either arm. Calla nodded, and the boy waved the girls away.

He walked over, the gold-trimmed bath towel covering his body. "Greetings, Father. How was your journey?"

"Long, and fucking tedious," Calla said.

Rani Conorax grunted and seated himself by the pool, his brown feet trailing in the water. "Did you kill any Shen?"

"No, but I spoke to a couple."

"Really?" Conorax, his third son, was sharper than the others. Except Genza the youngest, who was too sharp for his own good—how Calla detested that brat. But unlike most of their brothers, the twins Conorax and Caranax were loyal to a point, almost trustworthy, and good warriors at twenty-two winters. Whereas Caranax was charged with monitoring raids across the River Shen, his twin preferred city life to the front. Conorax ran affairs here when his father was away. One of the three sons who stayed put in Cardalis, the other six spending their days fighting at the frontier alongside their men. "Sounds intriguing," Conorax added lazily, while gazing at the girls working at the far side of the bathhouse.

Conorax didn't look intrigued.

"Sowing seeds," Calla grunted. He watched as one of the slave girls glided past. Dark-skinned and lithe. Yamondon, by her look. He would have that one in his chamber tonight, maybe a few others too. It had been a long, arduous journey back. "How fares Cardalis?"

"Nothing to report," Conorax said. "We received word of a Vendeli trader docking in Largos, on its way east. We confiscated its goods, and executed the captain and crew."

"Good," Calla said. "Those Vendel scum should get the message soon. They risk a high tariff, dealing with Shen."

For centuries, the southlands had traded riches with the Shen. Calla's forbears hadn't intervened often. But they were idle, basking in the glory of their famous forbearer. The Laregozan Ran, Carda, had risked all in his war against Ptarni. The escaped slave and gladiator had gambled and won—over three hundred years ago. Since that time, Calla's predecessors had conducted border raids and skirmishes, and ignored any conflict at sea, deeming that too much trouble.

Ran Calla was different. He had long studied history and knew how his people had been enslaved, not only by Ptarnians, but the other more distant lands, too. One of his first acts had been to construct a fleet and start intercepting the traders on route between Yamondo, Vendel, Permio, and Shen. The old southern trade routes a strategy that had paid rich dividends.

"What else?" he asked.

Conorax shrugged. "Genza grows tedious."

"Nothing new there," Calla grunted. Genza was his seventh son. A troubled child who had grown into a petulant violent man that his father didn't like, let alone trust. "What has the little prick done this time?"

"Genza tests my authority as ever, has a faction of followers and thugs among the youth in the lower city. Keeps him busy, but I want your permission to punish them should things get out of hand."

"Given freely," Calla said. "That boy's a boil in my arse. I'll most likes have to kill him one day."

Conorax nodded agreement. "Oh, and yes—there was something else. A . . . curiosity."

"Go on."

Conorax smiled. "A rider came, a Northman from distant Leeth. They have a new king who would parley with us."

"Leeth." Calla coughed amusement. "That shitty backwoods is filled with nothing but savages and werebears."

"Many of whom we're fighting at that river."

"Don't remind me." The Northmen were a sore point. They had caused havoc during the ceaseless fighting along Shen frontier. Calla considered them the Shen's greatest asset. He determined to put an end to them when the invasion took place.

"What did this rustic king want?"

"He offered fighting men in return for our help."

Calla blinked. "Northmen serve the Shen—always have. And those bastards pay well."

"We are as rich as the Shen, Father." Conorax smiled.

"Very well, I'm curious. What does this little king believe we can help him with?"

"Erlund," Conorax said.

"What?"

"The king's name is Erlund. His messenger said King Erlund was looking for a man. A legendary warrior from Shen. A Northman called Jaran Saerk."

"I have heard that name before."

Conorax nodded. "He's the king's nephew. One of Shen's best fighters, but a renegade and outlaw wanted in Leeth. Must have done something bad, because this King Erlund has sent his three sons out to kill him."

"What care I for their petty feuds and squabbles?" Calla glared at his son, wearying of the subject.

Conorax persisted carefully. "The messenger said that his ruler got word this Jaran fellow deserted and is heading for our city."

"Why would he do that—to enlist?" Calla laughed.

"No . . . he seeks his ancestors' country, some island off the coast of Leeth. Apparently ruled by a witch, Erlund's estranged wife. It was she that told Erlund this rogue Northman was heading our way. He wants him stopped and chained beneath the old temple, until his sons can get here and deal with the pest."

"What is he offering me in return?"

"Two hundred fighting Northmen, including his three sons —formidable warriors, the envoy said. Berserkers—you know, the worst kind we come up against. But fighting for us this time, Father. To help the war effort and counter those Northmen still defying us at the front."

Calla rubbed his beard. "Interesting, and a generous offer. That king must detest his nephew. I can sympathize. I hate most of my family." He stood up, the hot water spilling from his sinewy bulk, and his scarred, hairy chest reddened by the long plunge. Calla snapped his fingers for a towel, and a girl came running.

He grabbed the cloth from her and dried himself. "What do you know of this island the man's searching for? Does it have a connection with Cardalan—I mean, why enter my realm and risk his neck?"

"The archive Halls of Antiquity and its libraries, I suspect. Biggest in the world," Conorax said wryly.

Was the boy mocking him? Calla had never entered inside those hallowed walls.

"There are maps and charts, and ancient grimoires," Conorax added, his face carefully neutral.

"Hmm, makes sense. Well, keep an eye out, Con. And I'll talk to this messenger—one hundred Northmen would be useful, providing they remained loyal and didn't defect to the other side. Where are these princes he speaks of?"

"That I do not know," Conorax said, and his father dismissed it as unimportant. "Valkador," he added after a moment.

"What now?" Calla demanded figs on a tray from the closest slave. He was getting hungry. Next, he'd take some drink and rest his tired muscles, before some recreation with those girls.

"The island I mentioned—it's off Leeth, north of the Crystal Lands that lie beyond the Endless Grass."

Calla looked hard at his handsome son. "You spend too much time listening to fable-weavers in taverns," he said. "Nothing lies beyond that Grass—why it's called endless."

He laughed, as did Conorax. For centuries, the Ptarnian Empire had waged bloody wars with that mystery realm in the west. The final outcome was unsure. Carda the Conqueror had showed scant interest in countries so far away, however legendary. His descendants were the same. Including Calla, whose mandate had always been to destroy all those realms who had once been Laregoza's foes.

"Feed that messenger and tell him I'll receive him in the morning," Ran Calla said. "And get me Straban."

Conorax nodded. "As you wish, Father." Calla coolly surveyed his son, as Conorax strolled along the bathhouse, flicking the slave girl attendants' hair as he passed.

Calla would have to watch that one, too. But then none of his sons could be trusted fully. It ran in their blood. As a young man, Calla had stabbed his own father through the heart. Why should they not do the same to him, given half a chance?

He was drinking Laregozan brandy in the bathhouse study when Straban knocked on his door. The bloody man had taken his time, but not even Calla would risk upsetting Straban without cause. His warrior-shaman was as unpredictable as he was dangerous.

A huge man, and former gladiator from the arenas the Ptarnians had constructed to amuse the masses, still in use today. Straban stood well over six feet tall, bald and scarred, barrel chested and keen of eye.

"Great Ran, it's good to see you back."

"Any news of Kull?"

"His body lies punctured with arrows, as do his men's." Straban had the far-sight, and Calla had sent word his way for news concerning the raiding party he'd sent north past the Shen River, daring the Dunnehine Wastes.

"They failed." Calla swallowed brandy and struck the desk with his fist.

"Not entirely," Straban said, his voice was husky with smoke and his dark eyes moist. Aside from himself, Calla's warrior-priest was the most feared man in Cardalan. And he, at least, was loyal, as Calla had freed him from the arenas once he got word of his special gifts. The gifts of far-sight, scrying, and reading weaker men's minds.

"I saw through Storga's eyes for a short while. They sacked an outpost near Pol Shen, then rode to the coast. I saw enough to know that the coastline wouldn't serve our purpose. But then they stopped at a portage area, a flat region where boats were moored, the expanse of Pol Shen Bay beyond. I deemed that a suitable landing stage, should you wish to use it."

Calla smiled. "That's good to hear, Straban. I'll send word to the front, get better men across to scout out more thoroughly."

"There was a challenger."

"A what?"

"I felt a presence." Straban's hard face twisted with distaste.

"A confrontation . . . some power working against me. I had to withdraw, as I was vulnerable."

"What kind of presence?"

"Malevolent, hostile. A woman—a Dunnehine witch, I suspect. *Unva*—the wind sang her name to me. They have their own war going on up there, those crafty warlocks. We don't want to get involved, as they're always dabbling in things they shouldn't and crossing into the Faerie realms. And that's not safe for us mortals. If your army lingers in Dunnehine, I will need all my acolytes aiding me. We'll need to protect the entire region, while your carpenters construct crafts for invasion. It could prove touch and go."

Calla's smile broadened. "I'm sure you won't let us down. Thank you, Straban—you may leave." The warrior-priest nodded and dipped his head, the closest he got to a bow. Calla drained his brandy and poured another.

Invasion. He liked the word. The time had come at last when Cardalan would break through Shen's defense and shatter that brittle empire like the rotten egg it was. He ignored Straban's other comments. Faerie? *Absurd.* The province of dreams. But why fret about things you don't understand? Straban was there to shield them from otherworldly nonsense. That would suffice.

I'll start with Pol Shen. That sly weasel Chulan will help me. Once that great city was his, the army would move south and tear down the legendary walls of Ta Shen. The empire's sapphire city. A place of unparalleled riches and beauty, so they told him. Once the second city had tumbled, the rest would crumple and the entire country break apart between his squeezing fingers, like crusty dry leaves in winter.

Victory was close. It just required boldness, and a change of direction. That meant entering Dunnehine again. Satisfied that all was in hand, Calla drained his drink and shouted for the girls. He felt the need rising from below. He would achieve the impossible and be remembered as the greatest Cardalan Ran since the days of the Conqueror himself, perhaps even greater.

Within six months, Ran Calla would have the Sapphire Empress, proud Rasnei, brought before him naked and broken. He'd have that arrogant bitch sucking his cock before he let her die.

Almost there. Calla had his armies, Straban's far-sight and spell craft, and soon he would have some Northmen too. The slave girls arrived, and he decided he'd address the first one as Rasnei.

12

THE SLAVER'S VILLA

Vian surveyed the peaceful scene with dispassion. The ordered fields, the tiny figures at work down there. The neatly dammed river forking through, the mill wheels trapping water, the red roofed slave-sheds, stores and stables. All dominated by the white expanse of trellis and gardens, proud gable and lofty minaret that comprised the villa at the crest of the grassy hill.

A mile distant, Shateke's manse lay at the head of a valley surrounded by olive trees, a setting almost as beautiful as Vian's home had been, before the slaver's men torched it. Vian considered repaying that debt. But beauty was to be honored and cherished, no matter who had created it. Shateke may be a man of taste, but he'd not live to spend any more time in his private paradise.

He shouldered the Chiang spear and loped down through the ordered cluster of mulberry trees, the warm breeze lifting his hair, the sun throbbing scarlet as it dropped behind the villa ahead. A quiet evening where birds chirped and men worked ceaselessly, their scythes sweeping in unison, as they worked the masters' fields.

Vian left the trees behind and strolled out across the emerald fields. Dusk settled gently on the serene scene. He walked briskly with purpose, saw men watching him. Their eyes timid, and legs taut—ready for flight. He approached the nearest, a strong-looking man with a whip scar across his tanned face.

Vian pointed the Chiang spear toward the distant villa. "The master at home?" he asked the big slave, as the fellow dropped to his knees, eyes angry and glazed. This one was proud—a former fighter, he suspected.

"He is." The slave's voice was croak raw, but at least he still had a tongue in that head. Vian knew the Shen often removed tongues from their male slaves. The other slaves were watching, curiosity overcoming their fear.

"You know the house?"

"I do. I used to serve the old family. Good people, noble."

"What happened to them?"

"Shateke—the new master. He came with his men and killed them all. New money, he was gifted the villa and land by Magister Chulan himself. The old family had fallen out with the new administrators in Pol Shen."

"New leaders?" Vian's eyes scanned the fields and river ahead. No overseers in sight, but they'd be around—as would guards. He needed to move on, and quickly. But this man was sharp, and any knowledge about the great city in the north would pay dividends. "What of Rasnei, the Empress?"

"Blessed be her name." His reply was a mumble, but the pride showed in his eyes. "She is in peril, I fear. This country is rotting from within. I was a soldier once." Vian saw the other slaves had dropped to their knees after hearing Rasnei's name.

"I can tell," Vian said. On instinct, he unsheathed a Jian blade and tossed it to the slave. "Your name?"

"Lin Gu," the man said, catching the sword and swinging it deftly through the air. "A fine weapon," he said, his dark eyes bright with pride.

"You look like you know how to use it," Vian replied. "How many guards?" Vian's nod hinted the villa, already fading in the twilight.

"Twenty," Lin Gu said. "We cannot kill them all."

"*We . . .?*" Vian smiled.

"I assumed that's why you lent me this sword."

Before Vian could respond, one of the other slaves leapt to his feet and rushed their way. "Conra is coming!" he hissed.

"Who?" Vian's eyes flicked toward the villa. He saw a tall figure in a conical hat surrounded by three other men with whips tucked under their elbows. Vian smiled and traced a line along the flat of his spear head.

"I'll go meet this Conra," Vian said. "You men are free to choose your fate." He turned away and strode across the fields until reaching the stream where it was bridged by the wheel-house. The overseer and his men stopped and pointed when they saw Vian standing on the bridge. They walked briskly up.

"Who the fuck are you?" The overseer, Conra, placed a booted foot on the bridge.

"I am *Death*," Vian said, stepping forward with quicksilver grace and sweeping the Chiang spear in an elegant arc that sliced through Conra's neck and sent his head spinning into the sparkling green water below. It vanished beneath a floating mass of watercress.

Conra's men dropped their whips and reached for their swords. All three died before their hands touched the scabbards. Vian stepped over the corpses and started trotting up the lane toward the dusky villa. A deep voice reached him from behind.

"You, too, can use a weapon, it seems."

Vian stopped and turned, allowing the big former slave to catch up to him. Lin Gu was built like an ox, and his red face was flushed with angry pride. "Only twenty guards." Vian smiled at him.

"Easy." Lin Gu grinned back, showing even brown teeth. "Now that I'm here to help you."

SHATEKE RESTED IN HIS DIVAN, ALLOWING THE NAKED GIRL to place grapes in his mouth as he fondled her breasts. He'd have this one in an hour or so—no need to rush. She was one of the new girls, nervous and clumsy, the whip fresh to her dark southern skin. Perhaps fifteen. Shateke liked them young.

A beautiful evening outside. His gardens, the distant trickle of steam, the doves cooing in their tower cote close by. So serene. He bit on the grape, squirting out juice.

"I've done well," Shateke told the girl, smearing her terrified face with a grubby hand. "Tamanega is one of the finest villas in all Shen. Your master is favored beyond most men."

The girl stared at him. "Your name?" he asked. Shateke felt a brief flash of irritation at her doe-like vacant stare. Perhaps he'd use the whip on her tonight, after she'd served him, and depending on how good she was.

"Kuulla," the girl mumbled, her voice cracking and accent foreign.

"KooooLaaa," Shateke mocked as he made her place another

fruit in his mouth. "Unusual name, sounds Yamondon. Vendeli?"

The girl was about to answer, but Shateke leapt to his feet when he heard a man's scream somewhere close in gardens below.

"Guards, go see!" Shateke rushed into his antechamber, where four of his men had been playing cards and betting. These had grabbed their weapons and were already rushing out into the gardens. There was fighting out there—*in his gardens.* The dull clash of steel, two more death screams.

Shateke yelled at his men as more emerged from corridors and side rooms. Were the slaves rebelling? *Not those timid creatures.* Then what? The fighting was getting closer.

Shateke stumbled into his armory and grabbed his jeweled Jian blades. He gasped as two of his guards fell at the door by his feet. Their throats were sliced very neatly.

A slim figure rose from nowhere behind them, a long Chiang spear in his hands. Beyond, more fighting meant there were other assassins present too. The man rested his spear and leaned against it. He was small in build. The long, red hair didn't look natural. The calm smile was patrician cold, and those gold-flecked large brown eyes, keen as a cat's.

Shateke was no coward, but he knew a killer when he saw one. "Who sent you?" he demanded as he readied his twin blades. He was a fine swordsman, but knew it could go either way with this man.

The fighting ceased outside and a rough voice shouted. "Done."

"Good," the stranger said without turning his head, those weird dangerous eyes focused on Shateke, the spear quivering slightly as he spun the shaft through his hands.

"I asked who sent you, assassin?" Shateke braced his legs and made to strike. He was confused. He'd been so careful. Chulan and Soma Ghee, all those powerful men up there—he'd made sure they'd be on his side. The many gifts he'd sent. Even that vicious hell-cat the other week.

Then he felt an icy shiver. *The girl with the flame red hair who looked just like . . .*

The spear sliced through his right hand before he'd registered it moving. Shateke glanced down in horror as his severed limb spouted blood on the tiles, the Jian clanging alongside.

"No one sent me." The stranger smiled, placing the spear against the wall again. He reached for a curved dagger as Shateke sunk to his knees, dropping the other sword and grasping the ruined hand. He sobbed at the pain

"I have . . . *money.* Slaves."

"I think we both know that's not why we're here." Shateke saw a huge figure block the entrance to the door.

"You found him, then," a gruff voice said.

"You're certain they're all dead, Lin Gu?" The stranger's eyes still hadn't left Shateke, and he kept flicking that knife through his fingers.

"You killed seventeen," the deep voice croaked. "I merely did for the leftovers."

"I wasn't counting," the cat-eyed killer said.

"Please, I—" Shateke screamed as the knife jabbed into his left eye.

"'Tis but the start," the man said. "I can make this last hours, unless you prove helpful."

"I know nothing!" Shateke sobbed. The knife struck again, this time taking an ear.

"Where is my sister? You sent her north—why?"

Shateke slumped to his belly and started choking.

Savarna.

"She fought . . . *well* . . ." Shateke choked as blood from his gored face trickled into his mouth. "I sent her to Magister Chulan . . . a gift to the empress."

VIAN STEPPED FORWARD AND SLICED THE DAGGER ACROSS the slaver's throat. He watched the man twitch and kick without much interest. He reached over and studied Shateke's twin swords, one still gripped in the slaver's hand, as he'd reached out and grasped it before dying. Fine weapons, they were. He scooped up both blades and examined them closer.

Lin Gu returned, a rough smile on his face as he saw the dead slaver and the swords in Vian's grasp. "Twin Jians from the Ta Shen armories, by their look," the big man said. "Never seen a finer pair."

"Yours," Vian said, handing the weapons over. Lin Gu's brown eyes widened in surprise. He seemed lost for words, so Vian retrieved his own Jian, which he'd lent the big man, and left him. He also reclaimed his long-bladed spear. The Chiang was a good weapon, and one he hadn't used often before. He spun it through his hands and walked out into the gardens, gracefully strolling, passing the mangle and tangle of corpses like a ghost drifting in as darkness fell.

Vian walked for an hour until the moon rode high and silver above. Flanking its passage were four loyal stars. Vian found a flat rock cresting one of the hills, awarding starlit views of the neat valley below. He sat, neatly crossed his legs, and allowed his breath to slow in measured beats.

As the peaceful calm filled his mind, Vian reached inside his tunic and placed the silver flute between his lips. He played for hours as his mind wandered free, and on until the morning birds joined him in chorus and dawn's golden light filtered down through the valley. The thin twist of river sparkling amber over soft mist rising. Tomorrow, he would make for the city Pol Shen.

13

THE CITY OF THE CLOUDS

A RED GLOW lingered in the east. Jaran rolled free of his cloak and sat up, rubbing his eyes. He reached for the great axe Tyho had given him and stroked his fingers along the runes, his thoughts clearing as the wind whistled and clouds mustered in the shoulder of mountain above.

The woman was still sleeping, but Finvar yawned, stretched laboriously and then threw a wink his way. "Morning," he said. "Got a plan yet?"

"Food," Jaran said. "And ale would be nice."

"Be some in that city," Finvar said.

"Yep." Jaran glanced down at Savarna, who was stirring and rubbing sleep from her eyes.

"What I actually meant was, do you have a plan for getting into the city?"

"Thought I'd leave that to you—you're the master thief."

"What's happening?" Savarna pushed her hands through her red locks and tied them back with a cord from her belt.

"We're discussing how to enter Cardalis," Fin said. "Jaran

here is hungry and wants a beer, even though it's rather early. I'd settle for some porridge in this climate, myself. A hot mug. Thing is, we're not sure how to get through the gates."

"Fly," Savarna said, and the men looked at her.

"That's not overly helpful," Finvar said. "But thanks for the input."

Jaran looked at her face, no smirk curling chapped lips. "You're serious . . ."

Savarna flicked her gaze at Finvar. "He can do it."

"What?" Finvar stood up and flapped his arms. "Am I missing something, a joke?"

"I've seen you do it."

"Do what?"

"Fly."

Finvar stared hard at her, his eyebrows knotted. He shook his head. "I haven't a notion what you're fucking talking about."

"She dreamt you were a hawk," Jaran said.

"She *dreamt* it . . . and now I can fly." Finvar honked and spat, getting annoyed. "I think it's past time we had a serious conversation."

"You are the hawk, and Jaran is the bear. As I am the tiger— they are our spirit animals. I saw you fly, Fin. That's how you escaped the white dogs. I couldn't protect you and kill them all. You realized that and changed, took wing. The *Aikashi* know about these things."

Finvar's face was bleak. He turned to Jaran, his tattooed arm pointing at Savarna. "I haven't a bloody clue what she's on about. I saw her—or something like her—kill those dogs while hiding in the woods, but it happened so fast my memory's shot. I don't know about you daft pair, but I'm going to start walking towards

Cardalis, and maybe the guards will see how miserable I am and let me in."

"You could try flapping your wings." Jaran grinned, but Finvar was back on the road.

Savarna cuffed his ear. "I was being serious. He can do it— just doesn't realize that yet."

"*Aikashi*—what is that?"

"A discussion for another time." She clutched his hand with her own and smiled. "Suffice to say we three have some unique talents, Jaran Saerk. Let's catch Fin up before he gets more upset."

They walked for three hours, the dark mass of mountains hedging the right and the road winding higher, awarding sweeping views of the wide region below. It was warmer here despite the elevation, because the mountains blocked the winds. No snow glittered white below.

Jaran saw homesteads down there, roads and rivers dammed for fishing, the weirs rippling. A pale-blue sky painted the horizon.

They rounded a corner, and a wonder filled their eyes.

The city. Cardalis. They had reached it at last.

"Now there's a fine sight," Finvar said, having got over his sulk. "The City of the Clouds."

"Thought you'd been here?" Jaran said.

"Not from this direction," Finvar said. "I traveled on the great highways through Cardalan, entered through the lower gates. It's shitty down there. This is more impressive."

And it was. Floating ahead of them were the walls, towers, and twisted minarets of a huge city, hazy and sprawling. All that stone appeared to float on the horizon, white fluffy clouds billowing out on either side.

They walked closer, stopping to shelter behind a rock a hundred yards from the great iron gates. Jaran saw guards with long pikes. A closer look revealed more gazing down from the walls above. He recognized the conical helms and ornate shields. Cardalan Immortals—these were Calla's bodyguard. He'd killed a few on the border. Good fighters.

"So . . .?" Fin had his arms folded and was looking at him. Savarna seemed lost in thought.

"The wall," Savarna said

"Not flying over," Finvar said.

"We have knives," she said. "That wall's comprised of sandstone blocks, the joints should prove soft enough. Wiggle the blades in deep and pull ourselves up. Easy."

"She's an intelligent lass, ain't she?" Finvar smiled.

Savarna ignored that. "Let's get off this road and scour the cliffs until we find somewhere suitable."

"Is it really necessary?" Finvar said. "When I came here before, they just let me in at the gates. Maybe we should try."

"He's a Northman," Savarna said. "Stop making stupid suggestions."

"You're the one who mentioned all the flying stuff."

"Shut up, Fin," Jaran said. "Let's get moving."

After a strenuous hour climbing and creeping along the mountain's southern flank, they reached a place that awarded fine views of the city walls. Savarna pointed to a buttress thrusting out into the rock.

"We should be able to climb that easily," she said.

Jaran nodded. "I don't see many guards this far along." The buttress marked the northwest corner of the city. The walls ran south beyond, swallowed by cloud.

They clambered down, tripping occasionally, but taking great care not to be seen by anyone who might be looking their way. Jaran had lashed Tyho's gift to his back. His smaller axe and sword still hung at his side. They reached the buttress.

Savarna spat a knife into one hand and bit down on another she'd acquired from the Tseole camp. "I'll go first—don't want you pair falling on me." She tiptoed, poked the first dagger in a split between the stones and wriggled the blade. Once stuck, she used it to hoist her slim body up. Jaran watched her lissome form with fascination as Finvar poked his ribs.

"Nice little mover," Finvar said. "I'm thinking you might need a bigger knife, heavy as you are."

"I'll manage," Jaran said, as he and Finvar commenced working their own blades and climbing, following the girl up the walls. They regrouped at the top.

"Just the one guard." Savarna pointed to a distant figure leaning over the low wall that awarded view of the rooftops below. They stole the other way, quick as they could. It wasn't long before Fin spied a suitable place to jump down, via rooftop into a garden.

Once they'd settled beneath a fir tree, the three took stock and glanced around. Jaran saw a gate leading into the city streets beyond. He approached and opened it carefully. The street was empty—nothing stirred.

"Which way to the library?" Jaran asked Finvar.

"Halls of Antiquity. Follow me," the small man said. Savarna exchanged a wry glance with Jaran as they stepped out into the street. They kept walking until voices could be heard. They rounded a corner. Various groups of people emerged, but no soldiers were visible. They walked on, mingling with the city folk as best they could. Jaran's stomach grumbled, and he hoped they'd source some food very soon.

SAVARNA DIDN'T LIKE THIS PLACE. SHE FELT EDGY, TENSE, and wished they were back in the snow. Why was she here, when every fiber in her body urged her leave Cardalis while she still could?

She knew the answer, but refused to admit it. Instead, she focused on staying alert, her eyes flicking from side to side as she walked beside the two men.

Cardalis resembled a gray wedge of flat rock jutting out from the most southerly spur of the Urgo Ranges. As she walked, Savarna caught glimpses of the plains and forests far beyond. This elevated upper city was covered in decaying structures and overgrown vines trailing, spilling down to the tangled filthy maze of the lower, and much newer—Finvar told her—city. Down there, she could see a hive of broken roofs, ruined temples, overgrown gardens, and dried-up fountains—all that remained as a legacy of the Ptarnian Empire, he explained.

"This place was once a swelter pot of intrigue and vice, where murder and conspiracy were everyday events," Finvar said, talking quickly in a hushed voice. "Proud Caranaxis was rumored a place of color, and majesty, fear, corruption and lies. All fallen to memories and rising dust. Then renamed in honor of the Laregozan conqueror, Carda the Cruel. They say he butchered the last mad emperor in the central square after capturing the city."

"Shut up, Fin," Jaran said. "You're jarring my nerves."

"I thought you'd be interested."

"I was," Savarna flashed him a smile.

They kept moving, as Cardalis surrounded them, a succession of tall, leaning houses. Savarna passed taverns and temples, shops, alleys hinting more—even the odd brothel, and one with a late customer retching in the gutter. The city folk ignored them, a silent gray mass of faceless people hurrying along.

To Savarna, this upper city appeared as a huge trading station. People everywhere, but all hurrying about their morning, none chatting. Grim, silent figures passing along the ancient streets, their business their own, and not wanting to spare so much as a nod.

The reason for their furtive strides was obvious. The Immortals. Finvar had warned them about Calla's elite guard. As they entered the central region, the first of those soldiers appeared. Tough-looking individuals in gleaming ring mail and heavy fur cloaks. They carried short throwing spears and crossbows, and most had heavy curved swords hanging from their belts. A few favored maces, and she saw the odd axeman lurking at corners. Soon, Calla's Immortals were everywhere, milling around, lounging outside taverns, dicing or playing cards at tables in shrouded market squares. Heavily armed, swarthy and cruel-looking. The Laregozan invaders had so obliterated the old regime that the name Ptarni was never spoken. That race no longer existed.

Those few noble families who survived that terrible time called themselves Laregozan, Tseole—even Rundali. Anything rather than Ptarnian. Eventually, the entire region comprising Ptarni, Laregoza, and western Tseole became known simply as Greater Cardalan, again in honor of the conqueror from Largos.

Those ancient emperors had been mad, she'd heard Finvar say. Decadent, depraved, rotting fruit. Like the Shen were now, in her opinion. The Ptarnians had paid a high price for that depravity. Three hundred years ago, a seasoned fighting slave broke free from the games held in the city. This Laregozan gladiator, Carda, led a rebellion out in the fields. It spread like wildfires in late summer, as the rage, hunger, fear, age-long resentment, and bitter loathing combined into a melting pot, uniting Ptarni's many enemies and resulting in the obliteration of the old regime.

Carda re-entered the city as a warlord leading thirty thousand men. He killed everyone within the walls, women and children, newborn babes—even the beasts weren't spared. The emperor had been hung up by his own entrails, lashed tight around a stone effigy of Callanz, his depraved ancestor, the first of the self-styled God-Emperors.

She'd heard that Calla was a direct descendant of Carda, bent on destroying distant Shen, Cardalan's only remaining threat. A warlord—or Ran, as they were called—rumored every bit as brutal as his forefather had been. And even more ambitious.

"We're getting near," Finvar said. "Best we find a quiet spot, plan the next move."

They passed an alcove leading off from the main street and took hasty shelter. Savarna stared out beneath the arches where the three of them stood, shaded from the icy wind and hidden for the moment from those soldiers' questing eyes.

Why are we here? She shook her head quietly, as Finvar was chatting excitedly about the Halls of Antiquity where the archives could be found. It was the wrong question, she told herself. Should be—*Why am I here? Walking into the hornets' nest with these two madmen?* There was no logical answer to that. This was a detour—that's all. A distraction. She was going back to Shen, however long that took. She'd find Vian, and together they'd kill the empress of that country. Avenge her kin, or more likely perish trying. *A plan of sorts.*

But it no longer convinced her. Though she dared not admit it, Savarna's priorities had changed. Her entire perspective had shifted irrationally. And here she was, half a world away, caught up in something that didn't concern her. Accompanying two strangers, both lost strays, with no clear notion of what they were about. *I am such a fool.*

Renegades and lone wolves can perchance survive in the wilderness. But here, in this hostile, dangerous city—with her flame-colored hair and Jaran's size and belligerent glare? *Folly.* Every nerve in Savarna's body urged her to flee back to those walls, find a way out of Cardalis while she still could. Let these two fools seek their own destruction. Why should she care? She watched people passing by in silence. Fin was still chattering, Jaran staring moodily beside him.

But I do care . . .

The problem was they weren't strangers anymore. Something had happened in the frozen lands. A changing, deep inside her. Savarna still wanted her revenge, of course—and even more than that, she *needed* to see Vian again. She missed her twin, his cool, calm eyes and measured manner. Vian was the only one who could ease her inner storms. Until now . . .

But the long cold trek, that strange night in the camp with the Tseole, the words spoken by their shaman—all had left echoes. Then—far stranger—the dream-attack that had turned so terribly real. *Who had sent those dogs?* She needed to know that. Then seeing *Hawk*–Finvar take flight, knowing that he too was not all he seemed. Like the *Aikashi* spirit deep inside her, Finvar also denied his past.

But none of these were the true reasons she'd stayed. It was all Jaran Saerk. The blond Northman with the rough features and hideous chest scar. A savage who had surprised her with his wry humor and caring eyes. She'd felt his body against hers these past nights, sometimes woken and seen him gazing up at the moon, or else staring down at her with his whimsical, distant smile.

A barbarian, most civilized people would say, especially here or in Shen. But Savarna knew there was more to Jaran. He was as much a thinker as a fighter, and she realized that she was liking him more every day. Something that scared her deep inside. Nor was it sensible, because they would most likely die in this city.

But Savarna couldn't lie to herself any longer. There were too many coincidences and odd things happening. The three companions were forced together by fate. Unva the witch—or whatever she was—had told Jaran that, and now she believed it, too. Their destiny was entwined. And another witch had tried to kill them in Dunnehine. The aforementioned Sheega was now her enemy, too. Savarna rubbed her eyes. These thoughts were not helping.

"What are you discussing?" she asked Finvar, realizing she hadn't followed a word of their conversation.

"The way in—haven't you been listening? It's a mile up that hill." He motioned to Jaran, and she saw where Finvar was pointing. Almost humorous how Jaran towered over the smaller man, his face screwed up and eyes baffled as he listened to every detail. "There, on that corner—the sign reads: Street of Veils. Do you not see that? It's up there near the ruins of the great temple, the one Carda pulled down."

"I . . . see ugly rune shapes carved on stone," Jaran blinked at the distant street entrance.

"It's in plain sight," Finvar said. "What's wrong with your eyes?"

"A *mile*," Savarna cut in. "We won't get twenty feet without being spotted by an entire garrison. I've never seen so many fighting men in one place."

"Me neither." Jaran scowled. "Not even at the frontier. And these are his crack troops. Methinks Ran Calla's stepping up his game and planning invasion. It's why those bastards were in Ferrytown. Odel the Tseole shaman was right."

"Well, we can't go back, so we have to go forward," Finvar said. "That means you two waiting here until dark. One sly gawp at Jaran here, or a glimpse of your lustrous locks, sweetling, and we're in the shit, barrel deep. But don't fret—I can blend in nicely, even with these bastard Card Immortals lurking bored on every corner."

Savarna's eyes narrowed as she stared at Finvar. He caught her gaze and shrugged. "Food, and something to drink are necessities, I'm thinking. He needs his strength, and we need our brains." Finvar winked at Jaran, who was still looking at the distant sign. "I'll be quick as I can."

"Be careful . . ." she said.

He flashed her a grin. "*Careful's* my second name. Back soon!"

They watched him go. Jaran rubbed his face with a callused hand. He looked at Savarna, his gaze bleak. "Think I messed up, bringing us here. Maybe that old fox Odel was lying. But why?"

"I came of my own volition," she said.

"Happy to hear that, but I'm still puzzled by your change of heart." His shrewd blue eyes met hers, and Savarna shrugged.

"I cannot rule out stupidity at this point."

Jaran smiled. "That's why you fit in with us. And I'm glad you're here. More than glad, truth be told. And know this. Whatever happens with my own affairs, I will help you avenge your family if I can."

"After you've killed all yours." It was her turn to smile. "We have to stay together to succeed—I get that. It's what he said, the shaman. I don't think he was lying, but perhaps he knew more than he was letting on."

"I remember most of what Odel said, despite the Yunna. But I also know how much you miss your brother. *Vian?*" She nodded. "You call out to him in your sleep, you know. That and the *Aikashi* that I'm waiting to hear about. I've heard you talk with Vian as if he's lying right beside you. Makes me feel like I know him, too."

She felt awkward, not wanting to talk about Vian or the special thing they shared. "My brother isn't like me—he's calm like still water. *Deep*. A thinker who works problems through. Whereas, I rage—constantly—and hate enough for both of us. We are two sides of the same coin, and share the *Aikashi* blood."

"That word again." Jaran snorted. "You are a mystery like crafty Drolly Fin. I haven't worked him out yet either, but I do believe him a friend."

"Fin needs you—that much is apparent."

"And what about you, wild lady? Do *you* need me?"

She cuffed his ear. "You are conceited, Northman."

"And you are troublesome, woman. Life was simple a month ago, and you're partly to blame for changing that."

"Why . . .?"

"Because of the way I feel about you." They looked up as Finvar appeared with something wrapped and steaming in his hands.

14

THE HALLS OF ANTIQUITY

"Pies," he said. "They're fucking hot." He unwrapped the grubby cloth, and two steamy round meat pies fell into Savarna's hands. "I could only pilfer two, so me and you can share. Size of Jaran, think he'll need a whole one." He also produced a skin of wine and tossed it on a nearby bench.

"Cards were glugging this." Finvar bit the cork free and spat it out. "Probably shit, but it will wet the lips, maybe quench the thirst a bit." He took a glug and stared at them. "How fare you dreamboats?" Fin's sharp coaly eyes glanced at each of them in turn, a wry half-smile on his lips, as though he'd been listening in on their conversation from afar.

"We've a long wait," Jaran said, grumpily, after crunching down hard on the meat pie. Two bites and it was gone. "Best we take turns, get some shuteye."

"We cannot sleep here," Savarna said. "It's not safe. If one of those Immortals wanders past and looks in, they'd see us hiding here."

"I think they've other matters on their minds rather than exploring grubby alcoves," Finvar said. "I overheard a deal of interesting talk at the pie stall."

"Are you certain you weren't spotted?" Jaran asked.

"Of course I was spotted." Finvar snorted. "I'm not fucking invisible. But the art is to belong, Northman. To fit in, so that to any straying eye, I'm just another grubby tradesman busy about his affairs."

"Theft being your trade." Savarna smiled. "But thank you, Fin, I feel better. What were they saying, and who spoke?"

"Two of the Immortals, officers by their arrogant tones and manner—Calla's favorite fighting scum." Finvar shrugged. "Veterans, back from the front. Enjoying some tongue waggle as they slurped. Not caring who listened on. They confirmed our suspicions. Calla's attacking Shen from Ferrytown, or nearby. And soon. That reconnaissance crew dying didn't matter much. The warlord has a shaman helping him. A powerful one called Straban. Not much liked, judging by the Cards' hushed voices when they mentioned him. This Straban will protect them from any stray Dunnehine warlocks."

"What about us?" Savarna asked, crouching down and making herself as comfortable as was possible.

"The pie shop was only a stone's throw from the Halls. I took to strolling past. No one about, Cards not being overzealous readers. We should be able to slip in at dusk, latest."

Jaran took a slurp of wine and grunted. "We're looking for a map, something you can decipher?"

"Yep," Finvar said, "that's the plan." He munched on his pie. "This snippet caught my attention as well. I heard a couple of men talking, merchants by their look. They spoke in whispers in a side alley away from the Cards. One of Calla's sons is stirring up shit. Genza—you heard of him, Jaran?"

"Nope," Jaran said, and Savarna wondered where Finvar was going with this.

"Ran Calla has a lot of sons," Finvar said. "Most don't appear to like him that much. But this Genza is plotting some kind of coup, wants to overthrow his father. Judging by their tone and nervous faces, these two were involved in the plot. Such knowledge could prove useful to us." Savarna couldn't think why, but she was happy to listen as Finvar rambled on about Cardalis, the Card Immortals and their leader, Ran Calla, shedding light on the furtive time he'd spent here before.

"All the Ptarnians were murdered?" she interrupted Finvar at one point when he was twittering on about the old days, just passing the time. Jaran was stretched on the floor, his eyes closed —although she knew he was awake. It was late afternoon. They'd be moving soon. "That must have been horrific."

"All the nobles and princes, the entire emperor's family. *Butchered.* The priests suffered the worst, being hated the most. Nasty business—thousands died. I studied the demise of Ptarni in some detail when I was creeping about in the archives that time. Most of the common folk survived after the initial horror. A lot were forced into slavery, others fled the realm. But most Ptarnians stayed put, faded into the background. Changed their identity to survive. Ptarni disappeared. The survivors became Cards."

When, at last, the light faded to dusk and the first lantern was lit by a soldier at the corner of the street, Jaran opened an eye. He grinned at Savarna as she shuffled free from her blanket, another gift from the Tseole.

"Time to go," Jaran said, rising to his feet smoothly and reaching for Griner. "You want a sword?" he asked her. She nodded with a grin, and Jaran unsheathed his blade and passed it across.

"Thank you," she said, the sword heavy in her hands.

Finvar led the way through the almost-empty streets. Cardalis was silent at this hour, as the warlord had placed a curfew on the citizens. The odd Immortal still lurked, but these were half-drunk or too busy with a leman to notice the three passing by.

They reached the Halls of Antiquity and stole inside. It was dark, cold and airy. A chilly breeze hinted whispers, and the odd sconce cast flickering shadows through the empty rooms they passed. Finvar led them through doorways leading into cold spaces. The doors were broken, or missing altogether, some still hanging rotten on the hinges. Passing these, Savarna saw shelves covered in dust, the shapes of what might once have been books and scrolls, faded into ruin. All reduced to shapeless mounds of dust.

"Carda banned reading," Finvar said, as they passed a large one, the shelves broken and pulled down. "But his shamans convinced him to keep the histories, believing them important. All the other texts were burnt, or else left to rot like these we're passing. One of that conquering bastard's worst crimes, in my opinion."

They reached a stairway flanked by two tall stone pillars. A snarling griffin crouched on each, the glittering red eyes revealed rubies, sparkling in the torchlight. "Up here," Finvar said, taking the stone steps two at a time.

Savarna glanced at Jaran. He raised a brow. "After you," he said, motioning for her to follow Finvar's dark shape into the gloom above. She nodded fiercely and hefted the sword, ready to swing should someone appear. Jaran loomed behind her, the massive war axe gripped in both paws.

The wide stairs opened into a huge hallway. There were more candles here, and it looked like the rooms were used every day. Savarna saw the signs of recent occupants, half-empty drinking vessels, writing equipment, and other gear. The odd scurry of a mouse wasn't encouraging.

Finvar reached a large table and stopped. Savarna gazed down at a chaotic mass of parchments, papers, scrolls, and objects that meant nothing to her. Beside her, Jaran leaned on Griner and glared at the sconces warily. "Too fucking quiet in here," he muttered.

Finvar scrabbled about, muttering, his bow laid on a table, arrows close by. He pushed scrolls across the table for several minutes, while muttering profanities. Finally, he let out a hiss of satisfaction.

"Got something here," he said, pulling out a crumpled, faded, and badly burnt scroll.

"What is that?" Savarna asked.

"An old sea chart showing the Crystal Kingdoms, and the lands surrounding, including Leeth and, more importantly, Jaran's home." He looked across at Jaran, whose gaze was still on the flickering glow, as though he was expecting company.

"Here." Finvar motioned for them to come over. He had his

thumb covering a part of the scroll, the other hand pressing down. "Hold that end so he can see," Finvar said to Savarna.

She glared at him, but complied, resting Jaran's sword on the table. Jaran leaned closer. "I only see broken lines and shapes," he grumbled.

"Where my thumb is." Finvar grinned up at him. "Recognize that sign?"

"It's a rune." Jaran looked closer, placing the Griner against the table. "I've seen it before, though I can't recall when. Strange, I seldom forget things. Must have been back when I was very small."

"You were never small," Finvar said. "That mark—rune as you call it—is spread over this faded wiggly line. Faint, but clear enough. A seashore, defining an island. The rune says *Valkador*. I learnt how to read them in Dunnehine. Yet another talent I possess. I know you're impressed, so no need to comment. See, look!" He was excited, and Savarna looked closer at the faint wiggly lines. Not much to go by, in her opinion. "There's the coast of Leeth clearly drawn," Finvar whispered excitedly. "See, your little island is close to that western shore, Jaran. A quick hop across."

Finvar's hands worked across the scroll until they stopped on another mark. "Grimhold Castle," he said, risking a smile. "Easy. We find Grimhold first, and then fare due west. Reach the coast, steal a boat that doesn't leak, and sail over to your island. Once there, you can kill the witch and all her cronies, while me and the lass here take in the sights."

"That short crossing would prove harder than you think, Finvar the Droll."

Savarna whirled around as a mass of torches flickered into life, flooding the gloom with light and banishing shadows to the far end of the hall. The voice had been close, deep and resonant, though its tone but a whisper. A shape emerged from the far end of the room. Beside her, Jaran reached for Griner, and Finvar scrabbled for his bow. She picked up the sword and waited.

"Too late for that, Jaran Saerk." The shape approached until Savarna saw a tall figure clad in a long scarlet gown, his shaven head smooth and keen eyes, black as midnight, flashing with the torchlit glimmer. "I am Straban," the man said, and Savarna saw other figures emerging from the corners where they'd been lying in wait.

A trap. Why wasn't she surprised?

"You're the shaman." Finvar's face was terrified in the torchlight.

"I am." The voice resonated power, and the man stepped closer. "And you three strays are trespassing. That's punishable by slow death in Cardalis. But before I order that done, there are things I need to know. You can help me with them in my oubliette. Arrest these fools!" He turned and ushered for the shadows to approach with his hands.

Those silent figures leapt into action. Warriors rushed at them, twenty—maybe more. All bore swords and shields, and a few carried heavy pikes. They were surrounded in the cold dark. Savarna felt her mind turn black. What fools they'd been to come here.

IT HAD STARTED AS A FEELING, A SLIGHT SHUDDER RISING from deep inside. Jaran knew they were being watched, had felt the raw power of someone working against them. Then, when the man had appeared and spoke, he'd felt a withdrawal, a shifting into some other state.

This is how it starts . . .

His mind felt detached, distant. The warriors running at him slowed, as did the measured beating of his heart. He hefted the axe, and a part of him heard the weapon's voice.

Griner thirsts for blood.

Jaran smiled as the familiar rage rose up from inside—the *Northman's Gift*, they called it. Dimly, he'd watched Immortals, their limbs and weapons moving in slow motion, the yelling stifled by the throbbing drums inside his head. Their shouts were frozen as they leaped—so slowly—toward the table where he and his friends stood. Vaguely, Jaran saw the woman dive low beside him—she alone was moving fast—and then Finvar vanished like candlelight snuffed out at dawn.

Jaran stepped forward as the first attackers crashed upon him. Griner gripped in hands, his legs braced wide, the Northman laughed as he allowed the rage to rise up from within. The berserkergang was loose. He laughed and snarled, hefted the weapon, swung wide, swung out, swung down.

THE SCREAMS WERE ALL AROUND HER AS SAVARNA CRAWLED out from the table. The shaman had vanished, but more warriors had entered the room. Their dying screams resonated through the Halls of Antiquity. Caught between horror and fascination, she glimpsed a flicker of dark, looked up and saw a large golden-eyed hawk settle on a beam above.

This time, she ignored the bird. Another presence filled this dark place, and its roars echoed higher until they buried the screams of the dying. Jaran stood there, the great axe bloody in his hands, swinging and hewing, cutting men apart like a scythe cuts through reeds. She saw heads sail by, limbs hewn and hacked and ripped from bodies as he swung the long-hafted weapon back and forth. Heard him howl like a wolf, the tears streaming in his eyes. None of this was strange to her, for the *Aikashi* rage was rising inside her, too.

It was the vast shadow behind Jaran that almost stopped her breath and quelled her rising fires. A white shadow. Ghostly, and towering. A great snarling bear, rearing tall on its tree-thick hind legs. The white bear loomed over Jaran, and its huge rending paws moved with perfect unison as he struck out with the heavy axe.

Soon, there were no warriors left in the hall. Only their bodies, strewn torn and broken, like rag dolls ripped apart by a playful puppy. Blood was everywhere, dripping, seeping. Savarna saw the blur again, and Finvar emerged, eyes wide with fear and something else. A kind of wonder, horror.

"We need to go." His lips spoke the words, but she heard no sounds.

"Jaran." She glanced his way. The axe had stopped swinging, and the great bear was gone. "Jaran!" She shook his arm, he turned and gazed down at her. He seemed out of reach, lost in a dream. A different person altogether. She shuddered. Those familiar pale-blue eyes blazed like raging sapphires, burning into hers.

"Wake up—we need to leave here!" She struck his face. Jaran blinked at her, seemed to shrink. She struck him again, harder, her palm stinging.

"I'm ready," Jaran said, eyes glazing over, stepping over the pile of body parts littered around his feet. In the distance, she heard yells, the sounds of boots crashing on stone. "Hard fight to get free of here," he added, his voice breaking as the rage faded, and his shoulders shaking with exhaustion.

Savarna gripped the sword tighter. Where was Fin? He'd vanished again, replaced by the rush of feet as fresh Immortals flooded the hall.

STRABAN STEPPED OVER THE MANGLED BODIES OF HIS soldiers as he sped back through the corridors, his pace quickening by the second. He was badly shaken, not used to such surprises. But then he hadn't expected to witness what he'd just seen.

He'd known there was something unusual about the three infiltrators. And he knew Saerk's reputation—rumors of his berserk rages had reached the shaman from the front. But the woman and Finvar too? That had been a surprise. All three were touched by Faerie. But far worse had been the realization of what —or rather who—raged inside the Northman.

The White Bear.

Straban had seen the apparition clearly as snowfall in sunshine. A huge white bear, like those that ranged the frozen north of his country. Snarling, tearing and clawing at flesh, cocooning the man as a proud father protects his wayward son.

He'd seen the others change, too. The woman with the tiger's eye, her form shifting and shimmering. The small bird-man winging up to the rafters above. Three spirits from the Other-realm, united. But for what purpose? He passed more Immortals running the other way. Another hundred had entered the hall. He ignored their quizzical glances as they rushed by.

Straban reached the dark street outside, and once clear of the buildings sped toward the altar where he summoned his own spirits during moonless nights. Warding spirits for protection. He fell to his knees and uttered the words . . .

"LINK!"

The voice hurt her ear like a wasp sting. She saw Finvar again, his face shifting from man to bird, and back again. "I can't keep . . . *doing this alone* . . ." his words blurred and drifted. He was a hawk again, then a man, bow shouldered, eyes pleading.

Instinctively, Savarna tossed Jaran's sword away, and instead reached out and grabbed his hand, placing her other on Jaran's arm. Ahead, two-score warriors had entered the building, running in with grim faces, their pikes leveled as they prepared to move forward at a rush. More arrived, and these carried crossbows.

"Now!" Finvar said. Savarna blinked as an explosion of light filled her vision, and her head throbbed with violent, shuddering pain. She felt her body surge up, gagged and spewed, as the air rushed past her face, and she looked down seeing the figures of Cards panicking, rushing about far below, shooting up at them with wayward, misfired bolts.

What is happening . . .? Jaran . . . Fin . . .?

They crashed through the ceiling, out into the silent dark of night. She had no weight, a feather floating on the night breeze. Savarna saw Jaran gliding beside her, his eyes wide in disbelief. Above, she heard the rush of wings, drumming, beating faster each second. The darkness jabbed to bright light. Savarna shut her eyes as the stabbing glare stung her vision.

"I cannot do this any longer . . ." a voice said close by. She opened her eyes again as the glare subsided. "Help me!" she heard Finvar yell—then Savarna was falling, and fast. A white rolling mist rising up to swallow her. She couldn't see her companions.

Jaran!

The mist swallowed her whole. Savarna heard voices inside that fret. Deep thunderous shouts, the clang of hollow metal. Laughter, weeping, and cries of sudden pain. She saw faces rushing at her, then vanishing like exploding puffs of smoke. All had pale, milky-white features with blue-silver eyes that flickered and glowed. Cruel and beautiful, alien faces. There were distorted screams, more weird laughter, the constant cold shrieking rush of wind.

She heard another sound and realized it was her own voice crying out in terror. Then she saw his face. *Vian,* as he sat cross legged, the sea crashing at his feet. A world away, yet by her side.

Stay strong . . . sister . . .

Vian's calm voice surrounded her, filling her lungs and chasing back the terror.

Then the mist cleared like vapor and she fell through the gap. Below—far below—land and water rushed up to greet her. Savarna saw a white beach, the thin ribbon of a winding river greeting shoreline, and beyond its loops, a deep shadowy fortress thrusting out like eagle's claw reaching down into the waves.

The wind shrieked louder in her ears as fresh cold stung her face. Her eyes filled with water, blurring her sight. The clear last vision was of a large white bird gliding silently toward her, its yellow beak open and blood dripping from its wings.

Not that way . . .

Vian's voice somewhere close, sounding urgent this time.

Avoid the castle! The ground shifted as her body glided, dropped, and slid through thermals until the cold blue of ocean shimmered below. Savarna hit the water like a tossed pebble, and those cold clear waters sucked her down.

END OF PART ONE

PART TWO

***

The Empress and the Witch

15

THREE FALLS DOWN

"DON'T LET GO!"

Too late. His companions had vanished, and Finvar's fading shout sounded muffled as the wind tugged viciously at his garments. Jaran felt his hair whip around his face and lash his eyes. Dark and cold. He was falling, and fast.

Is this death?

He didn't think so. But what the fuck had happened? A blur of confusion and noises. He'd seen pale, pointed faces in fog, heard distant shrieks and screams. *The men I killed?* Again, he doubted that. The rage had left him weak and sickly, more so even than was normal. The gift of berserkergang came with a cost. Usually, he recovered an hour or so after the fights. This time it felt like days had passed, but it was hard to tell.

Jaran forced his mind calm as he tumbled through icy air. *I'm not dying. I can't perish without avenging my kin. But someone works against me.*

The bird came from nowhere. A huge white gull, sliding in,

and stabbing his face with its iron-hard beak. He knocked it aside, and the bird flew backward and vanished.

Jaran felt blood trickle from his face. He slowed his breath, willed himself to relax. He looked around as he fell. Sparks and shimmers—Jaran saw something shiny falling beside him, glinting and gleaming in the dark. *The axe, Griner!* Jaran reached out across that nothingness. Somehow, he grabbed the weapon and pulled it close. He felt a surge of joy and new energy flush through his veins. The darkness exploded into blazing light and he saw visions, multicolored shapes and objects dancing all around him. He gripped Griner in both hands and closed his eyes.

His body struck the ground. Jaran rolled on instinct, then tripped and fell face-first into what felt like wet sand. Jaran opened his eyes and saw water and rocks, his nose detecting brine. He sat up, blinked, and stared incredulously at the ocean. The sea, stretching out gray and distant, a blur of white caps rising, falling, fading into murk-light.

Jaran heard footsteps. He looked up and saw a tall figure approaching. A man, his features hidden beneath a wide brimmed hat.

"You . . ." Jaran recognized the Traveler. The mysterious roamer who had persuaded his mother to let the boy Jaran depart with him. A man who seemed to have a hold over Bera. A wizard, or enchanter—he'd helped Jaran recover from the wolves that day, and the bear attack that followed.

"You need to find the others," the Traveler said. "As three, you are strong enough to withstand her. Divided, you are vulnerable, even with His axe."

"Where am I?" Jaran clutched Griner, the knuckles white on his hand. "What is happening here?"

The Traveler showed a twisted grin. "Fabric's thin here, tearing apart. We cannot let them break through. Ranning is with her now. Others will follow."

"I don't understand your fucking riddles," Jaran lurched to his feet, swaying as his head felt suddenly giddy. "Why have you returned?" The Traveler's tall image faded and flickered, then dwindled to shadows.

"Find your friends—they can't be far. Hawk-Finvar can get you back across. He has the skill, though doubts himself. But you need to act quickly, you can't remain in this dimension long. I will see you in time . . ." The Traveler's shadow flickered one last time, and then that too was gone.

His dizzy spell faded. Jaran thrust the axe haft down into the sand and rested his hands on the heavy blade. Griner gave him strength, he realized that now. Tyho's gift was no normal weapon. But no doubt there would be a price to pay. The northern gods weren't known for their generosity.

Jaran blinked and took his bearings. Sea and sky, wind and clouds, rushing out over the gray ragged ocean. A thin wedge of birds gliding low across the darkening horizon. He heard a shout, turned, and grinned happily, seeing Finvar running toward him.

"I'm happy you're in one piece," Jaran said, as Finvar came to a crashing halt. The ex-thief's eyes were wild, and his smoky hair sticking out, as though he'd been struck by lightning—and perhaps he had, Jaran thought. "Where's our girl?"

"I . . ." Finvar moved his mouth around and mumbled. "*Can't* . . . speak . . . properly. Think we lost her mid-flight."

"You did that?"

Finvar glared at him for long moments. Eventually, he nodded. "I can't fucking control it. Happens when I'm stressed. Why Gurtei and his boys booted me out. Called me a weirdo.

They blamed it on my double-crossing them—an excuse. Load of bollocks. They saw me . . . *change.*" He shook his head. "And didn't like it very much."

"Fly," Jaran said. "They saw you *flying*—must have been quite a shock."

"I don't know how to control it." Finvar waved his hands about. "Neither when it happens or where the fuck I go. I just feel light and fluffy, distorted—can see for miles. But I've never taken people with me before, nor have I busted up through a ceiling. It just . . . *happened.*"

"You saved us, Fin," Jaran said. "Don't feel so glum." He reached across and patted Finvar's head as though he was a small, trusting hound. "That shaman Straban would most likes have us boiling in a vat of lard by now. I've heard what those twisted bastards are like when they get angry."

Finvar looked hard at Jaran's face and sunk to his knees. "I'm knackered," he said. "Worn out, and my poor wee nerves are shredded to buggery. And . . . where the fuck are we?"

"Don't know," Jaran responded. "But I've good reason to believe if we stay here much longer, we might die."

"That's encouraging." Finvar coughed up phlegm and spat it out. He reached into his jerkin and grinned. "Still got it." He showed Jaran the rolled parchment he'd pilfered from the Halls of Antiquity.

"That's going be useful." Jaran tried not to sound overly sarcastic, feeling sorry for his friend. "Come on—let's walk."

"Where?"

"Along this beach. We'll find a portal of sorts—some kind of gateway. I have it on good authority that you busted us through into another dimension, as well as splintering that ceiling. That's some rare talent you have, my small friend. Come on, step up, Birdy Fin—we need to find that lass."

"Dimensions? I have no idea what you're jabbering about. And don't call me that," Finvar said, but started walking beside him, as Jaran hoisted Griner and followed the thin white line of sand wedged between murmuring waves and towering dunes.

As they walked, Jaran told Fin of the Traveler and what little he knew about the man, and in turn, Fin shed more light on his unusual gift.

"It's why I sought you out," Finvar said. "I'd heard the bear thing. The rumors I mean, how men spoke of seeing a huge bear shadow over you when you fought. I figured you were *weird* like me, and might-but-could-use a mate."

Fin crashed into his back without realizing Jaran had stopped. "What the fuck is that?" he said, as they stared at the huge square mass of spidery stone ahead.

THE MIRROR EXPLODED INTO SHEEGA'S FACE AS THE goblin's metallic laughter filled the chamber, its echoes rattling off around her head. She mouthed a curse-rune and the mirror reassembled, the tiny fragments of glass whirring back into proper place. The twisted face in the mirror leered at her.

"He defeated you," Gantallian said, his metallic voice mocking and cruel.

Sheega wiped the blood from her mouth where Jaran's fist had struck her. The gull lay dead and broken a yard away. She'd need a new conduit.

"How was I to know they'd break through to a different

zone? That stupid mortal meddler Straban fucked things up. *Amateur.*" She spat the last word out in contempt. "The fool got the hawk inside the man excited. Now I've lost all three of them."

The mirror glass wobbled and threatened to shatter again. She ignored Gantallian. Sheega was used to his corrosive nature. She departed the hall and sought out Ranning by the shore.

Her lover was knee-deep in the icy water, his green, honey-tinged naked body gleaming with sweat and oil as he strode along the beach toward her.

"Thought I'd find you here." Sheega kept her tone level despite her inner rage. "We have a problem." Ranning drew alongside her and smiled. His milky shifting eyes were full of irony as she glared at him.

"I think you mean, *you* have a problem," Ranning said. "I felt the quiver through my veins, saw the shimmer in the sky. Your prey slipped the snare you set in Cardalan. He has a sky tracker with him. A Voidsurfer. That hawk-man has unusual talent for a mortal. Even in Faerie, such beings are uncommon."

"And how was I to know that?"

Ranning ignored her as he walked briskly along the beach, the cold wind drying his oily skin. He spoke a rune-spell, and next time she looked, his body was clothed in shimmering satin and velvet, of deep violet and green, the colors shifting back and forth, confusing her eyes. He stopped when reaching a tumbled pile of rocks. She caught up with him there.

Ranning surveyed her for a moment. "I suppose I could get involved," he said. "Though my own conflict lies beneath that water."

"You cannot fight Sensuata—even though He is much weakened from the last war in the galaxy. You are better off aiding me, so you can rule beside me when I return to Dunnehine and slaughter our enemies."

"Your enemies," he corrected her.

"Yours, too," Sheega said, reaching out and grabbing his arm. The need was on her again, and she slipped a hand inside his garment. "Mankind has always been Faerie's bitterest foe. Your people—the Faen, the Elementals, and my folk. All of us suffered at the hands of those clumsy short-lived fools. I think the Weaver created them out of purest spite to cause us pain, after we rebelled against Him. Men have souls—what a gift," she spat bitterly.

"I have no specific quarrel with mankind," Ranning said. "To hate, you have to care. *I don't.*"

"You will if Faerie is defeated." She worked her fingers deftly until he pulled her close, his damp lips smothering her own. "And it can be—anything is possible."

After they were done, Ranning rolled to his feet and glared down at her. "You think a paltry band of renegade warlocks are a match for my realm, and the original races of Ansu? You are naïve, witch."

"I'm not talking about those fools in Dunnehine." Sheega stood up beside him, slipping back into her warm clothes. "I mean Jaran Saerk—or more importantly, those aiding him. You know the Traveler is back from his—"

"—*travels.*" He smiled at her, his eyes cold as frosted glass. "Why should I care? That one is just another shadow from the past. Like his kin, he has no real power anymore."

"But still he has guile and cunning, and a long memory. And, far worse, Tyho's abroad in the land. That's never good. One-Arm gave the man the axe Griner. I felt its searing strength when I assailed him just now." Her time to smile, as the flicker of what could have been fear, quivered the muscles at the edge of his mouth. "The name Tyho got your attention, I see."

"Tyho plays His own game." Ranning's eyes flickered annoyance.

"Through Jaran Saerk this time—unless we can kill him and those other two wretched creatures."

"Your obsession pains me. I know you need to destroy him before the prophecy does for you. The White Bear's return. I know little of the others you hint at. Voidsurfer and the woman. They are small fry, even if talented for clumsy mortal folk."

"There is more." Sheega explained how Gantallian had revealed to her the spirit animals residing in Jaran's companions while her dogs attacked in Dunnehine. "You know about the bird man, but the woman Savarna has *Aikashi* blood running through her veins. She's half-breed, and worse, has a twin somewhere."

"Shen demons?"

She laughed. "*Aikashi* wouldn't thank you for calling them Shen—the race of men who put the original inhabitants to death. *Aikashi* are extinct, have been for years."

"A few obviously survived, but what's that to me? I know little of the peoples in the east. My waters are far from theirs."

"The *Aikashi* are killers, and that girl has some latent being inside her. Her *Aikashi*-spirit takes the form of a tiger, a great eastern cat. She defeated my dogs when I stole inside her dreams."

"What of the Voidsurfer?" Sheega could tell by his tone that Ranning was bored. His kind seldom focused for long. The reason why she'd never trust him. He was Faen, a creature of Faerie, like the elves and trolls. Not reliable allies, as already she'd learnt, and she partially blamed them for her own misfortunes.

"Finvar is interesting," she said eventually. "Whereas Jaran is a blunt tool of destruction, thus suitable for Tyho's purposes, and the girl simplistic and savage. Finvar Droll is more intriguing. Clever and quick. He reminds me of that rogue Lofhi the trickster who was banished beyond the great dark."

"So where are they, your new mortal friends? Which dimension did Finvar take them to?" The half-smile again.

"Scymara, or Galenki. Maybe Gwelan—it doesn't matter, as they won't be able to stay there. The very air in those realms is hostile to mortals."

"Probably Galenki," Ranning said. "Scymara was dissolved, and Gwelan destroyed by the steel Grogans."

"Point is—they'll be back, and probably nearer here, if Finvar gets a handle on his compass. That means I have to be ready for them. And you."

"What of your slug husband and those dotard sons you sent? Weren't they supposed to deal with the Northman?"

"I didn't know about Finvar when I sent them. If I had, I'd have bid them stay in Leeth. They are scant help to us in Cardalan now the game has shifted closer. As for Erlund—he might serve us best as bait. I know the Traveler got to Jaran before Bera could reveal his past, thus protecting him from me. But he knows about Erlund after that stupid mercenary failed to kill him."

"Time to unleash the Witch-Men, then," Ranning said.

"Are they ready, my Witch-Guard, schooled enough in lore?"

Ranning's smile was triumphant. "Our seeds have taken root. All twelve have become formidable warriors, more than a match for Saerk and his cronies. And their spellcraft will shatter any counter-illusions the mortals can muster." He turned away from her and started walking back toward the water. "I can scoop them from the water anytime. You know they prefer sleeping beneath the brine to the comfy cots inside your hall."

Sheega caught up with him and grabbed his arm. "Must you spend all your days in the deep?" She felt the need returning, as the joyful thought of Jaran's severed head being delivered by Ranning's new Witch-Men filled her with savage lust.

"I miss my home." He turned and stared at her. He was naked again, his honey skin gleaming. "I will send for the strongest, Stoon, this evening in the Hall." He kissed her hard and long. Sheega gasped for breath and pulled him closer. Together they writhed and tumbled as the sea lapped cold around their bodies.

16

SHIFTING DIMENSIONS

Savarna gasped as she surfaced, choking and coughing as the cold brine tossed her body around. She could see the shoreline scarce a hundred feet away. She was a good swimmer, and she cut bold, clean strokes through the chop until she staggered onto the pale, sandy strand, her clothes dripping beside her.

She ran on the spot, shook herself and stamped about, until the worst of the chill had gone, taking time to look around and study the alien terrain for any sign of movement. Her friends were gone, and she had no idea where. Worse, she didn't know where she was or what had happened.

Somehow Finvar had saved them from Straban's ambush. Blasted them through the roof—impossibly without any damage, at least to herself. But Fin had lost control, or had lost her anyway. Then that bird had attacked, but something must have driven it away before it reached her.

Another sending from the witch Sheega, she suspected. It was past time for payback. Finally warmed up enough to resume walking, Savarna headed along the strand until she saw the weird slab of rock sprawl into view. A castle. Or else some vast structure, forbidding and ominous.

Not that way . . . Ware the castle . . .

Vian's voice inside her head again. For the briefest moment, she saw his face, taut in concentration, then he'd gone.

"Brother—where is this place? Help me," she called out, but was answered by wind over dune grass and the wan distant cries of birds. She stared at the glistening pile of black rock, perhaps a mile distant. Grim to behold, vast and sheer. Jet black as the tar that coated ships' stays. A mass that seemed to swallow light. It drew her eyes like a magnet.

Vian had warned her to stay clear. *Twice.* But what else could she do? She had to find Jaran and Fin, and at the moment the castle seemed the only option.

"I have to," she muttered, and commenced walking again toward the looming monstrosity.

No!

His voice slammed hammer-hard inside her head. This time she heeded, sensing rare fear in her brother, who so seldom showed that emotion. *You win . . .* She turned, walked the other way, her heart heavy as leaden stone.

She had walked a mile, reached a turn when she came to a sudden stop. The black castle barred her way. Closer than it had been. And huger by far, swallowing light. She could make out lines of walls and turrets. But they, too, were hard to define.

Savarna turned away, climbing up through the dunes. She reached a stubby area of brush and kept walking until she saw a high ridge. She made for the slope and crested the rise, then turned to look back at the ocean.

It wasn't there. Instead, the castle rose huge and bleak in

front of where she stood again. Closer, and seated on a rock, was a man. He greeted her like an old friend.

"You're back," he said, smiling. Savarna saw a tanned, handsome face buried beneath disheveled beard and an unruly mass of hair. A madman, it seemed, clad in dun-colored shabby tunic and trousers, a long, curved knife at his belt. "Savarna." He was smiling, bidding her approach. "So happy to see you again. I got washed up here." His moist brown eyes were like a lost lover.

"Who are you, another wayward sorcerer?" Savarna strode up to confront him, her fists at her side, wishing she still had her knife, or Jaran's sword that she'd left in the Halls. "And where is this fucking place?"

"That I do not know." The man looked askance, baffled that she didn't recognize him. "Last time we met, you were less testy —friendly even. And where's that big northern bugger? Give him greetings from the shipwrecked sailor, Carlo Sarfe." He didn't look like a warlock, but rather a penniless vagabond, his clothes shredded and worn, and the shabby-looking knife at his side.

"I don't know you," Savarna said, "and have no notion as to how you think you know me."

"*Aw* . . . shit," the man calling himself Carlo Sarfe said, placing his hands on either side of his face. "It's happening again."

"What's *happening*—and what is that?" She pointed at the huge slab of rock glistening behind him.

"Time warps, a distortion. Probably caused by them in there." He hinted at the mass of rock without turning around.

"Are they wizards?"

"Don't know," he said miserably. "They wouldn't let me through their gates. See, I'm as lost as you are, lovely Savarna."

She changed tact. "Where were we when you saw us last?"

"Onboard my ship," he said. "Making for Valkador, where your big, fair-haired bear of a man had a rendezvous planned with a witch."

Before she could respond, Savarna heard a hoarse shout coming from the other way. She glanced past the mass of stone and saw two figures sprinting up a path toward her, the nearest half the size of the other one. She grinned, recognizing Finvar and Jaran. They'd found her again. "You'll have to explain that to Jaran." She turned and then gaped. The sailor Carlo Sarfe had vanished, as had the vast black tower of stone.

Instead, the sea churned close by, and a thin path threaded up from where the two men approached at breakneck speed.

"No time to explain," Finvar said, bow slung across his back, grabbing her sleeve and yanking her forward as Jaran loped up to join them. "Got to keep moving, else we'll miss our slot."

She shot a quizzical glance at Jaran, who showed a wry smile, the great axe gripped in one hand. "We are in need of haste," Jaran told her.

They ran, the path shrinking beneath their feet as dark trees loomed ahead. "Where are we going?" Savarna almost screamed the words out, as confusion, rage, and joy at seeing Jaran mingled inside her.

"In there." Finvar slammed to a halt and pointed. Savarna crashed into his back and then Jaran jolted hers, knocking her sprawling on top of Fin, and him face-first into the dirt.

"Sorry about that," Jaran said, as she looked up, gazed at the latest phenomena taking shape before her eyes. A jagged, multi-colored hole of light throbbed inside a door spanning the road, its hinges creaking slightly as it rocked back and forth. Vaguely oval, the hole's aura kept flashing and shifting, with deep blackness showing beyond.

"It's a portal," Fin yelled in her ear excitedly. "A gate!"

"Doesn't look like a gate to me," Jaran said. "Doors without surrounding buildings can't be right." Savarna regained her feet and threw him a quick hug. "Happy to see you, girl," he said.

"Stop that," Finvar glared at them. "We three need to link hands and jump through that doorway, else we're stuck here until something big eats us."

"It might be worse on the other side," Jaran said.

They both looked at him, until Finvar jabbed his hands out wide on either side. "We don't have any fucking choice," Finvar yelled.

"Any idea where this will take us?" Jaran asked wryly, after grabbing her hand in his and allowing Finvar to grasp his wrist beneath the axe haft.

"I'm aiming for Leeth, but we'll see," Finvar said. "Come on, for fuck's sake. Let's do this. On *three*. One . . . two . . . *jump!*"

17

KEEP THEM CLOSE

Vian counted nine men, all seated in various positions around their dismal campfire. A dark night, the misty freckle of snowflakes spinning down, winking then fading on the hard, dry ground. He leaned on the Chiang spear and listened in. The round-faced one with the heavy moustache was poking a stick in the sorry-looking fire. He must be the leader, as most were listening to his words in silence. If these were outlaw robbers —and surely, they must be—then they had fallen on hard times of late. All nine, lounging idle or seated on logs, looked hard done by, some recovering from wounds, their eyes bloodshot, the faces lean and hungry.

All looked exhausted, a few angry, a few more dangerous with shifting eyes, as though looking to blame someone for their plight. Vian smiled, sensing an opportunity here. They were angry, too, looking at their leader who was still poking the fire. Finally, a gaunt-faced, snarly-looking one couldn't hold back any longer. "We'll starve if we stay in this wood much longer. No fucking game to hunt, on account of the bastard Magister claiming it all for himself."

"I doubt Chulan's involved personally," the leader said, glancing around in the dark. Vian shifted his stance slightly and smiled. This older man was cleverer than the others. Calmer. A thinker, thus one to watch. He stopped poking the fire and glared at the thin one who'd just spoken. "What do you suggest, Roile? We stagger out into the fields and wave fucking flags? I don't fancy Chulan's rusty saw chewing into my neck."

"I'm just saying—stay here and we'll be a lot thinner, on account of being dead. Fuck Drolly and that red-haired bitch —left us to die."

"Doubt she had much choice," the older man said. "That Card patrol leader didn't look like the type who'd spare the sword on a woman. I miss the lass," he said after a moment's repose. "She was bright, feisty—and a lot better looking than you, Roile."

Vian chose that precise moment to walk out from his hide.

GURTEI LEAPED TO HIS FEET, AS DID MOST OF THE OTHERS, Roile included. A man had appeared from nowhere. A red-haired man who bore an uncanny resemblance to . . . Gurtei reached for his sabre, but the man didn't react. Instead, he leaned casually on his cruel-looking Chiang, his back against a tree.

Beside Gurtei, Roile and Corben cursed, and Truggan made ready with his axe. "Ease up." Gurtei waved at the lads to calm down. "Let's see what he has to say." He awarded the redhead a long, measured look. Smallish, calm and very confident. That confidence bordered on arrogance. He was neatly dressed in southern style, and two Jian blades hung across his back. Perhaps twenty-five winters, hard to tell. "Not polite," Gurtei said. "Creeping up on folk in the dead of night."

"I thought perhaps we might help each other." The man smiled. "I mean you no harm, and feel like I know you already." He rested his spear against the tree and folded his arms, smiled again. *Arrogant bastard*, thought Gurtei. *Brave, though.*

"Kill him quickly, I say," Roile muttered, and two of the other lads grunted approval. The redhead raised a brow.

"I doubt you'd succeed," he said. "But you can try if you want."

"Wait . . . you're . . ." Gurtei let go of his sabre and rubbed his moustache.

"Vian of Noble House Eltayn, from distant Rundali. And yes, Gurtei, I'm Savarna's brother."

"More like one of Gujun's assassins flushing out bandits," Roile said. "His archers are probably surrounding us."

"I'm alone," the man calling himself Vian said. He let his hands drop to his side.

"Then you are dead." Roile stepped forward, unsheathing his sabre. Gurtei made to stop him, but Vian waved him back. The smile had fled the redhead's face. His expression was cold, *a killer's*, thought Gurtei.

"My sister didn't care for you, overmuch. How's your hand?"

Roile glanced down at his right hand, now healed nicely, bar the missing half nubbin. "You got inside my head." His sword lunged for the newcomer. "And that sister of yours is a bitch." The lunge cut clean night air. Vian had danced out of reach, his arms were folded again, he'd moved so quickly Gurtei was still blinking. Roile spat, took a vicious swing aiming for Vian's neck.

With a speed Gurtei had never witnessed in all his forty-five years, the man called Vian ducked low below that sweep, leaned in, twisted, locked his hands around the Cutter, and threw Roile, together with his wildly swinging sword, over his right shoulder. Roile crumpled in a heap, started to rise, and then fell back again as Vian's suede boot kicked his jaw. He lay still.

Vian calmly stood over him, untied his drawstrings and emptied his bladder. "That's for insulting Savarna," he said, finishing off and neatly retying his strings. "Normally, you'd be dead for such behavior, but I've no wish to upset your leader." He turned to Gurtei, his green eyes glinting gold.

Savarna's brother. The same eyes, Gurtei realized. *Interesting pair.* Those eyes should have given him away. How had this man found them when Chulan's best hounds couldn't? *I must be getting stupid in my dotage.* No one spoke as Roile wheezed and leaked blood from his mouth. The other men, all standing, waited for Gurtei to say something.

He forced himself to relax, though the truth was that he felt anything but that. This Vian had made a fool of one of his best fighters. Roile was a prick, sure, but he was damn good with that sword of his. *Normally*, Gurtei thought wryly. Quite funny, watching that show.

"You have our full attention," Gurtei said, crunching on his moustache. "We are all ears."

Vian smiled. "Mind if I share your fire?"

"I'd offer you brandy, but we're a bit short at the moment."

"Ferrytown." Vian nodded. "I saw the mess."

Gurtei noted how his men paled, and some muttered. He kept his voice calm. "You share certain . . . *talents* with Savarna."

Vian perched on a log. The nearest men shuffled away from him, their eyes shifty and nervous. He said nothing for a while, his strange eyes viewing them in turn, as though weighing up their courage. Then Vian shot Gurtei a hard, sharp glance. "I am going to kill your empress, and her Magister," he said. "But first I'd like your help." Nervous laughter came from his men, but Gurtei bid them quit.

"He's insane," Sumil said, but Gurtei ignored him.

"I'm listening," he said to Vian. "First, tell me if your sister survived."

"Think you'd be alive if she didn't?" Vian said, his handsome features arrow-sharp again. "She's away west with the Northman and your old friend."

"Drolly's alive?" Sumil again. Again, he was ignored.

"Well, are you interested, Gurtei?" Vian folded his arms again. "I see how you're all faring so well these days. I heard Magister Chulan has tripled the price on your heads since the murder of Soma Ghee's aide. The Midnight Cutting Crew are out of luck, it seems."

Gurtei laughed softy. "We've had better days, but what you're proposing doesn't seem likely to improve our chance of survival."

"Best form of defense is attack." Vian smiled. "As you said, I've certain talents. Can see around corners, so to speak. I can assist you while you help me do my task. In return for your help, you'll be rich. I've money to spare and lands in the south that need workers, as most of the old ones were murdered by Shen slavers."

"What do you have in mind?"

For answer, Vian produced a silver flute and kneeled playing a short merry tune. "A night entertaining Imperial Rasnei in her chambers." He smiled as he stowed the flute and slipped a curved dagger into both hands. "No one will hear her scream," Vian said, and smiled. "So, are you in?"

GOST CHULAN, SEVENTY-THIRD HIGH MAGISTER OF POL Shen, surveyed his manicured lawns over the rim of his tea cup. Mint tea was his preferred beverage this early in the afternoon. A beautiful winter's day, sunny and clear, not too cold. The odd wren sang noisily.

Three slaves toiled silently, trimming and clearing, preparing for spring and the long Shen summer that followed. He watched them coolly for a moment. One was limping, he noted. The sight annoyed him, spoilt the moment. He'd send word for the man to be killed later. Garroted in the dark. He might choose to watch, depending on his mood. Sometimes killings made him melancholy, on other occasions they aroused him. Tonight could go either way—he'd have to wait and see.

The soft sound of slippers brushing the mosaics. He turned and glared at the servant, Hui San, currently bowing and hair sweeping low. "What?" Chulan said.

"The man to see you, Venerable One."

The man. He had a name, of course, but no one dared speak it. Perhaps the only individual more feared than Chulan himself. Gujun, his torturer. Also a skilled warrior, assassin and spy. Leader of the Silver Slayers. Useful, efficient and deadly.

"Fetch him." Chulan flicked his eyes at the woman, who bowed low again and vanished. Moments later, Gujun appeared behind him.

"How do you do that?" Chulan was always impressed how this killer could walk without making a sound or leaving a trace.

Gujun was a small, neat man, dark eyes, the hard face lined and leathery from years spent out in the wild. He wore his hair long, a silky black sheen, tied back neatly with a silver snake clasp. The tiny wasp tattoo on his left cheek hinted the street gangs where Chulan's people had discovered him. He'd risen through the gang's ranks swiftly, and soon led the Slayers. Chulan had bribed him first, and then bought the whole gang. It helped to have outlaws working on the inside.

The warrior bowed, a slight dip of his head. Such disrespect was intolerable, and were it any other individual, would result in a slow death. But Gujun and his master knew they needed each other.

"What news from the border?" Chulan asked him.

"Calla wants to meet with you," Gujun said, his black eyes revealing nothing.

"I thought he might." Chulan smiled and sipped his mint tea. "Who did you speak to?"

"Dagara, his fourth son—he's in charge at the front when his father's away."

"Ran Calla has returned to the City of the Clouds?"

"He has. Calla wants to meet with you in Ferrytown, but before that, he wants that bay area cleared of Tseole nomads. They attacked the scouting party he sent last month, killing all of them."

"It's not my jurisdiction, but I'll see what can be done." Chulan tugged at his thin mustaches. *Strange, the Tseole are usually timid.* "Calla should be more concerned about crossing through Dunnehine, even with an army."

Gujun shrugged, and Chulan let his mind peruse the matter for a moment. "Was there anything else?" he asked his henchman.

"The Cutting Crew have gone to ground."

"Flush them out. I'm weary of their nonsense. Why is this

taking so long? And what of the slave girl Ghee summoned, the one they abducted in their ambush?"

"No word. The Cutters must have sold her on—perhaps in Ferrytown or beyond." Gujun smiled slightly as though amused —it was always hard to tell with him. "You know the Cutters were in Ferrytown when the Cards arrived. Whatever happened up there with the Tseole or whomever, the brigand Gurtei lost most of his men in the crossfire. Wrong time, wrong place, I suspect." The half-smile again.

"THE REBEL, GURTEI, DOESN'T CONCERN ME, GU. I WANT that Rundali bitch apprehended. The empress showed an interest. And what of the renegade Northman, Jaran Saerk?"

"I spoke to Hranic, who knows nothing, but then they're always obtuse. Saerk must have fled with the thief who rescued him."

"Hranic cannot control his oafs." Chulan couldn't stand those Northmen. Rude, clumsy thugs. Hranic was better than most, but still a yokel from those rough lands. He couldn't be relied on. None of them could. Trouble was, they were needed, and Rasnei liked them.

"Clean this up. I don't want loose ends, Gujun."

Gujun bowed again, a hint of irony in that stoop. Chulan chose to ignore that. "I mentioned those miscreants to Dagara. Maybe they'll help us catch them over there."

"Good. You had best get to it." Chulan finished his cup and turned to survey the gardens again. A thin mist was settling over the lawns—it would be cold tonight. He'd order a boy brought in later, when he'd taken enough wine.

He'd turned to address Gujun again, but the man had gone.

No matter. Gujun was thorough, and once he'd confirmed the meeting at the border, the situation would improve. Ran Calla needed him, and in return he'd save Shen from annihilation. Chulan wasn't a fool. He knew Shen couldn't hold out much longer. Cardalan was on the rise, much like Shen itself had been three thousand years ago. A storm was coming, and it would blast apart the gates of Pol Shen. The empress was living on borrowed time, the old Shen regime soon would be no more. But Calla would need shrewd advisors in his new land. Chulan had thought it only sensible to offer his name up as Imperial Governor.

18

ERLUND'S BOYS

STRABAN PROSTRATED himself as the warlord glared down at him. He had failed, and Calla wasn't the forgiving kind. Any other shaman would have been slain already. Thirty men dead, and all had been veterans. Seasoned warriors and Immortals who'd fought beside the warlord himself. Calla was beyond furious, and even a man with Straban's influence and knowledge daren't risk rousing him further.

"Tell me what happened in there?" Calla was seated on the ancient Ptarni throne. The gaudily carved ebony chair, together with its glowing candles and ruby crustaceans. The God Emperors had been a very strange lot.

Straban rose, then bowed low again. "Sorcery," he said, after a moment working his lips.

"You *think* . . .?" Calla stood up and hurled an axe past Straban's head. The weapon struck a wall panel and cut off half the eagle's head. Straban bowed again, as the three servants remaining in the hall fled from sight.

"It was unexpected," Straban said. "The other man—he's a shapeshifter, a flyer."

"Don't test me, Straban."

"The Northman went berserk—I know they do that a lot, but this was different. I saw a bear, a spirit creature. Huge and white. And the woman was a shapeshifter, too. A great striped cat —she didn't manifest properly, but I saw she had the potential."

Calla glared at him and reached for a second axe. Straban chewed his lip. "The man became a hawk," he said, eyes on the axe. "It was him who broke through the roof. I don't know how —never encountered such a thing."

"What's the point in having a shaman who's crap at magic?" Calla said, tossing the axe his way. Straban ducked, bowed again. The axe broke off another chunk of tapestry. Calla sat back on the throne, his hand reaching for a flask. His face was almost purple, and his cheeks puffed out, but at least he seemed calmer, more reflective. Straban deemed the worst danger had passed, for the moment at least.

"Who are these people—and what's their quarrel with that witch in the north?"

"She's from northern Dunnehine," Straban said, edgy again. "An exile from the ice realm. Fell out with her kin. There's another war brewing, Great Ran. One that mirrors our own."

"Where?"

Straban paused for a moment. "Faerie," he replied in a whisper. "The Shadow Realm."

Calla slurped back wine and chuckled. Then he yelled for a slave to bring more. "You need to work harder, Straban. If I needed a joker, I'd geld one of the slaves, or Shen prisoners. I expect more from you, shaman. Piss off."

Straban bowed, but lingered.

"What . . .?" Calla's dark eyes narrowed dangerously.

"There is something else," Straban said. "Speaking of North-men, three have just arrived in the city. The guard reported back that they are looking for Jaran Saerk."

"Must be those brothers Con told me about," he said. "Send them here, I could use some new killers now that you've lost some of my best."

THE CITY WAS A HIVE. VALGARN LOPED UP FROM THE street, his two brothers beside him. Their horses had been stabled, and they'd eaten well. The Cardalan guard captain proved an affable host, once word came back from the warlord in the citadel.

"Mighty Calla will see you now," a stooped, bald man with a hawk nose announced, and led them into the great palace of the deceased emperors who'd reigned here long ago. Valgarn grinned at his brothers as they walked past rooms, their shields and axes clanking, and their boots staining the thick carpets with mud.

"Never imagined such a place existing." Valgarn's eyes watched the slaves milling around. Some of the girls were pretty. Beside him, Holtarn grinned.

"Makes Grimhold look like a cowshed," he said.

"That's because it is a fucking cowshed," Gorn said.

They came to a halt when their bald-headed guide reached a set of double doors. These were carved with weird intricate signs that, despite Valgarn's familiarity with his mother's tampering, lifted the hairs on the back of his neck.

"In there," the man said, and hinted they enter as a guard opened the doors. A wide hall spread out in full view, lanterns and candles flickered everywhere, and at the far end Valgarn saw a heavy-set man slumped on a huge, ugly chair.

They approached, and the man watched them in silence. Aside him, a few retainers and slaves fussed in the shadows. Valgarn and his brothers stopped at the foot of the dais. None thought to bow. The warlord didn't seem to mind.

"You must be Calla," Gorn said.

"I am he," the warlord said. "You three are welcome here."

"We've come to fight for you," Gorn said, but Valgarn stepped forward.

"Before that, we have a private matter to conclude. We believe our renegade cousin is in your city."

"Jaran Saerk. Yes, well—he just left." Calla sighed theatrically. "You boys arrived too late. I was hoping you'd kill him and be on your way back to the front. I need good lads like you out there to deal with Hranic's bastards. They say you Northmen favor gold over family. And your father promised me two hundred fighting men—"

"—where'd Jaran go?" Gorn stepped forward, his face red and flustered. "We've crossed half the world searching for that bastard. My axe is hungry for his neck."

Valgarn saw how Calla's eyes glittered dangerously and narrowed, and how every servant visible threw themselves to their knees. He kicked his brother in the shins. Gorn turned and glared at him.

"Gorn here's a touch hasty," Valgarn said. "He didn't mean to be rude. We three respect you, mighty Calla."

Calla's round face exploded with sudden laughter. "Get these lads ale and some wenches, and see they are given spacious quarters, with sweeping views of this fine city." He turned to survey the brothers again. Gorn still looked angry, Holtarn confused.

"I'm so happy you're here." Calla was still chuckling. "You don't know how wearisome it is, being surrounded by gutless worms. Even my scurvy sons steer clear of me these days, except to bitch about each other. At last—strong men who speak their mind. *Warriors.* As to your brother's question" —Calla's smile resembled a wolf—"I do not know the answer, but I have my best shaman working on it."

"We need to apprehend him," Valgarn said.

"Well of course, and I'll help—they caused some damage while they were here and will have to answer to that."

"Our mother wants all three of them dead—and quickly," Holtarn blurted out.

"Your . . . *mother.*" Calla's heavy brows linked as his face frowned. "What of your father, the king?"

"Him too." Valgarn glared at Holtarn. *Why were his brothers so stupid?* "But our mother is more persuasive."

"Ah, yes—Conorax mentioned a witch, as I recall. You Northmen are a queer race."

"Our mother is from Dunnehine," Valgarn said. "A queen of that land, but treated badly by her subjects. They sent this Jaran to kill her. He's a bastard by-blow of King Erlund's dead brother. An imposter who threatens the throne of Leeth, and worse, is planning to kill our mother. We three cannot let that happen."

Calla stared down at Valgarn and his brothers. "You must be weary, even men as tough as you. Here's what I suggest. We wait and see what Straban discovers concerning your cousin Saerk. In the meantime, you brothers relax in my city and await your fellow Northmen to arrive. When they come, you can journey with them to the Shen River where my army lies encamped, preparing for invasion. You youngsters can play a leading part in that, and reap the rewards a-plenty."

"What about Jaran Saerk?" Holtarn asked.

"Once we know his whereabouts, it shouldn't be difficult to arrange for his death. Doesn't have to be one of you. I doubt your father—or mother—would care who kills that rogue. Getting the job done should prove satisfactory. So why not let Straban deal with Jaran Saerk? As I said, he and his companions are now the enemies of Cardalan too."

"Our mother laid it on us—"

"—shut up, Holt," Valgarn said as his brother shuffled beside him. "We'll do as you suggest, great Calla. And await word from your shaman, or any other source concerning our foe. But, know this—if Jaran Saerk is still at large in this land, it will be one of us that kills him."

RAN CALLA HAD WATCHED THE THREE BROTHERS WITH interest. On the surface, they were clearly thugs, big brutish killers, good at what they did. Calla had scores of men like that ranked amongst his Immortals, though few as big or strong.

Gorn looked the most volatile of the three, probably the oldest, and had the worst temperament. Holtarn was the weakest, but no doubt still ferocious in battle. Valgarn was more interesting. He didn't seem swayed by his death-duty like the others. This brother might prove useful, should any of Calla's sons make a move against him after Shen fell. A move he half-expected, as he'd been so occupied with events in the east. It was something to consider.

Later that afternoon while the Ran was attending the bath houses, Straban appeared with three warriors. "I have news of the fugitives," Straban said, his lean face flushed with excitement. "A fissure erupted—that's where they'll be."

"A . . . what?"

"A hole in the world fabric," Straban said. "It's how Hawk-Finvar escaped. He shifted through the dimensions and took the others with him. But you can't survive long out there. Too many hazards. I knew it was only a matter of time before they broke back through. When I saw the vortex open, I delved closer."

"Well, stop jabbering about your spell-prowess, and tell me where they are."

"Hragglund," Straban said.

Calla smiled as he pondered the next move.

19

HRAGGLUND

"This doesn't look like Leeth," Jaran said as they stood gazing across a wide-open country strewn with glittering lakes. Blue, still waters were surrounded by spiky forests of emerald pines, their conical crowns dusted in snow.

"Hragglund," Finvar said. "Close enough. You've no idea how knackering it is, steering as well as flying."

"You'll have to tell us about it one day," Jaran said, as Savarna stretched her legs and jumped up and down in the snow beside him. Cold and bright, but at least they were back from . . . *wherever*, and there was no one unpleasant around.

"We have the map," Finvar said, pleased with himself. "We know Valkador's off that west coast, across from Grimhold. I say we find a road and make for that castle first."

"My uncle might be expecting us from this direction."

"He most likely thinks you're dead, or missing. Besides, with our combined talent, we can creep up on him—if that's what you still want to do."

"Sheega is the one we need to kill," Savarna said. "Or, rather, you do, Jaran. But since I seem to be temporarily stuck with you two, it's in my interest to help with that. Together we can withstand her, you said?"

"*He* said," Jaran grunted. "The Traveler, and I believe him. Odel, too. Sheega is the real foe, but Erlund needs to die as well. Be easier killing him first, I'm thinking. But the down side of that—it gives her more time to prepare a special welcome."

"Since we'll pass through Grimhold, we might as well start with him," Finvar said. "Plus, we can get supplies on route—as long as no one recognizes us."

Jaran shook his head. "Sheega and Erlund will be expecting us to call in at that castle. And I bet that witch will also know about what happened in Cardalis soon enough, what with her scrying powers. Plus, her sons must be scouring that area for me. I think it's wiser we skirt north of Grimhold Castle and strike out directly for the coast."

They both stared at him, Finvar grinning, Savarna more serious.

"We have our weapons—we can hunt," Jaran said, waving his arms.

"We'll be fine." Finvar nodded. "Of course we will. The first settlement or village on the coast will provide us with a boat. Then sail across—doesn't look far, so it should be easy enough —kill the hag, stuff her witchy head in a bag and claim your inheritance. You can pay me then, Northman. And send your new army of freed Valkador Jaran-worshippers to help this lass find her brother, while she murders everyone in Pol Shen. *Simple.*"

"Let's get moving," Savarna said, shaking her head. "Else your incessant tongue-wagging drain our reserves before we've even started."

"You say the sweetest things," Finvar said. "Lead on."

LATER, AFTER DARK, THEY WERE CAMPED AROUND A TINY fire. A ring of pines giving shelter, the dark glitter of lake water a half mile distant. Finvar kept watch on a rise shadowed by the nearest tree. Jaran could see him crouched up there, legs crossed, smoking the pipe he still retained alongside his bow. How he'd managed to hang on to those with all the shapeshifting and flapping about was beyond Jaran's pool of knowledge. He'd ask Fin about that one day.

Jaran's thoughts drifted as he sat on a log beside the woman. She looked far away, also lost in thought. Eventually she shuffled, as though she'd made some inner decision.

"I think Fin's deluded," Savarna said. "His optimism might well prove our ruin."

"You could be right," Jaran said. "But Finvar cheers me up. If it wasn't for him, I'd be dead, having killed a few hundred guards in Pol Shen, after they tried to flog me." He grinned at her, but Savarna's face was serious.

"Do you really believe a witch stole your inheritance? That you're some kind of lord—a prince?"

"Jarle. Never thought about it." Jaran shrugged. "My mother seldom spoke of our past, despite my prying. I knew my father Hrelgi had been killed, but not by whom. Or where we came from originally—she said that knowledge would destroy me. I raged at her often, but now I regret that. The witch Sheega probably had a hold on Bera too."

"Where is your mother now?"

Jaran shook his head. "Probably still in that cave, if she lives."

He felt a wash of sadness rush over him. "She helped sick folk in the nearby village. Bera had healing skills and was popular, though she never lingered where people were."

"A cave?" Savarna pressed her warm body closer to his, as the wind rose up and a deep chill entered their fold where they nestled. "You seldom mention your childhood, or that terrible scar."

"Both are like a dream to me," Jaran sighed. "*Surreal.*"

"Tell me," she smiled. "Best you can."

"Very well then, I'll start with the scar . . . I was hunting away in the hills, fourteen winters, I think. I'd argued with mother, yet again. She'd warned me not to go far, but I was angry. The wolves surrounded me, eventually attacked. I killed some, but the others tore upon me. I thought I was done for. Then that great white bear came from nowhere and the wolves fled."

"I thought it was the bear that scarred you?"

"It was," Jaran said. "A huge white creature, like out of a fable. I remember how it reared so tall over me. I heard it roar, then felt the pain ripping me apart. Next I remember waking and a hooded man standing over."

"The Traveler." She smiled. "And what of him? Who is he?"

"I don't know," Jaran said. "But Bera knew him and feared him, though she said we owed him everything. There was scant love between them." He sighed. "I traveled with him for a time, but he revealed little of himself. He's a trickster, or warlock. Perhaps even a god—who knows? I'll never understand these riddles."

"You will." She held his hand, smiled again. "Like Tyho, that Traveler needs you—so you'll learn the truth about him one day."

Jaran shrugged. "It took both of them months to heal me. He returned two years later, and after quarreling with mother again, I decided to journey with him. Bera had taught me some basic fighting skills she'd learnt from Hrelgi, who she said had been the best warrior she'd known. The Traveler schooled me in more.

"I was strong and fit, and learned quickly. He told me about Shen, how they'd employed Northmen for centuries. A good honorable career. We parted company and I rode east, enlisted in Hranic's Auxiliaries at the river. For ten years, I fought the Card Immortals along the frontier, mostly enjoying the life. Gromaki of Leeth insulted me, and everything changed."

"But how did Fin know about your past, and why would he care?"

"That I do not know. For such a big talker, he's a closed one." Jaran turned his head and stared hard into her gold-flecked eyes. "I'll find out eventually. Far more pressing to me is, why are you still here, Savarna?"

"I was hoping you might have worked that out by now." She smiled again. Jaran stroked her hair, the deep red color sparkling in the firelight. He glanced up to where Finvar sat smoking, his back to them. Then, on impulse, Jaran reached across and kissed her lips gently.

"That was nice," she said, responding eagerly, and pressing herself against him.

RAGAN GENZA SPURRED HIS HORSE ALONG THE HIGH mountain pass. He was angry and bitter, his father having insulted him by sending him out with this barbarian and such a small company of men. But no great surprise. Genza was convinced the Ran wanted him dead. The most troublesome of Calla's nine sons could meet with a convenient accident at any time. This rash trip into Leeth seemed like an ideal opportunity. For all he knew, Ran Calla might have ordered the vile Northmen riding at his side to slit his throat while they camped. A sober thought, and he'd keep his knives close.

Genza wasn't a warrior born like his father and grandfather before him. But he was no fool, being sharp of wit and clever. The current Ran was obsessed with his own glory, outdoing their magnificent forbear, the all-conquering Carda.

Fuck glory, thought Genza. What mattered was control, and in the places where you lived—not the other side of the world. Shen would most likely fall to them, *but so what?* They might get richer. They were stinking rich already. In his determination to overthrow an age-old foe, Calla had ignored the growing issues at home. Laregoza, their ancestral land, was falling apart. Most the towns and gardens, temples, libraries—all the culture created by his ancestors over so many centuries had been neglected.

And the people were ignored throughout the region known as Greater Cardalan, a cross-culture vastness loosely described as a republic. Calla's warriors did as they pleased wherever they went, living like heroes, while the common folk struggled to find enough food. Not that Genza gave a shit about that. But neglected people become dangerous over time. Carda the Conqueror knew that and made it serve a purpose. Genza's father had forgotten. And most his other sons were too stupid to think past their organs.

But not Genza. *I'm a survivor.* And if that meant usurping the old man, so be it. Suffice to say he wasn't much trusted by Calla. Chosen for this *worthy* task. A wild ride north into barbarian lands, to meet with some grubby, petty king and collect a squad of oafish Northman to help on the front. Fighting other Northmen.

They'll probably switch sides and kill us the moment they meet up. Calla glanced slyly sideways at the heavily bearded giant riding beside him. Holtarn, one of three brutish brothers who'd recently arrived in Cardalis. Youngest son of King Erlund, who had promised his father two hundred Northmen in return for Calla's help killing another Northman. Didn't make much sense.

Holtarn saw him staring and grunted. He sat on his horse like a sack of grain. Ungainly, scruffy, the great battle axe hanging from his waist, together with round shield slung across his back, spear and sword in saddle. A warrior born, *like father.*

The other two sons had opted for joining the invasion with Calla. But this monster seemed more loyal to his father. Loyalty, *fuck that.*

"We're in my country," Holtarn said, his accent strange to Genza's ears. Rough, deep and grating.

"Happy to hear it," Genza said, turning back, and making sure the score of soldiers were keeping close. Their captain, Magar, saluted him. Good man, Magar—his man, not not father's. "Thought this trip might take forever."

"You are city people. I prefer the wild lands," Holtarn said.

Well, that's a fucking surprise. "How far?"

"Day's ride—no more. We shall feast with my father by evening."

Probably on dog, or something equally ghastly. They'd ridden the long-twisted roads across the Urgo heights, then through the bleak moors and highlands of cold Rethen, skirted the dark lakes of Hragglund, and finally they were here, in this vast wooded mass of nothing. The realm of elk and bear, eagle and . . . *death.*

"I hope you can drink, Card." Holtarn laughed at his expression. The man was too obtuse to register the loathing Genza felt for him.

Drink. Of course I can drink. Most likely in Leeth that would mean stale beer—or worse, fermented milk from some cow's tit. "I prefer not to be addressed as Card," Genza said. "You weren't to know, but it's a derogatory term. I'm Laregozan, born there—by the warm sea. A thousand miles away." *Where people wash.* "Cardalan is just a confederation of several countries. *Cards* are things you lose money with."

Holtarn was smiling, looking up at the sun spilling out between the trees. "It's nice to be home . . . *Card.*" he grinned viciously at Genza.

And fuck you, too.

True to Holtarn's word, they reached Grimhold Castle late that evening. Genza's first impression was *shithole.* A rustic, ancient assemble of dark ugly stone. Crude crenulation and arrow slots. Portcullis and gate, and filthy frozen moat. A square set of circular towers, squeezed tight between two long ridges of hills. A sight about as welcoming as his last dose of crabs.

Once through the gates, they dismounted, and their horses were taken by grooms. Inside, the castle was even worse. Filthy, cold, the flags covered in shit. He saw miserable, ragged people huddled in alcoves, and hounds chasing each other and snarling over scraps. Even fowl, capering about, shitting and squawking. One crossed his path, so he gave it a sly boot, feathers and feet sailing off.

King Erlund met them in his hall. A dingy affair of dark recessed hearth, and darker stone. The walls draped depressing tapestries of some dismal hunt occurring in a wood. Long benches, longer tables, these flanking a half-lit trench fire, a choking mass of smoke without heat. Not nearly enough candles to dispel the murk.

"Welcome," the king said, as Genza was introduced by his son. "This is Grimhold Castle, ancient house of the Kings of Leeth." Erlund was a big man, though his son Holtarn dwarfed him. He looked hard and cynical, hair dark for a Northman. Blue eyes haunted, distrusting. *You'd have to be, living here. Even the sheep would probably knife you.*

"It's good to be here, Lord," Genza lied smoothly. He detected a flicker of doubt in the king's face. This rustic ruler looked brighter than his son. But also . . . *tortured.* As though something ate him from within. He was neatly bearded and graying at the temples. He wore expensive furs and a felt cap, unlike most of the men Genza had seen who were clad in iron. Erlund had a sword hanging from his belt, together with a hunting horn. Aside that, the gold chain around his neck was the only adornment.

"We will be holding a feast shortly," the king said. "First, I wanted to speak with you alone to discuss our . . . arrangement."

"Father didn't really enlighten me," Genza said, accepting a horn of ale. He sipped it. Wasn't completely horrible, so sipped again. "He just ordered me to collect your men and bring them back to Cardalis."

"What of Jaran Saerk? Is he apprehended?"

"If you mean the lout who tore up the ancient Halls of Antiquity, then *no*. He escaped."

King Erlund's face blanched white. "That is not good to hear."

"My father, the Ran, has promised to find him, deal with the rogue, and the other two individuals."

"You had best tell me what happened down there." Erlund's

blue eyes flashed anger. "Else I withdraw my loan of two hundred men."

"I'm only the fucking messenger," Genza said, but he told the king everything he knew.

AFTER THE FEAST, ERLUND SAT UPON HIS COLD THRONE alone with his thoughts. The fires had dwindled to flickers and faggots, the three great hounds sprawled sleeping on the ale-stained rugs. He was drunk and miserable. Didn't like the prick Ran Calla had sent.

One of his younger sons, and obviously not much loved, as he'd been sent up here. Erlund had promised that warlord two hundred fighting men. Northmen—the best warriors in the world. In return for an arrogant pup informing him that Jaran Saerk had sprung the net . . . again.

And where the fuck was his nephew?

Erlund glanced around the hall as though expecting Jaran Hrelgisson to burst through a wall, screaming vengeance for his father's death. It was *her* fault. *Sheega.* She could have worked harder, found the mother and murdered her, together with the child. Instead, she had insisted they do nothing until the appointed year. *This year.*

And Jaran Saerk was on the loose again. Getting stronger. Where else would he be but heading here to Grimhold to repay a debt long owed? He'd contemplated sending the whelp Genza back empty-handed—even better, lashed naked to a donkey. But after careful consideration, he believed it wise to stay in league with this Cardalan bastard. Ran Calla looked to be the next great leader in the known world. So why piss off Calla's slippery son when he'd already too many foes? And a promise must be kept. Erlund was a Northman. He might detest himself, but he did have that. *My word is good.*

The promised two hundred would ride out at dawn. Genza and his escort with them. Holtarn had opted to stay, which was a shame. But at least his brothers were far away. Holt on his own would prove manageable, if quarrelsome and surly.

Useful, in fact. He'd send the boy out with a raiding party, ranging the countryside, looking for any vagrants or travelers. Keep Holtarn busy, and maybe the boy would find Jaran before he reached Grimhold.

Then there was his wife to consider, and the milky-eyed lover who now shared her bed. Ranning had visited the castle in the depth of winter. He'd appeared like a ghoul in the dead of night, calmly introducing himself.

"Don't let us down," he'd said, before fading back inside the walls from whence he'd emerged. Erlund, terrified, had drunk himself dizzy. *They're up to something, that dreadful pair.* Sheega and Ranning. The witch from Dunnehine, and the . . . whatever he was. A watery, slippery being from some distant nightmare realm. Sheega had mentioned *Faerie* of course. Erlund had never believed in its existence. But since Ranning's appearance, he'd come to change his mind.

"I'm a king, but I might as well be a beggar," he said to the dogs at his feet. He slurped the last dregs of his ale and then tossed the horn against one of the ancient priceless tapestries of Enromer Forest, badly smearing the trace work.

Whatever has become of me, Hrelgi? You were the lucky one, dying that day. Would that it wasn't me who'd done the deed. I thought you but a bear . . .

He was morose, depressed and very drunk as always at this

hour. Erlund sobbed damp tears that nobody would hear. Tomorrow he would go hunting. Drive those demons back inside. After that, feast and get drunk again. A dismal cycle. What he did these days.

THE GIRL WAS SHAKING AS SHE STOOD WAITING IN THE cold rain. The healer's shabby hut was more of a hunter's hide, miles from anywhere, hidden deep in Enromer Forest. A half-day's walk from Grimhold village where she lived with her sickly father.

This wise-woman came to Grimhold sometimes to beg for food and necessaries. She'd helped several people who sought her out, easing tooth pain or young women's problems. Her father had heard of the healer's skills, and in desperation sent his daughter, Gunsala, to seek her out.

She loved her father, and so had wanted to help. But now she was here, in the terrifying Enromer Forests—a place about which she'd heard so many frightening tales—Gunsala was afraid. Standing cold and wet, surrounded by ancient oaks and ash, as the icy rain spilled and lightning speared between the slimy trunks of winter trees.

A faint light glimmered within. Gunsala took a deep breath and knocked on the moss-covered wattles that served as a door.

"Enter," a rough voice said. She forced the contraption of wood out the way and climbed inside.

"You've come from the village," the woman said, though that was obvious.

"My father . . ."

"Is dying, Gunsala—I'm sorry."

"You . . . How do you know? You haven't met him, don't know who we are."

"I know things I shouldn't. *Dark things*, sad." Gunsala strained her eyes to see the huddled shape more clearly.

"Peiter will die, child. But I can give you plants to ease his passing."

Gunsala failed to stop the tears. She wasn't surprised, knew this to be the truth. But she'd hoped this healer in her hide-shack could do something. "I'll take the plants then," she said. "What do you require in return?"

"I would have news," the healer woman said. "Anything you hear, but particularly about the king . . . and his wife."

"His . . . *wife?*" She shook her head, confused. "You wish me to come back here?" Gunsala felt a shudder building inside.

"Yes, and often," the woman said. "I grow old and clumsy. It's not so easy to travel, and Grimhold's guards hold no love for a beggar woman. In return, I'll teach you all I know about healing, and other things."

20

STOON

A SHIMMER of light partially blinded him, a flash of movement away on another hill. Then he saw the man, if man it was, a tall, powerful shape, clad only in trousers, the naked torso a greenish gray merging with honey-gold, and hair the color of kelp.

Finvar dropped to his belly, the sweat streaking his face, despite the icy chill of that Hragglund morning. He was out early hunting, the other two still stirring back at camp. He'd reached a ridge awarding excellent views of the lake strewn land. They'd done well and made good progress. Another distant ridge announced the border with Rethen, and not too far beyond that lay Leeth.

Finvar had been pleased. He was looking forward to reporting back and delivering the two rabbits he'd shot for break-fast. Then he'd seen the stabbing gleam of light, followed by this creature. Nothing about the experience had been good. Finvar shivered and sweated in dread. A childhood spent just seven miles off the Dunnehine coast ensured he'd always feared the unnatural. His family on Coolega and the fisher-folk frequenting that isle had told many stories, none of them good. And he'd seen things while living there, and heard worse things in the long black nights, as the bitter winds shrieked in from the sea, carrying with them all manner of ill-behaved spooks. But this was worse. Finvar sensed a challenge, felt like the man-thing was watching him, though he was out of sight and well hidden.

Despite his urge to run, he remained put. The man-creature was tall, very strong-looking. He couldn't see a face, the shaggy mass of kelpie hair occluding any features. He, or it, was standing rock still, staring off into the distance. Finvar took deep breaths. He counted to ten, then the figure shimmered and faded, and in moments was gone.

Finvar almost forgot the rabbits in his haste to depart the hill. He scooped them up, grabbed his bow and half-slid, half-stumbled back down the hill. Ahead, the lake country spread wide and flat for countless miles, the still waters flooded red by winter sunrise. The days were short this far north, and so late in the year. They needed to get going, but Finvar's legs were shaking badly.

Jaran stood waiting at their tiny camp close by the nearest lakeshore. Savarna was stretching her long legs and striking the air with her fists—her usual morning routine. Jaran grinned when he saw Finvar staggering, trying to run. The big North-man's blond hair was tied back, and his naked, scarred chest covered in sweat from his routine warm up with Griner.

"Seen a ghost?" Jaran laughed, as Finvar crashed into camp and tossed the rabbits by their fire. "Or was it something you ate?"

"Worse." Finvar glared at him, and Savarna wandered over, her nimble hands threading the cord through her thick hair, neatly tying it back.

"What's wrong with him?" Savarna asked.

"Something's out there," Finvar said. "We need to get rolling, save these coneys for tonight."

"I'm hungry now," Jaran said.

"I'm not fucking joking," Finvar yelled at him. "We need to move, else *that* . . . comes back."

"What did you see, Fin?" Savarna asked, as Jaran glanced at her, his face more serious, the smile having faded.

"A man," Finvar said. "Or at least that's what it resembled. But it was greenish."

"Greenish?" They both looked at him.

"Sort of, and gold sometimes. It shimmered." Finvar hunched down and warmed his hands by the remnant of the fire. "I hate fucking sorcery."

"Are you certain this was a sending, not a trick of the light?" Savarna asked.

"Yes! Bloody right I'm sure. Thing came from nowhere, blinded me. A glare that became a man, or something resembling one. Large oily bugger—even bigger than you, Jaran. Stood there staring into space, yards away from where I stood. Half bollock-naked, with greenish skin and long, messy hair."

"Steady." Jaran leaned down and shook Finvar's shoulder. "You look pale. Where is it now?"

"Gone," Finvar said. "Vanished the moment the sun rose. I don't think it saw me, but I felt like it was searching, sensing I was near."

"Sounds like one of Sheega's sendings," Savarna said, her face pale too, and eyes worried.

Beside her Jaran nodded. He glanced at the rabbits. "You think it will come back."

"How should I know?" Finvar tried to stop his body shaking.

"But I don't want to spend any more time discussing this. We need to move, and quickly."

His friends exchanged glances and nodded. Jaran donned tunic, mail, and cloak. He slung the great axe across his back and lashed the rabbits to his belt. Savarna kicked the fire to ashes and then stamped down on those until nothing remained.

Finvar rose shakily to his feet. "You all right?" Jaran glanced his way.

"I think so," Finvar said. "It was fucking green, Jaran." He didn't mention it again, or that they were nearing the border with Rethen. In fact, Finvar kept unusually quiet that entire day.

They saw no more sightings of anything untoward, just the odd lone elk staring at their passing from beneath the dark canopy of pines.

STOON STOOD ON THE PROW OF THE LONGSHIP, HIS KIN gathered beside him. Ten terrible men sailing for the distant shore. Only Gorvaron and Crane had remained to watch over their queen. Aside those two, Stoon was the strongest of the Witch-Guard. He alone had tested his powers by far-gazing, projecting his mind far across the wildlands. That had worked— he'd spied the archer crouched in those woods. A timid creature. One of the three they hunted. Stoon had enjoyed sensing the man's fear—he made sure his image was seen.

Stoon didn't know who he was, or where he'd come from. But, like his brothers, Stoon was filled with anger and rage. A hatred consumed him for all beings in this land. For he believed he'd been treated unfairly. Made from foul sorcery, with no thought or care as to whether he'd like a say in that. Stoon had no soul, they'd told him that. He was a creature fabricated from Faerie, made to resemble his creator Ranning. Crafted from bladder wrack and runes, grown strong and fast, tended by a canny witch and her elfin lover.

Ranning and Sheega had trained their Witch-Men well. From kelp sack to man, they had grown swiftly and strong. Fleet of foot, and lethal with sword, axe and spear. Hard to wound, let alone maim and kill. Clever, filled with Ranning's spite. Creatures from the ocean, as was he.

But Ranning well knew the risks. He and his leman had set the codicil, binding the invisible cords, so that neither Stoon or his brothers could turn against them—which they would have done happily in revenge for being born this way.

Their reason for existence was to find the renegade Northman Jaran Saerk and his companions. Kill them, collect their heads and then return to the island. After that . . .

Stoon was ready to think about that. He would do as charged, and enjoy it. To kill was the only pleasure he could imagine, so he'd take his time when he caught up with the prey. He knew where they were and kept the information to himself. That way, Stoon could deprive his brothers the kill and have some fun before returning to the island with the Northman's head.

THAT NIGHT, FINVAR COULDN'T SLEEP. HE SAT STARING AT their small fire, and where the other two lay half-hidden beneath firs, their camp high on the ridge that marked the boundary between Hragglund and Rethen.

Close by, Jaran snored rigorously and the woman shifted in

the big man's arms, the two lovers locked together. Normally, Finvar would smile at the joy his friends had discovered in each other. But not tonight. It was all he could do to stop himself jumping up and kicking Jaran, stopping that racket.

Fuck this. Finvar tossed the Tseole blanket aside. He stood flapping his arms, summoning warmth. High above, a crescent moon winked down at him through trees. No wind, the glimmer of ice coating the ridge, and slopes casting a ghostly silver sheen.

He gathered bow and knife. He walked for a time, hopping from ridge top to crest, passing beneath more trees. Wandering lost beneath their silent green canopy, the moon keeping pace above. He heard a sharp call and stopped, shivering, grasping the bow tighter. An owl, or some night bird hunting. Finvar walked on until the trees opened on wide views, the moon and stars allowing enough light to glimpse the wide realms beyond.

Finvar felt a strange sensation inside. The owl spoke again. *Hoo, hoo* . . . It was speaking to him— he could understand the words.

And Finvar answered. He didn't know how it happened, but then he never did. He felt his form shift, twist and morph. He changed, became a bird—arrow swift and keen of eye. Finvar lifted up into the cold empty night. Looking down, he could see his man-body standing there, bow in hand, a shadow cast by moonlight.

He cried out shrill and clear. The owl answered. *Hoo* . . . A surge of joy, Hawk-Finvar felt the night air rush past him, as he lifted—ever higher—winging up, soaring like a dart toward the silver moon. For long minutes, he held that course, until the owl spoke to him again, her voice a soft calm echo in his ear.

Hoo . . . *This way,* she said. *I will show you* . . .

Finvar replied with a shrill call and changed direction,

winging west, fast and light—a meteor, or lightning shaft blazing across the night sky. The joy of flight filled him, and he felt his wings lifted and ruffled, as the cold night-thermals tugged and pulled.

Finvar flew. The hills, forests and lakes were passing swiftly below. To his north, he glimpsed a wide mass of formless ice, sparkling and glinting back starlight, a shimmering sheen of translucent white. His man's mind registered that as Pack Ice Bay. Southwards ranged dark mountains. He'd reached Leeth. Hawk-Finvar surged lower, swooping, diving. He saw a dark line, and the distant craggy lump of towers resembling a castle thrust tight between hills.

That is Grimhold, the owl woman told him, her voice soft, yet loud enough fill his ears.

Finvar drifted on the thermals, let his wings guide him toward another distant gleam that grew until it filled the horizon. *The western ocean.* He'd reached it at last.

Finvar passed a broken line of cliffs and saw the thin, wavy worms of white water writhing far below. He dropped down there, plummeting at speed, then correcting, and skimming close to wave, leaving the dark shore of Leeth far behind.

Ahead loomed a fog, a murkiness where shapes shifted and moved around. The hawk slowed its flight, the man's mind inside felt a stab of fear and uncertainty.

Yes, the owl told him. *The mist hides Valkador. You must break through its maze, Finvar the Droll.*

I cannot go in there! The hawk banked, commenced circling. Hawk-Finvar felt heavy, his wings suddenly tired, struggling as fresh cold wind lashed them from the towering fog.

I won't! Fin called out to her, but the owl had gone. He felt the icy damp of that fret pulling him down like leaden weights lashed around his wings. Hawk-Finvar cried out once with the bird voice and then plunged into the mist-hidden water.

A thud, and crash. Finvar opened his eyes. He was a man again, prostrate, arms stretched wide, the bow lying beside him. He felt sick and frozen to the marrow. He staggered to his knees and spewed out seawater until his stomach retched empty, and he lurched forward in pain.

"What's happening to me?" Finvar said, as he stumbled to his feet, and bleary-eyed watched the sun rise above the myriad lakes of Hragglund far behind. He turned slowly, and for the briefest instant saw a woman watching him. A woman with gold-green eyes. He recognized her as the owl. *You must go back there, free the creature Rune,* her voice spoke inside his head.

"I cannot go back there."

You must . . .

"Who are you?" Before Finvar could blink, she had shimmered, faded and was gone—replaced by an owl that glided away, then settled on a branch and watched him with the same unblinking eyes.

Angry, Finvar glared at the creature, instinctively reaching for his bow. Wondering if that had been Sheega, come to pay him a visit. He stopped when a hoarse shout turned his head. Jaran Saerk was marching toward him, the heavy axe clung in both hands, and face red with exertion and fury.

"What the fuck are you doing out here?" Jaran stowed Griner and cuffed him, knocking Finvar to his knees. "Been searching the woods for you for over an hour—thought you were dead, or lost. Or your flashing spook had taken you."

Shaking, Finvar regained his feet and gave Jaran a measured look. "I'm in one piece. Though I'm no longer sure who I am, or what I'm becoming." Jaran looked at him sideways, saying nothing. Finvar managed a wry grin. "I've seen your island, North-man. Or at least the place where it's hidden in fog."

"You flew again." Savarna greeted them with a concerned expression when they loped back into camp. She had her gear ready, and they set off without further ado.

"It was the first time I knew what I was doing," Finvar said, after they had trekked for several hours. "In control, not a dream, and I wasn't being attacked. I knew exactly where I was going. There was an owl hooting, a woman—next minute, I'm talking to her and flying straight to the coast."

"You must be getting better." Savarna flashed him a grin.

"I don't know," Finvar said. "That woman could have been Sheega. She didn't seem unfriendly, so I'm not sure. She told me to go back."

"And you think you saw Valkador?" Jaran raised a brow at Savarna.

"I didn't see it—the island was covered in mist. Sheega's mist," he added. "There were faces in that nasty murk. I dared not penetrate, though the owl-woman told me I must."

Jaran scratched his head. "I wish I believed we're making the right choice. How can we kill this witch Sheega, if we cannot even get to Valkador?

"Rune—she mentioned him again," Finvar said. They stared at him with blank expressions. "Rune must be saved, she said. He can help us."

"We'll find a way," Savarna said, as Jaran rolled his eyes.

"I don't know what to suggest," Finvar said. "A more imme-diate problem is dealing with any wights or fetches she throws our way. It's a long walk to the coast. I'd love to fly us—but it doesn't work that way. Something brings it on. Long trek," he added to himself when they didn't respond. "A lot of bad things could happen on the way."

"I have thought on this," Jaran said. "We should turn north, make for Pack Ice Bay—it's not far, and won't cost us more than a day. There are fur stations up there. The northern Rethen do some trade with Hragglund and Leeth. They are strange people, distant and closed, unlike most Northmen—who are warm and friendly like me." He grinned at Finvar, while Savarna laughed and squeezed his hand.

"And also, strange," Finvar said, a wry smile creeping back, as he finally recovered from his recent frights.

"The Rethen are fur traders mostly," Jaran said. "They have camps near, and on the ice, where they drill holes and mine for minerals, salt and such. The Traveler and I passed through one of their trading stations when I was a lad. They had horses and wagons, some were for sale. They might have news of Sheega, too."

"We divert to the endless ice and hope to purchase a nag?" Finvar said. "Seems like a sketchy plan, big fellow."

"Be a lot easier if you flew us direct to my island, or at least the coast of Leeth." Jaran winked at him. Finvar scowled, not appreciating the joke.

"As I keep telling you—it doesn't work that way."

"But you could try, Fin," Savarna said.

"Not today. I'm bloody knackered."

SHEEGA WOKE AND LIT A CANDLE. SHE WAS ALONE IN THE hall, the bear furs cast aside from when Ranning had left. Doubt-less off to stroll the ocean again, as he always did during these long nights. Calling to his people deep below that churning water. She shivered, dressed quickly in furs and heavy gown, and made for her chamber at the end of the hall.

Gantallian's mocking face greeted her as soon as she had the candles lit. "Your Witch-Men have landed," the face inside the mirror said, the metal distorting again.

"Good. They will make for Grimhold, and snatch Jaran Hrelgisson and his friends when he seeks Erlund."

"Jaran is not making for that castle," Gantallian said, his imp voice grating her nerves. "He and his cohorts range north through Rethen—a predictable move had you thought over it. Ranning's abominable creation, Stoon, almost had the hawk-man in his sights."

"Stoon did what?"

"Travelled." Gantallian's steel claws tapped the inner surface of the mirror, rendering it quiver like a copper basin sending ripples down its length. "Dream-traveled. Didn't know they could do that—interesting."

"Shut up, imp." Sheega sent a sharp mind probe out to her Witch-Men. She sensed a blur—it mingled into faces. She saw her team. Ten huge figures loping down a track framed by ancient trees, spears slanted over shoulders, swords and axes hanging from belts, and serpent shields strapped to their backs.

Then a mind bolt blasted through the window and struck her shoulder, knocking Sheega to her knees. Stoon's angry face appeared, then faded away again. Sheega regained her feet, swearing vehemently as Gantallian's metallic laughter filled the room.

"I told you," he said. "That one's sentient."

Sheega ignored the imp in the mirror. Instead she reached out again, but this time shielded herself and dug deeper, mind-scoping and probing carefully inside Stoon's skull. She almost quavered when she felt the savage hatred stored in there.

What do you want with me . . . mother . . .?

"You have ranged far, Stoon, and alone. That was unwise. And why didn't you report back as was required? You are a team leader, not a lone agent."

I sensed their heat as I mind-traveled.

"You know where they are, then? It's as Gantallian tells me."

I shall pay them visit, Stoon's face flashed and faded—she'd lose him any moment.

"Go find them, you and your brothers." The air crackled and shutters rattled. She caught another brief glimpse of Stoon's heavy visage, then he vanished.

"Stoon won't tell the others you spoke to him," Gantallian said. "He's over-proud like his father. He wants Jaran all for himself."

"That doesn't matter if he succeeds, and why wouldn't he— with that loathing brimming like poison tar inside." She pinched the candles, left the murky face in the mirror behind, and walked out into the hall. Ranning stood there, naked and dripping.

Sheega unclasped her cloak and loosened her gown. He reached for her and pulled her down. "Stoon has the far-sight, and he can travel," she said huskily, then gasped as he forced himself upon her.

21

AT THE FRONTIER

VALGARN GRINNED at his older brother as they walked along the decking flanking the riverbank. The Shen River flowed and eddied a few feet away. A brown sludge of churning water, the far banks a vague haze over a mile distant. Ahead were staging crafts, storehouses, ferries—all manner of contraptions and sheds containing military equipment. They'd reached the frontier. A vast sprawl of camps and constant motion, where the warlord spearheaded his forces, preparing for winter's end and spring's invasion.

Ran Calla had explained their situation in grand, sweeping tones. Gesticulating and pointing, describing this skirmish and that great victory raid. The river had been a frontier for generations, centuries even. A convenient stalemate, where Shen politicians and generals staged strategic mini-plots, and the Cardalan generals replied with counter-strike and vengeful raids. A shallow, pointless business, Calla had explained as they walked along the foggy banks of the Shen in early morning. Cold and bright, the mist rising from the river to their right.

But the endless, fruitless strife was over, Calla had told Valgarn. He'd also introduced the Northman and his brother to three of his sons stationed at the camps. Dalgara was station commander, and Casca and Carasan, both generals—all three were tough-looking veterans who had summed up Valgarn and Gorn with cold, distaining eyes.

"Those are my best boys," Calla had said afterward, though Valgarn hadn't been impressed. They'd moved on from where his preferred offspring were discussing the planned move through Dunnehine, a tactic that Valgarn found most curious.

"Those lads are warriors born," Calla said, "not scheming connivers like Conorax and Raska, or treacherous shites like my youngest brat." The warlord had often spoken of his distrust for most his offspring. He had seven daughters, but seldom mentioned them. It was six of the nine sons that caused him concerns. The worst being Genza, the youngest. A spoilt turd whom Calla had ordered accompany Holtarn north to Grimhold to fetch Erlund's promised Northmen—much to Gorn and Valgarn's mirth. Holtarn had got what he deserved, fretting about father and not wanting to strike out alone. In Valgarn's opinion, Holtarn and Genza deserved each other.

They reached the nearest jetty, where a large raft had just moored. Ferrymen tied off and stowed their poles, as the small group of passengers disembarked carefully. They wore pointed conical hats and heavy furs. Their faces, when visible, were pale, and their eyes coaly black and deceitful.

"Excellent timing." Calla rubbed his hands and shouted to the guard captain authorizing their arrival with papers, standing tall outside a shed clearly built for the purpose. "Come with me, my new friends—you'll want to hear this."

Valgarn glanced at Gorn, who shrugged and grinned. Both

brothers were enjoying this morning tour. Ran Calla had been a good companion on the long ride east. He was also the perfect host—they'd had fresh girls every night, and plenty of good ale—brandy, too. Holtarn was most likes sleeping under a horse in Leeth. Valgarn returned his brother's grin. Both knew they chose well in coming here.

The ferry-guard captain saluted as Calla walked briskly up. "Greeting, Tolvar," he said, gruffly. Valgarn was impressed how the Ran knew all the officers' names. A warrior who led from the front. A man worth fighting for, providing the pay was as good as he'd promised. And why wouldn't it be?

The Shen lined up. Their thin, white faces looked awkward, their coaly eyes suspicious.

"Are you going to kill them?" Gorn asked, indiscreetly in Valgarn's opinion. *Stupid question*, even by his brother's standards. Obviously, this was some prearranged rendezvous. A parley before the game commenced. Calla wasn't fazed by Gorn's obtuse words, despite Valgarn's warning flash at his brother.

"No, no. We don't fight today." Calla waved his arms as he approached the dozen or so richly clad Shen. "These men are the Magister's people, therefore potential allies. Chulan is sensible for a Shen, and has promised aid in taking Pol Shen in return for some favors, the principle one keeping his head on his shoulders when we arrive through the city gates."

"Who's Chulan?" His brother again. Second stupid question inside a minute. Gorn was excelling himself this morning. Unlike Valgarn, Gorn hadn't shown much interest in the enemy. Valgarn liked to know who he'd be fighting in the coming weeks. He'd asked around and learnt all about the Shen hierarchy. The empress, her guard, the auxiliaries, and High Magister Chulan—the real power in Shen, now apparently owned by Calla. This was getting better all the time. Valgarn hoped there'd be enough killing and the great invasion wouldn't prove a disappointment. Small glory when the enemy begged at your feet.

He stopped close behind the Ran as they jumped down onto the jetty where the Shen retinue were lined up. Valgarn counted seven soldiers, heavily armored, their faces masked by steel-mesh veils. They carried curious spears, the blades long and curved, almost leaf shaped, and the edges serrated. Cruel, nasty-looking weapons. Valgarn liked the look of them.

Beside the warriors stood the officials in their robes and cloaks wriggling like irritable babes, the sheets torn off their cots. The leader was a thinnish individual with a narrow face, thinning hair, and long moustache. His hands were buried inside a woolen muff. He looked soft, unhappy, his white features taut. Valgarn wondered if he was constipated. He'd often seen that look in his father when Erlund spent hours in the privy.

The Shen bowed stiffly when Calla strode to meet them—all save one smallish man Valgarn hadn't noticed before. This one alone looked confident. Arrogant even, his dark eyes bored. He stood with feet braced and arms neatly folded, slightly away from the others. He caught Valgarn's gaze and smiled.

Valgarn whispered in the ferry-captain's ear when he drew alongside. "Who's the little fucker with the evil black eyes and those twin blades hanging from his back?"

"That's Gujun," the captain grunted. He shuffled and looked uncomfortable. "He's a killer." He turned away to attend his affairs.

"Welcome, ministers and secretaries. We are friends today." Calla spread his arms wide in greeting. The leading official stepped forward and bowed briefly again.

"Mighty Ran, I'm Secretary Ghee. I lead this conference

party and bid you sincere felicitations from Magister Chulan." Valgarn was still watching the killer Gujun. The small man looked amused by the secretary's words.

"He's one to watch," Valgarn muttered in Gorn's ear.

"More likely one to kill," Gorn coughed back. The man, Gujun, smiled again—as though he'd heard their words.

"Good to know," Calla said. "How fares the excellent Chulan? Is he busy preparing for our arrival?"

"He is, Great Ran—as are all his people, myself included. The empress and her regime are corrupt and decaying, like the ancient Ptarni who your noble ancestor destroyed. It's past time for regime change, and we will ensure the city is yours at the appropriate hour."

"Fine words." Calla's eyes were hard slots of violet. "But I'll need some assurance, a show of your loyalty to the cause."

"Name it." Secretary Ghee stiffened uncomfortably.

Calla smiled and turned to grab Valgarn and Gorn's cloaks. "Come forward, my friends, show yourselves to the good secretary here."

They complied and stood towering over the nervous Ghee. The other officials looked shocked, terrified even, and the soldiers tense, their steel gloves gripping those curious spears. The man Gujun was grinning openly, as though he was the only individual present who knew what was occurring here.

"You . . . have *Northmen* . . ." Soma Ghee said, his narrow eyes flicking over Valgarn and his brother.

"And more coming," Calla said. "The new king in Leeth has decided to aid the Cardalan cause. He no longer deems it appropriate to serve Shen, as his kin have for so many years. The loyal puppies have turned into wolves—isn't that right, Gorn? Valgarn?" Calla grinned across at them.

"We are here to kill Calla's enemies," Valgarn said, staring hard at Gujun, who shrugged indifference. *I'm starting with you, shithead.* Valgarn glared at the figure poised like a dancer at the end of the jetty.

Ghee seemed lost for words, so Calla continued. "So! Since we are discussing Northmen, you can prove useful by bringing me the head of one of yours?"

"Lord Ran?" Ghee's narrow face looked pinched.

"I speak of Hranic Finehair."

"The Auxiliary Captain?" Ghee looked openly shocked.

"I know who he is." Calla's eyes hardened again. "A constant thorn in my side, much like these mens' cousin, whom your Magister recently outlawed I believe."

"You mean Jaran Saerk? He's still alive?" Ghee's voice appeared on the brink of breaking.

"Roaming the Northlands, I believe." Calla laughed at the man's worried expression. "I've promised his head to their father. And you, Secretary Ghee, can go fetch me Hranic's."

"That will prove difficult." Soma Ghee whispered something to his fellow officials, who nodded sharply, their faces bleak. "But possible, yes. I will see to it in person."

"Excellent." Calla's broad face beamed mock joy. "I'll expect the trophy this time next week."

"I . . ." Ghee looked horrified, but Calla turned away and smiled at Valgarn and his brother. The party of Shen looked even more miserable, especially since a veil of cold rain had started spilling on the jetty deck.

"You can go back to your little foxholes." Calla waved a dismissive hand, and signaled to the captain to ready the ferry for departure again. "That went as planned." He grinned at the brothers.

"Who is this Northman, Hranic Finehair?" Valgarn asked Calla, as they left the jetty behind and made for one of the canteens, where the welcome smell of bacon meant breakfast. "Why not let us kill him? Why trust those little turds?"

"The Shen are crafty—don't underestimate them," Calla said. "But they are also cowards, and that man knows the lie of the land. Ghee wants to keep his head, and station, as does his master Chulan. Don't worry, there'll be plenty of Northmen left for you to fight and kill— honorable foes, unlike the scrawny Shen."

They entered the canteen and were served immediately. A full steaming plate of bacon, sausage, eggs, and mushrooms—all washed down with small beer and fermented yak milk, a favorite among the garrison stationed here.

After they'd eaten, a soldier appeared and quietly whispered in Calla's ear. "Gujun the Slayer waits outside, Lord Ran."

"Ah, yes—so he didn't depart with the others." He turned to Valgarn and Gorn and smiled. "Come with me."

Gujun waited quietly, until Ran Calla appeared with the two Northmen alongside. Huge brutes—even for that ungainly race. Blond, shaggy hair and rough forked beards. Unkempt, so unlike the neat styled Shen. Barbarian oafs for sure. These two were even uglier than normal, vicious-looking and heavily armed, with bearded axe and sword at waists, shields across backs and short spears clutched in fists. The pair glowered moodily at Gujun, and the biggest looked like he'd strike him at any moment, or at least try to.

Gujun calmly registered their loathing and waited for the

warlord to speak. Ran Calla was passing instructions to some of his officers outside the canteen, as the Northmen brothers and he waited. At last, done with his administrations, Calla turned and awarded Gujun a wry glance.

"Thought you'd returned with Ghee," he said. Gujun didn't respond, but folded his arms and nodded. "This is Gujun," Calla said to the brutish brothers. "He works for Chulan, therefore is useful to me. A go-between, with special skills. Think you could kill him, Gorn?"

Calla winked at the biggest of the brothers, who stepped forward and towered over Gujun. "Happy to." The Northman spat in the dirt before Gujun's feet.

Gujun stared up at him with disinterest. "Cocky little bugger." Gorn made a show of grabbing his axe in one hand, tugging it free of the loop hole. "Can I split him in two, Calla?"

"You can try." Calla smiled at the other brother, who seemed the brighter of the pair, *though of course all Northmen are stupid.* "Maybe you'll get to splatter your first Shen, Gorn. What say you, Valgarn—want a go, too?"

"I can wait," the other one said, mocking Gujun with his eyes and folding his arms and adding with a grin, "I prefer fighting warriors my own size."

"Ready to die, Gujun?" Calla asked. "I'm sure Chulan can replace you easily enough."

"Dying doesn't bother me," Gujun said. "But that's not going to happen here." He smiled at the biggest brother. "Why are Northmen all so ugly?"

Calla laughed, and the other brother swore, but Gorn's axe swung out, hard and fast for Gujun's neck. He danced aside and grinned up at the big man. "You're quite quick," Gujun said. "For a fat, lazy slug."

Gorn spat rage and swung again, from left to right. Gujun danced out of reach. Gorn stepped forward, panting with fury, face red and puffy. He swung up arcing, and then brought the axe down with a wild, vicious slash that would have split a young oak in two.

Again, Gujun stepped aside, but this time he darted in close, spun on his right foot and launched his left, kicking Gorn hard in the belly. Gorn buckled and cursed. He tugged his axe free from the ground, where the head had buried itself six inches deep.

The Northman swung again, wilder than before, the weapon slicing hard for Gujun's head. He ducked, sent a foot out, and hooked up behind Gorn's leg, twisting and lifting, sweeping the giant clumsy slug from his feet.

Gorn crashed onto his back with a clank and thud. He tried to rise, but Gujun jumped forward and placed his studded boot on Gorn's neck, forcing him down until the man's face reddened with fear. To his right, the other brother reached for his sword.

Valgarn stopped when he saw the knife appear in Gujun's hand, balanced beautifully and ready to fly.

"Enough, Gujun," Calla said, waving a dismissive hand. "You've proved your point."

Gujun nodded to the Ran and removed his foot from Gorn's neck, allowing the Northman, coughing and spewing, to regain his breath and eventually rise to his knees. He looked furious and stared at Gujun with a mixture of loathing and disbelief. The other brother looked more reflective. Yes, this one was bright for a Northman, Gujun thought. He bowed slightly to the Ran and stepped away, folding his arms neatly again.

"I told you not to underestimate the Shen," Calla said, as Gorn rose and glared down at Gujun.

"I was just warming up," the brother spat at him. Gujun considered skewering the oaf for that insult, but decided against it. There were more important matters here.

"Chulan sends apologies," Gujun said. "Secretary Ghee has proved a disappointment of late."

"I'm sure he'll pay for any carelessness," Ran Calla said. He turned to the towering Northmen. "You two go and find a wench or something else to do, and you clean yourself up, Gorn. I will meet with you later." The brothers gaped at him for a moment, obviously perturbed and shocked at being dismissed so out of hand.

The younger, brighter one nodded. "Come on, Gorn, let's go get some ale and leave the Ran to his busy day." Gorn nodded and turned, after awarding Gujun a final acidic glance.

Gujun waited until they were out of earshot. "You have more of these clowns coming?"

"Two hundred," the Ran nodded curtly. "I'll set them amongst Hranic's thugs. I've heard that Northmen like killing each other."

Gujun shrugged, bored with the subject. "You want me to deal with Finehair personally?"

"No, let Secretary Ghee sweat over that. I have a bigger task for you, assassin. The Empress Rasnei—how fares she?"

"Frail and alone, save for ten thousand overrated guards." Gujun grinned. "Who can be bribed."

Calla laughed. "Can you reach her, discreetly?"

"Of course. I can reach anyone, Ran. Though it might prove tricky staying alive afterward. So not much for me to get enthusiastic about, as I'd need considerable time to spend the vast amount of gold you'd be paying me."

"Hmm, yes." Calla nodded. "That's fair enough, and no need

to rush things. But I want her dead, and the family, too—at your convenience. But no later than spring. When Pol Shen tumbles, I want no freedom fighters rallying around a ruler."

"No problem," Gujun said. "Chulan sent me primarily to ask for your aid in the countryside surrounding the city. The Midnight Cutting Crew have reemerged, those same thugs who helped the Tseole kill some of your men In Ferrytown last month."

Calla looked irritated. "Can't Magister Chulan deal with his own internal affairs? Why must I do everything?" Then he smiled. "Let me think on this, Gu. It could be that I'll have a special task for those two brothers you just insulted. Send the Northmen across the river, let them fight each other, and then scour the lands for Gurtei's clowns."

"If you think them capable."

"Tell Chulan to expect my army inside two months," Calla said. "That gives him plenty of time to arrange everything. I trust the Magister will ensure everything is accomplished with his usual attention to detail."

"I'll pass on your wishes," Gujun said and turned, making for the second ferry. He'd pole that one across himself. Hard work, but Gujun would enjoy the exercise. He vaulted on to the ferry and reached for the pole. "See you soon, Ran." Gujun waved at Calla standing outside the canteen, his brawny fists resting on sword and ale flask.

"I'll expect you, and news of your accomplishments," Calla shouted across, then vanished inside the canteen. Gujun poled out, allowing the craft to ease into the steady brown flow of the Shen River. Once across, he'd report back to Chulan what the Ran had said.

22

THE ENTERTAINER

RASNEI LET her mind drift and wander as the soft music filled her world, took her far away and led her through a tangled maze of emotions. She strolled through leafy forests, sat naked beneath clear waterfalls, watched the sun fall from the sky, and then rise rose-gold again over distant eastern waters.

Her mind was free. Gone was this court, her servants and slaves, the soldiers—everything mundane that steered her world. The Magister, his people, the war, the enemy growing stronger each day. Also gone were her worries and concerns—driven to far places by the rising magic of the music.

Where did he come from—this uncanny player? A lone musician with a silver flute, sitting cross-legged, surrounded by candles. The flute was clutched in his hands, his deft fingers dancing along its length. Perhaps fifty feet from her dais where she held court, but easy to trap with her keen gaze and the spyglass she held. Rasnei had bid everyone else to leave, so she could hear him better. A small, distant figure clad in russet and green, his hair the sparkle of the sconces that flickered in timing with his song.

Her most trusted courtesan, Mawla Tei, had crept into her chambers this very afternoon, saying that one of the captains in her outer guard—the girl's occasional lover—had heard this singer-player in a crowded tavern. He had been so impressed he'd told her that the empress herself should hear this man. Rasnei, always ready for something new to ease her boredom, had bid Mawla Tei to summon him right away and arrange him to play for her—at a safe distance, of course.

The stranger had played for over an hour, unaccompanied. A beautiful collection of sweeping melodies that commanded her emotions, ruthlessly driving them from melancholy to joy to excitement, and back to melancholy again, as his deft hands worked the instrument and his clear, strong voice sung words she couldn't understand. An ancient alien language from some far-off land.

At last, he stopped, placed the flute in his lap. He bowed, waited.

Rasnei rose to her feet, she clapped once and beckoned the man nearer. "I would see your face, more clearly" Rasnei said, placing the spyglass down. The player nodded and rose to his feet in a swift fluid motion. He was small in build, she noted, but taller than herself. His hair was combed neatly, his face appealing though unusual. He walked toward the base of the dais, his long hair glistening the color of blazing embers.

The player stopped at the foot of the dais. He bowed low, and then stared up at her—a thing forbidden, but it excited Rasnei. She had only to speak loudly, or tug on her bell by the throne, and threescore guards would fall upon this stranger. She chose to do neither. Instead she studied the handsome, tanned features of the player.

"Who are you, minstrel? How is it that we haven't heard of you before?"

"I'm but a traveler, Exalted One. A man between countries, earning what coin he can from plying his trade."

"Where is your home?"

"Rundali, and beyond."

"And your name?"

"Eltayn Salcara."

"A strange name, and yet part of it sounds familiar. You play well, stranger. I would hear you again. Return tomorrow at dusk. My preferred courtesan, Mawla Tei, will escort you via the backrooms to my personal chambers. Once inside, you can play for me again, in private, and while I take my leisure. You may leave us now."

The man bowed again, turned on his toes and walked swiftly from the dais. She noted his balance, lithe graceful strides. In seconds, he had vanished beyond the candles, and the guards that emerged down there allowing him depart through the doors.

"He has talent and intrigues me," she told her servant as Mawla Tei brought her late-night tonic, readied her hands to massage Rasnei's body, and prepared the scented bath. "I've ordered him back tomorrow. Mawla, I need you to ensure he is allowed up into my chambers, without prying eyes."

"Exalted One, is this wise?" Mawla Tei's eyes were dark saucers. Rasnei indulged the girl too much. A weakness she had. She could have had Mawla Tei flayed for questioning her actions. But she liked Tei, who was fiercely loyal, unlike many of the others whom Rasnei suspected were controlled by Chulan. "He could be an assassin," the girl added nervously.

Rasnei said nothing. She drained her crystal vial, letting the strong, warm liquid settle. Then she retired to her inner chamber, casting off her clothes and stepping into the hot, steamy bath. She closed her eyes as the girl worked her nimble fingers along her neck and shoulders. Rasnei breathed deep and sighed as Tei's hands dropped lower, caressing her breasts, then further down, the nimble fingers slipping between her thighs, easing the tension she felt down there. Rasnei smiled and leaned back, allowing Mawla Tei to attend to her fully. She closed her eyes as her body trembled at the pleasure, and her thoughts drifted to the red-haired stranger and his busy silver flute.

GURTEI WATCHED THROUGH THE GRUBBY TAVERN WINDOW as rain beaded the glass. Two hours had passed since their new member had gone inside the palace. The men were edgy, especially Roile, who kept muttering about them all being damned fools, trusting in the Rundali.

An opinion easy to share. But Gurtei did trust Vian. He didn't know why—it wasn't logical. But then he knew the sister and had liked her, too. Unusual twins they made, with the flame red hair and their lethal skills. But, whereas Savarna had been wild and violent, Vian appeared patient and calm, a man who thought things through. Hence his bold idea to enter the palace alone had gone ahead with Gurtei's blessing.

Easy enough, since Truggen's sister had a friend working in the palace. A discreet woman, very well positioned, and apparently favored by Rasnei herself. Trug had spread the word of this amazing flute player who was performing in one of the taverns. Both his sister and the other girl had come to see. Said tavern was owned by a former Cutter. Grint had retired from the gang but kept a busy taproom. He'd changed his name, of course. No one in the city knew his former business, or where his sympathies lay. That said, the innkeep who went by the name Tar Mau was not overly happy about his old friends turning up and booking lodging. Neither had he liked the look of Vian.

"Stands out like a gonfalon flapping in the sunshine," he'd complained, when Gurtei had introduced that evening's entertainment. "Some fucking spy."

Gurtei had suggested Vian dye his hair black, but he'd refused, instead covering his features with a deep hood. He'd played in a dark corner of the inn, where none could see his face. Just two days later, word came from the same girl that Rasnei herself would hear this new troubadour.

Vian had left earlier this evening, a soft smile on his face, while the rest of them had sweated and fretted, drank too much brandy and rice wine, and wished they were anywhere else. It was almost midnight when the hooded and cloaked shape merged out from the lantern-lit gloom of that rainy Pol Shen night.

"He's back," Gurtei said to those Cutters still awake enough to hear. Groggy-faced, Roile and Truggen loomed close.

"Still got his head on—that's good," said Corben's gruff tone from somewhere behind. Gurtei got the door, looked about outside, and waited as Vian entered, his dark cloak shimmering with rain.

"My throat's dry," Vian said, entering the smoky taproom where the Cutters lurked with the odd girl. Gurtei bid Corben get him ale or wine.

"Success?"

"She liked my work." He smiled whimsically. "The empress appreciates the finer arts."

"Well I suppose that's good," Gurtei said, not knowing where this was going. "You couldn't get that close, I suppose? I mean, to make a move."

Vian smiled at him. "Small steps, Gurtei—she's invited me back tomorrow night. And via the backdoors, a secret entrance. She wants me all to herself, it seems."

Gurtei clapped the Rundali's shoulder. "You've done well, Vian. Tomorrow is the night then. How will you escape?"

"Hadn't given that a thought," Vian said, sipping the wine Corben produced. He smiled at the men standing gathered around him. "I'll find a way."

"He's got a fucking death wish," Roile muttered and retired to the corner. "That will trace back to us too, if we stick around here."

"Roile does have a point," Gurtei said. "Chulan's people are everywhere in this city. We daren't stay here much longer."

"No need." Vian placed a hand on Gurtei's shoulder. "You Cutters have done your part, for now. Leave the rest to me. I'll join you on the road south three days hence."

CHULAN WATCHED THE RIDER DISMOUNT AND LOPE UP THE hill. The servants lowered their gaze as he passed. Chulan smiled. They all dreaded Gujun, the black-clad killer with the twin blades slung across his back.

He approached, the afternoon sun blazing from behind him, the servants and slaves hard at work again. The waterfalls and fountains chiming, the small stream gleaming and sparkling as large blue butterflies danced above. An unusually warm day for this early in the year.

Chulan sat back in his divan and sipped his tea, as his messenger emerged through the wicker gates.

Gujun dipped his head. "It is done," he said. "Calla has promised aid mopping up, but he expects the city to be ready for him inside two months, and the empress dealt with during that time. He wants me to oblige him personally there."

"That's delicate." Chulan rubbed his long, drooping moustaches. "Even I can't get past Rasnei's guard without an entrance docket."

"We are talking about me, not you. I can get anywhere I want, and so can my gang. But getting out alive may prove harder, hence I need to bide my time, plan things to finite detail."

"Two months," Chulan said, only half-listening to his man. "That will pass quickly. And Calla still means to attack from Dunnehine, despite the rumors of that land?"

"He does, and wants your help eradicating any stray Tseole or other vagrants in the region. He's planning on setting up the main camp outside Ferrytown and commence building crafts for bay invasion. He'll also cross the river in several places."

Chulan chewed this over. He noted how Gujun looked poised, a half-smile on his hard face. "You have more news?"

"I do," Gujun said. "I met with two Northmen. Ungainly princes, by-blows of some rustic king out there. Their father is sending more, two hundred was the number I heard. Calla means to use these Northmen against Hranic's Auxiliaries. Apparently, they enjoy killing each other. He also promised their aid in dealing with the Midnight Cutters, though Shen soldiers should be able to stamp on those rebels easily enough."

"Ghee has proved tardy dealing with those maggots," Chulan

said. "Interesting about the Northmen, I'd always thought them loyal to Shen."

"What's next?" Gujun folded his arms.

"Hranic Finehair," Chulan said, smiling. "Time for you to pay that particular Northman a visit at the front. I'll need him interrogated, mind, not just murdered out of hand. Hranic might know where Saerk went with the thief and that runaway slave girl. He could be hiding all three of them."

"I've good cause to believe they are in Cardalan," Gujun said. "But I'll happily poke the Auxiliary Captain's arse with a hot iron, in case he does know something."

"Do so, then report back to me soon." Chulan waved the Slayer away and returned to his studies.

DUSK SETTLED THE STREETS OF POL SHEN. VIAN REACHED the back gates leading through the mile-long gardens of the Imperial Palace. The guards were informed of his arrival. A captain ordered the gates opened and insisted on escorting Vian through the intricate maze of green, toward the brightly painted walls of the palace.

The soldier looked hostile and hardly spoke. That suited Vian well enough, as he had time to examine the gardens as he walked, the golden flute clutched in one hand and his booklet of notes in the other. Just for show, as the music was in his head.

Vian gazed at the expanse of green as he walked. Even at this bleak time of year, the gardens were an exotic masterpiece. A design comprising intricate hedges, pristine verges, ornate trees positioned for maximum lighting and effect, and exotic flowers, their yellow and purple heads nodding to him as he passed. He saw wooden-arched bridges spanning chiming streams where brown trout darted below. Beyond these were flame-colored shrubs and bushes rising on earthy banks. There were lanterns winking from alcoves and corners. Vian saw nooks and grottoes half-hidden in twilight, where gentle folk could spend intimate hours together.

Everywhere, slaves toiled in busy silence. The gardens were a wonder to his mind. Such beauty, Vian thought. Soon to be destroyed by the brutish Calla. A great shame. Vian didn't care about the fate of the Shen, but these gardens were special. Without beauty, life was nothing.

Vian and his escort reached the back entrance. A retainer met them there, clad in gold and white, a silk square golden cap on his head, with three long tassels dangling. He and the officer spoke briefly. The official signaled to Vian to follow him inside, as the officer awarded him one last acidic stare before tapping his heels and stomping off back through the gardens.

"You are Rundali," the official said, his manner aloof and words condescending.

"I am, sir," Vian said. "But mostly I'm a traveler, plying my music for custom and coin."

"A high honor, performing for the empress in person." The man's cold tone made it very clear he didn't deserve it.

"Yes—I'm nervous," Vian lied.

"You will be searched thoroughly," the retainer said. They reached an archway leading to a pergola, passing beneath until a small door appeared, its yellow painted wood half-covered in vines. The retainer produced a large key from his satchel, hanging at his belt. He fumbled and fiddled, the key turned and the lock clicked. He opened the door. "Enter," he said, motioning for Vian to go inside. "I will await your return here."

"See you later, then." Vian smiled at the official, whose thin face stiffened in reply. These Shen needed to relax more, Vian thought, as he strode through a long, gloomy corridor toward another distant door.

This one opened as soon as he approached. A heavyset guard carrying a vicious-looking Chiang accosted him. "Spread your legs and arms wide," the man said.

Vian complied, after placing his flute and notes carefully on the floor. The guard signaled, and two others appeared. They searched him thoroughly for several minutes, until satisfied. The leader announced he could enter.

The three escorted Vian through a maze of rooms and chambers, until he reached yet another door. A woman stood there. Neat and pretty, garbed in silver and green silk of the finest quality. Her face was pale, the eyes shrewd black currants.

"You are expected," she said, and then looked at the guards. "You may leave us." They obeyed without hesitation, walking briskly back the way they'd come.

"The empress was impressed with your talent," the woman said. "That's a first since I've been her principal servant."

"You have a name?"

"I do," she said without revealing it. They reached more doors, passed through, then yet more corridors and rooms. Vian was impressed—he'd knew the palace was rumored huge, but this was more than he'd expected. Everywhere he looked, Vian saw gilded tapestries, priceless vases and busts, ornate mirrors, statues, internal fountains and miniature trees—all the fabled artifacts of an age-old culture.

At last, they reached the final doors. The woman awarded him a wry glance, then looked him up and down. "You can take your hood off, Vian Eltayn." She smiled slightly. "The empress knows who you are."

Vian masked his reaction, though inwardly he felt a stab of panic. He pushed the hood back, allowing his bright red hair to spill free.

"My name is Mawla Tei," she told him, and then rapped on the door three times.

"Let him in," a husky voice said from inside.

23

THE VILLAGE

THE DOGS WERE WORKING WELL, the sleigh sliding through the thickly packed snow, the world ahead a dazzling blend of steely blue and virgin white. Jaran was pleased with the progress. They'd done well in Rethen. Three weeks ago, Finvar had used both cunning and coin, acquiring more food and drink, new skis, and—most importantly—the eight dogs and the heavy sled they pulled.

The sleigh had been Savarna's idea. She'd watched a team racing over the ice north of the town where they'd stayed the night. A land of tents and roaring bonfires, the eerie green shimmering phenomena, the Giants' Dance, flickering across the moonless, starry sky.

Finvar had parted with most of his coin, Jaran with his old axe. He hadn't wanted to, but Griner needed both hands, and after the fight in Cardalis, he felt fully comfortable with the formidable weapon. The dark rune-energy locked inside the heavy weapon gave him strength. His other axe was mostly redundant, extra weight he didn't need. And Savarna had offered to share the night with a squinty-eyed, evil-looking trader. She hadn't delivered, but had succeeded in lifting all his coin during the process.

The dogs and sleigh had carried them far across Pack Ice Bay, cutting off a huge corner of Rethen and Leeth, enabling them to reach that latter land's far north and then enter the tundra wastes before heading southwest toward bleak ranging hills and distant gray ocean.

On the evening of the twentieth day after they'd departed Hragglund, they were greeted by a marvelous sight. The western ocean in plain view, sparkling and shimmering, the sun a disk of fire sinking and flooding those waters crimson.

"I was born for moments like this." Finvar brought the sled to a halt. The dogs were well-trained and he'd proved an excellent sled master, guiding and driving the apparatus with skill and precision. "Like the chariots of my ancestors," he'd told them proudly. Jaran had grinned at Savarna hearing that. Neither of them knew who Finvar's ancestors were.

"About ten miles, I'd say." Jaran squinted at the ocean. He felt a strange surge of pleasure, seeing that distant expanse of water. *A homecoming of sorts* . . . "Best we make camp and rest our pack before an early start. As I remember, there are a string of villages along the west coast, even the odd one this far north. Whaling towns, mostly. Once we reach a settlement, we can acquire a craft and plan the crossing to Valkador. You said it isn't far?" This to Finvar, who was urging the dogs toward a dark copse where they'd settle for the night, the first slopes of pine-studded hills rising beyond.

"I was flying, but it was a quick crossing—the distance quite short. The fog was another matter."

"We'll worry about that when we get there."

"Glad you've got this all worked out," Finvar said, and Savarna chuckled beside him. They'd stood arm in arm for most the rides, Finvar driving the craft in front of them, legs braced, hands gripping reins.

"You boys have done well." Finvar fussed at the dogs and fed them the meal they'd bought with the sled. He was fond of the beasts and mostly slept with them, which suited Jaran and Savarna well, as they were spending every night as intimately as was possible, under those bitter freezing starry skies.

Once the dogs had eaten and settled, Finvar fumbled with his pipe and leaned back against a tree. Savarna sat alongside, as Jaran left them to gather firewood. When he returned arms laden, the pair were deep in discussion. He worked the flint, got a blaze going and sat and joined them.

"How do you know they had chariots?" Savarna asked him, looking up and smiling at her lover.

"I don't—it's an educated guess." Finvar chewed on their remnants of jerky. The supplies had lasted well, but they needed to find a village soon or else they'd go hungry. "They got around a lot, always fighting each other."

"In your little island off Dunnehine?" Jaran asked, butting into their conversation.

"*Fuck*, no—I'm talking about my *ancestors*, Northman, thanks for joining us. They were heroic hunters from Khandol."

"I've not heard of it," Jaran said, reaching for the last piece of jerky.

"I think he just made the name up." Savarna smiled, and Finvar looked hurt.

"I most certainly did not." He glared at her, then grinned and winked slyly. "I come from good stock, I'll have you know."

"Where did these Candle people live?" Jaran asked, without much interest.

"Khandol," Finvar said firmly. "A land much like Dunnehine, and bordering Xandoria to its north." Jaran and Savarna exchanged glances. Finvar rolled his eyes.

"You pair really need to brush up on your history. It's why there's so many fuckups in the world—people keep making the same silly mistakes because the past is always forgotten."

"Then why not indulge us, Fin." Savarna awarded him her sunniest smile.

"It was called the Great Continent," Finvar said. "Thousands of years ago, ancient history. There was a big fucking disaster, Xandoria—an empire, and the main power at that time—was destroyed, and most people died. Tragic. The Khands fled . . . whatever *it* was. The thing. A fire dragon, I heard, or some monstrous beast from beneath the ground. My ancestors made boats, sailed west past Gol, watching as that land sunk beneath the water. Long sail, they feared falling off the world-rim of Ansu. Instead, the Khands found a dark shore and settled in what would become Dunnehine, only to be driven away to that skinny island by the warlocks and witches infesting the mainland. My story." He grinned.

Jaran was feeling sleepy, but Savarna nudged his arm, her gold-flecked dark eyes full of wonder. "Gol," she said. "The man I met, before you two found me. You know, in that other place. He said he was from Gol?"

Jaran and Finvar stared at her. "What are you talking about?" Jaran said. "You never mentioned a man, in that place, the weird spider castle?"

"I thought I did, must have slipped my mind," she said,

looking pensive. "So much has happened. I'd . . . forgotten about Carlo Sarfe, what he said."

"Who the fuck is Carlo Sarfe?" Finvar scratched his ear and glanced at Jaran. "Are we missing something?"

"Seems so," Jaran said, his eyes on Savarna. "You'd best explain."

She glared back at him. "Don't look at me like that."

"Didn't know I was," Jaran said. He turned to Finvar. "Help me out here."

"Nah, you're on your own, big lad." Finvar grinned. "I'm off to check on the dogs and get ready for a nice kip."

"You need to hear this, too." Savarna was still glaring at Jaran, her face flushed and angry. He had no idea why. He spread his hands and smiled, and Finvar stared at them both.

"Carlo Sarfe was seated on a rock outside that castle—you know the slimy, black, terrifying place where you found me." They nodded. "He said he was a shipwrecked sailor from Gol. He knew my name, and he asked how you were, Jaran."

"Doesn't make sense." Finvar looked edgy, as he always did around strangeness. "Gol drowned over two thousand years ago. Sounds like a madman, or rogue warlock perhaps."

"I thought the same thing, and asked him where he remembered us from."

"Good thinking," Finvar said. He winked at Jaran. "She's a bright girl."

Savarna rolled her eyes.

"Ignore him," Jaran said, irritated by the glib comments.

"Hard to." She forced a smile. "It was so strange, now I come to think of it. Carlo said he'd last seen us onboard his ship, making for Valkador. Where you, Jaran Saerk, had arranged a meeting with a witch. He described you perfectly, too." She looked almost vulnerable for a moment.

Jaran gripped her hand. "I'm glad you remembered now. Looks like we need to find this wayward sailor, or else hope he finds us."

"Stinks of witchcraft, or worse," Finvar spat. "Sheega could have sent the man, maybe a fetch, or spook—like that shiny thing I saw in Hragglund."

"He was just a man," Savarna said. "He looked as lost and confused as I felt. He also appeared sad."

"Well, another riddle," Jaran said, feeling tired and done with talking. "And I'm sure it won't be our last. Let's get some rest, I want to start at first light. The sooner we find a village on that coast, the happier I'll be."

"You mean you ate the last rations." Finvar cast him a bleak stare.

"Someone had to," Jaran said. "Good night, little man."

An hour later, he lay with Savarna sprawled over him, her hands stroking his chest. He gazed down, placed a soft kiss on her head. "Why were you angry with me?"

"I wasn't." She looked up at him, her large brown eyes unblinking.

"Yes, you were."

"Well, perhaps—a little. Your face, it accused me of hiding things from you. I'd never do that."

"I know." He smiled, and kissed her again. "I'm sorry. I was surprised, that's all."

"And I'm sorry I forgot about him." She smiled and kissed him back. "We are three lost souls, Jaran Saerk. I think he might be the fourth."

"Let's hope we can find him before Sheega finds us."

"We can but try—but where to look?"

"We'll start asking questions at the first village," he said, as though it would be easy. "After we've sourced some food. Good night, sweet girl. So happy you found me and decided to stick around."

"I could change my mind at any moment," she told him.

"True," Jaran said. "But you won't. I . . . whatever happens with me and that witch, and my bastard uncle—all of my enemies. I swear I will help you find your brother, even if that means returning to Shen."

"Don't worry," she said. "Knowing Vian as only I do, I'd wager he'll find us first. But thank you, Northman. It means a lot."

JARAN ROSE EARLY AND WOKE THE OTHERS. HE'D RESTED well and was keen to reach the ocean. "We should get there by dusk," he said as they set forth heading due west through another blue day. Late that afternoon, Jaran saw gulls swooping and detected the distant rumble of waves crashing against rocks.

He grinned when inhaling the salty air, hazy memories of his childhood rushing back. "We're here," he said, staring at the long line of slate gray cliffs falling away at either side, their edges sheer and the drop over two hundred feet.

At first, the sight was a disappointment—hard to imagine anyone dwelling in this desolate terrain. But Finvar cried out and grabbed Jaran's shoulder. "Look. Half-hidden down there, do you not see them?" He pointed excitedly and flapped his arms about.

"No," Jaran said, trying to make out why his excited friend was jumping about. "What am I supposed to see?"

"Lights," Savarna said, smiling. "Lanterns, down there—they've only just appeared, on account of it getting dusky."

"That's when they usually put them on," Jaran said, shielding his face from the sun's ebbing glare. Like the night before, it had sunk clear beneath the water, though this time more vivid and the darker hue of fresh-spilled blood. An ominous sign, should he choose to heed it as such. Jaran didn't.

At last, he saw what they were looking at. Tiny, winking eyes, like so many wolves or cats blinking at them from a long way off. But lamps they were, or lanterns. That meant a village. Jaran's stomach rumbled. He grinned—it meant food, too, and ale.

"Let's find a way down." It didn't take long before they found a deep cut in the cliffs. A scar where shale and mud had caused a slide, and where a rough track cut zig-zag down toward the distant twinkle of lights.

They daren't chance the sled down that slope. So instead, Finvar freed the dogs, he and Savarna carried their gear, while Jaran gripped the harness and grunted, settling for the toughest task.

"You sure you're all right with that?" Savarna looked concerned, but Jaran winked at her.

"It's downhill," he said. "Stopping will be the worst bit."

"He's a Northman." Finvar grinned back at them. "All muscle and bone, with a very small—"

"—shut up, Candle." Jaran had started calling his friend this after his story the other night. He couldn't pronounce Khandol right so had settled for something similar. For his part, Finvar hadn't seemed put out. "Else I hit you with my axe when we reach that village."

It took scarce twenty minutes before they arrived at a huddled mess of fishing huts and spilled nets, together with the briny stench. A lone track marked by the lanterns they'd spotted earlier hinted several dwellings, a rough harbor where two scraggy looking boats bounced on waves, and a bigger building that Jaran hoped might be a tavern, or such.

They made for the largest structure. Jaran noisily dropped the sled outside. He glanced around, seeing the odd wary face gazing out from murky windows. Finvar whistled the dogs in. These arrived tail-wagging and tongue-lolling, glad to be back with their new best friend.

Savarna awarded Jaran a wry look. "These people seem over-timid. We are but three strangers, though you are large, and with that giant hatchet to boot. I thought they were all wild savages in Leeth."

"Thanks." Jaran smiled. "The coast people are mostly fisher folk. I grew up along this coast, though that was further south, I think. We're a long way from Grimhold, or anywhere of account. And I don't care how timid they are, as long as they can cook."

Before he could reach the door, it was opened by a sandy-haired man, who stood with arms folded. He looked sturdy enough, perhaps fifty. If he was timid, he hid it well in Jaran's opinion, what with the thick brows, forked beard, and heavy axe gripped in his hands.

The man gave them all a long, searching look, studying their faces as if he was reading a map. He grunted to someone hidden behind. "Three strangers, Gild. One's a Northman. The other two are foreign. A scrawny shifty type, and a flame-headed wench." The man's voice was gruff as though he smoked too much.

"Well then, let them in, Dog," a women's peeved tones filtered through. "Where's your bloody manners?"

"You look hungry," the bearded, stocky fisher said, parting to let them in. He winked at Savarna, who—together with Finvar —looked put out at being described in such a way.

"I am," Jaran said, ignoring his companions.

A woman appeared, stocky and sandy-haired like her husband but lacking the beard. She wore long wooden earrings painted bright blue. She managed a gruff sort of smile. "I'm Gilda," the woman said. "That oaf is Doggan Stride. He's the sheriff of this territory."

Doggan grunted, "Hello."

"What territory is this?" Finvar asked, as Gilda filled three steamy bowls with fish chowder. Jaran dived in with both paws.

"I have spoons," Gilda said, her face alarmed. She turned to Finvar. "Are you lost? This is Garvaik Territory, of course—the most northerly district of glorious King Erlund's wonderful country."

"You don't much care for Erlund?" Jaran glanced up from his half-empty bowl. His tone was serious, and a flicker of fear flashed in her eyes.

"Never met the man, long way from here as I said. But the new king doesn't do much for us poor folk. My husband has to fend off beast, raider, and robber with only a few men. I don't think King Erlund's much interested in us."

"He's missing out," Finvar said cheerfully, his mouth full of chowder.

"Is that fellow simple in the head?" Gilda asked Jaran.

"I've often thought so," Jaran replied. "You get used to him."

"Thanks," Finvar said.

The woman looked at him. "I'll take your word for that."

"Just us here, and the lads' wives and children," Doggan said, taking a seat alongside. "You might have seen them gawping from their cottages." Jaran and Savarna nodded.

"Where are the men?" Savarna asked Doggan.

"Down in Skarness," Gilda answered, before her husband could open his mouth. "Selling fish and wasting valuable time."

"My six sons," Doggan said. "They took the carts south to sell our fish and shells, then purchase supplies in return. They go visit Skarness once a month."

"And are tardy coming back." Gilda smeared her apron with greasy hands. "You finished?" This to Savarna, who was busy draining her source. Gilda grabbed her wooden bowl before she could reply.

"We need a boat," Jaran said, rubbing his hands together and belching appreciatively.

"Bad time of year for fishing trips," Doggan said, while his wife raised a quizzical brow.

"I've a journey planned," Jaran said. "Need a sturdy craft." He looked at the woman sharply. "Do you know of a sailor called . . ." he glanced at Savarna.

"Carlo Sarfe," she said. Gilda rewarded both of them a blank stare.

"We've two boats," Doggan said, his expression slightly bemused.

"You're not welcome to either," Gilda said. "And we don't know anyone by that outlandish name."

"We need a canny craft to reach Valkador," Finvar said suddenly, his lean face keen in the lanternlight. "Preferably one owned by the aforementioned sailor."

Jaran felt a slight shiver. It seemed colder than it had been scarce seconds ago. He looked at the faces surrounding him. Savarna looked bleak, Finvar puzzled. But both Doggan and his wife looked terrified.

"How dare you bring evil into this house!" She stood up

clumsily, the retrieved bowls slipping through her fingers as an icy blast extinguished the lanterns.

Doggan sat with head in hands. "You've let her in. That name you spoke—it's forbidden."

They all looked up in alarm as something thudded outside. The dogs—tied to their sled and posts—broke out into a cacophony of growling yelps that turned into wailing howls. Jaran saw a weird shimmer of light. Then the door crashed open, and a man's shape stood there.

"I've come to kill you, Jaran Saerk," a deep voice said. The axe appeared from nowhere, glittering in the lamplight. Swiping —hard and fast. The man-thing became a huge shadow that jumped at Jaran, the axe swinging down.

THE PROPOSITION

VIAN BLINKED AS the door opened and a shadowy gloom awaited.

"Go inside," Mawla Tei said with a soft smile, as though she knew what awaited him. Vian thanked her and entered the room, the ornate door closing silently behind him.

He stood for a moment getting his bearings. Hard to see in here. Steamy and smoke-filled, the scent of candles burning incense. He detected lavender, frankincense, and a hint of lemongrass, too. He sniffed and took a step forward.

A large room, the windows blanked out with heavy velvet drapes, the color of summer oceans. He saw tables, the surfaces inlaid with parquetry and ornate carving. There were golden candelabras flickering at either end. More candles winked from the far corners of the room, casting shadowy light on priceless ornaments and artefacts of days gone by, more than a dozen yards away.

Vian paced slowly toward the center of the room, until he could make out a vague shape of a person resting idle on a divan.

The empress. He walked toward her, flute and papers in hand, stopping when she turned her head slightly to survey him.

Vian bowed as low as he could. He waited, keeping his gaze on the elaborate turquoise mosaics at his feet.

"I would see your face," the voice was cool, smooth and detached. A young woman's, hinting control and curiosity, and something else. Vian detected a mischievous edge to the tone.

He complied, dropping to one knee. He dared a glance at her features, seeing a smallish woman with jet hair, sleek coils, both long and perfumed. She wasn't beautiful in the traditional sense, but there was something enticing about her that tugged at him. Those seductive, clever dark eyes hinted both mischief and boredom. The empress was garbed in loose silk, the color of violets with silver-embroidered cranes stitched with sapphires, and more of the jewels studding the hem and flared sleeves, a golden silk sash gathering in the center hinting at hidden curves. Her skin was creamy, smooth as the silk she wore. A faint smile lifted from the corner of her mouth. She wore golden slippers adorned with yet more sapphires. Her long fingernails were painted blue.

So, you're Rasnei. He couldn't think why, but she wasn't what he'd expected.

"You play well, stranger." The empress shifted her body on the divan, revealing a length of pale thigh. Vian pretended not to notice. He stepped forward hesitantly and bowed again.

"I'm honored you think so, Exalted One." He made sure his voice was calm, the words measured. "I'm merely a wayfarer who plays the taverns and fairs throughout the lands."

"A talented one—we wonder how we have never heard mention of you before. *Salcara* is an unusual name." She smiled slightly. "But then, that's not your real name, is it?"

"It's my professional name, Exalted One." Vian controlled

the nervousness he felt inside. "It means 'player' in archaic Rundali." They knew who he was, so why hide inside another lie? "I am Vian of House Eltayn."

"And you have a sister, a twin?"

"I do—though I've not seen her these last months."

Rasnei said nothing. "Your hair gave you away, Vian of Rundali. If you meant to kill me then you should have dyed it, or else cropped it short. Perhaps vanity is your weakness . . . *Salcara*." The smile widened to a cruel smirk.

Vian said nothing, though inside he raged. He had lost his gambit. The guards would be coming for him. They were probably behind those drapes, armed with crossbows. They would pounce the moment he stepped toward their empress, wounding him just enough to slow his attack. Then they could drag him off for questioning and torture by Soma Ghee, or maybe the Magister himself. He'd heard all about Chulan's favorite pastimes.

"You have nothing to say?" Rasnei looked curious. "That proves your guilt. Why aren't you on your belly begging for your life?"

"I am not a beggar," Vian said. It was a shame—he'd so wanted to see Savarna again before he died. But life chooses the road, a man must follow best he can.

"Good," she said. "Glad we've got that out of the way. You can begin when you are ready."

"You still want me to play?" Vian failed to mask his surprise.

"It's why you're here, despite your other agenda. Your performance tonight will decide your fate. Play well, and who knows —we might prove lenient. We like good music."

Vian bowed again. He kept his mind neutral as he warmed up, scaling through the notes, working his mouth. Her dark eyes were on him the whole time, calm and cruel, faintly amused.

Vian worked the flute, forcing any panic or dread deep below. The music was in him—that was what mattered. He was the music—the Universe, life and death, the endless dance—all of it, the *music*.

Vian played long and perhaps better than he ever had, knowing this would be the last time. Throughout his flawless performance, Empress Rasnei reclined lazily on her divan, the faint smile hinting many things. Occasionally she would scoop a fig from an adjacent bowl, bite down hard, the juices smearing her pouty lips.

At last Vian was done, exhausted, his fingers aching and mouth dry. He bowed, offering the flute with both hands held toward her. Vian was pleased. Content. He'd played beautifully, and knew it. It wouldn't matter if they killed him. He had given all, but the game had shifted elsewhere. *Life is but a dream, a butterfly drifting through blue summer skies.* But the winter winds were always waiting. The only constant thing was change.

Vian bowed a final time and waited for the guards.

RASNEI HAD DRUNK IN THE PERFORMANCE. THIS BEAUTIFUL stranger. A man like no other she'd heard of. Cool and calm, radiating something she didn't understand. Her spies had soon got word of the Cutters' new member from the tavern they were frequenting. Intrigued, Rasnei had ensured the information stayed with her, and Chulan was kept well out of it. For now, at least—though, of course, it was naïve to expect that discretion to last.

Savarna's twin brother. Two proud Rundali from some noble family far to the south. Recently orphaned after one of the Ghee's slavers paid visit. Of course, they'd wanted revenge. She'd ordered Ghee summon Savarna after hearing of her prowess during capture. Rasnei was fascinated by a woman with such impressive skills, wishing she possessed them herself. She'd so wanted to meet this wild creature, Savarna. Then the unfortunate ambush had happened. The captive woman had disappeared, together with an illustrious Northman called Jaran Saerk and the infamous thief known as Finvar the Droll, a former Cutter. Strange business, unresolved. *Disappointing.* But now she had the brother all to herself. Time to decide his fate.

Rasnei gazed over his handsome features as Vian Eltayn offered out the flute, his gaze on the floor. "Look at me," she commanded.

Vian complied. His face revealed nothing, the enigmatic brown eyes, flecked with golden sparkles, that long fiery hair, burnished crimson by candlelight, and held back in place by a plain golden pin.

"A magnificent performance, even for such a maestro," Rasnei said, placing a fig in her mouth. "How can I reward you? A quick death? Perhaps a meal, some strong wine, before they take you away?"

"It was enough to play for you, Exalted One. I am at peace with myself, having done my best. I am ready to die."

She smiled. There was no fear in that voice. No pleading, so unlike the courtiers and courtesans that adorned her court like so many useless gaudy trinkets.

"I think that would be a waste of talent," Rasnei said. She smiled again. "I took a gamble allowing you to enter here. I knew you'd want to kill me for what they did to your family down in Rundali. But I wanted to tease you with something else instead."

"Go on," he said, the words flat and unadorned, portraying a hardness she hadn't noticed before. The real man behind the image. His gold-brown gaze revealed nothing, but she noted how his hands whitened on the flute.

"I have many enemies, Vian of Rundali—or should I still call you Salcara, the player?" Rasnei said. "Most of my foes live inside this city, a good amount within these gilded walls."

"Such are the perils of ruling an aging empire," Vian said, his feet braced like a dancer. Perhaps he would attack her, she thought. She really should have posted guards. But she'd needed the excitement. Also, she had to test this man, gauge him—and that meant offering him something, too. A chance.

"Indeed," she said, after studying his face for a time. "A ruler needs good instincts if she would keep her throne. A level head is paramount. And one has to trust the right people. Not easy. In Pol Shen, everyone has ears for the jingle of coin. That is why I've decided to trust you, Vian of Rundali." He straightened in surprise, and she laughed at the shock in his face. "Caught you off guard, at last."

"That strikes me as a rash decision, considering we both know why I came here," Vian said, a slight ironic smile raising the corner of his lip.

"To live is to gamble," Rasnei said. "I rule by my hunches, Rundali. My father had his army, whereas I have my spies, female intuition, and wondrous charms. Are you not . . . *charmed?*"

"Beyond words, Exalted One." His eyes looked shadowed, a hint of doubt flickering through. But that could have been the candlelight. Hard to tell—this was a confident fellow standing before her. She liked that.

"Here is my proposal." Rasnei shifted her legs on the divan, well aware of his eyes flicking that way. "We let you live—for now, at least." She smiled, and he bowed again. "Stop that, it's irritating after the first half-dozen times. I have more than enough fawning courtiers." His eyes widened but lips remained shut.

"We . . . I let you live." She smiled again, more intimately. "In return for such generosity, you promise not to stab me with that hairpin, or strangle me while I'm sleeping."

"Sleeping?" Vian raised a brow. She noted how his lips had parted slightly.

She cupped her hands under her chin and gazed into his fascinating eyes. He didn't blink, gave her look for look. "Your performance isn't over yet, Salcara. I still have other requirements." Again, his eyes widened. This time his smile was genuine.

"Agreed," Vian said. "For *now*, at least."

"You are impertinent," she said. "I like that, shows strong character. I also think you are a skilled killer. Had you ever considered why I wanted your sister here, once I heard of her capture?"

He shrugged. "I assumed as a curiosity. We twins have an unusual look. Or else an exotic trophy, or trinket to parade in court."

Her lips tightened hearing that. "That answer offends me," she said. "I do not care for trophies and trinkets. I value intellect and courage far more. But I forgive your words, however poorly spoken. You have very good reasons to hate me."

"I don't hate you," he said. "I despise what you represent. Your empire. What Shen has become, has always been." His eyes narrowed. "I killed the slaver your people sent."

"That is not of consequence. Nor do I have any interest in the affairs of slavers and their chattels. I rule as I see fit. Survive and thrive—sometimes the two get intertwined. I wanted Savarna here so I could speak with her," Rasnei said. "Yes, I was curious about this recently captured slave. But—I know how ridiculous this sounds—I wanted her as a friend, a person of rare strength that I could confide in. From another land, thus free of the cloying mindset of Imperial Shen. A breath of clean air in the fog. And she's a warrior, that's something I admire."

"Savarna would have killed you," Vian said.

"Would she? *You haven't.*"

"Yet . . ." He smiled at her smile, and deep inside Rasnei felt a shiver. He meant those words. The game here was just getting started. "Besides, my sister has a temper, whereas I'm placid and lazy by comparison."

"Then we will have to employ you instead."

"Employ?" He arched a quizzical brow.

"I want you on my side, Vian Eltayn. And Gurtei, with his Cutters." Her turn to smile again. "I know their names and what they eat, the girls they sleep with, and which woods they like to shelter in when Soma Ghee's soldiers come calling. It's in my interest to know these things. Why I'm still alive."

"What would you have us do?"

"Smuggle me out from Pol Shen." He looked genuinely startled hearing that. "Not the answer you expected?" Rasnei crossed her legs and sat up.

"I don't know what I expected."

"Survival, and a chance to plan a counterattack. Shen is dying slowly, painfully. And yes, you are right, Rundali, my country stinks of corruption, especially this court. The enemy beyond the river grows stronger each day. Calla is coming. But there are more devious players far closer who would sell us out, allowing the Cardalan wolves inside."

"Chulan? Soma Ghee?"

"The head of the serpent, and his prime executive. Soma Ghee is of small consequence, and won't be alive much longer —so my sources inform me. *No loss.* Gost Chulan, however, waxes more powerful each day. My spies number twenty, whereas he owns over two hundred."

"You think Magister Chulan wants to be emperor?"

"I am certain of it."

"Emperor of a fallen empire." Vian shrugged. "Seems pointless."

"Chulan is a practical man. He knows we cannot stop the torrent that is Calla. But, whereas I would fight tooth and nail for my country's protection, Chulan will capitulate. That serpent will sell his empress, and her people, to ensure his own pathetic survival, even reward, allowing himself retain the hollow title of emperor."

"So Chulan is a traitor as well as conniver."

"He is the worst of men, but also one of the cleverest I know of."

"Then we will have to be clever too." Vian flashed her a bright smile. "I hold Chulan ultimately responsible for my family's eradication. Soma Ghee is his man—as was that slaver I killed, Shateke, though indirectly."

"Then we are in accord?"

"I believe so."

"Good, I weary of conversation. We will retire to someplace more comfortable. Take some wine, and you can tell me all about Rundali, House Eltayn, and your bad-tempered, violent sister. Come, follow." Rasnei slipped from the divan and glided through the room. The panels at the far end were parted by invisible servants to allow her to pass. She heard his footsteps behind her. Felt a tremble of fear mixed with excitement. He could pounce at any time, with the gold hairpin. Her guards should have confiscated that.

She reached her inner chamber, the fountain chiming and yellow night birds trilling in their cage. Tei's girls had prepared the room for her private peruse. The courtesan knew what Rasnei liked. She made for her favorite couch, then turned to eye the man standing at the edge of the room.

"We won't be disturbed here," Rasnei told him. "Come closer —I would see you better." He complied with a smile and stopped a couple of feet from where she sat. She held out her hand and he offered the flute. She held it carefully and looked over the instrument. Then she placed it in her mouth and made a horrible squeak. He laughed, and she chuckled.

"Takes practice," Vian said.

"Most things do," Rasnei said. She placed the flute aside and turned to survey him. "Remove your clothing," Rasnei ordered with her best imperial tone. He blinked back surprise, but nodded. He stripped before her then stood naked, his eyes surprisingly calm.

Rasnei looked him up and down slowly. She smiled, reached out, and brushed her fingernails against his thighs.

"Time for you next performance, Salcara," the empress Rasnei told him.

SKARNESS

FINVAR DIVED LOW and crawled beneath the rocking table, as the room exploded with noise and weird flashing light. He heard the clang of steel on steel. Someone yelled. That sounded like Jaran, more like a bear's growl. Steel clanging again. Sparks flying . . .

A scream of rage—he recognized Savarna. Then the table lifted from above him and crashed into the wall. He looked up, blinking. A huge man-creature stood with legs braced apart. A warrior, half-naked, a heavy axe gripped in either hand. His face was distorted in the gloom, but one thing Finvar couldn't help noting—the axe-man's skin was a mixture of slimy green and greasy honey-gold.

You again. The creature he'd seen back in Hragglund. This time slavering over him like a famished hound.

Another shout. Jaran Saerk loomed into view, Griner swinging across at the creature whose axes were currently cutting down at Finvar.

He rolled clear, kicked out and struck the green man's legs.

That hurt, and the warrior didn't notice. The creature had turned to face Jaran, both his axes swinging in vicious circles. They glared at each other. Jaran's face was bloody, but he seemed unscathed thus far. Savarna appeared beside him.

They tried to get behind the brute as he smote blow after blow at Jaran's head. The lack of space and clutter meant most of those thudding into walls or shattering crockery.

"Jaran, please kill that thing," Finvar managed the words between gasps. He saw Jaran sweep in close, two hands parallel. The cunning stroke cut a deep slash along the creature's chest. The wound smoldered and puckered. No blood, just green sludgy steam venting out. It stank.

Jaran stood there blinking back sweat. "It should be dying," he said.

"You cannot kill me," the voice was deep and muffled, like a man trying to speak underwater. "I am Stoon—a creature of Faerie." The axes were swinging again, Jaran's held ready for their strike. "I have come to fetch your head, mortal."

Finvar dived forward on impulse, his head and shoulders ramming into Stoon's midriff from behind. Stars exploded in his head and Finvar crumpled. "Bastard's made of rock," Finvar said, as Savarna rushed in to help him up.

Movement to his right. Finvar—having regained his vision —saw Sheriff Doggan emerge, his face terrified, but both hands gripping a spear. Finvar waved him back.

Jaran was snarling, raining blow upon blow on the tall warrior, to no avail. Stoon countered most swipes with one axe while striking back with the other. He caught Jaran's arm, slicing up. Jaran hardly noticed. Finvar saw how his pale blue eyes were crazy-wild with madness.

"The berserkergang's on him," he said to Savarna beside him. "This is going to get rough."

"We have to help him," she yelled in his ear.

Finvar nodded. "It's more than that," he said. "*Three who are one*—we can defeat her magic if we are united."

"What?" She glared, readying her knife.

"On three," he yelled back. "Three for three!"

She blinked understanding.

"One . . . two . . . go!" Finvar and Savarna yelled and slammed their weapons into Stoon's exposed back, just as Jaran countered a wild sweep and, ducking low, slammed Griner's blade hard into Stoon's midriff.

Stoon rocked, his axes swung back and forth, but the blows were ill-aimed. He stumbled, dropped an axe.

"Again!" Finvar yelled. "Together we can kill him." He saw Jaran blink into some sort of comprehension, the rage fading back from his eyes. Savarna gripped her knife with both hands. "Now!" Finvar spat the words out with bloody phlegm.

Together they stabbed, thrust and hacked at Stoon. He stumbled again, more steamy ooze dripped from his torso, arms and legs. They struck out in unison a third time, and Stoon pitched head-first onto the floor.

Finvar staggered across to Jaran. "You all right?" he yelled. Jaran stared back at him with those crazy pale eyes. "I'll take that for a yes," Finvar said, as Savarna threw her arms around her lover. Jaran stared at her for a moment as the dust settled in the cottage, the only remaining candle allowing just enough light to hint at the mess.

"I think it's dead," Jaran said eventually, looking down at the green-honey colored dripping pile of man-shaped ooze.

"No shit," Finvar said. "Trouble is, it was most likely dead to begin with." They watched on, in fascinated horror as the remains of Stoon cracked open and shrank down like some rotten fly-blown fruit at summer's end.

"Fuck, but that's foul." Finvar squeezed his nostrils. He saw Savarna retch beside him. Jaran stood rock still, his hard face barely registering the stench.

The stench faded slowly, as the mess deliquesced, allowing a thick trail of vapor to rise up and creep through the walls and broken doorway. Within minutes, nothing remained of their attacker. "Gone," Jaran blinked down, stating the obvious.

"Not quite," Savarna said. She kicked a small round object into the light. "What is that?" she asked her friends.

"Looks like a seed," Finvar said, relieved that the terrible smell had dissipated.

Jaran nodded. "Kelp bubble. This Stoon must have come from the sea."

"A sending from Sheega, or Faerie—whatever that is. Or maybe both." Finvar scratched his head. He saw Gilda appear behind her husband's shadow. "Sorry about the mess."

The pair blinked back at him, faces ashen and eyes filled with disbelief.

"Are you hurt?" Savarna called across to them. Doggan shook his head. The wife was still blinking.

"Got any ale?" Jaran asked.

"Not enough to drown out what I've just witnessed." Doggan signaled to Gilda to bring sustenance for all. For once, she nodded, lost for words. She returned with five large mugs. "Barrels are outside in the shed," Doggan coughed. "Think I've aged ten years in the last half-hour."

The ale was good, strong enough to stop his hands shaking

uncontrollably, as they had since the thing called Stoon departed in vapor.

"I feel a bit queasy, truth be told," Finvar told the Northman, as Jaran sat with Savarna in the deep dark outside the cottage. Doggan joined them, then his wife, both chugging hard at ale. Nobody wanted to go back inside, despite the bitter chill.

FINVAR DRANK STEADILY UNTIL DAWN'S PINK GLOW CREPT down from the hills. His hands were still shaking and his head hurt. *At least we're alive.* He glanced at his friends. Jaran's face was unreadable. The Northman was seated on a wall with Savarna held close.

Finvar left them be and wandered off to stand staring at the churning waves close by. He returned minutes later and saw that Sheriff Doggan and Gilda remained as close to the ale barrel as was possible. Finvar grunted at them, but they ignored him. No one had said much since the unwelcome visit. *Hardly surprising.* He took seat on the wall and rocked back and forth, his mind racing and head throbbing badly. *Bugger this.* Finvar replenished his ale and drank it down quickly until his head felt numb.

Slowly the light grew, the pink hue turned golden, and sunlight's bright kiss promising a decent day. Spring was approaching, though you'd never know it this far north.

Finvar stood up, his legs shaky but head clearer and full of good ale. *Time to move on.* There were things they had to do.

"Well . . .?" Finvar stared at his friends. Savarna looked half-asleep, but Jaran's eyes were blazing. "What's next?"

Jaran grinned wolfishly at him. "We kill the witch on my island before she sends another Stoon, or something even worse."

"Worse?" Finvar said, shaking his head. "And first we need to get there."

Sheriff Doggan proved helpful with that. Finvar suspected it was mainly because he wanted rid of his guests, in case they drew in more bad things like Stoon the Weedman—which on reflection, Finvar thought, they most probably would.

"Twenty miles to Skarness," Doggan told them, as Gilda rustled up some food for breakfast, having finally faced the horror of returning inside her cottage. "The road leads to a fjord. There's a landing stage with a jetty, a raft tied up. The old pilot sleeps there. You'll need to pay him good coin to ferry you across. He's an odd sort, so be polite. Town's due south across the water. Keep an eye out for my sons when you are there. Big fair-headed lads, most likely be drinking or scrapping. Tell 'em we need them back home soonest."

"Thank you," Jaran said, as he, Finvar and Savarna all tucked in to Gilda's stew. Jaran emptied his bowl three times.

"We'll starve if he lingers another hour," Gilda complained.

"Answer one question, then we'll leave you be," Jaran said, not unkindly.

Gilda nodded, as her husband went back for more ale. "Ask away."

"Why was the name of my island such cause for concern?"

Gilda's shrewd eyes narrowed. "*Your* island?" Finvar saw Jaran nod—his big friend's eyes were keen this morning, missing little. She stared at him for a long time, her expression resigned. Doggan returned.

"Have I missed something?" he asked, seeing the resignation on her face, the three of them gathered close awaiting a response.

"I should bloody well say so." Gilda glared at him. "You might want to put that mug down, else you drop it." He did as she suggested, eyes bemused. "He's the one the Traveler told us was coming."

"What traveler?" Jaran grabbed her arm before Doggan could answer. Gilda didn't respond.

"Your being here can only bring bad luck, Jaran Saerk," Doggan said, his eyes bleak. "Sheega will soon know what happened here."

"You know who I am?"

"We do." Gilda nodded. "The Traveler told us. But we're forbidden from saying more, lest her sendings return."

"I'm going to kill this Sheega." Jaran stood up, his face flushed, and hair badly tangled after the long, rough night. "Then I'm going to deal with my uncle, your king."

"You had best go with them, Doggan," Gilda said. "Make sure they get that raft across, even if you have to pay yourself. I want them gone from here. No offense." She awarded Jaran a quirky grin.

"None taken. We're ready when you are, Sheriff," Finvar said. He'd wanted to linger for one more ale but decided that a bad idea. Doggan nodded at him. The sheriff looked dazed and ale-befuddled, still chewing over what he'd heard. He glanced at his wife who stood with fists on hips, wearing a sour expression.

"See you tonight, then," Doggan told her, and stumbled out of the cottage. He returned with a spear in hands, a short-hafted axe swinging from his belt, and a large round shield slung across his back.

"Let's get moving," Doggan told them, his florid face sober, as morning waxed bright.

Poor bugger, thought Finvar. *He'll do anything for a peaceful life.*

As compensation, Jaran suggested leaving the dogs and sled.

Finvar was sorry to part with the animals but realized it was necessary. They weren't needed anymore, and the original plan was to sell them before leaving Leeth. Doggan liked the idea, looking happy for the first time that morning.

They walked, the road hard underfoot. Ice-packed and exposed, the raw sea wind cutting across from the west. Finvar gazed that way often as they journeyed. The ocean churned and surged a few hundred yards to their right. This sea was different from the one he'd grown up by. The waves were taller, the color and hue a bluish green rather than the inky purple he remembered from the coves around Coolega Island.

Hills flanked their left, the snow crowning their tops, and the glittering pines flanking below. Finvar saw eagles gliding far away. He felt a tugging inside, as though he needed to be there, flying with them. Close his eyes, lift up. Join the hunt.

What is happening to me? He forced the birds from his mind, and instead focused on the road ahead. For miles, the way steepened—a long, winding climb that had even Jaran puffing. By late afternoon, they'd crested that steep rise. They rested at the crown, gazing down on the sparkle of water far below.

A deeper blue, the fjord's smooth surface glittered as the sunlight danced over. Rested, they made the way down. The track had narrowed to a steep mix of shale and pebbles, hazardous underfoot.

They reached the water's edge, and Finvar saw a hut with a scruffy dock of sorts beyond, a craft creaking and bobbing at the end. Sheriff Doggan led them across until Finvar descried another roof, with smoke drifting from the center. A cottage with a bright blue door, and a tall stooped figure watching them from the railings leading up to it.

"Your pilot, I assume?" Finvar said.

"Gurn is a strange one," Doggan said. "Not easy company, but he'll ferry us across if I speak to him." The sheriff walked over, approached the stooping figure, who had produced a long pipe and was blowing smoke in their direction.

"Doggan tells me you've business in Skarness." The pilot's face was long and craggy. The skin sallow, his graying hair and beard matted and dirty. The eyes were a violet blue shiftiness.

This old one's trouble, Finvar thought.

"Our business is our affair," Jaran said.

The old man nodded. "It will cost you," he said. "I wasn't planning on crossing today. Have other matters to attend."

Jaran hinted to Finvar, who nodded painfully and reached inside his tunic where he kept what coin he still retained.

"I've got this," Doggan said, placing a small leather bag in the pilot's grubby hands.

Gurn tossed the bag and caught it deftly. "Sufficient," he said, without glancing inside. "Wait here, I'll go get the raft ready." He signaled them over a few minutes later.

"You coming, too?" Finvar was shocked seeing Doggan clamber onto the lashed pine trunks comprising the heavy structure of the raft.

Doggan shrugged. "I've come this far." Finvar decided against pressing him further.

The raft was roughly square in shape, the pines cut in fifteen-foot lengths, and equally wide. The timbers were lashed expertly with animal gut and tar. A single mast with yard supported a wide, square sail, the blood-red cloth shabby and plain.

A tiller at one end hinted the stern.

Gurn poled away from the bank, his pipe gripped in his mouth and canny eyes flickering back along the shore, as though he was waiting for someone else to appear.

The wind whipped chill as they drifted out from the shore. The fjord sides rose dark and tall, with steep banks and cliffs frowning down on the fat finger of clear water they were crossing. Out to the west, Finvar saw whitecaps. The ocean, scarce five miles distant.

Skarness smudged into view. A straggle of huts, with turfed roofs leaking smoke. He could see tall pines framing the edge of the town. At the southern end lay a square jetty and dock. Tiny figures were running around there. He guessed they were children, but it was hard to be sure. They'd gone by the time Gurn guided the raft into its dock at the end of the harbor. The pilot said nothing as the three jumped from the raft and followed Doggan into the town. Finvar, glancing back, saw Gurn watching them beneath his floppy hat.

"That old bugger is up to something," Finvar muttered in Savarna's ear. She nodded, but didn't reply. "Time we got busy," he added. "See if there's a sailor called Carlo Sarfe in town."

SHEEGA SAW THE WRACK OF WEED DRIFT INTO THE SHORE. She walked closer, curious, knowing something had happened. She watched as Ranning reached down and scooped up a handful. He sniffed at it and turned to watch her approach.

"Stoon is gone," Ranning said, his milky eyes distant, a look almost like pain on his face. "They proved too much for him."

"He was meant to stay with the others."

"Almost as rebellious as your sons," Ranning laughed cruelly. "The other Witch-Men will be primed accordingly. They'll want revenge. Jaran Hrelgisson will try to cross from Skarness—it's near where Stoon found them." He dropped the wrack of weed and watched it drift off, vanishing beneath the murky water.

"They cannot cross without help," Sheega said. "We've reached a stalemate. Jaran's slain Stoon, so realizes we're on to him. He'll be wary, ready for anything. I need to get to him before he finds a way to crack the code—or worse, frees Rune from my nets. It's not impossible. His two companions possess rare skills. Then there is the Traveler. He cannot intervene directly, but that's never stopped him interfering whenever he can."

"Your old enemy." Ranning's cold eyes glittered as he gazed at her.

"He is also the enemy of Faerie, thus your foe, too," she said matching his gaze, as her own mood darkened. "As is Rune."

"Why don't you kill that sorry creature?"

"I cannot—Rune is potent. My sorcery renders him latent. But if I attacked him directly, it would backfire on us all. Besides, I need Rune. Only he can unlock the dimensions and travel through them freely."

"A renegade from Faerie." Ranning's tone was disapproving.

"He is much more than that."

Ranning shrugged, and Sheega let the matter rest. She would reach out and find her sons tonight. She was angry with two of them. Gorn and Valgarn had disobeyed her orders. She wouldn't tolerate that. But Holtarn alone might prove enough.

The Witch-Guard would wend north, while Holtarn made his way across from Grimhold with a squad of fighters. Hrelgisson and his friends would be caught in the mix, crushed like grain between millstones.

She forced a smile as she strolled the beach beside her lover. *You won't escape me this time, Jaran Saerk.*

FLUTE AND DAGGER

DORTHAR STARED through the thick fog rising from the river. A mile across, and scarce three yards visible. He blew on his hands and rubbed them together. He had a bad feeling this morning. It was too quiet, and that cursed mist cheated both vision and sound.

Two weeks, and nothing from the enemy. The slimy Soma Ghee had returned without comment from the sortie across the river. Captain Hranic had raged about this, but Chulan had ordered him say nothing, allowing Ghee and his people full access to all they needed and a pass to cross the river.

Dorthar spat on the frosted grass. The Northman shared his captain's view that Ghee and his master were up to something. *Selling us out, most likely.* Hranic had muttered to his closest officers that he suspected Chulan was planning a coup, with Cardalan aid. The Auxiliaries would be caught in the middle.

That stank. Dorthar, like all his comrades, had left behind the life they were born to and travelled the relentless miles to enlist in this army, like their fathers and grandfathers had done.

But they had been rewarded well. In those days, the Shen looked after their Northmen, as they had back when Dorthar enlisted, nearly fifteen years ago.

He had been fiery and proud, killing Cards, Rundali, Tseole —anyone who ranged too close. Defending this brown slug of a river that marked Shen's western borders. But the Cards had kept coming, and then Ran Calla had bolstered his camps along the river. That had led to more and more raids—good days, those had been. Plenty of time to gain glory and honor, butchering those Cards. Winning renown and good coin from the empress.

But something had changed. He'd noticed a shift in mood these recent years. The empress had withdrawn deeper into her chambers. The auxiliaries had always been rewarded by her favor, in gratitude for their good work and devout loyalty. He'd even been addressed by Imperial Rasnei personally once. A young, sharp-looking woman—he'd been very proud that day.

Then slippery Chulan had smeared his slime over the court at Shen. Everyone was in his pocket. And the Magister hated Hranic Finehair and his Northmen more than anyone. He resented the intimacy her foreign warriors had always received from their empress, and her father before.

Months had passed. Dorthar had been worried for a time, believing something was amiss in Pol Shen. Then Jaran Saerk had disappeared, and Hranic returned days after, his face bleak—and not a mention of that legendary warrior.

Was Saerk dead? Dorthar didn't believe that. Jaran was unkillable, in his opinion. A man he'd fought beside on so many occasions. An inspiration. A berserker who had killed scores of enemies. But a man of honor and respect, and a good comrade, too, with his gruff sense of humor. What had happened in Pol Shen, and where was Jaran Saerk now?

Dorthar shifted, stamped his boots on the damp grass, blew on his hands again. Two more hours, and he'd be off stag. He could return to camp for a hot brew and a blissful hour in his blanket before the dawn bells rang.

He removed his helmet, rubbing his temples as the headache came back. Tension headache, caused by the many blows he'd received over the years. That, and worry. Northmen weren't prone to worrying, being fatalistic in outlook. But Dorthar was a thinker like Jaran Saerk. This morning, he decided that a curse.

The fog was rolling back. White, billowing clouds rippled over the last sludge comprising the river's surface. The Shen was a fat, lazy snake. He could see better, perhaps forty yards. Far above him, a single star winked out in defiance of that fret.

Dorthar tensed, hearing a distant sound. He leaned on his spear, rammed the helm back on his head and buckled the chin strap. He heard it again. A distant splash and plop, like some river creature breaking free of the dirty water.

And again, closer. Getting nearer, and over there too. Then he saw them. Dark shapes, blurring out of the mist. Three rafts crossing from the other side. Dorthar rubbed his eyes in disbelief. After weeks of nothing they were under attack.

He waited long enough to register the men standing on those rafts. There were over a score on each, all carrying spears and round shields. They didn't look like Cards. Then Dorthar gasped, as a wave of horror and disbelief hit him like a mallet between the eyes. These were Northmen. They must have rowed across from Calla's camp. Dorthar cursed as the realization shook him. *The Cards have Northmen.* Ran Calla had sent the treacherous bastards to kill their kinsmen.

HRANIC FINEHAIR ROLLED TO HIS FEET AND GRABBED HIS weapons. Close by, the warning bell tolled. A deafening racket, the operator must've been swinging from the bell-cord. Hranic pulled his boots on, slid the mail vest down over his torso, and grabbed his thick wool cloak.

He pulled the tent flap back and stepped outside. He heard distant shouts and a mist was clearing. Then Dorthar's hard-scarred face appeared out the gloom.

"What is it, Dorth?"

"Northmen," Dorthar spat. "Attacking us."

Before he could respond, Hranic saw a score of fighters emerge from the dissipating fog. Big, hard men, their faces framed by steel helmets. Spears and axes grabbed in gloved fists. Shields slung across their backs.

The bell tolled and tolled. Hranic watched in disbelief as a warrior leapt out of the mist. A great brute of a man. He yelled and threw his spear. Hranic saw it arc high and then dive, skewering Haigi as he pulled on the bell cord. The spear passed clean through Haigi's body, pinning him to the bell house wall.

The warrior who'd killed him was smiling as he walked calmly toward them. Beside him Dorthar spat. "It cannot be —Jaran Saerk?"

Hranic had that sinking feeling. Saerk had said he'd fight for the enemy, but Hranic had never believed it. He felt an odd sense of relief when the warrior's face was lit by torchlight as he approached. Not Jaran Saerk. But similar, and just as large. A berserker by the look, the rage showing in his eyes.

Another Northman emerged beside him. Almost the same size. Both carried axes, and round shields held ready. These men were clearly brothers, and they bore an uncanny resemblance to Saerk. Their hair, trailing out from those helmets, was a shade darker, the hate-filled eyes, a moodier, grayer blue than Jaran's.

The two had stopped, a host of others appearing and filing out at either side.

"You must be Hranic Finehair, the auxiliary leader," the second brother spoke. This one looked more cunning. He was slightly shorter than his sibling, though still a huge man. The other one was snarling, biting the rim of his shield, his berserker-gang having taken hold.

"And who might you be?" Hranic stepped forward. "Murderer and Kinslayer?"

The taller brother made to step forward, but the one who'd spoken stopped him with his axe, striking the other man's shield.

"You are not our kin." The contempt in his voice was treacle-thick. "You are Shen puppies, at their beck and call. Doing their dirty work and drinking their piss. You're not fit to be North-men. That's why we've come to kill you."

Hranic forced himself to be calm, though he raged inside. What madness was this? There were more than a hundred, he guessed—a strong force, though not enough to overrun the camp. This was clearly a show of arms meant to shock them. His own warriors were lined up behind him. A tough fight would follow, but they would prevail.

"I am Valgarn Erlundsson," the man addressing him said. "This is my brother, Gorn. We are King Erlund's sons from Leeth. You should throw down your weapons, bow to your princes and hope to keep your sorry heads."

"Your petty king has no power here," Hranic said. "If it's true that Erlund sent you on Calla's behalf, then he must be the Ran's puppy, and you his mangy whelps. Strikes me as a touch hypo-critical, accusing us of serving Shen."

"I weary of this conversation," Valgarn Erlundsson said to his brother, whose mouth was frothing and eyes blinking rage. "Let's deal with these traitors—what say you, brother?"

"I'm ready," Gorn growled, and spat chunky phlegm in the dirt.

"Shield wall!" Hranic roared as his men pushed close, their round shields protecting their neighbor. "Come and greet us then, treacherous kin-killing bastards." Hranic leaned back, tossing his spear and striking one of the men standing beside the brothers. The brothers' Northmen were lined up like Hranic's men, with shields overlapped and spears thrust forward.

"Kill them all!" the giant Gorn yelled through his helmet, as the berserker, his brother and their wild-eyed warriors, yelled and clanged spears on shields, before charging head on at Hranic's waiting men.

Time slowed. He saw them coming, the gloom almost gone, as predawn light revealed the hatred on their faces. Hranic saw spears cast, axes rise and fall. He felt the anger rise up inside, saw Dorthar's hard face tense beside him.

The enemy faces loomed close, their axes swinging down. "Hold!" Hranic growled at his men. Then the crash, thud and stampede began. A dance of death and fury, where Northman butchered Northman.

SECRETARY GHEE WATCHED THE SUN RISE FROM HIS solarium. Outside, his lawns were studied with glittering rime. A cold morning, but the blue irises and yellow crocus and narcissi promised spring would soon be here.

He was ready. This winter had proved tricky. He had always

considered himself important in the scheme of things. Second only to Chulan, himself only to the empress. But that situation had changed. The embarrassment across the river. Calla had scared him. The Ran's eyes had been filled with contempt. And now he had Northmen, too? What would become of Soma Ghee, his beautiful home, his privileged lifestyle, the slaves, his concubines? Despite Magister Chulan's assurance, Soma Ghee suspected all he possessed would be taken from him. His power and possessions blasted into oblivion, like winter leaves in a storm.

Did I back the wrong horse? What choice had he had? The empress was a girl who had no real power. Chulan *was* Shen. But the Magister had sold himself to Calla, and that meant selling his loyal deputy alongside. For the first time in his privileged comfortable existence, Secretary Soma Ghee felt very alone. *Alone and scared.* Terrified, if truth be told.

Kill Hranic Finehair, the Ran had told him. The empress's beloved auxiliary leader. *His task.* Not Chulan's or his sinister servant Gujun's. *His . . .* A show of loyalty to the new ruler. *A test.*

He turned sharply when a soft sound ruffled the drapes behind him. Gujun the Slayer stood there. It was though his worried thoughts had conjured the killer from nowhere.

"What is it?" Soma Ghee felt a stab of fear in his loins. Why was Chulan's man here, and at this early hour?

"A brief message from the Magister." Gujun's dark eyes were on the frosted grass beyond his windows. Out there, a solitary bird was piping bravely, as pale skies promised a clear bright day.

"You had best deliver it, then," Soma Ghee forced authority into his voice. He was Secretary, and this man—though terrifying—was only a servant. *They need me, all of them.*

Gujun smiled. He turned briskly, and Soma Ghee gasped when he saw the slim golden dagger in the killer's left hand. "Finehair is dead," Gujun said. "Therefore, you are no longer needed, *Secretary*."

Soma Ghee turned, made for the door, as panic surged through his veins. Gujun blocked his escape. He leaped the other way, crashing through the glass of his solar, lacerating his body as the shards dug deep. He stumbled, fell to his knees. Gujun appeared in front of him.

"Please!" Soma Ghee saw the dagger glint, as the morning sunshine trapped its golden light. He screamed as the world turned dark, and red, the raw agony ripping him open and then itself engulfed by blackness and nothing.

GUJUN STOOD OVER THE SECRETARY'S CORPSE. HE crouched low and worked the dagger, sawing through Ghee's neck, yanking the head free and placing it in a bag that he tied to his belt. Task done, Gujun wiped the golden dagger clean. A gift from Ran Calla, beautifully crafted, a Laregozan stiletto inlaid with filigree gold over highly polished steel. A fine weapon worthy of his skills.

Those stupid blustering Northmen had put the Ran in a rare bad mood. Gujun had traveled between Chulan and his new master, as the Magister tried to calm Calla's rising rage. Chulan was desperate to repair the rift. The brutish brothers hadn't consulted with Calla before leading their freshly arrived countrymen in a rash and bold attack against Hranic's auxiliaries.

The fools had inflicted a lot of damage. Hranic Finehair himself had been killed in the fray. But then so had two thirds of

Calla's new warriors. He retained but sixty Northmen. The rest were crow food in that camp by the river.

Calla had raged when he'd received news of the stupid butchery. Especially as the oldest brother had boasted of the incident. The thug, Gorn, had laughed, tossing Finehair's severed head before Calla's feet, saying that it had been a "good fight." Calla had sent them back to Cardalis, lest he order his men to kill them and lose another score warriors doing so. A senseless business. But what could you expect of such ungainly folk?

Chulan had been swift to act. He'd ordered Gujun to kill the Secretary and send Ghee's head to Calla as compensation, a show of their continuing commitment—as Ghee was meant to deal with Hranic Finehair and had failed at that. And Chulan had had concerns about the Secretary lately. He hoped Ran Calla would take the message as a sign that the Magister was cleaning the mess at their end.

Gujun left the estate without sound. Servants and slaves stayed hidden as he returned to his fast horse, leapt in the saddle, and bid the mare canter north, back to Pol Shen. He met the soldier at the crossroads a mile beyond Ghee's estate and handed over a bloody bag.

"Take this to Ran Calla." The soldier nodded and departed in the opposite direction. The next task awaited. Chulan was afraid the unpredictable Calla would act faster than he'd said, and spring was only weeks away.

Thus, they'd had to step up their plans. He'd return to Pol Shen arriving at dusk, and the golden dagger would strike a second time that day.

"SHE WANTS US TO DO WHAT?" GURTEI'S FACE WAS ALMOST comical, his eyes bulged froglike in disbelief. Vian explained again to the Cutters gathered around him, save the three guarding the way through the forest.

"She wants me to return tonight and the following night. Says that I'm a good performer." He'd found them on the road as planned, leaving the palace by secret doors before dawn. He'd borrowed a horse from the innkeep and cantered south to the prearranged place, a cave at the edge of a steep line of hills.

Vian had imparted most of what Rasnei had told him, though he'd kept the more intimate parts of that conversation hidden. "She needs our help," he said.

"I thought you hated her and everything she stands for," Gurtei snorted.

"I do . . . or rather, *I did*. But things have changed." Vian forced a placating smile. "I didn't know the layout, the thin veneer that hides the cracks in Shen society. The real villain's Chulan, though I suspected it were so. Rasnei's a pawn in her Magister's power play. She's retains a few loyal servants in that palace, but most are in his pay. Her days are numbered unless we can help her. Aside those loyal in the city, Rasnei has the Northmen at the river. Her preferred auxiliaries. You need to go fetch Hranic Finehair. Inform the Auxiliary Captain that the empress's life is under threat."

"I can't believe I'm hearing this," Roile said, getting up and pacing about. Vian stared at their faces. Some were puzzled, a few looked angry like Roile. But Gurtei looked faintly amused.

"You, Rundali, are full of surprises."

"That may well be so, but our game has changed."

"Your game," Roile spat the words out. "Seriously, are you listening to this?" he asked Gurtei.

"Shut up and sit down," Gurtei said, and glaring, Roile obliged reluctantly. "Let's hear our new best friend out."

"Thank you," Vian said. "I went to the palace to kill Rasnei. That wasn't personal, but rather back-payment for her people killing or enslaving my kin, and capturing my twin sister."

"This we know," Gurtei said.

"Rasnei was aware of *our* intentions." Vian smiled. "That much you didn't know. The empress is not a fool, which is good considering the challenges she faces. She gave me an opportunity to do as I'd planned. It was a test—not only of myself, but of her own courage I believe. We were alone. I thought there'd be guards ready to pounce. There weren't. She'd heard from her spies how the Midnight Cutting Crew were involved with my sister's escape, an event that had caused considerable irritation to both Chulan and his puppet Ghee. The two men she loathes more than any other."

"Rasnei hates Chulan—what of it?" Gurtei asked.

"She has promised to pardon you all, and the other gangs— the Shadow Stalkers and Gray Ghosts. All of them except the Silver Slayers, who are apparently in Chulan's pocket."

"Why would Rasnei do this?" Gurtei's eyes narrowed.

"Because she needs your help, Gurtei," Vian said. "And strange as that may seem to you Cutters, I for one intend to comply." They looked at him askance. Roile had his head in his hands. Gurtei's eyes were blank.

Vian sighed. "There's more . . ."

"Thought there might be," Gurtei said.

"She . . . *we* . . ."

"You shafted the empress, and no longer feel you can carry out the task." Gurtei laughed abruptly. "Understandable, but hardly professional."

"Partly true, but it's not that." Vian stood up. "My instincts are telling me the only way for you to survive is to help her. Chulan and this Calla are the real enemies. I thought Rasnei was, but I was wrong. As long as she's alive, the empress is a threat to Chulan. He's done some deal with Cardalan. I fear the next move will be against Rasnei directly, insuring his own survival as Calla attacks."

Roile rolled his eyes, Truggan swore, and a few of the others cursed, too. Gurtei said nothing.

"It's up to you whether you trust her word," Vian said. "*I do.* That's why I'm riding back into that city to save her."

THE COURTESAN MAWLA TEI LET HIM THROUGH THE DOOR. Vian smiled and nodded as she handed him the candle.

"No one knows you are here," she said. "The empress wants to keep the arrangement discreet."

"Naturally," Vian said, producing the flute as proof of purpose. "My music is for her ears alone." He walked through the gilded doors into the musk- and incense-filled chamber.

Rasnei waited for him at the place where they'd made love the night before. Her dark eyes were moist. "I dreamed of you," she said. "You were a dragon with golden eyes. I was riding on your back, through vermillion skies while booming voices called out to us in a language I couldn't understand."

Vian smiled. "Stranger things are possible," he said. "Care for some flute music?" He flourished the flute between his fingers.

"I'd sooner talk," she said, reclining on her divan, the hint of a smile on her face.

"Funny you should say that." Vian stowed the instrument inside his tunic. "We do need to talk."

"Gurtei, his men?"

"They are yours," Vian said. "Though they don't know it yet. I told them you'd pardon them. Make them heroes. They'll come around. Everyone hates Chulan."

She nodded. "Good. What of us, then? I've decided I like your company, Salcara—so I'd prefer not to lose you anytime soon. Regrettably, I"—she paused, looked awkward—"cannot protect you from Chulan, or his people."

"Fortunately, you won't have to." Vian smiled. "Because I've come here to save you instead."

She stared at him, her glossy lips parted slightly. "Save *me* . . .?" She looked amused and was about to respond further, when the nearest candle flickered as a shadow crossed the room.

"Down!"

Vian shoved Rasnei to the floor and dived low after her, rolling sideways, as a figure emerged from the drapes brandishing a dagger. A masked man obscured in black. He struck out at Vian with the knife.

Vian rolled to a crouch, braced his feet beneath him and rose swiftly, kicking out with his left leg. The assassin dodged that kick and stabbed at Vian's outstretched leg. Vian twisted, spun around, then launched a spinning side-kick with his right, his heel ramming into the masked man's head, knocking him back against the bed.

He saw Rasnei clamber to her feet. "Stay down," Vian said, waving her back. "There could be more." The masked intruder leveled his knife. The man was skilled with the blade. A professional who clearly hadn't expected to be challenged, but seemed unfazed by Vian's counterattack.

He stepped forward, warily, then lunged for Vian's throat, hard and fast. Vian's hand slipped inside his tunic as he danced back out of reach. He produced the flute. The assailant darted forward again, stabbing and slicing in smooth arcs, this time for his stomach.

Vian blocked the blade with his flute, knocking the dagger aside. Stepping in fast, he brought the flute's mouthpiece up under the assassin's chin, crunching his head back, at the same time jabbing his other hand, middle knuckle extended, into the side of the masked face.

The assailant crumpled. Vian leaned over him, pulling the mask off his face. A dark-skinned man, scarred and hard looking, a bone earring in his right ear. "Is he dead?" Rasnei asked, leaning over. He noted the lack of fear in her face.

"Yes." Vian stowed his flute again. "Do you recognize him?"

She nodded. "One of Gujun's men. That's the leader of the Silent Slayers, and works covertly for Chulan. That bone earring marks this man clearly as a member of Gujun's gang. I expect he has membership ranking tattoos branded on his flesh, though I prefer not to look."

"Seems everyone is in Chulan's pay," Vian said, leaning over the corpse. He looked at the door, hearing a muffled scream cut short. More attackers were imminent. "It's time we left your palace, Empress."

"That's not possible."

Vian smiled. "Everything is possible. And I've decided I like you company, too." More screams, the sound of clashing steel. "We're done talking. Time to move, Empress." He grabbed her warm hand in his.

She nodded. "It would appear so."

They fled the chamber. Rasnei screamed once when she saw

Mawla Tei's neat body pooling blood by the door, her pretty dark eyes glazed, the throat slit wide open.

They reached the secret corridors and ran on through. More corpses littered the stairs. Guards—doubtless stabbed by the attacker on his way up, their dead eyes staring up in disbelief.

Vian paused by the last one. He listened for pursuit. No one followed close. The screams and fighting were fading off inside the palace. "Come on," he said, grabbing her small smooth hand again. They reached the gardens. Vian pushed the doors open and stepped outside into the dark canopy of foliage. He stopped when he saw a man standing beneath a cherry tree. Arms folded neatly, a small figure clad in black, shiny leather, with two immaculate Jian blades slung across his back.

"That is Gujun," Rasnei said, her voice at last showing fear. "He is a killer." The smiling figure glided toward them.

Vian gripped his flute. "I need you to run, Empress," he said, calmly. "I will join you at the gates."

THE FIRST CROSSING

SKARNESS WAS a ribbon of stone wedged between steep, dark slopes and the cold, lapping water of the fjord. They stood, taking in the sights, as Sheriff Doggan made his way along the jetty. Close by, a few people were milling around in what looked like a market. Jaran saw traders' stalls and smoke drifting up from firepits. He detected the rich aroma of roast pork, and his nostrils tingled.

"This way," Doggan said, making for the nearest buildings. "We'll get some food and inquire about boats, and then you're on your own."

"Sounds like a plan," Finvar said behind him. "The food part anyway." They walked briskly, eyes on everything and anyone. Jaran felt tense. The creature Stoon had shaken him more than he had admitted. Sheega and Erlund. They both had to die, and quickly.

He'd wanted to deal with Erlund first. But Savarna was right, the witch was the real threat. King Erlund could rot in Grimhold until he paid him a visit. If Sheega sent more of those seaweed creatures, they were in real trouble.

I am coming for you, witch.

Jaran slung Griner over his left shoulder as he walked, Savarna's small hand gripped in his. She hadn't spoken much today, still looking pensive after the attack in Doggan's cottage. Even Finvar kept his thoughts inside his head.

They reached the marketplace where men stood talking, bartering and discussing their various woes. Children chased and laughed. He saw dogs lounging, women bickering in a corner, one stood scalding her man. Jaran almost laughed when he saw her strike him with a water urn.

Doggan stopped at a stall where a rotund, shaven-headed man stood roasting hog on a spit. The sheriff addressed the man, who nodded, tore off chunks of meat, and passed them over. Doggan parted with more coin.

Jaran thanked him when he threw some of the hot meat his way. He chomped down. It was delicious, and more kept coming. They ate better than they had in days.

"Hulmgar here says Graftin is your best bet," Doggan told them as he worried the pork through his brown teeth. "Graftin's a local fisher. Wilder than most. He'll most likely let you purchase one of his craft for enough coin."

"Purchase?" Jaran said, looking at Finvar, who shrugged. "Doubt we can afford that. I'd sooner borrow boat and skipper."

"Good luck trying," Doggan laughed. "I'm off to the taverns, where I'm fairly confident I'll find my sons. Once I've banged their heads enough, I'll be heading home. I'll not linger long, Gurn doesn't tarry at the dock when light fades."

They thanked him and looked around. Finvar yawned. "Best

we find this Graftin and do a deal—or else just steal his boat while he isn't looking."

"What of Carlo Sarfe?" Savarna asked.

Jaran shook his head. "I don't think your mystery sailor's here. Nor should we waste hours scouring this town and countryside for him. We need to cross that water before she finds us again." Savarna nodded, though she looked unhappy.

"It will work out," Jaran told her, gripping her hand. "'Tis destined. And, I'm ready to see my island."

She nodded, managed a tight smile.

They found Graftin mending nets at the northern end of town. He was a skinny fellow, with scraggy gray beard and long tangled hair. He glanced their way with flinty blue eyes.

"You three look like trouble," he said, his accent thick and salty.

"Only for those who court it," Finvar said, as they walked up to where the fisher worked on his nets.

"The island," Jaran said. "I need to get there."

Graftin's eyes were veiled. "There are lots of islands off this coast. Most are inhabited by seals and such."

"I'm speaking of a large island, perhaps a day's sail offshore. You know of it, I'm sure—though I'll not mention the name."

"No one sails near that place," Graftin spat, his eyes hostile. "You are fools, or else under the glamour of she who dwells there."

"What do you know of her?"

Graftin spat again. He looked miserable and stared hard at Jaran, as though he recognized him from somewhere. "You have the look," he said eventually.

"What do you mean by that?" Jaran reached down and

grabbed his coat. "Speak." He lifted Graftin to his feet with one hand. The fisher glared at him and shook his head.

"I dare not," he said. "I knew you were fucking trouble."

"What do you know about Val—"

"Don't say it!" Graftin cut in, his eyes wide with fear. "She is always listening," he muttered in a quieter voice. "Her reach is long, her memory longer."

"You're from there, aren't you?" Savarna said quietly. Jaran glanced her way in surprise. "I see it in his face. The sorrow, loathing and fear."

Graftin nodded. "I was born there. The island was my home. I was one of the lucky few that escaped after she came and changed everything."

"I'm Jaran Saerk. I was born there. I mean to kill the witch who caused my people so much pain."

"I know who you are, Jaran Hrelgisson," Graftin said. "We all feared you would return one day and stir everything up. There were rumors concerning Hrelgi's lost wife and son. None thought them dead on the island, though the witch had ordered it so. You look like the Jarle's eldest son, and you're the right age." He spat down on his hands and shuddered. "But I'm not the one who can help you."

"Then who can?"

"Gurn the ferryman."

Jaran looked up when Savarna nudged him. "There's something flashing on the side of that mountain," she said. He gazed past the roofs and woods until his eyes saw what she was pointing at. A shimmering contortion moving down the side of the hill, perhaps four or five miles distant.

"What is that?" Savarna asked, and then her face paled.

Finvar cursed. "What I saw in fucking Hragglund," he said. "Looks like we'll soon have more company."

They watched in fascinated dread, as the shimmering lights became a glittering worm, wending down the steep sides of the mountain. The fiery worm broke apart, becoming distant figures. Jaran counted nine. Tall and manlike, clad in what looked to be green mail, and outlandish helmets. They all carried axes and shields, with short stabbing-spears sloped across shoulders, and were marching toward the town at alarming speed.

"It appears Stoon has brothers," Jaran said, his voice grim. "We need your boat, fisher."

Graftin's eyes were on the hill. He looked terrified. "*She* sent them," he muttered. "Ghosts from the mirror-lands. We're all going to die."

"Shut up and untie that craft." Jaran pointed at the nearest vessel. A single-sailed lean hulled craft, some sixty foot in length.

"I'll take you," a gruff voice said. Jaran wasn't overly surprised to see Gurn sanding at the water's edge. The boatman smiled. "For a price."

The distant green-clad warriors had reached the base of the mountain, and were trotting along the thin ribbon of road toward Skarness. Graftin sat with his head in hands, but Gurn walked past him and hopped across onto the waiting ship. He untied the mooring ropes and signaled them to jump onboard. They complied without hesitation. Graftin joined them, seeing the strange-looking warriors reach the furthest houses of the town.

"You two, go raise the sail," Gurn shouted across at Jaran. Jaran placed his axe aside, and Finvar joined him. Together they hauled up yard and cloth, as Gurn poled off and then worked the tiller. Savarna stood watching him, and Graftin stared with blank eyes as the dock slipped away.

They heard screams, shouts, and dogs baying. Mercifully, the noises faded quickly as they drifted out across the water. Jaran and Finvar untied the gaskets and let the sail drop, before lashing its trailing ropes to the stays.

The ship caught breeze and current, its speed increasing, clipping a pace through that clear, clean water. Skarness and its horrors faded far behind. Gurn swung the tiller and Graftin's ship turned seaward.

Jaran gazed that way for a time, then went and joined Savarna. Her face was bleak, a glint of tears lined her eyes.

"What is wrong?" he asked, placing an arm around her shoulders.

"The townsfolk—they're all going to die at the hands of those . . . monsters. That's because of us, Jaran. We leave corpses wherever we go."

"That's why I have to kill that witch," Jaran's voice was grim. He'd hated leaving the village to those fiends—but what choice had they had? "It's me she wants. I'm sorry you're involved, Savarna. I was happy at first, but I'd change that now if I could. You should have gone your own way, when you could."

"I'm staying put," she said, but the tears streamed down her cheeks. "I miss him, Jaran. *Vian*. Especially at times like this. We were always so close. These days, I can't even see his face, despite trying every night. My brother is gone from me. I'm not losing you, too."

"We'll soon have answers," Finvar said, sitting down beside them, his keen dark eyes on the helmsman. "I, for one, would like to know why that shifty old bugger is helping us, and what payment he's expecting."

"Gurn reminds me of someone else," Jaran said. "Doubtless he'll show his hand at some point. It doesn't matter. Once we beach ashore, I'm seeking her out. Sheega's rule is coming to an abrupt and unpleasant end."

"You think it will be that easy?" Savarna asked him.

"I prefer not to think," he answered, "but rather to do. Tyho gave me this blade for a reason, the Traveler was helping me for another. The old shaman, Odel, in that Tseole camp said we three are stronger together and a match for that witch. Let's not worry about how, but rather focus on where she's hiding, and dig her out."

"The Great Hall," a faint voice said. Jaran turned and saw Graftin staring bleakly across. "She took it over after Hrund the old Jarle died. She lived there with his surviving son Erlund, before she sent him away, preferring her faerie lover."

They all looked across at him. Finvar's jaw had dropped in surprise. "Faerie lover?" he said, as Savarna and Jaran exchanged puzzled glances. It seemed Graftin had got over his dread of speaking about Valkador, or at least thought it no longer mattered, as he was doomed anyway.

"Ranning, he is called." Graftin hawked and spat. "He came out from the sea, the same month I escaped through the island's nets—more by kind chance than skillful navigation. Few get through Sheega's fret."

"Is he some kind of fish?" Finvar asked. Jaran and Savarna stared at him. "It's a fair question."

"Ranning is a creature of Faerie, the Otherrealm—or 'mirror-lands' as we called them," Graftin muttered. "He is most danger-ous. Sheega was bad enough on her own, but when Ranning arrived, things got far worse. Those families who dared fled to the far corners of the island, scratching out what meagre living they could, anything to survive, while being far away as possible from those two.

"Sheega and her lover keep mostly to the hall. She had her dark arts, while the elf-man walked the seashore alone at night. I saw Ranning once, when returning from night-fishing by the lake. He was standing on the beach staring out across the ocean, a long ash pole gripped in his hands, a horse's skull mounted at the top. He was singing in a weird, high voice, chanting something. A summoning of sorts, I suspected. The sound made the hairs stand up on my neck. The following day, I planned my escape from the island."

"And now you're going back," Finvar said, cheerfully.

"Seems possible." Graftin nodded, his face white and eyes lost.

They cleared the fjord and entered open water, the chop growing and a swell rising that broke hard across the bow. Graftin's ship cut clean through the rising waves, heading due west beneath clear blue skies.

Jaran glanced over at the grim-faced Gurn. Why was the shifty old man so familiar? He pulled a face then knelt forward, kissing Savarna on her cheek. "Get some sleep while you can," he told her. "I've no doubt we will need all our strength and extra resourcefulness when we land."

She nodded, her red hair spilling across her face as the wind stiffened and salt air chilled. Finvar was nodding off, his back braced against a stack of oars. Graftin sat staring into space, his eyes haunted, as though he were caught halfway between reality and nightmare. Jaran approached the wily tillerman. Gurn grunted as he stepped alongside.

"Want me to take her for a spell, give you a break?"

"I enjoy this work," Gurn said, shaking his head. "Miss the

merry days, dancing over the many oceans of this troubled world."

"You weren't always a ferryman, then?"

Gurn laughed, a crow's croak of wry amusement. "No. I've pursued lots of trades over the years. Plied the seas, fought in foreign wars. I've had a very long and interesting life." He flashed Jaran a sharp, silvery stare.

"You remind me of someone," Jaran said.

"There's a good reason for that." Gurn awarded him another sharp look.

"Who are you?"

Gurn shrugged. "Nobody much."

"Why offer your services on this perilous trip? You know where we are going."

Gurn gazed across the water. "We haven't got there yet. This is a test of your resolve, my young friend."

Jaran stared hard at him for a moment and then shrugged. "You're a strange fellow, Gurn. Can't say I like you much. Keep your riddles as you will—I'll learn the truth soon enough." He left Gurn without waiting for a response. The man was up to something. Perhaps he worked for Sheega and would betray them? *I'll be watching, sly one.*

Thoughts grim, Jaran walked along the ship's length, stopping at the prow. Once there, Jaran stood gazing west for the next hour. He watched in brooding silence as the sun set, flooding both sky and water with pinkish gold then crimson.

"I hope we get there before dark." Savarna joined him and slipped an arm around his waist.

"Finvar said it isn't far." He smiled, glad she was with him, and glanced back along the ship's length. The cliffs of Leeth were far behind. They stood silently watching as light faded, until Savarna nudged his arm again.

"I see something over there." A mist was rising in the distance, a murkiness that swallowed the remaining light.

"That must be it," Jaran said. "The fog Fin mentioned." As soon as he spoke, the ship changed tack and pitched hard toward the growing blanket of mist.

"Looks like we're going to be eaten alive by that fret." Fin grinned as he joined them. "I had to join you, couldn't bear Graftin's miserable face any longer. Poor fellow—he's convinced we're going to die."

"Everyone dies," Jaran said. *Not our turn yet.* They watched as the darkness swelled like a broiling storm ahead. Jaran went aft and claimed his axe, Finvar slipped the bow from his shoulders, knocking arrow to string. Savarna bit her bottom lip. The mist was a smoky tower leaning high over them, beckoning them to come inside its shifting walls.

"You must hold to courage," a strange voice said from behind. It could have been Gurn speaking, but it was hard to tell. The blackness billowed and swelled. Jaran saw fingers of fog wrapping themselves around the ship's hull as though pulling her in.

A deep chill and silence surrounded them, as utter darkness cloaked sky and ship. Jaran gripped his axe. "I hope you're ready, Sheega," he said. Then the fog swallowed them whole.

28

SHEEGA'S CHILDREN

ERLUND GASPED as the bolt of light blinded him and the sudden gust extinguished the sconces. He staggered from the throne where he'd been dazing, the ale spilling from his tankard. The lightning flicked and vanished, replaced by darkness and bitter chill. The hall was empty—the hour was early, dusk having fled west beneath scurrying storm clouds.

The hounds had fled. Erlund had the hall to himself. He clambered on the throne, spilling more ale, and gripping the heavy wooden arms until his giddiness relented enough for him to see straight again. He refilled his tankard from the large ale jug his steward had left.

The lightning flashed again, this time farther off. The thunder rumbled and shook the tables. The storm was passing like a thousand horses galloping through the sky.

A third strike, and another. He drained his ale, reached for the jug again, then stopped as Sheega's fiery face blurred and flickered at him from the hearth. Erlund blanched and shivered, seeing the faggots sucked dry of heat, the fires dwindle and fizz, and choked smoke trail off to dissipate above his head.

Her blazing eyes pinned him to the throne, the smoky hair filling the hearth and coiling like worms in well-rotted soil. "He is coming," Sheega said, her words were steely knives scraping inside his skull. "The nemesis, and yet you do nothing."

Erlund choked on his ale and, coughing, threw the tankard at her face in the fire. Her eyes blazed angrily, then faded back to mocking glints of blue. "I sent Holtarn forth with some of my best men," Erlund yelled at her, "looking for Hrelgisson, and the others. What else could I do? You're the one with scrying powers."

"Holtarn was riding in the wrong direction," she sneered. "The boy's almost as stupid as his father." Her voice surged louder, blasting ash out from the hearth. Erlund shivered again, pulled his cloak around his shoulders. *Freezing in here.*

"Then I'll send Holtarn out again when he returns, and with more men." He reached for the ale jug.

"Don't bother," Sheega mocked him. "We do not need your aid, Ranning and I. And I will deal with our sons, in due course. A sorry tale, how they retained some of your obtuse stubbornness, despite all my work on them. Blunt tools they've proved."

"You should have schooled them better," he said, wincing as those eyes bore into his. It was always hazardous risking her rage.

"And don't worry about Holtarn," she said, ignoring his feeble retaliation with the flicker of a smile. "You won't see him again, unless I send him to kill you, which I might one day."

"I'll be waiting for him, sword honed and ready."

"You . . .?" Her mouth twisted in a cruel smile. "I doubt you've the strength to wield a sword these days, pathetic creature that you are."

"Fuck you."

She laughed. "I corrected our youngest son's course—he is riding for the coast. I've ordered Holtarn to return to my island. He will prove useful here if Hrelgisson breaks through. But he's small fry, as I have other, more reliable fighters." Her white face flickered and faded, leaving behind a dead fire and bitter damp chill.

Erlund reached for the jug again. He grabbed it with both shaking hands and poured the entire contents in his mouth, spilling most onto the floor. *Fuck . . . you . . .*

"Look what you've become . . ." Her voice faded, as the beautiful face flickered along the walls before vanishing, replaced by silence and more bitter chill.

"It's what you made me, witch!" Erlund hurled the jug across the hall. He stood, grabbed his sword where it rested close by. *Enough.* He would ride out, find Jaran Hrelgisson and kill him, or be killed in the process. It didn't matter. He'd not spend another night alone with ghosts and shadows.

"THE KING IS LEAVING GRIMHOLD," GUNSALA SAID, AS SHE studied the runes spread across the shabby table. "He means to depart in the morning."

The vagabond healer watched her and showed her crooked smile. "You've done well, child," her voice croaked. "You learn quickly. The king will pass through this wood on the way to the coast. Tomorrow."

"He rides for the coast?"

"Erlund rides to meet his destiny," the woman smiled again. "It is past time, Gunsala." Her blue eyes narrowed. "There are certain things I need you to get before morning. After waiting so long, time is running out."

Gunsala nodded. She was used to running errands for the healer, fetching this or that herb, and delivering poultices secretly to those in need. She never questioned the woman unless told to, but always listened. The healer-woman's eyes were hollow. She looked eaten up inside. Gunsala suspected she was sickly. A healer who couldn't save herself. Perhaps Gunsala could save her instead.

"I will go," she said.

HOLTARN REINED IN AT THE CLIFF EDGE, HIS FATHER'S thirty borrowed thanes alongside. They'd reached the southern rim of Lothargon Fjord. Clear, blue water danced far below. Holtarn smiled, pleased with himself. He was his mother's favorite. Gorn and Valgarn had abandoned the cause. He alone remained loyal. He'd be well rewarded on return to Valkador.

His keen gaze turned west where the distant glimmer of ocean greeted the fjord's mouth. He saw the ribbon of houses, recognizing Skarness from his younger days, when he and his brothers had crossed from Valkador, hired horses in that town, and then rode like madmen across the desolate country comprising the coastal region of Leeth.

Holtarn grinned. There would be vessels down there. He and Erlund's men would help themselves. No need to rush. They'd drink the taverns dry first, and then plough any wenches they could muster up.

An hour later, thirsty, his mind on ale, Holtarn led his riders along the narrow road beneath the stark pines toward the first huts of Skarness town. He saw no smoke rising, heard no sounds. That struck him as strange. There should be people, animals, the sounds of hammers and saws, men at work. He bid his mare pick up her pace, the men bunching behind. Holtarn reached the first houses and reined in sharply.

Three corpses were strewn across the road, the eyes missing and faces crow-pecked. He could see more past the next house. The bodies were mutilated and torn apart, as though some giant rabid beast had fallen upon them.

He dismounted and took a closer look, seeing the severed limbs and missing heads where axes had done their work. Axes meant men had done this. But who?

What happened here?

Holtarn wasn't the caring sort. But what he saw in Skarness struck him as reckless and wasteful. Villagers had uses. They could be taxed and bullied, the women ploughed. And there were always ale and food to plunder.

He walked past the first corpses entering the main part of town. Crows lifted like storm clouds. They drifted away and settled further off, their dark voices mocking his clumsy approach. Holtarn saw the fear in his men's faces. *Sorcery.* The only explanation. His mother must have conjured up something very bad.

The men dismounted and tied their beasts to fences. They accompanied him, shields held ready, and spears and axes gripped with white knuckles. Holtarn unslung his own heavy axe. He wasn't afraid. Instead, he was angry, and he wanted to wreck havoc on the deranged sendings who'd done this.

Skarness was empty of life. No living soul in sight, save the crows who still mocked him from the turfed rooftops or distant pines.

There was no food. The only ale barrels he saw were drained and broken apart, again by axes. *Who would do that?* Holtarn had never witnessed such wanton destruction. Worse, there were no ships in the small harbor, and the lone dock that used to hold the Lothargon ferry was broken, the planks ripped up and missing in places.

"What now?" Grim-faced Torgan stared at him. Erlund's captain was no craven, but his eyes were wild as he looked about in horror and disbelief.

Holtarn shrugged. "It must be the Saerk's work. My mother says my cousin is most dangerous, perhaps insane. We will hunt Jaran Saerk down and kill the rabid mangy beast he's become."

He knew his cousin couldn't have done this. But why tell his father's men? This way, they would gladly assist him in trapping the renegade and deal with his friends while Holtarn butchered his cousin. Holtarn would present his mother with Saerk's head. She'd bestow a small kingdom on him for that. One in the eye for Gorn and Val.

CRANE'S MILKY EYES FLICKERED AS HE WATCHED THE SHIP slip from view into the haze which always shrouded Valkador. His eight brothers stood silently beside him, their faces hidden beneath the masks hanging from their kettle helms.

It had been good to kill the humans in that village. Mankind had always been the enemy of Faerie, or the Faen, as his father Ranning called their people. They were the original occupants of this world, Ansu.

But the wretched creature called man had crawled from the earth, copulating and spreading like disease, or countless plague beetles. They'd destroyed everything in their path, forcing the ancient races take shelter in the dark and flee to the hidden corners of the world, driven to exile and near extinction. And also to the fathomless depths of the ocean, where his father's people had built their underwater castles. They were Rann's dark children, who served her father the old sea god, Sensuata.

Spawned from spilled seed and weed, bound by runes and spellcraft, Crane was a creature of hate. He was also new to this earthly existence, his solid form created from sorcery fused with loathing, as were the eight tall warriors standing beside him, and the other remaining two who'd stayed on the island, ensuring their guardians came to no harm.

Their schooling had been swift, their ability to learn quicker. Crane was clever, as were his siblings. Ranning had taught them the history of their world, where they came from, and how their forbearers' inheritance had been robbed by mankind, long before the Witch-Guard—as he called the twelve—were born. And their foster mother, the witch Sheega, had placed all her hatred, bitterness and savagery inside their hearts.

They were cunning and ruthless and filled with a keen desire to kill—it was their only purpose. But one had failed already. Stoon had died. He'd abandoned his brothers and struck out against the enemy alone. But the enemy, the one their mother feared and hated, the man she called Hrelgisson, was rumored powerful, hard to kill. Thus, Stoon had been broken, and the other Witch-Guard learnt what sorrow meant when they stumbled upon his body in that village.

They'd found people there, and the killing had started. It continued in the town Skarness, but their quarry had escaped. Crane had seen him and the others departing in a ship. He'd mind-signaled his mother, who had told him to await her command on that shore.

And so, Crane and his brothers waited in brooding silence as the day's light faded, and clouds scurried like torn banners in the darkening skies above.

THE MIST CONTAINED VOICES AND SHAPES. SAVARNA SAW huge figures lumbering past, heard the screams and shouts of the dying on some distant battlefield. She saw triangular birds flying up, and exploding into puffs of light. Beneath and all around them was the constant, grinding roar of gray nothingness.

Jaran gripped her hand in his, his other fist wrapped around Griner's ash haft. Finvar stood beside them, his lean face taut, and eyes wide with apprehension. She couldn't see Graftin, but Gurn's dour shape loomed out from the passing shadow as he steered the craft forward.

Above her head, the sail dripped limp, but Savarna could tell they were moving—or, rather, something was drawing them in. She saw faces emerging from the white gloom. These glared at her, then faded back into nothing. Once, close by, Savarna heard the clear tolling of a solitary bell, and then later the eerie sound of harp song trailing off into the distance.

Hold to courage, the helmsman Gurn had said. She was determined to do just that, and not show the fear and dread she felt rising from below. Gurn—whoever he really was—was taking them deeper into a world of shifting nothingness.

The passage through the mist had taken hours, or so it seemed to her. She saw nothing substantial in that fret. No island raised its rocky shores. The noises and sounds came and went, the faces and shapes, too. Time dragged. Then a hoarse voice boomed off to her right.

"Ware, the rocks . . ."

The mist had dispersed, revealing a long, broken line of cliffs and the rocky strand comprising beach and shoreline, yards away. The sea was crashing and surging, the white breakers foaming and beating hard against those cliffs.

Gurn yanked hard on the tiller. The vessel lurched to starboard, allowing cold waves to drench the deck as the ship tilted badly. Savarna was tossed aside like a broken doll, the waves drenching her and pulling her down. She tried to yell, but her mouth filled with seawater. Her body was sinking. She saw Vian's taut face for an instant.

Vian . . .

Then Savarna felt a scrape along her side, and screamed inwardly as her body was thrown free of the waves and spewed up on that strand. She vomited brine and crawled clear of the spume.

She heard a shout and saw Jaran running toward her, his blond hair soaked and trailing behind, and his hands gripping Tyho's axe.

He pulled her to her feet. "Are you hurt?" His pale blue eyes were wild.

"No," she said, gazing around half-stunned. "I don't think so. Where is Fin?"

"Up there." Jaran pointed to the dark sky above where thunder clouds were passing like a host heading west. She glimpsed a brown speck, saw the hawk settle on the beach beside them. The bird shimmered and blurred, then Finvar stood where it had been.

"Is this Valkador?" Savarna gazed around, looking for somewhere they could climb to escape from this narrow beach.

Jaran shook his head. "I do not know," he said. They looked up as Gurn emerged from the sea, walking calmly toward them, his hair and beard dripping and eyes doleful.

"He is dead." Finvar shuddered. "See how he moves through those waves?"

Gurn stopped yards away, the waves passing over and through him. Then his face peeled away like dry parchment scorched by cinders. "I told you this was a test . . ." the voice didn't belong to Gurn. It sounded distant and faint. The doleful tone trailed off like spume, and Gurn's body imploded into water, blood, and bones blending with the waves.

You must find Rune . . . the strange voice sounded very far away. *Only he can help you break through her fence . . .*

"We must be back in Leeth then," Savarna said. "That spell-fret turned us around. What's the matter?" She saw the wild look in Jaran's eye.

"It was him," he said. "The Traveler."

"Are you sure?" Finvar asked him.

"I'd recognize that voice anywhere," Jaran said. "I knew there was something *wrong* about Gurn."

"We can't help that," Savarna said. "And this is not the time for solving riddles."

"You're right—we need to find a way off this beach before it vanishes under water," Jaran said. "That tide's coming in swiftly."

They walked, drenched along the dark broken shore, until the morning light revealed a break in the cliffs where a small cove allowed them to clamber up rocks and rest exhausted amid bird droppings and gannets' nests.

"Graftin must be drowned," Finvar said, miserably. "His ship's in splinters and gone."

"Then we have to acquire another one," Jaran said.

"We have to find the sailor Carlo Sarfe," Savarna told them, and her friends gazed at her. "What do you know about Rune, Fin?"

"No more than you." Finvar looked glummer than before. "Heard the name mentioned before. Another bloody mystery, same as me not knowing how and when I change into a bird. It's stressing me out."

"Never mind that—you're alive," Jaran told him, as his large hand squeezed Savarna's. "It's a brief setback, that's all. Whatever he is up to, the Traveler is no friend of Sheega. We should take comfort from that. We will fare south along this coast until we reach another town or settlement. We'll find a ship and try again. We'll do this right, with or without your mystery sailor's assistance, and the aforementioned Rune creature." He smiled at her. "The witch has won the first round. But Sheega has no idea how persistent I am."

They waited until well rested, and then started climbing over the maze of rocks toward the break in the cliffs ahead. A long scramble and climb, until at last they reached dry ground and a level plateau of cliff, jutting out two hundred feet below the main clifftops.

They walked for a mile, the sea glinting below and to their right as they trod. Savarna was frozen, her limbs stiff and heavy. She was also badly bruised. Jaran looked unscathed by their shipwreck, and Finvar too, though his dark eyes were wild and the hair strewn across his thin face.

They reached a place where the cliffs were lower, and a long shale slide awarded enough purchase for them to climb swiftly.

They gained the clifftops proper and stood panting as the

cold wind stung their faces, and Savarna's hair whipped into her eyes. She blinked, tugged her damp locks free and stared.

The cliffs ranged south for mile upon mile, merging into a haze that meant no habitation close by. A wide, empty grassland spread east as far as the eyes could see. Something glittered out there. It vanished, then reappeared, glinting again.

Jaran saw it, too, and his eyes narrowed. "I think we might have company," he said, and Finvar cursed as he saw the shimmer in the distance.

"Stoon's brothers have found us," he said. "Old Gurn must have dropped us back where we started. Nice of the old boy."

"We had better push on," Jaran said, moving forward and grabbing Savarna's hand. He froze when the sound of hoofbeats and shouting announced more company coming from the other direction.

"What now?" Finvar squinted and shielded his eyes, gazing north along the cliff line. "Oh, I see them. This just keeps getting better. A score of riders, perhaps more. Warriors bearing shields and spears. Ugly buggers, especially the one at the front. Looks like your uncle got wind of your whereabouts, Jaran Saerk."

Jaran let go of Savarna's hand and gripped Griner in both hands. "Let them come." His pale eyes were filled with fury.

Savarna watched as the riders thundered closer. She counted thirty Northmen, all heavily armed, in bright mail shirts and woolen cloaks that billowed in the wind.

"Thirty against three," Finvar confirmed her count. "Then there's that lot." His head nudged to where the distant shimmer had split into several tall greenish shapes heading their way.

"What do you suggest?" Savarna stared at Jaran, the horsemen nearly upon them. "Fin?" The smaller man looked in pain, as though he fought with himself.

"I'll kill most of them," Jaran's blue eyes were blurry. He bit into the haft of his axe.

"That's not overly helpful, lover," Savarna said, wishing she retained a weapon other than her knife. The riders came to a halt thirty yards away. The leader broke off from the main group and urged his mount closer. He stopped twenty feet from where the three of them stood.

"The rabbits are snared," the Northman said. He looked like Jaran, though cruel of features, and his hair a shade darker. A big man who sat upon his horse with arrogant ease.

"Who the fuck are you?" Jaran spat in the soil, and then gnawed on his axe handle again.

"Your death, Hrelgisson," the rider laughed. "I'm your long-lost cousin, Holtarn Erlundsson. I bring special greetings from my mother, and the king too." He slipped from the saddle, producing a double-headed axe and sliding the round shield into his other arm. "Time to die, Jaran Saerk."

The other Northmen had ridden up beside him and also were dismounting. Savarna's eyes caught a glint of movement—she flicked her gaze inland and saw the green-gold warriors were almost upon them, too.

"I can do this," a voice said behind her. "I *can* fucking do this."

Jaran stepped forward, the axe swinging slowly.

"Grab his arm, girl."

"What?" She turned and saw Finvar staring at her like a man possessed.

"Grab—him, Savarna. We need to do this now."

She nodded, reached out and locked an arm around Jaran's shoulders. He was oblivious, Griner raised in mid-swing. The weight of its motion nearly lifted her from her feet. She hung on, felt Finvar's rough hand grip her other one.

"Hold on!" He yelled in her ear. "Don't let go this time."

Savarna felt the ground lurch, then yelled as sudden pain jabbed in her ears. Jaran's axe cut through air. She heard him roar and curse. Then the ground fell away. She heard shouts of fear beneath her, and one of rage. She looked down, as the cold air shredded her hair and half-blinded her. Holtarn Erlundsson stood gazing up, the double-headed axe held high.

"You cannot escape me, cousin. My axe hungers for your neck!" The ground tilted, Holtarn and his men vanished, the cliffs fell away and she fell with them.

"Hold tight!" She heard Finvar yelling beside her. She gripped his hand tight as she could and leant close into Jaran's side as they tunneled down through winter skies, the sea rushing up to meet them.

Savarna braced herself for impact, but she was jolted back as Finvar changed course and angled out across the waves, skimming over their frothing crowns. The morning blurred into murk, the water shrank back, and the towering veil of mist rose up forbidding in the distance.

"I cannot pierce that," Finvar yelled in her ear. Then he pulled her close and Savarna felt her body spinning. They were circling high over the water again. In the distance, a mile beyond the fog, she saw a ship, a schooner plunging west.

Finvar muttered something and they lurched in that direction. They sailed through clouds, descending again until the ship grew in size. "This might be bad—*stopping is the hard part*," she heard Finvar say. The ship was beneath them, swelling as they tumbled. They were falling again, drifting down like splinters from the sky.

"Change!" Finvar yelled in her ear. Savarna blinked, then her body hit the deck and she crumpled in pain. Jaran still gripped her arm. Savarna blinked again and rolled to her knees.

A man loomed over them. A handsome face, deeply tanned.

"We meet again, Carlo Sarfe," Savarna said, before passing out unconscious on the deck.

29

AIKASHI

AN IMAGE of Savarna's face flashed through his head, and Vian heard her cry out in pain. Then the blur of steel jabbed at his throat, and he dived low.

He rolled sideways, kicked out, and saw movement to his right. He rolled again, as steel dug in the ground where he'd been.

"You're quick," a dark voice said. "That won't save you." Vian could see the man watching him, a Jian blade resting on each shoulder, a half smile on his lips. Vian rolled to a crouch, rising slowly, his eyes on the other man.

"That's a matter of opinion," Vian said, slipping the flute into his hands. The man in black leather smiled when he saw that. Then with lightning precision, he danced forward, the Jian blades swinging across, one at Vian's neck, the other lower, aiming for a disembowel.

Instead of diving back, Vian caught his enemy off-guard by jumping straight at him, close enough to avoid both blades slicing, and quick enough to strike the man's head with his flute.

He darted to his right, as the swords swung again. "You must be Chulan's henchman," Vian said, stepping back out of range, as the other watched him with impassive dark eyes. "You're overrated."

"I'm Gujun the Slayer," the black-clad swordsman said. "I'm going to take my time killing you. First, I'm going to retrieve that instrument and shove it up your arse." He levelled the Jian blades again, but stopped when shouts and the rush of feet announced more guards had finally arrived.

"Another time then, Rundali," Gujun dipped his head. "Regrettable, but I can't let my real quarry escape."

"I won't let you have her." Vian locked eyes with Gujun for a moment, then both of them cut off in different directions as the first guard arrived crashing through the bushes.

Vian ran, ducking beneath vines, crisscrossing through trees, and vaulting over flower beds, his lithe form dancing around statues, sprinting under fountains. Soon he was lost in the mass of tangled foliage, the sky occluded above, the shouts of guards fading off again.

He stopped and caught his breath. She'd be at the gate, if she wasn't the one who sent those guards. Clearly, they weren't Chulan's—or else his assassin wouldn't have fled like a thief in the darkness. Vian walked slowly out from that undergrowth. So hard to see. Somewhere close, an owl hooted twice. Vian thought of Savarna's face—the first time he'd seen her image in days. She must be in trouble.

Stay strong . . .

He mouthed the words with eyes closed, sending his thought out into the void. He took deep breaths, allowing his mind to settle and his heart beats to slow. The gate was over there, the latent creature inside him said. *That way . . .* Vian sped out from the bushes, weaving and sprinting, head down. Minutes later, he saw the iron rungs and locks that kept the populace out of the Imperial Gardens. *Thank you*, he whispered to the Aikashi spirit within him.

A shadow loomed from the bushes beside the gate. Rasnei's face was pale in the dark, her big eyes wild. "I thought you were dead," she told him. "That the only joy I've ever known was lost as quickly as I'd found it."

Vain smiled, and threw his arms around her. "I'm not that easy to kill," he said.

"That was Gujun," she said. "He sent that assassin."

"I'm sure there are others creeping all over the palace," Vian said. "Gujun hasn't given up. I doubt your guards are a match for him. We need to get out before either find us."

Rasnei placed a hand on his arm, her eyes were sad. "My brave adventurer, this game is up. You cannot hope to escape with the Empress of Shen in tow. You'd best take your chances and allow me to take mine. I know these gardens better than most. The Slayer and his assassins won't find me before dawn, and by then Hranic's auxiliaries will have been alerted. The captain has a squad stationed nearby." She let go of his hand.

"I'm not going without you." Vian turned, tugged at the gate.

"It's not negotiable." She traced a line across his mouth. "*Shame.* I would feel you inside me again."

"That does it." Vian had the gate open. He turned to face the empress, saw her standing there. She looked frail and afraid. The first time he'd seen her like this. "No time to argue." He reached across and grabbed her beneath her arms and under a leg. He hoisted her over a shoulder, as though she were a sack of grain.

"Consider yourself kidnapped, Empress Rasnei."

"You are a fool," she said, but didn't struggle, as he shifted her weight over his shoulders and ran through the dark, leaving the hidden gates behind. Ahead were buildings and the lower walls of the outer city. Vian reached the closest street.

"Put me down," Rasnei said. She started laughing, despite their predicament.

"No," he replied, laughing, too. "You're my captive."

"You are a madman."

Vian reached the stable outside the tavern. He allowed the empress to slip to the ground. "Don't run off," he said.

She stood there grinning at him. "This is a game to you, isn't it?"

Vian shook his head. He turned, kicked the door through, shearing the lock.

"You're very violent," she said.

"You haven't met my sister," he replied, stealing inside to where the horse he'd borrowed stood in silence. "Come on, boy." Vian led the beast out into the street. "You'd best clamber on that saddle, Empress."

"I cannot ride," she said.

He hoisted her onto the big animal's back. The mare snorted but remained calm. "Easy," Vian whispered in her ear. "This is your empress, horse, so be polite—and no snorting."

Rasnei made a weird sound that could have been a giggle. She sat rigid, her eyes wide. "This is most uncomfortable," Rasnei said, as Vian vaulted up beside her.

"You'll get used to it," he told her, and urged the mare to trot out into the street. Behind, the sounds of shouts and steel clashing announced that the auxiliaries had been alerted, and soon the entire city would be in uproar once it was realized that the empress was missing.

They reached the gates, and two guards blocked the way, long Chiang spears crossed to bar their passage. "Sit still." Vian squeezed her sides and slid off the horse. Calmly, he approached the guards.

"I need you to let us out of the city," he said, walking calmly toward them. He couldn't see their faces beneath the heavy helms. Neither spoke, but the nearest levelled his Chiang and jabbed forward to stop Vian.

Vian stepped aside, and then leaped forward, grasping the Chiang by its shaft below where the guard gripped it. He twisted his grip, wrenched it from the startled guard's grasp, and at the same time, spun the shaft around and struck the soldier on the side of his neck, just below the helmet. He fell to his knees. Vian jabbed down with the base and sent the man sprawling.

His companion leaped forward, his Chiang swinging out at Vian's neck. Vian ducked beneath the swipe, moved in close and then brought the spear's butt up under the guard's chin strap. The second man crumpled and fell across his comrade.

Vian approached the gates. No more guards were visible. But behind, back in the city, the sound of fighting had intensified. He unbolted the gates, then removed the iron key from the nearest guard, who was still trying to recover from Vian's blow. His comrade was worse off, face down in the mud, unconscious.

Vian jabbed the key into the great door, twisted and wriggled until it clanged and clicked. He pushed hard at the heavy oak and iron, until a horse-sized gap appeared. He vaulted up on the horse's back, the Chiang blade gripped in one hand.

"Your empress is safe," Vian yelled at the conscious guard, currently staggering to his feet. "Make sure Chulan finds out. And tell the Magister I'm coming for him next." He spurred the horse through the gap in the gates, and then allowed her to trot into the lantern-lit high road outside, as the southern walls of Pol Shen faded back into the gloom.

"How is that possible?" Gost Chulan rose from his divan, his eyes blazing, the tea cup falling from his grasp. "The empress gone? How—*tell me!* She has to be at large in the city, damn you."

Gujun shrugged. "The flute player, I suspect."

"What are you talking about?" Chulan summoned patience and tried to steady his hands. His nervous system was shot this morning. He'd woken to horns and marching men. A troop of Hranic's Auxiliaries beat at his townhouse doors, demanding he attend them.

His own guards had seen them off, but not before it had turned nasty—the Northmen having accused him of treachery and collusion with the enemy. *True enough,* but he didn't need to hear it from them, particularly before taking his morning walk and tea.

Gujun had appeared a while later. The Slayer's customary coolness had made things worse. Chulan prided himself with his control, but this morning that calm demeanor had gone to rat shit. "What flute player?"

"She summoned him to her chambers," Gujun said, looking bored. "Twice, and kept his identity hidden from you."

"From your informants, you mean. You are my head of police, Gujun. This . . . calamity is on you." Chulan stood, poured himself another cup of the piping liquid to calm his nerves. *Unbelievable.* Rasnei had slipped their net. The empress who never left her palace had vanished like a spirit-owl in the dead of night—not only from her chambers but the entire city, too. And now this mystery flute player. *A secret lover*, somehow, she'd kept that from him too.

Rasnei had outplayed him. Chulan had badly underestimated her guile. *Lesson learned.* He turned on Gujun, his face hot and flustered. "I'm hearing this right? Rasnei smuggled in a lover. A flutist, you say? A man she must have seen performing in court, and then summoned to her chambers. Well?"

Chulan stroked his long moustaches. The Slayer said nothing, his inscrutable eyes on the door. "You have let me down, Slayer. I expected better from you."

Gujun's eyes flashed annoyance, but he said nothing.

Careful . . . Chulan told himself, taking his ease on the divan again. Pointless getting Gujun riled. The man had failed him, but the damage was done. Gujun was still his best servant by a mile, but also unpredictable and deadly. No need to test him further today, lest the Slayer find a new master and turn against him.

"Tell me all you know," Chulan sipped his tea again.

Gujun shrugged. "Not much about where they went. But the guards reported a breakthrough at the South Gate. A rider with a girl—their words—accompanying him. One horse. Had to be them."

"I'll interview those guards personally, then flay the flesh from their bones."

"Too late," Gujun said. "I ordered them hung by their ankles from the gates they were meant to guard."

"Good," Chulan snapped. "Past time the Imperial Guard woke up in this city. We're about to be invaded." He rubbed his eyes and squinted as the headache worsened. This hadn't been an enjoyable morning. But it wasn't crucial. Rasnei evaded them at the moment, but Gujun would find her, of that he'd no doubt.

The Slayer despised failure even more than he did. After brief consideration, Chulan was content to allow Gujun free rein again. *Enough for now.*

"What news of Calla?"

"He's at Ferrytown, or thereabouts," Gujun said. "Moving his entire army that way along the river's northern banks. Think he's almost ready for the big day."

Chulan digested this. "And the city?"

Gujun shrugged his shoulders again—such an annoying habit of his. "Confused, afraid—we are feeding that. Spreading rumors of Calla's savagery. With Hranic Finehair dead, the Auxiliaries are scattered. They suffered heavy losses at the river."

"What happened there?" Chulan had heard about the attack. Northmen from across the river, raiding their own kin. Hadn't made much sense. *Convenient though.*

"The Leeth king's sons raided Hranic's camp without consulting Calla." Gujun grinned. "They lost half their men in the raid, but at least Hranic died—and many other veterans from the border wars. Those remaining auxiliaries won't give us much trouble, whether at the river or in the city. And Rasnei's personal guard are in disarray. I had the servants in her palace slain." His smile broadened.

"We'll spread word in the city that Rasnei was murdered by the Midnight Cutting Crew, who sent an assassin into her chamber. Those outlaws are still lurking somewhere. Once word spreads that they are responsible for our empress's sorry demise, Shen will be in uproar. They will be flushed out, hooked up and left to dry."

"Good," Chulan said, and drained his tea cup. He felt better. The situation had corrected itself. He'd been badly shaken that Rasnei had stolen a march on him. But it was a small matter.

She'd fled. *Her gambit.* The empress was no longer the ruler in this city. Ran Calla would arrive soon, and he, Chulan, would ensure he'd play his part well, welcoming the Ran inside the gates. He'd report Rasnei's death out of hand. *An unfortunate accident*—that should do it. He smiled, seeing beauty in the morning again.

"You may leave, Slayer." Gujun lingered by the door, his dark eyes hooded. "There is more?"

"Something struck me as odd, last night," Gujun said. "I met with the flute player in the gardens, albeit briefly. He is trained. An adept of the fighting arts. I think it was always his plan to infiltrate the palace. As to why, of that I'm not certain. But I do have a hunch."

"Go on," Chulan said.

"He was Rundali, noble born. You know how they look. And his hair was the color of those embers in your fireplace. Sound familiar?"

Gujun bowed slightly, turned and left the room. Chulan remembered Soma Ghee telling him about his man Shateke's murder. How the slaver had been found butchered, and his guards, too. Word was, a flame-haired Rundali had been the killer. *Coincidence? Unlikely.*

That killer was lurking here in Pol Shen, or somewhere close. And he had abducted the empress. *Why?* Then he remembered Ghee telling him about the wild Rundali girl who had been summoned to court a few months back. A flame-haired tigress, caught by slavers—Shateke's people. Ghee had ordered her fetched as a curiosity for court. But she had escaped, with the assistance of none other than the Midnight Cutting Crew. Chulan felt a cold shiver of doubt run down his spine, as morning's bright promise faded back again.

GURTEI JUMPED TO HIS FEET AS THE SOUND OF HOOFBEATS thundered close. His men grabbed their weapons and surrounded the rider, as Vian guided the horse into the deep glade where they hid their camp, several miles off the highway in a hidden forest hemmed by dark hills.

Vian slipped from the horse's back. Gurtei saw a woman seated on the saddle, a dark shape hard to define. She gazed across at the men with a strange expression.

"The Midnight Cutters," the woman said. "I've always wanted to meet my country's most illustrious outlaw band."

"Behold your empress, Imperial Rasnei." Vian bowed low as he swept an arm her way.

"Nah," Truggan said. "You're pulling our puds."

"He's playing us for fools." Predictably, that was Roile. But Gurtei strode forward and grasped the horse's harness. He looked up, straight into the eyes of Rasnei Ti–Shen, whom he'd glimpsed from a distance at her court once long ago. Gurtei dropped to his knees. The others, seeing his expression, followed suit.

"Stand up, all of you. This world has turned upside down," Rasnei said. "Our trusted Magister and his people have betrayed us. My loyal followers conspired against my August Person. Your empress is alone in the realm."

"We are yours, Empress Rasnei—if you will have us," Gurtei said, a tear lining his eye.

She smiled down at him. "I was going to pardon you anyway," she said, winking at Vian, who stood grinning beside the men, their faces white as ghosts. "With that in mind, I might as well employ your skills."

LATER AT THEIR CAMP, MORNING LIGHT FILTERED THROUGH trees and the first song thrush announced spring's final arrival with clear piping tones, its cheerful calls promising a new hope and better days to come. Rasnei rolled in her blanket and saw Vian standing over her.

"I have to leave for a time," the Rundali said.

"But why?" She looked up. He placed a kiss on his hand, and then brushed his fingers against her face.

"You are safe for the moment, Empress. Gurtei and his men will take you south to Ta Shen. That city remains loyal, so I hear. I'll join you there, or on the road south."

"Again, why must you leave?" She stared up at him, a tear tracing an eye.

"My twin sister Savarna has need of me," he said. Before she could respond, he placed a hand on her shoulder and squeezed. "Farwell, brave Rasnei."

Vian turned away, fading off like a cherished dream through the rising vapor of the early morning mist.

AN HOUR LATER, VIAN CRESTED THE TOP OF THE NEAREST hill. The outlaws' camp lay far below. He felt weary and drained, knowing what had to be done. Spirit-travel came with hazards.

Damn your timing, sister.

Vian felt torn. He'd found something unexpected here in Shen, and it hurt to leave. He would worry about Rasnei—but there was no helping that. Savarna had called him through the void. His sister was in trouble. Vian had to save her. *And that meant . . .*

I am coming. He breathed the words, pushing them out across the ether.

Vian straightened the Jian blades across his back. He folded his legs beneath him and seated himself neatly upon the rock, closing his eyes.

He summoned inner calm. *Focus hard, concentrate.* He'd only done this once before at such a great distance, and the effort had almost destroyed him. Time to summon his darker self. The creature who dwelt latent inside him, as another similar soul lived within his sister. Hers took on the form of a tiger. But Vian Eltayn's *Aikashi* was a dragon.

He slowed his breath, focused, and then spoke the words in his head.

Aikashi, we have need of you.

A stirring below. Vian felt is body rock and shake. The familiar sickness came and went, the pounding head, the giddiness. And then, in his mind's eye, Vian lifted high above, feather light. A leaf on the wind. Floating, and drifting—the hills and woods so far below. *Focus . . . fly.*

Vian felt the angry spirit stir inside. The dragon took form in his mind. A huge, scaled creature from a long-forgotten age. Vian felt it beneath him, lifting him higher. *Fly!*

The *Aikashi* spirit was free. He felt its fury and joy—the heat rising from the manifestation below. He also felt its violence, the reckless hate he could barely control. *Harness the power,* his grandfather had taught Savarna and himself. *You cannot let your Aikashi spirit control you. That way lies oblivion.*

Vian chanted the mantra inside his head, soothing the rage

rising from below. *Dragon and man—we're a team.* Two sides of a coin, each half cannot exist without the other.

I am stronger than you, mortal. Vian heard the *Aikashi* spirit burning beneath him. *One day, I shall break free.*

Vian spoke the containing words inside his head, over and over, and the dragon beneath him grew sullenly silent. He felt its vast wings thudding like a thousand drumbeats. Vian looked out with his mind's eye. He soared through skies on the *Aikashi-dragon's* back, a blazing arrow of sparkling blue, green and gold.

Dragon and rider sped west through the fading winter air, as that day dwindled to evening. Vian saw the sun set beyond distant water. To the north, an uncanny sea fret rose like a sentient beast and rushed toward him. *That way,* he told the dragon.

And the *Aikashi-dragon* veered and swooped fast, sailing down through the darkening skies and plunging into the wall of fog that swallowed them whole.

INTO THE MIST

"Fog rising fast," a voice yelled from above. Savarna came to slowly, head spinning and body throbbing with pain. She still gripped Jaran's hand and saw him gazing down at her, eyes worried.

She nodded and staggered to her feet. "I'm fine." The ship's deck rolled beneath her. She felt sick. Close by, the man called Carlo Sarfe stood silent, his eyes mistrusting and a hand on his curved sword.

"What trickery is this?" Carlo Sarfe said. "Where did you . . . *people* come from?"

"You don't remember me." Savarna saw the mist spreading across the water, its wispy fingers reaching out toward them. "But then I didn't know you the last time, so no great surprise there."

"This is your mystery sailor." Jaran loomed close, and Carlo tugged at his sword. "Easy, fellow—we are not wraiths conjured from that mist."

Carlo glanced around, registering the fog for the first time.

"What is happening here?" he asked, his brown eyes incredulous and edgy.

"The mist is pulling us in," Jaran said, reaching for her hand again.

"Captain!" Savarna heard the muffled shout from above, then the mist rolled over them, swallowing ship and wave, hiding their faces from each other. She heard Carlo's muffled yells but could no longer see him.

Then a familiar voice announced Finvar had survived the crash landing. "Don't you ever ask me to do anything like that again," he said. They didn't respond. "We're back inside the fog," he added, as if stating the obvious was helpful, at least to him. "I suppose that's a good thing."

"You did well, Candle," Jaran said.

"Don't fucking call me that."

The fog had deepened to white smoke. Savarna could scarcely make out Jaran's face although he stood beside her, his big hand clasping hers, the other gripping Griner.

"I wonder what that witch has waiting for us," Jaran said.

"I'd sooner not dwell on that," Savarna said. Then she gasped, and shook all over as Vian's face appeared in the fret and then vanished almost immediately.

I am coming . . . Savarna heard his voice, then the distant muffled sound of wingbeats approaching from far away.

"What is wrong?" Jaran's pale eyes were concerned. "We have to hold together—you too, Fin. Be prepared for anything she may throw at us."

"Thanks for including me in this," Finvar muttered from somewhere close. Savarna heard muffled yells and glimpsed movement, the sailors trying to deal with the strangeness that had happened.

"Are you sorcerers?" Carlo Sarfe loomed up from nowhere, his brown eyes filled with loathing.

"We are your friends," Savarna said without knowing how to respond. "It's a sorcerer we're after. A witch, truth be told. She has stolen Jaran here's island, and covered it in this awful mist."

"I think this is yet another dream," Carlo Sarfe said. "My visions returning again."

"We are real, Carlo Sarfe, as is the mist," Savarna said. "We met outside that dark, creepy castle." She gazed at his face, as both Jaran and the sailor stared back at her. "That is how I know your name."

"What dark, creepy castle?"

Savarna shook her head and turned away. There were shapes moving in the whiteness. She heard voices, same as before—some close, others distant. They were strange to her ears, metallic and eerie. Then a blur shimmered a few yards away. Savarna saw a horned figure rushing toward them. It vanished, and somewhere to her left she heard laughter.

Then the mist shifted and broke enough to reveal a length of deck, and the three men standing beside her. Briefly Savarna glimpsed a distant shore, before the curtains of fret rolled back in again and she could see nothing, not even her hand.

"Did you see the shoreline?" Finvar's voice was excited. "We are nearly through."

Then a huge jolt shook the ship's side, and Carlo's schooner lurched to larboard. Savarna fell to her knees, striking her head against the rail. She heard Jaran shout her name.

"I'm all right," she said, but another jolt sent her sprawling and slipping, and then icy water plunged over the deck and soaked her to the bone. The last wave threw her overboard.

No . . . not this again . . .

She thrashed about as the cold water pulled her down. She saw Vian's face again and vaguely heard Jaran shouting her name. Then the numb cold penetrated her mind, and she drifted into darkness . . .

"Savarna!"

Jaran had lost purchase on Savarna's arm. For a terrible moment, he'd seen her sliding across the deck, a great wave having drenched them both and washed her from him. Seconds later, she was gone, replaced by more fog and dim shapes that rose up from the whiteness all around.

Jaran yelled her name again, but Savarna was gone. He'd lost her to the ocean. Jaran gripped Griner and leaped onto the rail, but another wave knocked him backward onto the deck again.

Jaran heard Finvar yell, and somewhere further away a sailor screamed in pain. Dark shapes were manifesting in that fret. He saw savage faces, horns sprouting out between hair. They were under attack. Jaran yelled at Finvar to get ready as he found his feet, braced as the ship rolled, and hefted Griner into both hands.

Gantallian's face rippled on the surface of the mirror. "He is coming for you." His hollow metallic laughter echoed through the hall, until Sheega slapped the glass with her hand, making it wobble and stilling the goblin inside.

"Be silent, imp," she said, as Gantallian's face glared out at her, with bug eyes and lolling tongue. "I tire of your incessant rambunctiousness. You are my servant, tasked to obey." The face sulked, and faded back from the glass.

"That's better," Sheega said. "Now then, Gantallian—be useful for once, and inform me of their whereabouts."

"Hrelgisson is close—"

"I know where he is," she cut in, annoyed that he was still playing games. "I need to know where my creatures are, the Witch-Guard and my stupid youngest son and his borrowed men. All are needed here."

Gantallian's face loomed close again, his golden eyes were full of mischief. "I would help you more if you freed me from this mirror."

"You know I cannot do that until I have safely defeated the warlocks in Dunnehine," Sheega said. "And before I tackle that scum, I have to deal with Hrelgi's brat, lest his father's ghost—or, worse, the spirit of his ancestor Barin—rise up and aid him in destroying everything I've built."

"You have Ranning to help you." The goblin was sulking again, and sounded hurt.

"My lover has his own affairs to attend. Moreover, Ranning is busy tempting King Aldorian. We need the elves to rally to the cause, as well as Rumgrold's trolls and your own stunted folk. We are the friends of Faerie, not your foes. There is much at stake here, so I need you to grasp the importance of ensuring I'm not thwarted by some petty, vengeful mortal."

"Gorn and Valgarn are crossing Cardalan on their way back to the city, their tails between legs, having upset their new master."

"I cannot pull them back from there." Sheega slapped the

mirror again, sending ripples that blurred his face. "Forget those miscreants—I meant Holtarn." She would deal with the older pair once the business with the Hrelgisson was over. "What of my youngest? And Crane and the rest of Ranning's Witch-Guard? I cannot find them and need them back here soonest, in case by some quirk of fate Jaran Hrelgisson breaks through my mist."

"I thought he needed a specific spellcraft to unlock your codes."

"Not if Rune appears and tells him the combination."

"Ah, yes," Gantallian's face was a blurry smear. "I almost forgot about Rune. Ranning is right—you should have killed that creature. Is Rune still trapped inside your fret, somewhere even you can't find him? He'll wreck havoc if he escapes."

"Rune won't escape—he's trapped on a different dimension."

"Holtarn sent a mind-signal." Gantallian's face shimmered gold. "He's ready for you to pull him across. You need to do that quickly, as he is under attack."

"By whom?"

"Crane, and his brothers." Gantallian stuck his tongue through the mirror's surface and his metallic laughter rang out again, reverberating across her chamber. "You should train your minions better, witch."

STOP THAT!

The voice fell from the sky like a shaft of lightning. Crane glanced up and saw his mother's face floating through clouds, her ice-blue eyes filled with fury.

That is my son—you must aid him.

Crane lowered his axe, and his brothers followed suit. The men facing looked to attack again, but the leader walked forward and slammed his double-headed axe into the dirt.

"Stupid green fuckers, you've slain half my men." Then he glanced over at the sea in sudden shock as a gust whipped the hair around his face, and Crane, turning, saw Sheega's fret racing to the shore. That broiling mist surrounded both Witch-Guard and mortals. Crane felt himself lifted and carried through space.

I need you back here, his mother's voice shrieked like the gale surrounding them.

SAVARNA WAS SINKING DOWN THROUGH BLACKNESS, AS A part of her mind registered, *I'm dying . . .*

It wasn't a bad feeling—she felt peaceful and surprisingly warm, like she was cocooned and wrapped as a swaddling child. Then she heard his voice, calling her from far away.

Savarna.

Jaran? She felt a stir, the chill returning for a brief moment, until her memory faded back. *I'm sorry, my Northman . . .*

Savarna.

Now it sounded like her brother calling out to her across the void. Vian's voice urgent, impatient—unusual for him. *You cannot reach me Vian, not this time.*

Savarna, awaken! We are not ready to die yet.

The shout came from inside her. Savarna's eyes blinked open. She stood in a cave, water all around her, but Savarna was dry and felt no pain. Then she saw the tiger prowling at the cave mouth. Huge and striped, he turned her way, and she saw her own face staring back at her.

It was you that spoke. *Aikashi.*

We have to go back to the realm of men. Limbo will destroy us if we linger here. The tiger faded and was gone. But she knew he was all around her, and inside. Her *Aikashi* spirit had saved her.

"I do not know how to go back without drowning first," she said, her voice lost in that place without sounds.

"I can help your lover, for a price," she felt rather than heard the voice. A creature stood before her, the face hard to define. The body was manlike, but covered in silver fur, and large horns curled out from either side of its head.

"Who are you?" Savarna asked, her mind slowly waking. "Where is my *Aikashi?*"

"Gone for now," the silver creature said, his voice a muffle. "As you must. But first you have to free me from here."

"How do I do that?"

"Say my name."

"You haven't told me what it is yet."

"It is all around you, pluck it from the air. Speak my name, Savarna Eltayn, and your brother can save you. And you, in turn, can save your lover from Sheega's nets. That witch's spider's web has caught us all. Free me, and you, too, can be free. Jaran Saerk can get his revenge. Say my name!"

"I cannot! *How can I?*" The creature faded back into darkness. Outside the cave, the water glistened and shimmered, and she realized she stood within a huge bubble of air.

"This is Ranning's place." The silver creature appeared again, this time beside her. "He will know you are here before long. You can save us both, Savarna. Only with my help can your lover navigate the dimensions and reach Valkador safely. Look at the walls—what do you see?"

Savarna did as the creature suggested, but saw nothing but the ripples of the water outside, and the dark featureless rock surrounding her. She closed her eyes, the cold and pain from her shipwreck were coming back. The near-death experience fading.

Damn this . . .

Savarna opened her eyes again and scanned the cave walls. Then walked closer, brushing her hands against the damp stone. The creature shrank back into shadow, his face still hidden. Her fingers ruffled over a groove. She found another, then a third. She leaned close, pressed her forefinger down the length of each groove.

"These are words, Northern symbols." Then it grasped her. *Runes.* Jaran had spoken of their power in the northlands. "You are called Rune," Savarna said, then gasped as the cave wall collapsed, and icy water rushed in. Savarna was battered and tossed, flushed out from that cave, but high above a light filtered down. Savarna knew she had to reach it.

She swam up, the *Aikashi* inside her lending her strength. At last, she broke through the surface, and strong hands pulled her clear of the waves. A long, white beach stretched for miles on either side. Vian stood before her, his face tired and strained. "We cannot linger here," he said.

"Brother . . ." She reached for his arms but felt nothing.

"I have to return to my body. I cannot hold this much longer —my *Aikashi* waits in the skies above." She gazed up and saw a shimmering flash of blue and green and gold, a huge creature flickering and fading.

"Yours is a dragon spirit—I never knew."

"I cannot linger, Savarna," Vian told her. "I'm sorry. I have failed you. The creature Rune will aid you and Jaran against the witch. You must do as he says, sister."

"Vian?" His beautiful face was fading, the red hair lifting in the wind.

"I must return, else I'll perish on that hill. Stay strong, whatever happens." Vian gave her a last, desperate smile, and disappeared. For the glimmer of a second, she saw the dragon circle the sky in a rainbow of colors above—then his *Aikashi* too was gone.

Vian . . .?

Savarna felt tears of loneliness and frustration trace down her cheeks. *I'm still lost, and now he's gone.* She turned and saw a tall, horned figure standing on the beach, the features strange and ancient, the strong-looking body covered with silky, silver fur.

"What now?" Savarna asked the creature called Rune. He looked at her with sad, golden eyes, and then turned and walked slowly and purposely along the beach. Savarna followed, as the sun was lost behind clouds and the wind blew colder.

THE SHIP STRUCK ROCKS AS FINVAR CLUNG TO THE STERN rails. He saw men falling broken on the jagged stone. Their attackers had gone, fading back into the mist. But Carlo Sarfe's ship had lost all control, and then the rocks had risen out of the mist.

That mist had gone. So had Jaran Saerk, Savarna, and everyone else. Finvar stood alone on an empty beach. He heard a groan. Felt a flush of relief seeing the schooner's captain, the man Savarna had named Carlo Sarfe, sitting on the sand, head held in his hands.

"My ship," he moaned. "*My crew*." He saw Finvar gazing at him. "Your fucking sorcery, was it?"

"No," Finvar told him. "And you need to stop whining, sailor. *Shit happens*, but we're both breathing."

"Where is this strange shore?"

"I'm hoping It's an island called Valkador," Finvar told him, as he walked up and lifted Carlo to his feet. "Once a proud kingdom, now in the cruel clutches of a witch. My friends will be around somewhere," he added, trying to convince himself. "Jaran is home at last."

"I think you are a madman," Carlo said. He reached down, and looked relieved seeing his curved blade still at his side. "Where did that demon fret come from?"

"It's Sheega's fog—the witch. We have to go find her. Jaran will need our help."

"I'm not going anywhere," Carlo Sarfe said.

"I think you might have to." Finvar gestured past the sailor, where figures had appeared in the distance. Tall, shimmering warriors, running toward them with spears and shields gleaming, their armor shifting in hue from the deep green-blue of the ocean to a rich honey-gold glow. "You don't want to meet these boys." Finvar grabbed his arm. "Come, on, sailor—we've work to do."

JARAN OPENED HIS EYES. THE SEA SURGED CLOSE, AND Carlo Sarfe's broken ship splintered and cracked—much like Graftin's had done before, and just as mysteriously. One moment, Jaran had been fighting figures in the mist—then he'd been sailing through the air and crashing into wet sand. He stood on a beach, the schooner breaking apart beside him.

Were they all dead?

He didn't believe it so. Nor did Jaran have time to dwell on the matter, as the tall figure of a warrior strode into view, a shield slung across his back, spear gripped in one hand, a double-headed war axe in the other.

"We've unfinished business, Hrelgisson," Holtarn Erlundsson said.

KINSMEN

JARAN STOOPED and rubbed sand into his palms. He waited for Holtarn to approach, and then cursed, seeing another dozen men appear behind him. Jaran recognized some of the faces from the riders on the coast before Finvar had saved them. How they came to be here, Jaran had no idea. *Sorcery*—the answer to everything at the moment.

He shrugged, heaved Griner into both hands, and feigned a bored expression. Holtarn stopped a few yards away, and the other Northmen hung well back, letting their leader deal with his cousin and not wanting to mess with a blood feud. Jaran saw they all carried spears and axes—some swords, too. He smiled, but cursed inwardly. Where was Finvar? And Savarna—had she drowned?

Jaran shut those nagging thoughts from his mind and focused instead on the hard-looking man smiling at him. *My cousin . . .*

"What I don't understand," he said, as he readied his axe, "is what I've done to you and your father to earn such loathing. Seems to me that you're holding a grudge against someone who's never caused you ill. Why is that, cousin?"

"Because my mother fears you, Jaran Hrelgisson," Holtarn said. "Therefore, King Erlund, too—as he's shit-scared of his wife, and anything bad happening to her will surely rebound on him. You're a threat to them both as long as you're breathing. The prophecy—it runs two ways."

"I know of no prophecy."

Holtarn spat and laughed. He unslung the heavy, round shield from his back and thrust his spear butt down in the sand. "That's a nice-looking axe," he said, staring at Griner. "I shall enjoy using it to cut off your head and deliver it to my mother. It's not personal, cousin, but I'd sooner it be me who kills you, and not my brothers."

"What is this prophecy you speak of? Enlighten me, *cousin*. So once I've dealt with you and your timid men there, I can take it up personally with your mother."

Holtarn spat again. Beyond him, Jaran noted how his men looked puzzled. They also appeared edgy. *That all be the sorcery.* They didn't appear overly committed to Holtarn's cause.

Jaran smiled. *Keep the conversation going.* Then kill him quickly, and those men would scatter. They looked troubled and uncertain—confused, too. Sheega must have intervened, maybe messed with their sorry heads.

"You haven't heard the stories, cousin?" Holtarn laughed. "Or perhaps you lost your memory when that bear shafted your mother. I heard the rumors—stories by the river. A great white bear carved you up nicely, they said. The brute must have erased your memory—not a day went by when my mother wouldn't mention your name, Hrelgisson, and how we brothers needed to kill you. Especially after our father failed."

He stepped forward, hoisted the spear and hurled it at Jaran. A ferocious throw, accurate and fast. Jaran knocked the spear contemptuously aside with his axe as though he were swatting a wasp. Holtarn grinned at him. "Just warming up," he said, the axe in his right hand, round shield held ready in the other.

"Crap throw," Jaran said. "I hope your brothers are more impressive. Hardly worth the trouble, having a feud with kin too feeble to toss a spear." He felt the rage building inside, as Holtarn's face reddened.

"We're done talking, Hrelgisson," Holtarn said, and charged toward him with a yell.

"WHERE DID THOSE BIG GREEN BASTARDS COME FROM?" THE sailor Carlo Sarfe yelled in Finvar's ear as they sprinted along the beach, the odd spear sailing past their heads and sticking, point first, in the sand beside them.

"You're asking me?" Finvar yelled back at him. "I've been confused all fucking month." He dodged another spear as it sailed past his head. "Where were you sailing to before we dropped by?" He pulled Carlo toward him as yet another spear flew past, the closest yet. Finvar's legs were aching, but Stoon's brethren were slipping back. *Must be all that ugly green metal weighing them down.*

"Trying to get home." Carlo glanced back. "They're fucking green. Gold too, and flickering like sparks. It's not natural."

"Nothing here is natural." Finvar dared a look back. They'd

reached the high dunes, affording some protection. The pursuers had slipped out of sight. Finvar and Carlo scurried up the steep banks of sand. "My legs are done with running," Finvar said, reaching for his bow, still stubbornly wedged around his shoulders despite the many hazards he'd faced, and the sack of shafts hanging limp from his belt.

Carlo Sarfe slipped his heavy scimitar free of the scabbard. "Mine, too."

They waited, but aside from seabirds and wind, and the sea crashing below, heard nothing. "Perhaps they got lost." Finvar smiled. "The one we met earlier didn't seem that bright."

Carlo looked at him askance. "Who—what are they?"

"*Her* things," Finvar said. "Man-shaped chunks of evil seaweed. Products of sorcery."

"Her . . .?"

"Sheega. The witch we told you about."

"I don't recall you telling me much. I just remember you three crashing on my deck, and then that awful fog. And then . . ."

"Yes . . ." Finvar placed his bow down and rubbed his eyes, exhaustion digging in. "Sorry about your schooner and crew, mate. Savarna said you were from Gol. That's strange too."

"Why?"

Finvar shrugged. "I'm too knackered to explain. Suffice to say, I don't think you'll see your home again, even with a new, shiny vessel."

Carlo gave him a sideways look. "You people are very strange."

Finvar nodded. "It's been said before. Oh, *super*, here they come—best we get moving, Sailor Sarfe. I need to catch up with that big Northman. We've a witch to kill and a lass to recover.

And you might as well join our merry team—you'll fit right in. At least until you source another ship."

Carlo Sarfe didn't respond. He was already yards ahead sprinting over the dunes.

THE DOUBLE-HEADED AXE SAILED FOR HIS HEAD. JARAN blocked with Griner, wrenching backwards, sliding his axe blade down until it trapped Holtarn's shield rim, and then wrenched back hard.

That trick had fooled many an enemy during the border skirmishes. It didn't fool Holtarn. He dropped to one knee, allowing the shield to slide free, and cut out and upward again with his own axe at the same time, striking Griner's haft above Jaran's hands and knocking Jaran from his feet.

Holtarn yelled and swung the axe down. Jaran rolled and shot a leg up, catching Holtarn in the balls. His cousin fell on top of him, the axe thudding into the sand, his shield battering Jaran's head.

Jaran followed through with a knee into Holtarn's belly, then he rolled free from underneath. He regained his feet and readied Griner.

Holtarn leaped up and backed off as Jaran's swing went wide. Holtarn spat, cursed, and came running in again, hard—his axe cutting low and the shield guarding his face.

Jaran barely caught the axe in time, trapping a blade with Griner's steel beard and knocking the weapon aside. He braced as Holtarn followed through, ramming his shield into Jaran's chest, trying to knock him backward. He couldn't.

Jaran grinned. He leaned down and chewed at Holtarn's ear until part of it fell off. Holtarn hollered and brought his knee up into Jaran's groin, sending a wave of sickness through his guts, though the nausea and pain subsided as his battle fury took hold again.

Jaran wrenched and butted, Holtarn blocking with shield, trying to get lucky with his axe. Jaran stamped on his leg, and with no room to swing and hands held apart, Jaran rammed Griner's haft tip over the top of Holtarn's shield, breaking his nose.

Caught off balance, Holtarn broke free, the blood streaming down his face. "You're even uglier now, cousin," Jaran said, following through with a wicked blow that would have cleaved him from shoulder to groin, had Holtarn not caught it with his shield. Even so, that blow knocked him to his knees.

Jaran stepped closer, swung again. Holtarn stared up at him. "Fuck you," he said, before Griner struck his face, slicing half of it away. Holtarn's body twisted and tumbled.

Jaran, the berserkergang tearing open inside him, hacked down, cleaving Holtarn's body in two. He struck a third time, and then again until all that remained of Holtarn Erlundsson was a mangled mess of blood and brains and scattered limbs.

At last done, panting and shaking, the rage fading slowly, Jaran's wild gaze fell on the men watching with spears held ready.

"Who's next for dying?" Jaran said, tugging the axe free of Holtarn's corpse, a trail of blood dripping from the beard.

They didn't move. Jaran counted eleven. "Come on!" he said, bracing his legs wide and gripping Griner with both hands parallel. "Come and embrace Tyho's gift. Griner longs for your sorry heads."

An older warrior stepped forward. He cast his spear to the ground at his feet. "We are not your enemies," he said. "We served King Erlund, not yonder corpse. Holtarn was the king's son but we hardly knew him. And liked him less."

The other men followed suit, placing spears on the sand. "I'm going to kill King Erlund, too," Jaran said, the rage finally subsiding, replaced by the wave of sadness and exhaustion he always felt after killing. "So you better try and kill me anyway."

They still didn't move.

"Are you cowards?" Jaran was too tired to fight well, but Northmen had to hold on to their reputation. Though this group didn't seem that fussed about protecting their king, or their honor.

The speaker unslung his axe. "I am Gunard, King Erlund's captain at arms. You insult us unfairly, so I will fight you happily, Jaran Hrelgisson. First, though—understand this. King Erlund is weak. That witch sapped his courage and stole his manhood. Leeth Is breaking apart. I will fight you, kinsman—but I'd sooner serve you as the rightful King of Valkador. Brave Hrelgi's only son." He unslung the shield from his shoulder and readied his axe.

The younger man next to him drew his sword. "You kill my father and I will kill you next," this one said. The other nine watched in silence.

"Well, get ready," Jaran said. "Because unless you all get on your knees, I'm going to start hitting Gunard here with Tyho's cleaver." He made to step forward, then stopped, hearing Finvar's frantic yell from somewhere behind.

"Good of you to join us," Jaran said as Finvar and Carlo crashed in upon the circle of spearmen surrounding him.

"What's this, a Northman convention?" Finvar skidded to his heels, the bow aimed and ready, Carlo Sarfe had his curved sword at his side.

"Took your time, Candle," Jaran said, looking at him, a half-smile on his face. "We're finishing up some business here."

"Well, I'm happy for you—but you might want to know that Stoon's nasty brothers are back and trying to catch me and my best new friend Carlo Shipless here." As though to prove his point, Gunard's Northmen started shouting and pointing.

"It's those green bastards, Gun," one of them yelled. "The sendings that did for Ailfe and Strogey, and the other boys."

"WHERE ARE YOU GOING?" SAVARNA CALLED OUT TO THE creature Rune.

He stopped and turned, his huge golden eyes filled with sorrow. "We cannot avoid her," Rune said. "She is everywhere, and this island is not the one you need."

"Sheega? What do you mean, this is not the same island? This must be Valkador—what other island is there out here?" She caught up with him, and the creature Rune stared down at her with mournful gaze. An ancient being. She saw both sorrow and wisdom in those hypnotic golden discs.

"It's a different Valkador," Rune said. "That fret was more than mist and fog. Sheega wanted to make sure Jaran couldn't reach her. She shifted the fabric of time around the island. I can shift it back—but only if you three are with me."

"Then we must find my friends, Fin and Jaran Saerk."

"That we must, and before she finds us."

"You are too late," a woman's harsh voice called across. Savarna looked around but saw nothing but beach and sea and sky. Then she heard a splash, and something emerged from the water. She gasped, recognizing the lean, hard body of a man, his long green-silver hair trailing down, and his eyes large and milky without pupils. A creature from the Otherrealm, like Rune. But whereas Rune bore no malice, this creature looked crueler than the slavers who had raided her family.

Rune shivered beside her. "I cannot help you now," he said. She saw his body ripple and vanish, leaving her alone with the naked man on the beach.

He strode toward her, as a woman's harsh laugh filled the air, and the voice accompanying it was everywhere. "Catch her!" the woman almost screamed.

Before she could turn and run, the man accosting her scooped something from the shallow water and tossed it over her. A net, weighed down with shells and stones. Savarna thrashed and wriggled, but the trap worked tighter.

The fishy-man approached her, leaned over. He struck her once between the eyes, and she faded into a black and merciless dream.

Sheega smiled when her lover entered the hall, his wet feet leaving damp footprints as he dragged the net containing the unconscious prisoner and laid it at her feet.

Ranning grinned. "Look what I caught, while taking my morning swim."

"Rune got away."

"He is harmless against we two. A weak creature, for all his lore."

"I'd sooner he was dead. Rune's the only one who can unravel my codes."

"I shall kill him, eventually." Ranning shrugged. "You want

to take a look at this?" He kicked the girl in the net until she groaned and opened an eye.

"Savarna." Sheega smiled, feeling a warm glow inside. "You're a strange-looking creature. *Only half-human.* A bit like us—eh, lover?"

He said nothing, and Sheega leaned over the net. The girl was stirring, her crimson hair a mess across her face.

"Jaran Saerk is coming to kill you, witch." The girl's eyes were huge with loathing, the gold flecks sparkling inside the brown irises.

"He will fail," Sheega said. "You are his weakness, Savarna. Your lover cannot hurt me while I have your spirit as my prisoner. Your *Aikashi.*" Sheega smiled and spoke the words, reaching down and pressing her white hand against Savarna's face. The girl screamed and blacked out again.

"You have taken her soul?" Ranning's face was curious.

"Only the *Aikashi*, the non-human half. But without it she will fade over time. More importantly, that spirit-tiger is chained, and I retain the only key. We shall use Savarna as bait to draw him in. But not here"—Sheega smiled—"Dunnehine."

"You are ready to return and deal with the real enemy?"

"I am," Sheega said. "We cannot allow Jaran to set foot on his land, else the illusion shatters and the memory of his family's past returns—worse, the vengeful ancestors rise up and aid him. Their spirits detest me, Ranning. They lurk in every corner of this cursed island. In Dunnehine, I can protect myself and draw him in with this girl. And with King Aldorian's promised help, we will destroy Unva and the others, and pave the way for the return of Faerie.

"But first, I need to set the bait that will ensure he follows."

King Erlund struggled into his mail shirt and heaved on his heavy boots. His head was aching as normal. The hour was much earlier than he usually rose, the pink sky hinting dawn was yet to approach. His warriors would be waiting for him, ready to ride west to deal with the man his son had failed to find, and thus help free him of his bitch-wife's continual pestilence.

The king reached over to the table and drained a flagon of stale ale, reviving him enough to walk outside, over to where the men were gathered near the gates.

Tomsag stood with Halfti, a young girl struggling between them. Curious, he walked over. "What's happening here?" Erlund demanded.

"This wastrel girl claims she knows where Hrelgisson lurks." Tomsag shook the girl, who glared at him. Erlund half-recognized her as someone from the village outside his walls.

"Let her go," he said. "I doubt she's capable of harm." The men obeyed, though their faces looked disapproving.

"Who are you, wench, and what's is this about?" he demanded. "Why are you upsetting my thanes? Speak, girl—I've a busy day ahead."

"I'm Gunsala," she said quietly, glancing warily at the two huge men still looming close. Erlund bid them relax. She looked at him, her young face tense and afraid. "I know where he is, Your Highness. The one they call Jaran Saerk."

"You know where Hrelgisson is?" Erlund laughed. "How is that possible when no one else can find him, none of my carles, Prince Holtarn, Calla the Cruel. No one."

"He is wounded and taking shelter in the woods close by. The healer woman . . ."

"What fucking healer woman?" Erlund, his mood darkening, reached across and grabbed her chin, lifting it up. "Out with it, wench—else I'll have these boys whip your scrawny hide." He turned to Halfti. "What nonsense is this?"

"A beggar woman—claims to be a healer. A stinking, horrid creature who scratches a living out in the forest. Some of the villagers go to her when they are sickly."

"Why have I not heard of this woman?"

Halfti shrugged. "Nothing to tell. She arrived months back. Some of the men chased her off for begging in the village."

He turned to the girl again. "And you're saying the legendary warrior called Jaran Saerk is sheltering with this grubby ragamuffin?"

"He is, Highness. I have seen him but yesterday."

"Do you know what you risk lying to me?" Erlund grabbed her chin again and forced it back. "Can you imagine a blood eagle carved from your back?"

She sobbed, and Erlund let go. *Damn this nonsense.* "Where is this hideout in the woods?" he asked Halfti and Tomsag, but they shrugged.

"I can show you," the girl Gunsala said. "It is not far, an hour's walk. No more."

Erlund stared long and hard at her face. At last, he nodded. "She speaks the truth, as far as she believes it. It's most likely some rogue outlaw. But no harm looking into it. Tell the men we'll return in two hours, and they better be ready. You two can accompany me on me on this mystery walk through the woods."

"Shouldn't we take our horses?" Tomsag asked.

"The woods are too dense," Gunsala responded before Erlund could think to reply. "But it's easy on the feet."

They set out as morning filled the hills and countryside around, the first scent of spring promising a final end to the relentless northern winter. After twenty minutes crossing his fields beyond castle and town, the king and his two thanes had followed the girl into deep woods.

Erlund glanced around as he walked. He didn't like woods—they reminded him of his wife. Too busy, hard to define. Woods seeped Faerie and wrongness. Creatures from the twilight, elves and goblins—the *Otherrealm*.

Gunsala was right—these woods were deep and dense, the sky above blotted out by heavy oak and ash, the creak of willow beneath, hazel and hawthorn, and briar whipping his face.

Their young guide stopped when a shabby wooden hut emerged through the loamy gloom. Erlund gave her a sharp look, and Gunsala nodded.

"Hrelgi's long-lost son—is it possible?" Erlund muttered beneath his breath. Despite his doubt, he felt a sudden rush of excitement. *I get to kill him for you, Sheega. I do your dirty work like always—that's got to be worth something.*

The king approached, the thanes at either side, their faces dark with suspicion, the forest closing in around them. "I'll make sure they are still inside," Gunsala said.

"Wait," Erlund barked at her, and she stopped. He gazed around, feeling a strange tension. *It's just these fucking trees.* "Go on then, wench—and be quick about it." His men slid their axes free and looked at him warily.

Before the girl Gunsala could reach the tangled mess of moss and rotted stumps, a woman emerged. She stooped, her clothes were dismal rags, and her face was hidden by a gray thatch of unruly thick hair.

Erlund felt a quiver of fear. Could she be a witch? He'd had his fill of those for one lifetime. *Unlikely though*—Sheega would have sensed such a presence this close to the castle. "Stay here, and keep alert," Erlund said to his men. He walked over to the ghastly harridan, caught wind of her and scowled. *Healer*—more probably a madwoman.

"You have something to show me," the king said. "A gift."

"A gift it is, and a long time in coming." The woman turned and stared at him, and he felt a shock of recognition. "But I'm the one fucking claiming it."

A flash of steel, the dagger came from nowhere. King Erlund gasped as that cold metal stabbed deep into his side. He slumped to his knees, and she stabbed down at him, again and again.

Bera . . . I'm sorry . . .

"That's for Hrelgi, your brother," she said, laughing, before the thanes were on her, hacking her frail body in two.

GUNSALA SCREAMED WHEN SHE SAW THE KING FALL, AND again when the wise woman was hacked to pieces by those two men. The nearest turned her way, his face red with rage. Gunsala ran, fleet of foot, the low branches and thorns lashing her face, her legs burning with exertion. She heard their shouts as they tried to follow, but Gunsala soon lost them in the woods.

She stopped by a stream and washed blood from her face. She shivered and then turned, the hairs on the back of her neck tingling. For the briefest instant, Gunsala thought she saw the healer woman standing by the stream, her hair neatly ordered and face as beautiful as the smile upon it. Then she was gone like fading whispers, and Gunsala was alone in the forest.

She walked throughout that day and into the next, taking what meagre fare she could along the way. The healer had taught her much. Gunsala knew well how to survive in the wild. *But where to go?* The dead king's men would never stop looking for her. No point worrying about that. *Keep walking and survive.* She reached the mountains and started climbing.

3 2

RUNE

VIAN JOLTED back inside his body. He lay crumpled for a time on the hill, willing the pain away. When it subsided enough for him to breath normally, Vian crawled to his knees and spewed, his stomach cramping and the bright world spinning in his eyes.

Savarna, I'm sorry—I lack the strength to return.

She was in need again, a far worse trouble than when he'd helped her. The *Aikashi* spirit inside him had seen the witch and her accomplice, been a witness to their schemes. The mysterious creature Rune had tapped into his dragon-spirit somehow, and explained to him how Sheega had trapped him inside the void, knowing that Rune was the only one who could break the codes surrounding Sheega's mist.

With Rune compromised and Jaran Saerk busy fighting her warriors, Sheega had concentrated her cunning on snaring Savarna as she entered her domain by mischance, the fret pulling her in. They had her—that terrible pair, Sheega and Ranning. And he, Vian, could do nothing. He wept tears of sheer frustration. After all that effort—waking the *Aikashi*, the mind-journey halfway across the known world, saving her from limbo. *All useless.*

Enough.

Vian closed his eyes, feeling his strength return. The Dragon-*Aikashi* had vanished the moment he'd regained his body. For a while, its spirit lingered in the air—then that faded, too, as the fiery being's soul slipped back inside Vian's self.

He would not help Savarna by weeping on this hill. And there was Rasnei, the woman he realized he cared for deeply. She needed him, too, and Gurtei—they all needed Vian's skills. Chulan and his people, led by the killer Gujun, would be after the empress on the long road to Ta Shen—that shining city in the south—a perilous path where ambushes could occur anywhere.

Rasnei was key to the survival of this corner of the earth. She was also the woman he cared for. But Savarna was Vian's twin. His other *self*—who, like him shared her soul with a spirit from the ancient world. Something that occasionally happened in their family since the time of his Rundali forefathers—the Eltayn who, alone of mankind, had formed a bond with the terrible spirits called *Aikashi.*

Vian let the wave of emotions flood his mind, allowing it wander free. Once the thoughts slowed and his breath deepened, he forced inner calm into his mind. The right thing to do. Savarna was strong. Strong enough to survive in the short term —the witch's prey was Jaran Saerk, not her. And Rune had told Savarna that Sheega could not kill Saerk in Valkador, as his ancestors' ghosts would protect him.

Thus, Sheega would return to Dunnehine, her old country, and harness her powers. And Rune had told his *Aikashi* that Sheega had enemies there who would thwart her. Warlocks were not a match for her and Ranning, but together they would be strong. *And with Vian's help . . .*

He opened his eyes, stood arms held out wide, the world turning beneath him. Vian smiled, watching as a buzzard lifted on the thermals and rose higher, circling amidst the clear blue.

"I will journey north into Dunnehine," he told the heavens. "But first, my path lies in the other direction." He picked up his Jian blades, lying on the grass beside him, sheathed them in the scabbards, and commenced trotting down the hill. Hard to be sure how long he'd been away, but Vian suspected only a couple of days.

Vian found the road, then ran for a time until reaching a village. He laid low till dusk, then stole a horse from a stable. He rode the south road throughout that night, the stars and a horned moon matching his pace through the shadow of trees beyond.

Stay alive, sister—I will see you in time . . .

RAN CALLA WATCHED FROM THE JETTY AS HIS RAFTS drifted out across Pol Shen Bay. A thousand crafts bobbing on that water, each afloat with fifty warriors, their armor and weapons glistening in the sun.

A fine spring day, the wind was light and the sun warming his face from above. The Magister Chulan stood beside him, as did three of his sons. Chulan had informed him that the gates would be open and all was well. He had also told him that Rasnei was dead, and the Ti-Shen dynasty ended forever.

"A clean break." Calla smiled wolfishly. Chulan would prove useful, in the short term at least. Once Calla understood how

Shen worked, he'd have Gujun murder the Magister, who was too damn clever for his own good. In a year or two, once things had settled down.

They would set up camp in Pol Shen, and he'd allow his warriors any women or booty they found. He'd spare the useful but order any resisting soldiers killed on sight–flayed over hot coals to prove he meant business. Then he'd mop up the country-side, scouring it free of outlaws, and other scum like the infa-mous Midnight Cutting Crew. He'd start with them.

Once northern Shen was under his heel, Calla would send his army south to that other great city. Ta Shen was rumored beautiful beyond words, the climate kind, and its women demure and sultry, with eastern charms beyond compare. It was also said to be the richest city in the world.

Ta Shen will be mine inside six months.

Ran Calla nodded to his men, who were readying the final raft for his crossing. The invasion of Shen was finally underway.

RAGAN CONORAX RESTED HIS ELBOWS ON THE TILES AS HIS brown body allowed the steaming water to soak. The girl had departed for more wine. Just the two of them this evening. His favorite slave, some candles, and the best wine in Cardalis.

There were advantages to staying behind. His father was gone, as were most of his brothers. This ancient city his to rule. And Ran Calla wouldn't be back anytime soon. That meant Conorax could while away the days in luxury and rule western Cardalan as he saw fit.

He opened his eyes lazily and studied the room, the water

lapping as he paddled and kicked. *Where was she?* Kiaza should be back by now.

He heard a distant scream—a woman's death cry. Vexed, Conorax forced his wet body free of the water.

What is this?

He reached for a towel, but froze when three shadows emerged from the far side of the bathhouse. They blurred into view, and he recognized Genza, his youngest brother, standing there, with two giant Northmen flanking him on either side.

Genza was grinning as he and the big men walked up and surrounded Conorax. "These valiant Northmen work for me now, brother." His smile broadened. "They arrived back in the city, but recently. Gorn and Valgarn complained they were bored, so I put them to good work killing some of father's lesser shamans, and a good few of his household guard."

"Genza, you treacherous—" The nearest Northman produced a dagger and jabbed down with sudden violence. Conorax gurgled as his throat was sliced wide open. He staggered to his knees, blood pooling on the tiles, the steam surrounding him fading as the world went dark.

VALGARN STOOD OVER THE CORPSE OF CALLA'S FAVORITE son. They'd returned a week ago, and Ragan Genza's people had sought them out. The youngest son was ambitious, it seemed. He'd returned from Leeth and decided on supplanting his father's rule.

"Calla holds the east," the little turd had told Valgarn and his brother. "I will rule throughout Greater Cardalan and the west, while father languishes in sultry Shen, hopefully catching some foul pestilence. You two Northmen can be my generals. What say you?"

They had agreed readily. Calla had no love for them after the raid on Finehair's camp. The brothers could reap fine rewards serving this treacherous son. Then, when wealthy enough, they'd return to Grimhold and cast out their father, the king, to rule as brothers in his stead.

But the only constant in life was change. Later that evening, the two brothers caroused from their balcony, formally Conorax's and now bestowed very generously on them. They had women a-plenty, more than enough wine, and slaves to satisfy all other needs.

The pair drank long into that night, the warmth of early spring allowing them to stay comfortable on that balcony and watch the city sleeping below.

Valgarn was drunk, his words slurring, with a wench asleep in his arms. He'd humped her twice and was happy to sit drinking quietly, enjoying the fine view of city lanterns sparkling and winking far below.

Gorn was standing by the balcony, a wolf-skin cloak about his shoulders. His brother was restless for some reason. Obviously he hadn't drank enough.

"What ails you?" Valgarn yawned, and poured himself another glass, spinning the clear crystal in his rough hand. He'd seen nothing like it in rustic Leeth. *I could get used to this life.*

Gorn turned and glared at him. "This isn't our land."

"You prefer living in freezing, dreary Grimhold, or remote Valkador?" Valgarn scoffed. "You're never fucking happy, brother. Relax, have another drink. This wine is exquisite."

"You'll end up soft like Holt, or worse—these fucking Cards," Gorn said, rounding on his brother. "Ran Calla won't take kindly to us aiding his shithead son. And our men can't see us getting soft on southern wines. Good Northmen need action. We should return north to consult with Mother."

"I no longer need your help." Sheega's voice was clear and sharp, the cold wind accompanying it sent table cloths and drapes flying. The girl woke and screamed, running inside the palace. Sheega stood at the balcony, wrapped in a blue cloak that lifted in the sudden breeze. Her sharp features were pale, and glare icy as she surveyed Valgarn and his brother.

"Your brother is dead," Sheega said. "Slain by your cousin. Holtarn failed in his task, but at least he tried. You two knaves are worse than useless. Fat, idle slugs swilling wine. I despise you and need you no more. *Don't return to Valkador*—you are not welcome there."

"We will avenge Holtarn," Valgarn said, standing up and spilling wine. "We'll find Saerk and carve a blood eagle on his back."

"You never loved Holtarn," she sneered. "And Hrelgisson is mine—or will be soon enough. And don't go running to your father, because he's fucking dead, too, owing to something we both overlooked. But just as well. Erlund failed me, as have you." Her ice-blue eyes narrowed, and a faint smile showed. "You are tainted with his weakness and thus no longer needed. Go snap at the heels of your new master." She laughed for a moment, raised her hands and clapped, her form exploding and releasing a score of doves that flew above Valgarn's head before vanishing from sight.

"Fuck." Gorn stared at him, mouth open. "Mother's not happy, is she? And Father's dead—Holt, too? That bastard Hrelgisson did for them both? I knew something bad was brewing, Val. What should we do?"

"Ride north and avenge our brother." Valgarn yawned. "Mother didn't mean those harsh words." He sipped his wine and smiled at Gorn's worried face. "King Erlund is dead," he hiccupped. "A shame, but shit happens. And there's an empty throne to fill. I'll arm-wrestle you for it, Gorn."

"You would lose."

"Not if I kicked you in the bollocks at the same time." Valgarn snorted in his wine. "Fuck it—I like it here, Gorn. And we stand to get rich. But honor is honor, and we do have to avenge Father and Holt, despite what Mother says." He smiled slyly at Gorn. "Or maybe you should do that, big brother. That way you can be the uncontested King of Leeth, as is your right as oldest son."

"We are Northmen," Gorn agreed. "But we are also brothers —we can rule Leeth together. Mother won't interfere once that bastard Hrelgisson is dead. I say we leave at first light, get back home and take control. Then see what she's up to on the island."

"I'm not going back there," Valgarn said. "If Mother lets you kill Hrelgisson, that's good news. The blood feud is settled. You don't need my help. But Ragan Genza does—and unlike you, brother, he's generous."

"I said we can share the throne."

"Nah, be sensible, Gorn. We're not big sharers. You would cut my throat in the night and take my half of the kingdom, unless I got to you first."

"You're probably right," Gorn said, and the pair of them laughed out loud.

"To King Gorn the Terrible"—Valgarn hiccupped as he raised his glass—"May your reign be as brutal and glorious as it is long."

"I'm going to skin Jaran Hrelgisson's hide from his bones and hang it in the feasting hall over the fires."

"Sounds like a plan." Valgarn grinned. "And do call on Mother when that's done—she loves us really, *especially you*." He poured another glass from the jug and hiccupped again. "You had best bugger off, brother. You've an early start and lots to do. *As for me . . .*" He smiled and leaned back in the comfortable chair, the city lights still winking far below. "I will be just fine."

"YOU SHOULD HAVE DROWNED THOSE WHELPS AT BIRTH." Gantallian's golden face winked out at her from the mirror. "Ungrateful brats, they've proved."

"It is a small matter," Sheega said after returning to her chamber, her mind busy on other things. "I have the *Aikashi* part of the woman Savarna's soul."

"The useful part." Gantallian nodded, sending ripples through the glass. "Best you do away with the human shell."

"Eventually," Sheega said. "First, we'll have some fun, then I'll depart this island for a time and set up camp on the ice rim."

"I don't like it there." The goblin made an obscene face. "Free me, and I can aid you from here, alongside Ranning while he waits for Faerie assistance."

"You're coming with me, imp. And just because Ranning shares my bed doesn't mean I trust him. He's of Faerie, as are you —we are good allies, but hardly friends."

"Poor Ranning, unloved as well as exiled."

Sheega snorted derision. "Be useful, Gantallian. Find our enemy, and tell me where Rune's lurking. I cannot have that wayward creature ruining my plans."

"Rune cannot act alone. He is the key, but needs willing hands to turn it."

"Jaran Saerk has the hands," Sheega said. "That's why I cannot let him reach Valkador. But there's no harm in allowing him to think that he has—hence my deception with the beach. I trapped them into a different dimension, using the fret to pull them in. Things got a bit confused when that sailor from lost Gol appeared, and then Savana's twin tried to intervene. But that's what happens when you mess with time and its dimensions."

"Tricky and hazardous," Gantallian agreed.

"But useful, too," Sheega said. "Now for the fun part! Set the bait and lure him in."

JARAN SIGHED AND LEVELLED HIS AXE AGAIN. SHEEGA'S sendings were loping toward them along the beach—tall, slimy warriors in green. Almost identical to Stoon, though the nearest was even bigger.

"I haven't got time for this," Jaran said. "I need to find Savarna and kill that witch. I don't know why, Fin—but something warns me if I don't seek Sheega out alone, and now, we are all going to die."

"Go then, off with you," Finvar said. "Do your stuff, but be quick about it." The Northmen were lining up on the dunes waiting for the Sheega's creatures to arrive. These slowed when they saw them. The leader—or the biggest at the front—pointed and hoisted his spear.

"Round three," Finvar said, and then squinted up at Jaran. "You still here, big man?"

"I'm not happy about leaving you with them."

"I've got your new hairy friends helping me—*we've got this.* Go, kill the bitch-witch!"

Jaran nodded. "Keep that skin on your back, Candle," he said, and turned for the woods framing the beach.

"He's coming back—don't worry," Jaran heard Finvar say to the fighters gathered. Moments later, the shouts came, and then the clash of steel. *Curse you, Sheega.*

Jaran loped through the trees, Griner gripped in his left hand, his right fending off branches and thorns. He reached a lone hut, stopped and stared. A wash of emotion flooded through him.

I know this place. A small, lonely garth surrounded by a tinkling stream, the sea's crash mixing with the sound of steel a half-mile distant.

Jaran passed the thatched cottage. Nothing stirred inside. He ran out of the trees and entered an open area leading to distant hills. Ahead, a wide lake dominated a valley, a track cut clean along its closest shore. Beyond that, on a low rise, the bigger hills behind, Jaran saw a large building. A great construction of stone and wood, the roof steep, and snarling beasts carved on pillars and apex. The Great Hall.

That had to be where Sheega waited. Before he killed her, Jaran would make her tell him where Savarna was. She was alive somewhere—Jaran knew it was so.

Jaran picked up speed, running toward the lake as soft rain pitted its silver surface. He slowed to a walk as he reached the shore, eager to get this done but not wanting to use up all his strength. He didn't doubt she was expecting him. Perhaps more of Stoon's kin were waiting, or something worse.

He left the lake behind and slung Griner across his back, winding up the track until the great wooden building rose up to block his way. A magnificent square structure wrought from hewn logs. He hardly noticed it. Jaran's eyes were on the woman seated on a rock, her legs neatly crossed, and a long pole held in her hands. She was beautiful and frightening, with pale features, icy blue eyes and a cold but welcoming smile.

Jaran stopped and lowered the axe. The woman's smile deepened. She stood, thrusting the pole into the soil at her feet. Jaran noticed the horse's skull mounted on the top, the dead eyes gazing directly at him. A challenge for certain. She leaned gracefully against the pole, still smiling.

Jaran slowed his walk, forcing calm into his veins and keeping his eyes sharp. He could feel the malice emanating from that horse skull. Already she was working against him.

Jaran stopped a dozen yards from where she stood. The wind had got up, and her jet hair was blowing, tossing around her face. Large, slanted eyes filled with irony, the color of northern ice. They sparkled with malice.

Beautiful and deadly, she appeared to him. Her long ermine cloak and silky gown ruffled by that wind.

"Greetings, Jaran Hrelgisson," the woman said, her voice deep and husky. "I'm so glad you came. It gets lonely out here."

"I've come to kill you, witch." Jaran dropped Griner into both hands and took a step forward. She didn't seem to notice.

"Your people shun me, you know. It's not polite." Her mouth quivered, and flint eyes sharpened. "And as for your ancestors—how their bold spirits rage throughout this land! They don't like my kind, Jaran. This island has a long, troubled history."

"Tell me where Savarna is, and I'll slay you quickly."

"Ha, yes—*Savarna*." The woman smiled. "Not part of the original plan, but interesting. As is your small friend the hawk-man—soon to perish beneath the blades of my valiant Witch-Guard. *Shame*—such a waste of talent."

"Tell me where Savarna is." Jaran struggled to keep his cool. "Else I'll cleave you in two with this axe. Recognize it, Sheega? *Griner.* A gift from Tyho Himself."

Her eyes were hooded for a moment. "*Griner,* yes—I know that blade. It also has a long history. And not a happy one. There is always a price for accepting gifts from the gods, Hrelgisson. Tyho is not a kindly deity. He will want his cut."

"Last chance." Jaran stepped forward again. "Where is Savarna? Tell me!"

Sheega's smile was perfection. "I can do better than that, Jaran Saerk. *Much better.*" She whispered something, the wind cried shrill and then, *incredibly*—he saw her.

Savarna.

For barely a second, before she vanished, leaving Jaran alone with the woman again. She'd been caged, her red hair covering her face. He'd noticed how her arms were bleeding and feet lacerated.

"You bitch!" He raised Griner and stepped forward.

"Yes, she is ours," Sheega said, hands white on the pole. "A fiery little creature. That will be the *Aikashi* spirit residing inside her. I'll free the tiger after you're dead, then feed the girl's mortal flesh to my death-hounds. Do you remember those, Jaran Saerk?"

He roared and ran at her, her white face mocking his assault with laughter. Jaran swung back, then out, striking at Sheega wildly with Griner—a blow meant to cleave her in two. He swung wide, lost balance, and Griner thudded into the dirt. The impact sent a jolt up his arm. Jaran tugged the axe free, as laughter surrounded him. *Where was she?* A blast in his ears. He staggered, clung to the axe.

Then, sudden lightning stabbed his eyes, dazzling him, as the accompanying thunder exploded in the atmosphere above. Momentarily blinded and jolted badly, Jaran staggered and almost fell. He blinked, saw her standing there again, still laughing. Then Sheega vanished and the sky turned black, as freezing hail struck his face like tiny sharp hammers.

Jaran ignored the stinging ice-rain. So dark, he couldn't see his hands. He heard a sound like distant laughter, fading further away. Then Jaran felt his body lifted and carried, before crashing down onto hard, bare ground. He rolled with Griner ready, opened his eyes while blinking frantically. The dark sky above crackled and sparked, spilling more hail, its color changing from black to cobalt, through green, then dark red to purple.

Jaran staggered to his feet and hoisted Griner. He was back on that beach. The Giants' Dance filled the sky above. Sheega and the hall, the lake and countryside were gone. Then Jaran heard her voice reach him from all around.

I have your woman, Hrelgisson. I'm taking her to Dunnehine. You are welcome to seek us out . . .

Jaran stared up at that shifting brooding sky. He heard a familiar curse and turned, seeing Finvar standing behind him, his freckled face covered in blood. "They've gone," he said. "Those honey-green fuckers. *Vanished.*"

Jaran didn't respond, his addled mind still grasping what had happened. "Most of your kinsmen are dead, I'm afraid," Finvar said. "Good fighters. And Carlo Sarfe's gone, disappeared—like the green ones. This whole place stinks of sorcery, Jaran. I don't think we're where we should be."

"She has Savarna," Jaran said. "That witch tricked me. You are right, Fin. Wherever this place is, it's not Valkador."

"You are in Limbo—the place between worlds." They turned, and Jaran saw a strange figure walking toward them. "Sheega trapped you with her cunning mist, luring you in—as she has done to many before. Myself included. But Sheega could not allow you near the hall. Instead, she altered the dimensions, and what you saw was an illusion of Valkador."

"Who or what are you, exactly—should we be worried?" Finvar said, as the vaguely man-like creature approached slowly. Tall and stooping, the entire body covered in dense, silvery fur. The face was almost human, the eyes large golden hypnotic discs, filled with wisdom and sorrow. There were long, curved horns protruding from either side his head.

"I am Rune," the being said. "My race came from the frozen wastelands. Originally of Faerie kin, they were hunted to extinction by Sheega's forebears. I survived because of the lore I still retain. The world-key that unlocks dimensions. Your friend, the *Aikashi*, freed me from Sheega's trap. Therefore, I am in your debt."

"You know where she took Savarna?" Jaran glared at the strange being.

"I do," Rune said. "For it was once my realm." His eyes were watery, almost tearful. "Ours was a gentle race, before the warlocks of Zorne arrived to enslave us. Fell wizards fleeing the flames that Ashmali the Elemental wrought upon their land."

"Tell me how to get there, and I'll avenge you, too." Jaran hefted Griner and spat on the sand at his feet. Finvar shifted awkwardly beside him.

"I can save you from this place," Rune said. "But for both our sakes, you must help me in return—and you, Hawk-Man.

Sheega is a terrible foe. If you don't kill her, she will rise up more powerful than ever."

"Then tell me how to catch up with the bitch and cut out her heart," Jaran said.

"You cannot kill her until the appointed time, nor could she kill you—hence her illusions." The creature Rune leaned close to him—the smell of his breath wasn't good. He resembled some kind of great silver ape, though not as bulky. Jaran had seen one once, way down on the Rundali border, while scouting Cardalan raiders.

"That's why she sent her creatures, instead of dealing with you directly." Rune loomed close. "Ranning's Witch-Men departed with her when she left."

"Is that what those slimy green bastards were? Stoon's kinfolk, created by sorcery?" Finvar stared at Jaran. "I think we should trust this hairy fellow—what choice do we have? And, if this is not Valkador—then where the fuck is it?"

"Nowhere," the creature Rune replied. "A different dimension, not dissimilar to that other place you happened upon after escaping Cardalis."

"How do you know about that?" Jaran hefted Griner at Rune. "I don't share Finvar's optimism. You could be another gift from the witch."

"I could be—but I'm not." The creature's eyes flickered annoyance. "I am *Rune. The key.* I alone can unlock Sheega's hold on your island, shatter a hole in her mist. She knew that, so she had me imprisoned by her guile. But I cannot achieve that from here, and not without your helping me at the proper time, and with Savarna-*Aikashi* too. I am the key, and you three are the hands needed to turn it."

"Thanks for making that clear," Finvar said, as Jaran lowered the axe and rubbed his eyes, feeling suddenly very weary.

"You need to return to the world of men," Rune said. "I will help you with that, and with killing the witch, if I can. Allow Rune to thread the path through Sheega's nets. But first, you must assist me, and to do that you will need help from afar."

"Go on," Finvar said. "We're listening."

"There is something else," the creature said, his golden eyes moist.

"Always." Finvar nodded, but Jaran hushed him.

"A lost soul I encountered on her way to the Halls of the Dead. She knew my purpose and demanded she speak with you."

"This gets better by the minute," Finvar said. "I wish I had my tobacco close by."

But Jaran didn't hear his friend. He was looking at a shadowy shape appearing beside Rune. A woman draped in fur, a shawl hiding her features. She pushed it back revealing a handsome face, proud and strong—though heavily lined by the worries of a troubled life. Her pale blue eyes were filled with passion, yearning, and something else. *Love . . .*

Jaran almost stumbled when he recognized her.

Mother . . .?

Bera smiled. "I had to see you one last time, before crossing through the gates and joining your father."

"Mother—*Gods*, what happened to you?" He reached for her. "I'm so sorry I left you to perish, for dead you must be."

"I killed your uncle." Her smile was fierce. "Our Hrelgi is avenged at last. That means I'm finally free to move on. I'm ready, *so tired.* But you still have work to do, my son. You are Jarle Hrelgisson. Valkador is your heritage, Jaran. *Your destiny.*"

"Why didn't you tell me—I'd have stayed."

"The Traveler warned me that if I mentioned a word about

what happened, she would find you. I couldn't lose you too, Jaran. Sheega fears you. Knows that you will kill her one day soon, unless she can get you first."

"Oh, Mother . . ."

"Mourn me not, brave son. My task on Ansu is complete, and our family's blood feud over, save for those two brothers. You must deal with Gorn and Valgarn in time, for they are Sheega's brats as well as Erlund's. Therefore, most dangerous.

"Stay alive, Jaran Saerk, whom the White Bear blessed with his claws. Kill the witch, and save your girl. And know that I shall always love you, dearest son." She smiled, but her face was fading, beach and ocean showing through her body.

"How can I do that when I cannot reach her, and Sheega holds Savarna captive?"

Bera's form was fading fast, gossamer thin. "Seek out he who saved you from the wolves, all those years ago."

"The Traveler—I know not where he is?"

"Not that trickster. I mean the *White Bear*, who has always looked over you. He who left his mark, enabling him could guide your axe all these years. Your protector, Jaran. Your *shadow* . . . you must call on his aid at last."

"It was a white bear that gored me that day, Mother. But the Traveler killed it, or so he said."

"The body, yes. Not the spirit who controlled it. Your ancestor Barin is the *White Bear*. You must find him first and set him free from the confines that bind him. Free Barin, and this creature Rune, whose soul is no longer his own. You will need both their help to save Savarna. And save her you must, before any harm can come to Sheega."

"For what it's worth, I'm with you, too," Finvar said in a quiet voice that Jaran barely registered.

"Trust in Rune's guidance. *I will see you in time.*" Her faint image faded from view.

"Mother!" Jaran hefted Griner and slammed the heavy axe into the sand. Bera had gone. He stood beside Finvar on that empty beach. Jaran wiped salty tears from his eyes. "I left her to die, Fin. *Alone.* I thought only of myself. All those years—I could have helped her."

"You were guided by another, as was Bera." Rune loomed close again, his golden eyes showing something akin to sympathy. "The Traveler is not who he seems. Like Tyho, he has reasons for wanting you to succeed. A war is brewing. Sheega and Ranning have powerful allies. The *Otherrealm* is waking. *Faerie.* An ancient score is about to be settled. Sheega is the bridge between your world and the shifting chaos of Faerie. And you, Jaran Saerk, and your friends are the only ones who can stop her opening the doors of Yffarn to let them in."

Jaran stared hard at Rune. Eventually, he nodded.

"That's a lot to take in," Finvar said beside him. "Perhaps we should chew it over while you provide a way out of here."

Rune nodded. "It is time—though time itself has no meaning here. I will open a vent in the world fabric, a link through to the past. One thousand years. Once safely across, you must seek Barin, your ancestor, as your mother said. His soul is held captive inside a mountain. With Barin's help, and the Hawk-Man's here, I can stall Sheega's plans, and divert her attentions while you save Savarna. Then as three-who-are-one, you can defeat the witch's cunning and shatter the nets to your island, claiming your inheritance at last."

Rune turned away. He made a mark with his claws. A large hole appeared in the air—a tear revealing dazzling lights and nothingness beyond. "That is the Void," Rune said. "Jump through quickly. I will see you on the other side."

Rune vanished inside the rent. They both stared at the ragged, gaping hole resembling a painting slashed apart with a knife. Finvar looked at him and gripped his bow. Jaran nodded.

"On three," Finvar said, gripping his friend's hand. "One . . . two . . . *Jump!*"

Jaran leaped, and heard Finvar yell beside him. Then the vent closed behind them, and they fell into the warm nothingness of the Void.

As he fell, Jaran's right hand gripped Finvar's left. It seemed to Jaran that something huge was falling beside them. He looked across that emptiness, and for the briefest instant gazed into the knowing blue eyes of a huge white bear. The bear faded, as a yawning chasm of fire rose up from below and swallowed them whole.

"This doesn't look good," he heard Finvar yell, before huge tongues of flame surrounded them, pulling them in. Jaran closed his eyes and focused on her face, as searing heat reached up to engulf him.

Stay alive—I will find you . . .

Jaran heard Finvar scream out as the heat tore upon them and darkness enveloped them whole.

Savarna jolted awake and saw the massive shadow looming at the edge of the cave where she was imprisoned, a metal chain tied to her feet, the bitter cold gnawing and chafing. The shadow loomed closer. A huge white bear with Jaran's pale eyes.

Stay alive—I will find you.

The words reached her from somewhere very far away. Savarna smiled. Sheega might be winning, but this game was far from over. She'd dreamed of Vian last night, and heard his soft voice in the dark. And now her lover's spirit guardian had found her, too.

A yellow light grew in the cave. She saw Sheega's white face emerge. She looked the other way, and the great bear was gone.

"He's coming for you," Savarna said to the pale face gazing at her behind that candle. "You time is running out, witch."

"Our time is always running out, my dear." The beautiful face pressed against the cage. A cold hand reached in and touched her cheek. Savarna shivered. "As for your lover, he's expected. But I need for him to hurry. I have more pressing matters to attend to, and cannot move forward until Jaran Hrelgisson is dead."

"You cannot kill him."

"I won't need to," she said, laughing. "The changeling I summoned from Yffarn will do that. Good night, poor, lost Savarna." Sheega's flinty eyes faded back from the light and her face vanished.

Savarna clutched the chains at her feet. *I'll not wait here like some sacrifice.* She'd never done it before but knew it was past time. Savarna closed her eyes and summoned the *Aikashi.*

"I need your help," she whispered as the tiger's spirit stirred inside her.

I cannot help us, the *Aikashi* voice rose up from deep within her. *The witch has my soul . . .*

"Then I shall save us both," Savarna said, and closed her eyes.

Would you trade your soul to save your life?

The Crimson Lady knows that her soul may be the price she has to pay to get revenge.

If you enjoyed *Blood Feud*, you will love this new tale, *The Crimson Lady*. It's available free for newsletter members only. Don't miss out! Join our fun newsletter the JW Webb VIP Lounge. *Subscribe today!*

GLOSSARY

Valkador

Jarle Hrund: Ruler of Valkador

Sheega: his new wife

Hrelgi Hrundsson

Bera: Hrelgi's wife

Erlund Hrundsson

Gorn Erlundsson

Valgarn Erlundsson

Holtarn Erlundsson

Leeth

Doggan: a district sheriff

Gilda: his wife

Gurn: a dour ferryman

Graftin: a fisherman

Gunsala: a girl from Grimhold Village

Tomsag: a thane

Halfti: a thane

Gromaki: a mercenary

Easec: Gromaki's kerne

Helga Kregat: a legendary witch

Shen

Rasnei Cai Ti-Shen: The Sapphire Empress

Magister Chulan: her enforcer

Gujun: an assassin in Chulan's pay, leader of the Silent Slayers

Soma Ghee: First Secretary of Pol Shen

Tin Lous: an official in Ghee's office

Mawla Tei: Rasnei's chief courtesan

Hranic Finehair: Imperial Auxiliary Guard Captain

Jaran Saerk/Hrelgisson: a famous auxiliary serving under Hranic Finehair

Dorthar: a veteran auxiliary serving under Hranic Finehair

Finvar the Droll: a former thief wanted by the Midnight Cutting Crew (MCC)

Gurtei: MCC leader

Roile: a robber in the MCC

Truggan: a robber in the MCC

Corben: a robber in the MCC

Mulci: a robber in the MCC

Dorley: a robber in the MCC

Rosin: a robber in the MCC

Sumil: a robber in the MCC

Shateke: a wealthy slaver

Conra: his overseer

Lin Gu: a slave

Kuulla: a slave girl

Rundali

Savarna Eltayn: a nobleman's daughter

Vian Eltayn: her twin brother

Elafan: a legendary warrior

Chiarra: a slave freed by Vian

Mjorde: a slave freed by Vian

Hulo: a retainer at House Eltayn

Coru: his son

Cardalan

Ran Carda the Destroyer – legendary Laregozan hero and conqueror of Ptarni

Ran Calla: his descendant, present ruler of Cardalan

The Ragans: Calla's nine sons

Casla

Calgara

Conorax

Caranax

Casca

Daigar

Racara

Uzcara

Genza

Straban: Calla's shaman

Tolvar: a captain at the frontier

Storga Kull: an officer in Calla's Immortals

Baltarg: his second

Tseole

Cuile: a nomad

Odel: a shaman

Others

The Traveler: a mysterious warlock

Unva: a witch from Dunnehine; enemy of Sheega

Carlo Sarfe: a sailor

Deities and Creatures from the Otherrealm

Tyho: The War God

Kullaan: The Wind God

Aldorian: Faerie Elf King

Rann: A daughter of Sensuata, The Sea God

Ranning: A banished Faen from Sensuata's Realm

Gantallian: a goblin imprisoned inside a mirror, forced to serve Sheega

Rune: A mystery being from the frozen wastelands

Stoon: A Witch-Guard

Crane: A Witch-Guard

ENJOY THIS BOOK? THEN HELP SPREAD THE WORD!

Reviews are one the most powerful tools in my arsenal when it comes to getting readers for my books. Much as I'd like to, I don't have the financial muscle of a New York publisher. I can't take out full-page ads in the newspaper or put posters on the subway.

(Not yet, anyway.)

But I do have something much more powerful and effective than that, and it's something that those publishers would kill to get their hands on:

A committed and loyal bunch of readers.

If you have enjoyed this book, I would be so grateful if you could spend just a few minutes leaving a review, either on Amazon or Goodreads or wherever you bought it. And I'd love if if you'd like to email me a link to the review! ansureviews@gmail.com

Thank you so very much!

ABOUT THE AUTHOR

J. W. Webb is an English writer living in Georgia. Mostly he writes fantasy, though sometimes diverts in even stranger directions. His epic saga , The Legends of Ansu, blends the mystic grandeur of JRR Tolkien with the gritty realism of GRR Martin. Webb's characters are three dimensional and flawed, their world a tapestry of vivid color and constant motion. All the books feature beautiful bespoke sketches by the late Tolkien illustrator, Roger Garland.